In *Autumn's Break*, Ma and its impact on two tale of love, hope, and forgiveness as she carries you into the marriage of Gar and Autumn. Opening with raw emotions, their story captured my interest from the start and didn't let up. Theirs is a fragile relationship complicated by years of infertility, and this poignant romance is sometimes touching, sometimes humorous, sometimes bittersweet. Readers will find themselves rooting for Gar and Autumn's broken hearts to heal and their marriage to be restored. Mary's beautifully written novel is a joy to read and will satisfy any romance lover. I thoroughly enjoyed the road to renewed romance in *Autumn's Break*, an uplifting tale of hope for tomorrow and the power of second chances. You will want to read it from front to back without putting it down.

Paula McGrew
Author of *My Heart Beats for You*

Autumn's Break

Second Chance 4

Mary E Hanks

www.maryehanks.com

Visit Mary's website and sign up for her newsletter at

www.maryehanks.com

You can write Mary at

maryhanks@maryehanks.com.

For Jason

Forty years and our romance keeps getting sweeter.

Thanks for asking me to marry you.

Here's to many more years of laughter and kisses.

For Shem

The day you were born the world became a brighter place.

You add so much joy and laughter and fun to our family.

Love you always.

Above all, love each other deeply,

because love covers over a multitude of sins.

I Peter 4:8

One

Gar

After the disastrous school board meeting ended, Garth Bevere stormed out of the auditorium in pursuit of his boss, Principal Ben Whiffleman. Blood boiled in his veins and pulsed in his ears. If he didn't exercise restraint, his career as a teacher at Everett Christian High School would end tonight. But didn't the board already kick him out the door by sabotaging his drama program?

A knot twisted in his gut. He had to make Ben see his viewpoint. He poured too much of his life into theater at the school for the whole thing to be flushed down the toilet now. "This isn't finished," he called to the retreating man. "We need to talk."

"Don't push me or *you'll* be finished too." The principal unlocked his office door, his fingers fumbling with the key. He escaped inside and shoved on the door as if to keep Gar out.

Gar wouldn't be put off like that. Not when his career was at stake. Not when the only thing that made sense in his life right now was being ripped apart. He rammed his loafer into the opening. "Come on, Ben, I've worked here for ten years. That's got to count for something." The principal harrumphed but let him enter the small office. "Sure it does. You're a great English teacher, Gar. Your theater program has been a shining light in our community. But it's over. The board's decision is final. You can file an appeal at next month's meeting."

"It's over" pounded through his thoughts. Gar had the urge to take out his frustrations by kicking something. Instead, he inhaled deeply, then exhaled. Didn't Autumn warn him before he left the house to stay calm? Didn't she accuse him of being more hot-tempered lately?

With the way the board terminated his theater program, he had to find a way to convince Ben to talk to the board members again. Gar had given his time and dedication to directing twenty productions in the last ten years. Couldn't they see the good he did? It couldn't end like this. "Nobody's stopping my shows." Maybe that wasn't the best way to say it, but that's the way it came out.

Ben pursed his lips. "*Your* shows. *Your* actors. Listen to yourself. Is any of this about the kids? The Lord? Or is everything about you, now?"

How could he say such a thing after Gar's years of service? "Of course, it's for the kids."

"I wonder." Ben squeezed the bridge of his nose. Dark circles puffed up beneath the man's eyes, making him appear older than sixty. He heaved a sigh. "It boils down to this—we can no longer afford the program."

"Why?" Where were the school's funds going? Into sports, no doubt. The philosophy of athletics taking precedence over every other extra-curricular activity gnawed at Gar. "What's the real issue, Ben?"

"Money—"

"Stop blaming it on money." Irritation hammered in his

chest. Just like teachers all over the country, Gar had donated plenty of his own money toward improving his classroom and making his productions at ECHS better. "I want to know why you and the board made this decision." His voice rose. Every muscle in his shoulders tightened.

"It's about the students." Ben ran his hand over his thinning hair. "If we don't get our budget fixed, the school will close. End of story."

"Cut football or basketball. Reduce office staff." Gar huffed out a breath. "Don't pull the plug on theater and music. Platform skills could be the most important thing we teach here."

"The most important—?" Ben tossed his hands in the air. "Above the Bible? The basics? This theater business has gone to your head, Gar. Something to feed your ego. Then, there's the matter of Sasha Delaney."

The sound of the woman's name filled the room like smoke. Gar gritted his teeth. "What are you talking about?" He was a married man, for goodness' sake. His stage designer happened to be one of the best in the Northwest. She'd helped him with every show he directed at ECHS. She was his partner in crime, so to speak. An instigator of creative genius. Not his—

"There've been rumors. And I saw you *alone* with her at a coffee shop in Edmonds, laughing and carrying on." Ben crossed his arms and squinted at Gar.

"Carrying on?" Gar knew teachers in Christian schools were expected to live by a high moral standard. But by what Ben was saying, he might as well have said "having an affair." "She's my coworker. Nothing m-more." That shake in his voice was from indignation, not guilt.

"A leave of absence might be necessary." Ben cleared his throat. "Married teachers on staff going through something like this might be a poor example to the students."

"Something like what?" Gar nearly shouted. "Is that why

you recommended dropping a program the kids love? Because of your concern about my marriage? Autumn and I are fine." The white lie burned across his tongue. His marriage had been on rocky ground for the last six months, but that wasn't any of Ben's business. And it had nothing to do with Sasha Delaney. Just because she was a gorgeous blond, whom he enjoyed working with, didn't mean he'd been unfaithful to Autumn. Guilt raced up his spine and made the back of his neck itch.

With jerky movements, Ben straightened papers on his desk, then grabbed his coat. "Meeting adjourned. Go home. Accept what you can't change."

How could Gar accept the theater program he'd dreamed into existence was washed up? That the job he loved was over because someone saw him *laughing* with a woman in a coffee shop? "I'll do anything you say to keep my job—get counseling, whatever." Even though he didn't think he needed it. "What can I do to get theater reinstated? Donate more money?" Maybe he could get a loan. Sell the house.

Ben shook his head. "It's over."

"No," Gar yelled, "you don't realize how important this is to me. I mean, to the kids."

Ben's eyebrows arched. "Your productions were successful, but they're finished." With his hand on Gar's shoulder, Ben nudged him toward the exit.

This was dirty politics, nothing more. Rage burned through Gar like a wildfire, devouring every ounce of self-control. He whirled around and jabbed his index finger against Ben's chest. "You should have stuck up for me. I've worked hard as a teacher. Sacrificed. Put the students first. Why couldn't you stand up to the board for once?"

Ben's gaze turned steely. "I suggest you leave before I suspend you."

Suspend?

Foul words Gar hadn't said in years pounded in his brain. Wounded pride fueled the flames of injustice churning in his chest.

A leave of absence. Suspension. Finished. Washed up.

He'd put up with Ben Whiffleman's pathetic leadership long enough. He was sick of being taken for granted. Disgusted with Ben for kowtowing to every whim of the school board's— at the students' and teachers' expense. Someone needed to show him how wrong he was. He grabbed the man's shirt and shoved him backward, his other fist raised. But Gar came to his senses before he hit him—what was he doing?—and released him. However, the harm was done.

"G-get out!" the principal sputtered.

As if someone had dumped ice water over his head, Gar's adrenaline tanked. He gulped. "I, uh—" Regret filled the tight places his anger vacated. "Look, I'm—"

"I s-said *get out!* You're fired!"

Heat infused Gar's face. "I thought—" What did he think? That he could grab the principal and nearly hit him, and continue teaching senior English? He'd blown it. What could he say? That he was sorry? "I shouldn't have—"

"In ten seconds, if you're still standing here, I'm calling the police."

Ben had really fired him. What would Autumn say now? What would his students think of him? He backed out the doorway. After Gar shut the door with its engraved plaque that read *Principal's Office*, he stared at streaks of grain in the wood until they blurred.

Oh, no. What have I done?

Two

Autumn

Autumn stretched in the Adirondack chair in her small backyard, feeling thankful for the late July sunshine and relieved the first day of school was still six weeks away. Not that she could sit idle for too long. Soon she'd have to prepare for her fall classes. Only on a beautiful blue-sky day like today, she preferred to curl up with her mocha and a novel, instead of reading Beau Johnson's *Teach a Reader, Grow a Nation*. As good of an educator as Mr. Whiffleman said the author was, she couldn't coax herself into academia yet. The upcoming school year would be her ninth as a freshman and sophomore English teacher at Everett Christian High School. But so far, she wasn't experiencing a fraction of the excitement she had about teaching in previous years.

She took a sip of her chocolaty drink, thinking her lack of zeal was probably due to the things that had gone wrong in her life lately. The dreams she carried in her heart since she was a girl—like having children and enjoying a great marriage—had all but shriveled up and died. Maybe she'd put too much stock in dreams.

She couldn't place the exact time when her relationship with Gar took a dive. Perhaps it was the day she found out she couldn't conceive, and the world became a darker place. Maybe it was after he returned from a teacher's conference in Las Vegas last spring and seemed to have lost interest in her. Either way, an icy chill now occupied their home—and their hearts.

The awkwardness between them wasn't entirely his fault. She'd felt the growing distance for months and hadn't done anything to improve it. On the rare occasion he put his arm over her shoulder, she found some reason to pull away. She avoided the things they used to love to do together—canoeing in the sound, taking walks around the park, eating breakfast in Edmonds on Saturday mornings—and she didn't know why.

Maybe it was her guilt over disappointing him. He told her he wanted children often enough. How could they ever find their way back to being a passionate husband and wife, now that she couldn't give him the dreams of his heart?

Gar was spending more time away from her too. He used any excuse to be gone from the house—other than to sleep, shower, and change his clothes.

Had her aloofness encouraged his? She swallowed down regrets. She didn't want their marriage to turn out like this.

She remembered in their early years when the slightest glimpse of his gaze meeting hers across the room shot a powerful jolt through her. The touch of his fingers caressing her shoulder melted her into his arms. And his kisses were so tender and sweet. How long had it been since she even wanted him to hug her or for her to lay her cheek against his chest?

Last night, even though she was nursing a headache, she should have gone to the school board's summer meeting and supported Gar. At least, then, she might have kept him from making a fool of himself. After the session, he stormed into the house ranting about the evils of working at *that* school and how he'd be better off finding another job. It took some coaxing, but finally, she pulled the truth from him. She was appalled to learn he'd been fired, and why.

How could he have been so spiteful toward Ben? And now, without his salary, how would they keep up with the house payments and the medical bills for the infertility treatments they still owed? She didn't feel much sympathy toward Gar's situation, but maybe she should have kept her mouth shut about how ridiculous she thought he acted. How childish.

He slept in the guest room. Inconsolable, he moaned that he was a failure, and he needed time alone to contemplate his miserable life. That was fine with her. She was relieved to sleep by herself.

Her cell phone rang, yanking her out of her melancholy thoughts.

She tapped the screen. "Hello."

"Mrs. Bevere?" Principal Whiffleman's voice.

"Yes." She sat up straighter to speak with her boss. She attended a teacher's planning meeting that morning, and the air had been ripe with hushed whispers. Would the principal fire her because of what Gar did to him?

"I'm calling to assure you that we still want you to teach at ECHS." Ben sniffed.

"Oh, good." She expelled a breath.

"In fact, I have an offer for you."

Autumn swallowed. "An offer?"

"I want you to consider teaching junior and senior English. You have seniority."

Her teach Gar's classes? She sucked in a long breath.

"What do you think?"

"I-I don't know." Her mind whirled with thoughts as heavy as if she were weighted down with boots in the sound. What would Gar say? Would he be furious?

"It comes with a raise." Mr. Whiffleman's voice lightened.

She could use a raise, especially with Gar out of work and no unemployment compensation coming, since he'd been fired.

"You're a wonderful teacher, Mrs. Bevere." The principal cleared his throat. "This bad blood between Gar and the school board could hurt the unity of our ECHS family. Your stepping up and taking his place will smooth ruffled feathers."

He thought she could do all that? How?

"So—?" His question dangled between them.

"Can I think about it?" She should probably talk with Gar. Even though he wasn't acting like himself, he was her husband. Sure, he'd rant and rave. In the end, he'd tell her to do whatever she thought was best, like he usually did. And they needed the money.

"If you're not interested in the position, I'll place an advertisement online today." He sighed. "You've been with us for eight years. You've made a real impact on the kids' lives."

Had she? That's what she hoped to do when she trained to become a teacher. It was encouraging to hear someone say something nice about her work. Gar was the one who usually received the accolades.

"I'm sorry to pressure you," Ben continued, "but in light of Gar's actions, I'm obligated to seek his replacement immediately. I thought I'd ask you first."

"You need my decision now?" She gulped. Without talking to her husband?

"Due to the circumstances, yes. I apologize for pressuring you. It's just—"

"I understand." Thanks to Gar's behavior, he was in the awkward position of asking Gar's wife to take on the job. A test of loyalty? Yet, she wondered if preparing for and teaching the new classes might help pull her out of her funk. Maybe even cheer her up?

A charge of electricity rushed up her spine. She couldn't say no to the opportunity just because Gar would be perturbed, right?

"I'll do it." She agreed before she had a chance to talk herself out of it—or to seriously ponder what Gar might think of her making such a hasty decision. Her heart hammered against her ribcage.

"Excellent." She could almost hear Ben's smile. "Stop by my office, and we'll go over your new duties. There are forms to sign."

"I will. Thank you for considering me, Mr. Whiffleman."

"You're welcome." He ended the call.

Autumn stared at her tiny backyard lined with rosebushes and perennial greenery, and all the colors seemed brighter than before she took the call. Her heart felt a smidge lighter too. She was going to be the junior and senior English teacher. She dropped her novel and picked up Beau's educational book.

Then the truth smacked her in the face. Tonight, when Gar came home from wherever he'd spent the day—most likely, somewhere feeling sorry for himself—she'd have to break the news to him. She was his replacement. She would be doing the job he loved.

Did she just make the worst mistake of her life?

Three

Autumn

"I'm leaving." Gar dropped his suitcase on the floor beside him.

"What?" Autumn shot out of her chair, glaring at the man who'd become even more of a stranger in the last two weeks. She was sick of his mood swings, his temper flares, his sullenness. One minute he was pouting and giving her the cold shoulder, the next, slamming doors and yelling. The temptation to leave him had been on her mind, too. But he was the one who caused the trouble with the school and got himself—them—into this mess. "Leave, for all I care." She barely recognized the grit in her tone.

Not that she'd choose for him to walk out on their marriage. She loved him as her husband, even though she hadn't felt *loving* toward him in a long time. She still hoped things would work out between them. But something had to give. They needed to break the cycle. Yes, she promised "for richer or for poorer," but when she said those words, she never imagined sharing the house with a man who'd fallen out of love with her. A man who turned into a jerk she barely recognized as the man she married. Yep, they needed a break. She . . . needed time away from him.

His dark brown eyes squinted at her and turned coal black. "I still can't believe you stole my job." His jaw jutted out. "I never thought you capable of such devious behavior."

"Devious?" That was a laugh coming from him.

His curled lips and mocking glare made her want to slap him. Instead, she smirked. Phooey with male pride. "Gar, you were tossed out on your backside—for good cause. The school had to find someone to replace you. Why not me?" She glared at him, daring him to say something critical about her being chosen. She might not be as qualified as him, since she hadn't finished her master's program, but she was a good teacher. A faithful employee. The school wouldn't have to worry about her grabbing someone and pushing him.

Gar rolled his eyes.

Her anger boiled. "You don't think I can do it?"

His lids lowered to half-mast as if he didn't care. "You'll see how hard it is."

"So what?" Every job had its difficult days. "At least, *I* have people skills."

Gar snorted. "That I don't, you mean?"

"You said it."

He shook his head, his dark eyes filled with mirth, and she had the urge to kick him in the shin and leave a bruise. Something to remember her by when he was sleeping alone in some dingy motel on Broadway Avenue.

"Look at all the times you argued with Ben Whiffleman." Her voice turned snarly again. "Or with parents in the PTA."

"So?"

"Who does that to their boss? To the parents of the kids they teach? Especially in a *Christian* school? We're supposed to be different. A light in a dark world." Although, the storm brewing in her heart could hardly be called Christ-like, either. Ever since she'd been working through the disappointment of not having kids, she'd struggled with her faith. Why didn't God answer her prayers? Why couldn't she bear a child of her own body, while some aborted the hope of their womb as if the baby didn't matter? It was so . . . tragic. She ached inside every time she thought of her loss.

Gar made a rude sound that smacked of cussing without saying the word.

Oh, he infuriated her.

Where was the nice guy she married fifteen years ago? What about the life of service they committed to, especially to children? He'd changed so much. The arguments, the heated exchanges, the separate bedrooms for the last two weeks. The damage was irreparable. Midlife crisis or not, maybe it *was* best if he left.

"So, you think I deserved to be fired?" A tick throbbed beneath his eye. "For my reputation to be ruined?"

Yes. But she knew not to say so out loud.

He hadn't shaved in days. His roguish look emphasized the dark circles under his eyes. Too much caffeine? Or lack of sleep?

Gar obviously couldn't fathom her ability to continue working for the people who he thought mistreated him. Perhaps he was right about one thing—Ben didn't see value Gar's years of service as something worth standing up for. But was that reason enough for him to make a stink that would be discussed for years to come?

"If you were so concerned about your job, your *reputation*"— she said it like it was a dirty word—"you should have thought twice before shoving Ben."

"And you shouldn't have taken the position without talking to me first. That was the last straw."

No, they hit the last straw months ago, sometime after they stopped medical efforts to have kids. Ever since, she'd been walking around like a zombie, in shock or denial. She wanted to continue exploring every possible avenue toward conceiving and had begged Gar to let her try other hormone therapies. But he said no—they'd been at it for years, their funds were gone, their lives a mess. They were finished being lab experiments.

A tiny part of her even agreed with him. She was tired of charts and needles and embarrassing questions too. And probably depressed. They needed to get on with living. But the internal mommy in her still ached to hold a baby of her own.

Was that the main reason their marriage was falling apart—because of her infertility? Or was Gar's turbulent behavior due to him losing his job?

"You can't let what happened go, can you?" She stared at the man she used to adore, the one who wouldn't look her in the eyes now.

"No, I can't," he said quieter than she expected. He swiveled away and sniffled, his head bent as if he were crying. Gar, emotional? Hadn't he told her plenty of times that he was too tough to shed tears?

Something dug at her. "Would you have asked *me*?"

"Asked you what?" He didn't face her.

She stared at his stiff shoulders and knew she should be quiet. Still, her teeth clamped tight, and she shook at the release of inner strife. "If you had been the one offered the promotion, the raise, would *you* have talked to me first?" She knew the answer.

He turned around so fast his elbow hit the hurricane lamp on the end table, sending it crashing to the floor.

"No!" She reached for the favored antique. Too late.

Broken pieces of amber glass scattered at her feet.

"You're not hurt, are you?" The flash of tenderness in his eyes surprised her.

She pulled her arms in close to herself so he wouldn't touch her. "I'm fine."

He dropped to his knees and picked up chunks of glass. He laid them on the end table next to his dust-covered Bible.

They'd purchased the vintage lamp with its 60's poppy pattern in Montana when they vacationed in Yellowstone for their tenth anniversary. She enjoyed finding mementos to mark special occasions. Like the Kinkade painting of a snowy village they purchased and hung above the electric fireplace to celebrate five years together. The giant shell on the bookshelf from Hawaii for their first anniversary. After he left, would she want such reminders in plain view? Maybe she'd store them in the garage.

Golden shards peppered the floor, the brass base lay forlorn, but her feet remained stationary as she awaited his answer. The mess could be cleaned later.

Finally, he stood. "Of course, I would have told you."

She laughed. "You're kidding, right?"

He threw up his hands. "When did I ever *not* talk over something with you first?"

Oh, he had such a high opinion of himself.

His eyes glared at her with fiery angst, and she stared him down with equal venom. At least they were talking. Saying something was better than their usual silent warfare.

"How about before you railed at Principal Whiffleman, the school board, the parents' association?"

"Oh, that."

"Yeah, *that*. How do you think I felt walking into school for a teacher's meeting the next morning after you made such a debacle over the loss of your *precious* theater program?" Her voice rose, and she didn't care. "Funding was cut. So what? Big deal."

With each point, he jerked like she hit him.

"Grow up, Gar. The same thing's happening all over the country. Budgets are tight. It isn't personal. And you'd still have a job." She thrust her hands through her hair, but her temper

21

wasn't spent. "Maybe this whole theater fiasco had more to do with your ego than anything about kids losing drama."

He clutched his hands together as if restraining himself from hitting something. Not her. He'd never been abusive. But he shook his head like she was the daftest person on the planet. "You wouldn't understand."

She crossed her arms, mimicking his stance. "Try me."

"What does it matter now?"

"Because I'm your wife!"

"So you are." He sneered. "As my *wife,* if you cared, if you loved me at all, why would you take my job?"

Why? Because she was offered a promotion, a little prestige, finally.

Without waiting for her answer, he bent over and grabbed his travel bag. Then he strode toward the door.

She blinked back tears. Why the gripping emotion? This was for the best, *him* leaving her. The way he broke things off with the school, colleagues were already questioning her loyalty. Still, after fifteen years she never thought it would end like this.

But there he stood, suitcase in hand, looking like a kid running away from home. The home they built together.

"I do love you, you know."

Then, with a click of the door's closing, he was gone.

She rushed to the window, couldn't keep herself from watching the morbid unraveling of their wedding vows. Gar threw his navy bag into the back of his CRV, then hopped into the vehicle and gunned it out of the driveway.

She wanted to yell at him to slow down. Children were playing nearby.

Children.

But not theirs.

A cold ache gripped her. Would Gar divorce her and find someone more suitable to bear his children? Someone young and

fertile? A hot breath seared her throat. Was he ~~~~ troubled by
their personal failures than he let on? He wouldn't talk to her. He
kept everything bottled up. Instead of communicating and sharing,
he withdrew into work. Into other areas of his life—where she
wasn't allowed. And she sank deeper into her own despair.

During her last checkup, Doctor Walters told her she was
probably in mourning. She'd gained weight and secretly hoped
they overlooked something. Maybe she *was* pregnant. She even
dreamed she was. Her anticipation rose high, then crashed and
burned, for the hundredth time. Her body had deceived her.
She wasn't pregnant. Never would be. She had to rise above the
loss and find a way to care about something else again. Maybe
exercise more. Stop eating treats. Try to be happy. But how could
she when her husband was leaving and breaking her heart?

If she hadn't accepted his vacant position, would he have
stayed and tried to work through their difficulties? Was this all
her fault?

No, Gar was caught up in his own story, his need to have
center stage. In leaving, he kept the spotlight on himself. Wasn't
that how it always was?

She swallowed the raw emotion threatening to consume
her. Their marriage had been like a Broadway production that
ran its course. The finale came and went. The show was over.

But it hadn't always been that way.

She pictured him on their wedding day—so handsome—
decked out in his rich brown tones, promising to love her for
the rest of his life. She imagined the way he used to grin at her,
their gazes locked, and how those moments stole her breath
away. She thought she was the luckiest girl in the state of
Washington, if not the world, when he married her. She'd loved
him completely.

Now, she was left standing alone, wondering what happened
to them when they used to love each other so much. Had
promised forever. How could all those feelings be gone?

Four

Gar

Three hours of driving and Gar's temper hadn't slackened. He'd sped halfway across the state of Washington, en route to his cousin Kyle's house in Idaho, as if daring cops to pull him over. Near George, he got his wish. A hefty fine and a serious warning, and then he spent the next ten minutes yelling accusations at Autumn, God, and himself. Now he was hungry and tired of sitting.

With a half hour to go until he hit another city, his thoughts wandered to places he'd told himself never to think about. Memories seeped into his brain like a fog. He pictured Autumn when they were newly married, how sweet she used to be, the way she smiled at him all the time. How cold she'd become. A snapshot of another woman flashed across his mind. A younger lady with short-cropped hair who laughed at all his jokes and grinned at him like he was a movie star. A beautiful woman he knew for three days. Yet in five months hadn't forgotten her. Even though he prayed to forget her face, her lips.

Another unanswered prayer.

Sometimes he dreamed of her. Of that day he gave in to

her coaxing and spent the afternoon sightseeing with her. How they strolled through the shops on the Las Vegas Strip, laughing and kidding around. There were mornings since then when he'd wake up in a cold sweat, guilt clawing at him like a monster determined to kill him. During the daytime, shame wrapped a chain so tightly around his neck he'd been choking. And the chasm between him and Autumn had widened until they could barely talk civilly to each other.

How did life get so messed up? Him, a married man, flirting with another woman? Letting things go further than he ever thought they would? But it wasn't all his fault. When did Autumn last treat him like he was someone she wanted to be around, let alone flirt with or have fun together? Life with her had become a task on an endless checklist. Do this. Fix that. Change. Don't expect anything. Don't touch her. Stay away.

So he did.

Then love ebbed like the tide. Somewhere between the agony of waiting in doctor's offices and trying too hard to have a child, they lost what they had in search of something unattainable.

Even though it wasn't his fault they couldn't have kids, she acted as if she blamed him. Gave him the silent treatment. Said romance didn't matter anymore. What was the purpose? Who was she kidding? It mattered a whole lot to him.

Maybe he was to blame. He'd been the one to say enough was enough. They'd endured all the medical rigmarole he was willing to put himself, and her, through. Not to mention the horrific fees. It was time to put the idea of having their own kids behind them. Unless they adopted. And lately, she didn't even want to talk about that. A taboo subject.

They'd drifted so far apart they might as well be living in separate houses. Sure, both of them were busy. He was preoccupied with theater, his one oasis. She kept her nose in books and work. But they weren't connecting on any level, other than the weekly checklist. Mortgage paid? Check. Garage door fixed? Check. Canoe cleaned? Check. Stay two feet away. Check.

He smacked the steering wheel. Why was he thinking about this junk? All marriages went downhill after ten years, right? The hot fires of passion doused with the cold waters of boredom? Maybe his wife's chill justified his flirtations. Most men indulged a little, didn't they? If certain lines weren't crossed—and they hadn't been—what was the harm? After all, his mother raised a gentleman. And then, there was the matter of God seeing, and knowing all.

He tried to shake free of the guilt, to forget that one kiss. A small indiscretion that plagued him for five months.

Heat crept up his spine, his neck.

If only he hadn't attended the teacher's conference in Vegas. If he hadn't gone to dinner with Elaine, the young teacher he met there. Except, during that one day he felt ten years younger. Desirable to a woman. Excited by possibilities, even if he'd never act on them. But ever since, he carried a wheelbarrow load of guilt and doubt. If he'd stayed at the conference another day, would he have done something he would have regretted for the rest of his life?

That's what gnawed at him. Chinked away at his faith. How could a man who professed to be following God and loving his wife have been so tempted? So lured by a skirt?

He swallowed hard.

The attraction between him and Autumn had wilted and died. She didn't make time for him. He rarely spent evenings or weekends doing the things they used to enjoy together. Because of his guilty conscience? Or because of all the struggles they went through to try to have kids?

He couldn't believe how long they attempted to conceive

before they realized something was wrong. He could remember them praying about children when they were younger. Asking God to bless them with "a quiver full."

Autumn blamed a lack of pregnancy on their schedules, her irregular cycles, bad timing. Then, when they discovered her egg count was extremely low, she wept. But through the whole process, she didn't doubt. "It will happen. God will heal me." She tried all kinds of medicines and procedures, to no avail. Finally, they gave up. He gave up. And she grew away from him.

So he submerged himself in planning productions. He studied longer for his classes. Their paths rarely crossed, except for in the hall at school or at a teacher's meeting. He spent more sessions with Sasha, avoiding the house and the woman he used to love.

One day, he woke up with a heavy sensation of dread, like the world passed him by, like someone died. Like a fragment of himself. Or maybe hope. He had nothing to show for his life. He was a high school teacher—and he enjoyed that. He was a director and producer of amateur productions—and it seemed he couldn't live without the rush. But something had altered in his spirit. Something was stifling him. Even thinking about it as he drove made his chest ache.

On the outskirts of Moses Lake, he pulled into a gas station and filled up the tank. His CRV was as empty as he felt. Where was a good hamburger joint? Or a steak house? He could use a double dose of red meat.

He hopped back into the car and drove down the street, looking for a cheap eatery or pub. Funds were tight. He had enough gas money to get him to Coeur d'Alene and his cousin's automotive shop, where Kyle said he could pick up an entry-level position. Not that he'd choose something so below his education, but for now, he was grateful for any kind of work.

The wind had picked up. Tumbleweeds rolled across the street in front of him. He braked, and at the same time, glanced right. A sign on an archaic-looking building read "Freddy's Grill."

Perfect.

He pulled into the parking lot, and as soon as he parked, he jumped out. Taking fast strides that matched his agitation, he marched into the establishment that would have seemed questionable under normal circumstances. But when a man was hungry, he'd eat at any old dive. Surely Freddy's Grill had an edible burger on the menu.

Inside, the dimly lit restaurant smelled odd, like old tennies.

"Sit where you want," a nasally female voice called from the kitchen.

He plopped down at the counter, certain he'd get served faster there. No other customers were present. What was with this joint? Where was the server? He was in a hurry and starved. He cleared his throat—the universal "I'm waiting" signal.

Nothing.

He spotted a menu at the far end of the counter. Standing, he took several steps and grabbed the plastic folder, his fingers skidding through grease or slime. Disgusting. He rubbed his hand over the thigh of his jeans.

"What can I get you for?" A gray-haired woman who had to be in her late seventies shuffled into the room.

"Food, and fast."

"Hungry?"

"Yep." Gar opened the menu. Hamburgers were listed with cutesy names he hated. *Dungaree Burger. Whale of a Tail Burger. Sail the Seven Seas Burger.* Couldn't a burger be a burger? "Red meat here" were all the words he needed.

The woman whose name tag read "Sal" stood on the opposite side of the counter, staring at him. "Coffee?"

"Got anything stronger?" He hadn't had alcohol in years, but with the way he was feeling . . .

"Can't afford a liquor license." She snorted. "Can barely keep this place open." She grabbed a fly swatter from somewhere in the caverns of the long counter and whacked the grainy surface.

Gar jumped.

"Stevie," she yelled toward the kitchen, "flies are back."

Great. Gar was feeling less hungry all the time.

"Special's meatloaf."

He remembered how Autumn would sometimes laugh when he chose that entree. She'd take on a funny voice and talk about what was being served in "the home." He sighed. Meatloaf sounded as good as anything else. "I'll take the special."

"Coffee?" She grabbed a carafe with black coffee that looked thick enough to be yesterday's brew.

"No, thanks."

"One Number One!" she barked toward the cooking area. When she grinned, he saw she had one front tooth missing. Something green—broccoli or spinach?—was hanging in the gap.

"I'll take a Coke." He needed some liquid to swig down since his stomach acids had been churning for hours. A headache pounded behind his eyes. Not that more caffeine would help.

Sal grabbed a clear glass, far from smudge-free, and dropped in a couple of chunks of ice he seriously wondered about. Then she cracked open a soda and poured the bubbling drink into the glass. The snapping and fizzing made his stomach gurgle and his mouth water.

A mischievous sparkle in her eye, the woman laughed and tossed the glass of soda across the counter's surface. As if in slow motion, he watched the spinning glass hiccup in a dent in the Formica, tip, then the drink sloshed over the rim, pouring straight at him. Before he could react, brown cola splashed over the counter and down the front of his pants. He leaped off the stool.

"Oh, no." He brushed moisture off his clothes, but the damage was done. The stain looked like he'd had an embarrassing accident. "Just great."

Sal cackled. "Second time that's happened this week. I used to be better at that." She grabbed a dishtowel and sponged up the mess on the counter. Then she tossed the sopping wet towel at him. "Wipe down that stool, will ya? I'll fetch another Coke."

He should just leave. The service here was unbelievable. Yet, he did what she asked, and hoped his food would arrive faster since he was the only customer. He used some napkins on his pants, not that it improved the situation. When he sat back down, his legs felt sticky.

Like a bad dream, he watched her go through the process again—dirty glass, questionable ice, and fizzing drink. When she sent the glass spinning toward him, like some fail-proof barroom trick, he reached out and grabbed it. Was she insane? Her ruckus laughter confirmed his suspicions. He guzzled down the soda and wished he'd kept driving. What compelled him to choose this dive?

Finally, a bell dinged. A slim hand placed a white plate on the shelf at the serving window. "One's up," the young-sounding cook called.

Gar's mouth watered. He imagined how the meatloaf would taste slathered in ketchup.

The server carried the plate between both hands and stared at it like she was afraid of dropping it. The thought "what else could go wrong?" crossed his mind. A half-step before delivery, Sal inhaled loudly, then burst out the juiciest sneeze he ever heard.

She dropped the plate in front of him, wiping spit off the edge of the plate. He couldn't believe his misfortune. Like before, she didn't even say sorry.

"That all?" She smiled, and the green stuff from her tooth was gone. Probably came out in the sneeze on his plate.

In a daze, he stared at the meatloaf. All he could picture was the greenery his food had been baptized in. "Check, please?"

Still hungry and irritated, he slapped money on the counter. The woman didn't deserve a gratuity, but she probably needed one. He stomped out the door. Halfway across the parking lot, he realized his car looked horrible. Why was it leaning on its rear? He sprinted to his vehicle.

Oh, man. The back tires were gone! Tires, rims, everything.

He smacked the hood of the vehicle. He stared up at the cloudy sky. "Why?" Why was everything in his life going wrong?

Was this punishment for the way he left Autumn? How he yelled at her? How he knew she'd been going through an awful time, and maybe, he hadn't been supportive enough? He groaned.

He yanked his cell phone out of his jacket pocket and punched in 9-1-1. After he explained to the operator what happened outside of Freddy's, he paced. Was this a setup? Did Sal stall him while some henchmen—maybe the cook and his accomplice—destroyed his ride? He wanted to kick something. And he was still hungry!

He simmered down enough to call his auto club and get the number for a service that would deliver and install tires—a pretty penny's worth. Not to mention, it would be an hour's wait. He paced again.

Finally, a tall, thin policewoman arrived in an official-looking black vehicle. She sauntered toward him like she had all day. "I'm Officer Willus."

"Gar Bevere."

"This your vehicle?"

"As you can see by the missing tires." No use snapping at her, but he couldn't seem to help himself.

Officer Willus glanced at his pants with a frown.

He'd forgotten about that. He yanked his jacket closed.

She scribbled on her paper, then squinted at him. "Been drinking?"

"Nope. The clumsy server spilled soda on me."

"Hmm."

She didn't believe him? Oh, what did he care?

At the back of the car, she took pictures of the gaping cavities where the wheels used to sit. She stepped to the front tire and peering down, copied numbers. "Not much we can do. Other than submitting all the information. Anything else missing?"

Anything—? "I don't know." He didn't think to look. "My car was—" Usually locked. Did he forget to secure it before trotting into the restaurant? He opened the door without using his key. Not a good sign. Leaning in, he checked the back compartment where he stashed his travel bag. Gone. Everything he brought vanished? He wanted to yell. To swear. To rant at someone.

"What is it?" Her kindly voice annoyed him.

"My bag. It's gone." *Like my life.* Part of him wanted to turn around and drive home. To beg Autumn to take him back. To tell her he made an abominable mistake. But he wouldn't. Even if he had to sleep right here in his car, he couldn't return to Everett today.

"Valuables?" She clutched her notepad.

"Just . . . stuff. Clothes, books, shaving gear." His treasured Shakespeare book. His favorite tennies.

She nodded toward his stained pants. "Looks like you'll need a change of apparel."

She had to bring that up.

He covered his face with both hands, breathing deeply. Good thing he had his wallet. He patted his back pocket. It was there. But anger over his losses rose to the surface like a windstorm. "I suspect these people." He stabbed his index finger toward Freddy's Grill.

The policewoman, with her hair pulled into a ponytail and a police cap on her head scrunched up her face. "Why is that?"

"A suspicious series of events. They had to be in on it." Wasn't Sal too over the top to be a real server? Didn't his food take too long considering he was the only customer? Probably a criminal ring going down right here.

"I'll question them, but you shouldn't be quick to pass judgment."

"Why not?"

"You left your car unlocked?"

He had. "What about the tires?"

"We've had a string of similar crimes all over the city. They're calling the thieves the Vanishing Tire Gang. They're quick at their dirty business, then disappear. We think it's junior high kids."

"You've got to be kidding." Junior highers?

"I'll process your information. I'm sorry for your misfortune." She nodded at him. "Good day, Mr. Bevere."

He watched her walk into Freddy's, and he was tempted to follow. He'd like to see exactly who was in the kitchen cooking meatloaf. A junior high student?

That riled him.

But his tires should arrive any minute. A cost he hadn't foreseen when he started this little road trip. The insurance company would reimburse him, but for now, he had to cover the costs. On top of that, he had to buy new clothes. One downward glance verified his next stop would be a men's clothing department.

Autumn would never believe his bad luck if he told her. Which seemed unlikely. They were on a break. A long one, if he had his way. It was time he figured his life out before he could ever hope to face her again.

Five

Autumn

Autumn steered her Accent into the driveway of their suburban home, a half mile from Legend Park. The grass could use mowing. A light in the garage needed to be replaced. She hadn't rolled the garbage containers back into their spot. The rose bushes needed trimming. But she didn't have any desire to do outside tasks. Or inside chores, for that matter. Since Gar left, she hadn't done one load of laundry, dishes, vacuuming, or hiding those objects that reminded her of him. Good thing school wasn't in session yet.

She spent most of the last seven days curled up on the couch, watching old movies, eating snacks, and wishing Gar would come home and say he was sorry. If he did, they could put this awful time behind them. Maybe go in for counseling. He could get a different job. She'd finish out her year at ECHS, and then they could do something else. Like move to a different state and start over.

She could call and tell him how badly she missed him. How sorry she was for her part in their conflict. But didn't he make it obvious he wasn't interested in being with her? In loving her? She wasn't going to beg him to come home.

Although, in the middle of the night, she was tempted to do that very thing.

Around two in the morning, a blustery wind caused tree limbs to scrape the windows at the back of the house where the master bedroom was. The rattling and screeching freaked her out and kept her awake for hours. Was someone trying to get in? When she realized it was only a tree, she wondered if the branches might come crashing through the panes. What would she do if there was an emergency and she was alone?

She needed her husband. He couldn't take off and stay away as long as he wanted as if he didn't have adult obligations. As if their marriage didn't matter. But that's what he did.

Too many nights in the past, she sat home alone while he worked on staging, or whatever, with Sasha. The woman's name twisted angst in her stomach. Now that Gar had left, she was sifting through their past like a seamstress searching for a missing pattern piece. She had to figure out what went wrong. Was it possible his coolness toward her was because he sinned against their wedding vows? She held that thought close for a few moments, then shook her head. Wouldn't she have known if he cheated on her? He hadn't been acting himself but straying like that seemed too out of character.

Nights were the worst. She tossed and turned, fuming at Gar for leaving and hurting her, then crying into her pillow, so sorry she caused such a rift. Gar had every right to feel betrayed and angry. If the circumstances were reversed, wouldn't she be upset? But what could she do now? Quitting her job was out of the question. Losing the house wasn't an option. The school had already hired someone to fill the freshman and sophomore English classes. There was no going back to the way things were.

Somehow, she had to pull herself together. She had a ton of classroom prep. She needed to read a stack of English books that sat on the living room coffee table. And she had new grading software to learn. But nothing mattered unless Gar came home. How could she go back to life as usual when everything felt so wrong?

Dr. Walters said she needed to find something to focus on. Maybe if she stayed busy, distracted herself, her desire to get ready for the school year might naturally kick in.

So far, only one thing sounded remotely interesting—learning how to make fudge. Last night, she searched online and found a bunch of recipes—white chocolate, two-layered varieties, raspberry, caramel, and dark chocolate fudge. Her mouth watered at the possibilities. A chocoholic under normal circumstances, her recent turmoil made her even more susceptible to indulging.

She carried two plastic bags filled with candy-making supplies into the kitchen and dropped them on the counter. She tossed her jacket over a chair, then pulled out a large mixing bowl and measuring cups. Glancing over the array of instructions she'd spread out on the counter, she squinted at the lists of ingredients. Wow. Fudge took a lot of sugar.

She emptied the grocery bags but left the contents sprawled out. She ripped open the twenty-five-pound bag of white sugar and measured an exorbitant amount and dumped it in the bowl. She set a large pan on the burner, dropped in three cubes of butter, then poured in a can of evaporated milk. She couldn't wait to test the double-chocolate recipe.

She bet Gar would love her fudge. But she shouldn't think about him. Her work area needed to be a no-Gar zone. Because if she kept contemplating what she'd say to him if she got the chance, what she should or shouldn't have done about the job, or how she'd like to go searching for him, she'd go crazy.

She stirred the milk and butter and sugar over medium heat, and her thoughts strayed into the zone she was avoiding. For too long, she'd been lost in her sadness. Gar probably felt neglected, shunned even, by her. She never meant to make him feel that way. Could she just tell him that? Apologize?

No. He left her. He was the one who should ask *her* forgiveness. If he came back.

And if he didn't, would they get a divorce?

The word hurt.

More destroyed hopes and dreams.

She groaned. This was supposed to be a no-Gar zone. *Stop thinking of him.*

She did love chocolate . . . and so did he. She wanted to make the best killer fudge—the kind he'd never forget.

Wait, what was that awful smell? The pungent scent of scorched milk reached her nose. Oh, no. The ingredients were burning already!

Six

Gar

Gar shoved the eighteen-inch-wide dust broom across the cement floor of Kyle's mechanic shop in Coeur d'Alene, Idaho. Dust and tiny shards of metal skittered across the floor ahead of the bristles. *Why am I working in a place like this?* He groaned at the question he'd asked himself every day for the last week.

He was thankful for Kyle's hospitality and offer of employment but working as a mechanic flunky was monotonous and boring. In the past, creativity and enthusiasm for the next stage production, or preparing for his college preparatory English classes, had charged him. Now he spent his days doing mundane chores, brainless tasks a fourteen-year-old could do. It was enough to drive an educated man insane.

But working in the shop was a way to thank Kyle for providing shelter and food. The manual labor gave him tasks to fill his hours. Still, forty hours a week pushing a broom and parking cars? His brain was going crazy for something challenging.

Of course, it beat the alternative. Hanging around Kyle's house every day would be exasperating. Especially with Lacey, his wife, throwing zingers every chance she got. *Isn't it time you headed home? Is this any way for a Christian man to act? Don't you think Autumn's lonely without you?*

How should he know whether his estranged wife was lonely? He wasn't going to call and ask. Yes, some might call him stubborn. But he had his pride. Other than shooting her a text telling her he'd send money to help with the house payment as soon as he could, he hadn't contacted her.

The edge of the broom hit a butter bucket filled with screws and sent them sliding across the floor. He groaned and bent over to retrieve the metal pieces.

He needed to find a higher-paying job. Renting an apartment—and helping with the house in Everett—on his pittance of a salary would be difficult. It wasn't like he'd arranged a backup plan for losing his job and leaving his wife. After his tire purchase and the new duds in Moses Lake, and his speeding ticket, their previously insignificant savings account was non-existent.

Before his firing, he and Autumn were throwing any extra cash they could dig up at their medical bills for the infertility treatments. Now he wouldn't even be able to do that.

Anger sparked through his chest.

He sacrificed to work at that school. He could have had a higher-paying job in the public school system, instead of the non-profit position he filled at ECHS. Maybe that's the route he should have pursued. But he'd been excited to build something meaningful in a small school. A place where kids might not have gotten the chance to perform in top-notch productions. All those years, he thought he was making a difference in kids' lives.

But Ben and the school board didn't care about that. All Principal Whiffleman could see was some trumped-up accusation about Gar and Sasha. Good thing he didn't know about Gar's time in Vegas.

He shoved the broom hard against a red sports car's tire. Time to think about something else.

He drew comfort by imagining himself on the front pages of the *Herald* and the *Tribune*. Both papers had given him outstanding reviews for his productions, not only about his brilliant actors but about his and Sasha's remarkable stages. A warm feeling centered in his chest and radiated out. There was nothing like reading the editor's praises the morning following Opening Night. *Gar Bevere and Sasha Delaney Did it Again! A Remarkable Duo.* He smiled at the remembered headlines, despite the tension bunching up in his shoulders. The two of them liked trying to outdo past productions. They usually did too.

A lot of that success was due to Sasha. Younger than him, art was her passion. Her creativity amazed him. He loved talking about staging with her, spending hours in the cafeteria or one of the nearby coffee shops, throwing around ideas. It was like they were batteries revving up on each other's artistic vibes. How could they make the set better? The lighting more spectacular? Wasn't it in one of those sessions that she shared her dream of using a pulley system and ropes to make Peter Pan fly across the stage, even though it was a low-budget play?

The crowd went wild. Both newspapers raved about their theatrical exploits.

He shook his head and grinned. Sasha had been so pleased. He loved watching her eyes sparkle like fireworks on the Fourth of July, the way she hugged him after an encore. Boy, he'd miss her. But more than anything, he ached over the loss of his arts program as if he grieved for a loved one.

"What's going on?" Kyle stood in front of him, blocking his broom's movement.

"What do you mean?"

"You're standing there with that old broom like it's a dance partner."

Gar realized he *was* clutching the broom, standing statue-still in the corner of the shop, staring at the wall. Did his cousin think he was going bonkers? He lifted his shoulders. "Just thinking."

Kyle grabbed a wrench from the shelf. "Talk to Autumn today?"

"Nah." His usual answer. Gar forced his attention back to cleaning the floor.

Kyle's cell chirped. With greasy fingers, he picked it up. "Yello?" He scrubbed his hands over his dirt splattered overalls. "Hey, Ty. What's up?"

Ty. Gar groaned at the mention of Kyle's brother-in-law who was also co-owner of TK Automotive. That morning, Kyle told him Ty and his wife, Winter, were coming to the house for a barbecue. Marriage-retreat speakers. A coincidence? Or was Kyle setting him up for some impromptu counseling? Gar wanted nothing to do with yakking to strangers about his broken marriage. No thanks. He didn't need psychological babble from people who had it all together.

As soon as Kyle said they were finished for the day, Gar planned to take off for a long hike by the lake or to check out a movie. Anything to avoid what would surely be arm-twisting tactics to get him and Autumn back together.

For that to happen, it would take a miracle. And he'd lost faith in miracles. Didn't he pray for a son or daughter for years? That didn't happen. He'd prayed for his marriage. It disintegrated. He begged God to forgive him for being tempted by another woman. To make his life better. Look what transpired between him and the school. Between him and his wife.

Time had come for him to take matters into his own hands and to look for another teaching job, at least temporarily. One of the high schools or community colleges in the area might be interested in someone with his credentials. Then again, what was to keep him in the Northwest? If he and Autumn split for good, he could live anywhere. He grew up in Seattle. His mom and two brothers still lived there. Autumn lived a little north of them. Maybe the time had come for a complete break.

He was thirty-seven. Itching for something new. This might be the perfect opportunity to escape his guilt and dissatisfaction and find new passion elsewhere. How about one of those English teaching positions in Japan? He didn't have a reference from his last job. A firing would look bad. But with his master's degree and years of experience, they surely wouldn't turn him down.

There had to be new challenges out there. If not, his life felt over. All used up. He needed to feel . . . well, needed. Important to someone. Good at something. For years, that's what being a teacher and director had been to him.

Now, thanks to the school board, Ben, and Autumn, that was taken from him. His gut clenched at the mental picture of his wife in charge of his classes.

Where could he go from here?

Come to Me. My yoke is easy, and My burden is light.

Gar startled at the still small voice. He hadn't heard that in months. Years? For a moment, he didn't know how to respond. Maybe he was remembering a Bible verse. That couldn't be God. Where had He been when Gar and Autumn found out they couldn't have children? When their love faded to ashes? When he was nearly tempted by a beautiful woman beyond his ability to decline?

He didn't want to think about God or Elaine or his wife. What he needed was a distraction. Kyle normally played country music on the radio. Maybe Gar could blast the volume loud enough for his thoughts to be purged. Or he could recite his favorite Shakespearian sonnets. But that would just be a reminder of Autumn. Years ago, she said she loved his poetic voice, especially when he held her in his arms and whispered the words near her ear. She'd listen and relax against his chest, sometimes fall asleep. Or initiate kissing.

Blood pounded in his ears, and he was startled by his reaction. Perhaps his feelings for his wife were stronger than he imagined, even if he would carry this annoyance with her for the rest of his life. He'd better get his work finished. Five o'clock couldn't come fast enough. Then he'd slip out the back door.

Talking with Ty was out of the question. Gar had left Autumn. He needed a new beginning, somewhere else. Maybe, with someone else.

With a mix of longing and regret, he did what he told himself not to do—daydream about his three days in Vegas. And Elaine.

Seven

Gar

Five months ago, on that plane ride from Seattle to Las Vegas, Gar begrudged his boss for pushing him to attend another teacher's conference during the school year. Sure, the speakers were usually great. But he was up to his neck in deadlines. *Cinderella* opened in two weeks, which meant daily practices. Sasha was directing the volunteers with staging, but he was still involved in texting and fielding questions. He was behind in grading several classes of essays. That was the hardest part about being an English teacher—he always had stacks of written papers and online assignments to read and grade. And he was tired. Exhausted, more like. He'd been out of sorts with Autumn, lately. They were running on separate schedules. Staying up late and getting up early never worked well for him.

Now he was arriving at the Hotel Del Marco Oro at ten p.m., Monday night, after having worked all day. He rolled his carry-on luggage to the hotel's check-in counter and noticed his reflection in the gilded mirror behind the blond clerk. Gar's hair was poking up oddly, his face looked almost gray with fatigue, and he spotted a smudge on his cheek. He rubbed at it, frowning.

"May I help?"

He turned to find a twenty-something woman, who appeared to be a fellow traveler, with short-cropped brown hair and shimmering eyes that seemed to disperse light flecks around her, standing beside him. She smelled delicious, reminiscent of cherries on a summer day. Before he could answer, due to his jetlag fog, she reached up and wiped whatever it was off him. She smiled and something magical sparked between them. *Better watch out.*

"You look how I feel." The woman laughed musically. "I just arrived from Boston. Endless day of travel. Can't wait to take a bath." Her cheeks hued rosy. "I mean, get cleaned up after a long day in jets and airports, you know."

He nodded, warming at her friendliness. Something enticing about her made him lean in a little closer, if only to smell her feminine scent.

"I'm Elaine Hansen, by the way."

"Thanks for that." He pointed to his cheek. How many strangers would offer to wipe a smudge off someone's face?

"Checking in?" the female clerk with long golden earrings asked. "Name?"

"Yes." Gar had to think for a second, almost too frazzled and worn out to remember his own name. "Gar Bevere."

Elaine stepped closer. Their arms brushed. "You here for the teacher's conference?"

"Yes. I'm from Everett, Washington."

"Ahhh. I've been to Seattle a few times." She smiled that radiance again. "Gotta love the rain."

Gar laughed like she said something funny. "Or endure it."

"Going to hit the casino?" She nodded toward the opposite end of the lobby. Loud music pulsed in their direction.

"No, it's not my style." He shrugged. He'd been attending conferences here for years and never even stepped inside the hotel's gambling room.

The clerk had him sign a paper he didn't read, then handed him a keycard. She pointed toward the elevators and gave him directions to his room on the fifteenth floor.

"Looks like we'll be neighbors. Fifteen for me too."

He swallowed a lump of dryness in his throat. Elaine was more outgoing than most of the teachers he worked with at ECHS. More like Sasha. The comparison made him do a double-take. Something to ponder later.

When the elevator opened, he stepped in and held the doors apart while the younger teacher preceded him.

As if she were giving an elevator pitch, from the main floor to the fifteenth, she talked about being a history teacher at a public school in the burbs of Boston. How she loved the city. Was wild about living in the East. They stepped onto plush dark brown and gold carpeting and walked down the hallway side by side. She checked the door numbers and stopped beside one marked 1510. He paused also.

"Here's mine." She nodded toward the gold-trimmed number.

"Mine's down this way. It was nice meeting you."

"Want to get coffee later?" She laughed like maybe she was a little embarrassed. "Or a drink?"

There was that dry lump in his throat again. "I'd better take a rain check. I'm beat." He hoped she wouldn't take offense at his rejection, and he continued down the hall.

That was weird. He hadn't been around a pushy woman like that since his college days. And yet, she'd been pleasant. Nice to talk with. The skin around his wedding ring itched. He pushed his thumb against the gold piece and twirled the band. It had gotten tighter in the last couple of years. Sometimes he took it off to ease the discomfort. He might have to do that tonight. He really should get it resized.

He slipped the keycard into the slot and entered the chilly room. Perhaps he should order room service and stay away from the hotel hallway. A nice hot meal would hit the spot. Or he could collapse on the bed and sleep off his fatigue. He used the bathroom with its gold fixtures, slipped out of his clothes, and crawled under the comforter and sheets. He should call Autumn and let her know he arrived safely, but knowing her early-to-bed tendency as he did after fifteen years of marriage, she was probably asleep back home.

His eyes closed, and the woman prancing across the screen of his imagination wasn't his wife. Instead, he envisioned a young brown-haired woman with a bright smile and twinkling eyes wiping a spot of dirt off his cheek.

The next morning, Gar barely had time to get ready and arrive at the first session of the conference. Who in their right mind planned an eight a.m. class for teachers? He was sure the other travelers needed extra sleep as much as he did. Even if the keynote speaker was Beau Johnson, a brilliant scholar in the field of creative classroom development, why start at eight in the morning? Gar stopped by the coffeepot in the lobby and poured himself a cup. Two sugars and a bunch of creamer and it tasted acceptable. He was getting too coddled by hitting coffee shops every morning on his way to work. A mocha was his favorite. Probably due to Autumn's love affair with chocolate. Of course, those coffee stops were perfect opportunities for him and Sasha to meet and run over the day's plans for the stage.

He dropped into a seat near the back of the packed conference room, trying to settle in quietly as the speaker was introduced. In the next second, Elaine slipped into the chair beside him, a coffee cup that matched his in her hand.

"Morning. I see we had the same idea." She held up her cup.

He nodded, then tuned in to Beau who was making an introductory joke. Still, Gar took one more glance at the woman beside him, feeling a bit flattered over her attention. He caught her staring at his ringless finger surrounding the to-go mug. He'd left his wedding ring on the dresser back in his room because of tightness, not as an invitation. The slight lift of her eyebrow made him think she may have misunderstood. Ah, what would it hurt to enjoy a woman's admiration for the short time he'd be in Vegas? Three days. Nothing would happen. He faced forward, giving his full attention to the speaker behind the podium, but his heart was beating a faster rhythm than usual.

Over the next two days, the two of them fell into a pattern, rushing between conference rooms, hitting the coffee stand, hurrying to the next class, sitting together. Did she line up her sessions to match his? Or was it accidental they attended the exact same classes? Serendipitous?

Gar couldn't snuff out his guilty feelings. He was a married man, after all. He loved his wife. Even if they were stuck in a rut, and their marriage had digressed to boring.

"Want to get out of here and take in the Strip?" Elaine whispered in his ear the second day.

He gulped.

"I'd like to shop. We could find food." She nudged him with her arm.

He *was* hungry. The current session was a big snore, presented by a teacher who'd written a book about keeping enthusiasm alive in the classroom. How ironic was that?

"What do you think?"

Skipping one class wouldn't hurt. He was mainly at the teacher's convention to hear Beau speak, anyway. And he wouldn't keynote again until after dinner.

Elaine nodded toward the door and raised one eyebrow.

Gar noticed her freckles and reminded himself she was much younger than him. Autumn wouldn't mind if he took in the sights with a woman barely out of the classroom herself. Almost like a field trip. He deserved a little pleasure in seeing Vegas, right?

He followed Elaine out the back door, and they ran down the hallway. Gar laughed so hard he paused to catch his breath, not even knowing why what they were doing seemed so funny.

"We're playing hooky." She giggled.

"Exactly."

She grabbed his hand and pulled him toward the revolving glass door. He slid his hand free of hers. None of that.

What are you doing with her? He swallowed the warning down. He wasn't doing anything wrong. Hadn't he pulled his hand away? What was the crime in spending the afternoon with another teacher? Maybe they'd talk about school stuff. Exchange ideas.

Yeah, sure.

They bought hotdogs from a vendor, then window-shopped along the Strip, taking in the glitzy boutiques. Nothing appealed to him, but Elaine oohed and aahed over everything.

"Let's check out this one." She dodged into a jewelry and souvenir store and hurried right over to a case of necklaces and rings. She asked the clerk to pull out a box of samples.

Gar strolled around the store filled with a plethora of items brandishing the words "Las Vegas." He should buy something for Autumn. Maybe he'd come back later when he wasn't with Elaine. Purchasing a gift for his wife in front of another woman felt weird. Still, he perused the t-shirts on the wall. He especially liked a teal one with a castle and "Las Vegas" written in a medieval font. What size did Autumn wear now? Hadn't she gone from a medium to a large? He couldn't be sure. Maybe a mug would be better.

He felt someone beside him, brushing against his side.

"Anything interesting?" Elaine giggled.

He gulped, realizing he was feeling way more interested in her than he should. "Not really."

She tugged on his arm. At least not his hand, this time. Even friends sometimes strolled arm in arm, right?

They continued window-shopping. She ran into a store and purchased a frog that made *ree-deep* sounds. She said it would be an ice-breaker for her class. For the next couple of hours, Gar had fun hanging out with her and laughing. It seemed like forever since he' joked around like that. One missed session turned into two. They ate an early dinner, walked some more, then hit a coffee shop and shared more about their classes. As teachers, they had so much in common. As a man, he enjoyed her smile, the way her gaze danced when she explained about helping her students write their family's history.

He checked his cell. Uh-oh. If they didn't hurry, they'd miss Beau's main session on keeping high school students engaged, the precise reason Gar was attending. He had to report back to Ben on what he learned. If he missed out because he was spending time off-campus with a female teacher from Boston, that would be a difficult scenario to explain.

"It's late. I can't skip the next meeting." He noticed he'd missed a call and a couple of texts from Autumn. That knot of guilt kept twisting in his throat.

"Let's run. I don't want to miss it, either. You game?"

Gar nodded, bedazzled. Good thing she didn't ask for something more personal. Otherwise, he was afraid he might cross some invisible line after how comfortable he'd become spending the day with her. Him and a beautiful woman in a distant city? Who would know?

In his heart, Gar realized *he* would know—and probably hate himself. And God would know. But he swept concerns away. Nothing was going to happen. And if he set things straight right now, he'd miss her company for the rest of the conference. Tomorrow night he planned to see the Broadway hit *Newsies.* Maybe Elaine would be interested in watching the show with him.

Dashing between the revolving doors, she almost tripped. Gar caught her, tugged her safely away from the moving doors, and held her close for a moment. It was the gentlemanly thing to do. But as he kept her next to him longer than was required, her sky blue eyes stared up at him dreamily. Heat infused his chest. He released her, but not soon enough.

"I need to change my clothes." Elaine swiped her hand over a ketchup stain on her sleeve. "It will only take a minute."

"Sure." He shouldn't go up to her room. He could tell her he'd see her later at the conference. What time was it, anyway? Had the speaker started? He didn't want to check his cell and be reminded that Autumn had been trying to contact him. For just a few more minutes, he wanted to forget responsibilities, and enjoy a young woman hanging on his arm, attracted to him as a man.

And the woman beside him? She was breathtaking.

She stopped in front of her door on the fifteenth floor, and he was fascinated by her every move. Like a dancer, her fingers slid her keycard through the slot, then swished in the air. Her enticing gaze met his. She smiled coyly. Her eyes sparkled with mischief or attraction. "Come in? It'll only take a second."

At her question, his world stopped spinning.

They stared at each other. Her hand, soft and warm, slipped into his.

Was she asking what he thought she was?

She opened the door, revealing her room decorated in gold and maroon. She tugged on his hand. His heart beat so fast as if it were about to leap from his chest.

Then he found his voice. "I can't." He drew in a ragged breath of air. "I-I'm married."

"I know that, silly." She let go of his hand and toyed with a button on his shirt.

He didn't back away. He should have, but he didn't.

Slowly, as if in a dream, she leaned up on tiptoe and her lips teased his. It didn't take much before he gave in to the kiss, exploring her mouth in ways that would haunt him for days to come.

But then, as if a loud horn—maybe a trumpet—blasted in his head, he broke away, stumbled backward. What was he doing? How stupid could he be? He wasn't going to—

He turned away and sprinted to his room, without glancing back. Inside, he slammed the door and leaned against it, breathing like he ran a marathon. Something wretched and heart-stopping had happened. He just gave in to temptation in a way he never would have imagined himself capable of doing.

He rubbed his hands over his face, his recently kissed mouth, reeling with regret.

What have I done?

Eight

Autumn

Autumn avoided prepping her new classroom until the last Friday before school started. Gar's old classroom, which still had his posters and humorous quotes on the wall, had to be transformed into hers. But as she replaced his charts with her grammar tips and pictures of famous authors, she felt like she was betraying him all over again. How could she not think of her husband while she redecorated his classroom? How could she teach in his room without picturing him standing in that exact place, sharing his love for literature with the students in his dramatic way?

She dropped into the chair behind his—her—desk and filled two drawers with personal supplies—Kleenex, pens, legal pads, and several boxes of pre-wrapped snacks, and her weakness, chocolate. Although, she knew she'd better go easy on the treats or she'd turn into a blimp. Ever since Gar left five weeks ago, she'd hardly exercised. Instead, she sat home alone watching TV, reading sappy love stories, cooking fudge, and eating her successes and failures. Even if the candy didn't set right—and a lot of her first efforts didn't—it still tasted delicious. She had the gained weight to prove it. But she lacked the self-discipline to curb her appetite. Once classes started, she promised herself, she'd get back on schedule, dieting and exercising.

Maybe fudge was the wrong kind of distraction to indulge in, but she sure enjoyed it.

What would Gar think of her taking over his space? He'd probably resent it, and her even more.

Lacey, Gar's cousin's wife who lived in Coeur d'Alene, made it her mission to keep Autumn informed on Gar's where-abouts. At first, Autumn was eager to hear every detail. How he'd crashed at their place since the day he left her. How he was working in Kyle's mechanic shop. Gar, all greasy and filthy? She had a hard time picturing that. Lacey complained about the guys sitting around all weekend, watching preseason football and belching. But if her friend didn't fill her in, thanks to Gar not taking her calls, she wouldn't know where he landed, or if he was even alive. Lacey assured her he was miserable. Which Autumn doubted. If he were feeling any sense of remorse, wouldn't he contact her?

She missed him every day. As much as she'd thought he should leave, she didn't like living without him this long. She missed the sound of his laughter over something funny on TV, or him chatting with her during a meal or lying beside her on the couch like they used to do. In the past, they discussed a lot of school events. How his or her classes were going. What new ideas he and Sasha had drummed up.

Now, the house was silent.

Maybe she could ask her sister to move in with her until Gar returned. But then she'd have to clean the kitchen. She pictured the stack of pans and utensils she left in the sink after making a layered fudge of white chocolate and peanut butter two nights ago. Boy had that been amazing. Although, she had trouble getting the concoction to stay at the perfect temperature for five minutes. Some fudge scorched easily—especially the ones where the marshmallow creme was added first. Other varieties turned out dry and grainy because she overcooked them.

She pushed her hair over her ears and leaned closer to her laptop, studying her class rosters. Twenty-five students in her first English period. Twenty-one in the second. And—

Shelley Pollard, a cheerleader and junior class president, burst into the room like a ray of sunshine. Right behind her, Jewel, her five-foot-tall mother, strode toward Autumn like a fast-moving locomotive on four-inch heels. Anxiety churned in Autumn's belly. Jewel Pollard might be small in stature, but she had a reputation for being a stinker. Behind closed doors, Autumn had heard frustrated teachers call her a troublemaker.

Autumn stood to meet them. "Hello." With her knee, she nudged the drawer filled with snacks closed. No use Jewel getting the impression she was a snack food junkie.

"Hi, Mrs. Bevere." Shelley grinned, her braces gleaming under the room's fluorescent lighting. "Looks different in here."

"I'm changing a few things. How may I help you?"

Jewel's sculpted eyebrow quirked. "We are here to discuss *your* theatrical plans, Mrs. Bevere."

Surely, she knew the drama program was canceled. "I have no theater plans."

Jewel didn't bat an eyelash. "I heard about that dreadful demonstration with your husband and the board." She tsk-tsked. "*I* was out of town, or things might have turned out differently." Jewel slid her sequin-covered purse strap higher on her shoulder. "I can assure you, I was put out when I heard Gar quit."

"He didn't quit. He was fired." Autumn didn't approve of the way Gar acted, but she wouldn't let the truth get twisted.

Jewel glanced at her daughter. "Yes, well, however you want to phrase it, what's done is done. Shelley and I are here to find out what you're going to do about it."

"There's nothing to *do*. Funding was cut." She tried to keep her tone modulated, but she felt a snarky reaction coming on.

Jewel strode forward until her pointy-toed shoes almost touched Autumn's pumps.

She inhaled the woman's tangy perfume and was tempted to cover her nose.

Jewel leaned her hand against one corner of the desk, making her muscled arm taut. No doubt, she worked out at the gym. Did Zumba, or something.

Maybe Autumn should get a membership at one of the local workout joints. She needed to ease the tension in her life. And relieve the pudgy feeling in her belly and thighs.

"Forgive me if I misunderstood." Jewel's green eyes followed Autumn's every move. "Are you implying there won't be drama this fall?" The way she said "drama" sounded more like "draaama."

Autumn wished Jewel would have kept this conversation between the two adults. But it couldn't be helped now. "That's exactly what I'm saying. No program in the fall. No spring production."

Shelley whimpered.

Jewel clutched the silver necklace at her chest. "I don't believe it."

What wasn't to believe?

Shelley swiped at something under her eyes. Tears?

Autumn hadn't considered the impact the absence of theater and music might have on some students. She probably should have cared more about that. Them. Still, it wasn't her concern.

Jewel enveloped Shelley in an embrace. "There, there. Don't worry, baby doll, Mommy will work this out."

She would? How?

As fast as Jewel released her daughter, she grabbed hold of Autumn's wrist. The woman's eyes peered at her as if reading every nuance on Autumn's face. "Tell me, what do we need to do? I'll do anything. Name your price."

Autumn disengaged the parent's grasp. Whatever Jewel thought she could do, she couldn't.

"How much do you need?" Jewel opened her purse and withdrew a checkbook.

Seriously? A trip to Hawaii. A yacht. "Nothing."

"Our school needs a play." Jewel tapped her foot.

Why was she telling Autumn this? "No funding means no play."

"That's absurd." With her plum-colored nails, Jewel picked at a speck of dust on her sweater.

"Perhaps, but that's how things turned out." Gar would still be home if the board hadn't made such a drastic decision. He wouldn't have shoved Ben in his tirade. He'd still have his job. She'd be the freshman and sophomore teacher—which would be fine with her. And she'd be the one *not* having this awkward conversation.

She crossed the white and gray checkered linoleum toward the door, hoping the women would follow. She had important things to do. Like finishing the bulletin board. Like calming herself and trying out the snacks in her drawer. Tension always gave her the munchies. Too bad she didn't bring the cherry and almond fudge for lunch. "Thanks for stopping by." She forced a smile, hoping it didn't appear contrived.

Jewel's heels clicked across the floor. Her thick red lipstick exaggerated her frown. "You haven't heard the last of this, Mrs. Bevere. In fact, if there isn't a play for my Shelley"—she raised her chin a notch—"I'll remove her from this school."

Shelley gasped. Apparently, this was the first time the teenager knew of the ultimatum. "Mom—"

"My generous funding will vanish." Her trump card? Mr. Whiffleman would hate that.

"I'm not the one you should be talking to." Autumn kept her hand on the doorknob. "Perhaps you should take this up with the principal?"

"I believe I shall." Jewel stomped out of the classroom, her purse hitting the doorframe. Her heels click-clacked down the hallway, but the perfumed air remained pungent.

"Goodbye, Mrs. Bevere." Shelley waved, her cheeks flushed like she might be embarrassed. Then she scurried after her mother.

"Goodbye." Autumn shut the door and leaned against it. Good grief, why did Jewel assume she'd take on drama? Did she think it Autumn's obligation to assume all of Gar's roles? But what if that happened? What if she was forced to take on Gar's program without him? Anxiety twirled in her stomach and raced up her chest. She shook her head. No, she wasn't tempted to resurrect theater. It caused enough trouble in her life, thank you very much.

With a harrumph, she returned to the desk. Only one thing to do—she opened the second drawer and grabbed a frosting covered brownie. She closed her eyes and savored the chocolate. Frustration like this might require two.

Needing something to get her mind off Jewel, she resumed decorating the walls. She checked online for more authors' quotes to print off. After trimming the edges around each sentence or phrase, she stapled them to the green construction paper on the wall. Despite her intent to stay focused on her classroom, her afternoon was peppered with interruptions. Two more parents visited. Five calls came in. Each parent was asking—demanding—that theater be reinstated. Why wouldn't they believe there was nothing she could do?

Why didn't the "concerned" parents speak up for Gar at

that meeting? Why did they let the board reject the thing that supposedly meant so much to them?

No way would she volunteer a bazillion hours to something she didn't care about. If she had time to donate, she'd choose her own organization. Like helping feed the homeless in Everett. Her friend, Marny Blakely, who worked in the school office, was always trying to get her to join the soup-and-sandwich ministry at her church. She'd been planning to help, but something always interfered.

She pushed a thumbtack into the wall, securing a poster with the words "Authors' Quotes." She'd have the students in her four English classes display Post-its all around the perimeter, listing their favorite authors and quotes. Satisfied, she stepped back to admire her work.

The classroom door squeaked open. If that was another parent asking about—

"Mrs. Bevere, may I speak with you?" The principal's voice.

She tensed, then plastered on her professional face. "Mr. Whiffleman, welcome." She swayed her hand toward the walls. "I'm almost ready for classes."

"Good. Got a minute?" The salt-and-pepper haired man ran his fingers over his thin strands like he was taming down frustration.

"Sure."

When he sat down at a student's desk, she took another. She crossed her legs at her ankles, interlaced her fingers, and waited.

He twiddled his thumbs, his gray eyes appraising her. "How are you doing? Things must be difficult without Gar." His voice sounded kind.

She swallowed a cotton ball of dryness. "I'm . . . okay." She doubted he wanted to hear how lonely she'd been. How she cried herself to sleep last night. Well, every night. How she buried herself in fudge and memories.

"My phone's been ringing off the wall."

His abrupt change in conversation confused her.

"For the life of me, I can't understand why parents are calling today." He pinched the bridge of his nose like he had a horrific headache.

"I've gotten a few of those calls myself." Not that she took them seriously.

"We may have to give in to them."

What? Start Gar's program back up? "But I thought—"

He held up his hand. "I know. Zero funding for theater. We're over budget. Hopefully, the auction in December will be successful. But that's for salaries and fixing the roof."

"Explain that to the parents." *Good luck telling Jewel.* She blew out the breath she'd been holding. He could ask for Gar's help. Her husband would probably do it even without a stipend. She sat up straighter. Would Ben consider offering Gar his old position? If he did, would Gar come home? "The board's decision was final, right?"

"Based on a lack of money and other reasons, yes." He rubbed his forehead. "But five of our most influential families have threatened to withdraw if we don't provide a theatrical outlet for their children."

"Five?" "Influential families" paid her salary, right? In a way, they owned the school and could make demands. She felt a noose tightening around her neck.

"They give generously at the auction and other fundraisers and feel they should have a say." He spread his hands wide. "What am I to do?"

"Tell them no?"

He shook his head and stood. "Jewel Pollard was firm. Same as the others. They'll leave. I'll take this up with the board tonight, but I know what has to happen."

She stood also. "What's that, sir?"

He pointed at her, his eyes sparkling. He seemed more animated, like his old self, now. Less rattled. "It's all up to you."

"Me?" He couldn't be saying what she thought he was.

"You'll put on a show, and everything will be fine. You know, smooth out those ruffled feathers." He clapped his hands as if she'd agreed to the preposterous suggestion. He strode toward the door.

"Wait." She rushed after him. "I can't do that. I'm not a theater major." What was he thinking? "That's Gar's line of work." Why did people assume married couples shared the same talents and skills?

At the doorway, he eyed her over his glasses. "And you have his position, don't you?"

That wasn't fair. She took the job of an English teacher, not the drama director. She sucked in a deep breath, her airways feeling inflamed. "What about production costs?" *If* she could pull off a show. "Who's going to back this play?" She couldn't. Not since she had a house payment to make without Gar's regular income.

"You'll think of something." He marched out the door whistling a cheery tune.

She groaned in disbelief, then faced the room she'd been trying so hard to make her own. The one Gar taught in for ten years. The one that now felt like her enemy.

How could Ben suggest that she direct a show? She had enough responsibilities with teaching four high school English classes, plus health. How could she fulfill all her obligations and put on a grand production like Ben and the parents would expect? How could she take over one more thing that had been Gar's? She . . . just . . . couldn't. She sank into her chair and grabbed an almond and yogurt bar from the drawer. She gobbled it up so fast she barely tasted it.

Tears pooled in her eyes, but she blinked rapidly and buried the threatening emotions. She had to forget all this theater stuff and focus on the work in front of her. Otherwise, resigning seemed like a viable option. Until she remembered she was dependent on her paycheck to cover her house payments, especially since Gar was a minimum-wage broom operator in Idaho.

God, help. What have I gotten myself into?

Nine

Autumn

On the first day of school, Autumn stood by her desk and welcomed back the students. She always enjoyed the excitement of opening week. As the juniors filled her room during the first period, several stopped at her desk.

"I'm pumped you're going to do a play, Mrs. Bevere." Sandy Thompson grinned.

"Me too, Mrs. Bevere," Shelley chirped from a front-row chair. "I hope we do a spectacular musical."

Not a musical. Not with all the voice coaching and choreography it entailed. Autumn shuddered.

"That would be awesome."

"I'm all in."

Several voices called out in agreement.

A performance was the main topic of the morning. However, it was the last thing on her mind.

"What about Shakespeare?" Todd Meyers suggested as he brushed past her desk.

She smiled at the last stragglers rushing to find seats.

"Welcome to eleventh grade English. In case you don't know, my name is Mrs. Bevere."

"Mr. Bevere's *wife*," someone in the back whispered.

Yes, that too. *He* wasn't far from her thoughts.

A red-haired girl chewing gum in the back raised her hand. "Yes?"

"I'm Dani. This is my third year at Everett Christian."

Autumn recognized her from last year's sophomore English class. "Yes, Dani?"

"Did Mr. Bevere really grab Principal Whiffleman and shove him?" Her eyes widened.

Autumn had anticipated that question.

Chattering erupted around the room.

"I heard—"

"My mom said—"

"Students. Students." Sticking with her plan, Autumn picked up her copy of Shakespeare's sonnets. "If I could have your attention?" Without addressing Dani's question, she pried the pages of the book apart and found Sonnet 116. "'Let me not to the marriage of true minds admit impediments. Love is not love which alters when it alteration finds, or bends with the remover to remove: O no; it is an ever-fixed mark, that looks on tempests, and is never shaken.'"

She continued reading, but her mind was stuck on Gar and the times he held her in his arms and quoted this poem. She could still hear his gentle voice whispering in her ear. "'Love alters not with his brief hours and weeks, but bears it out even to the edge of doom.'" When Gar thought of those words, did he think of her like she was thinking of him right now?

She closed the book and sighed.

"I love poetry, as you'll discover by the things I read in class. I thrill to a good novel as well. Dickens, Austen, C. S. Lewis, to modern day, Grisham and Rivers." As Autumn spoke, she walked back and forth at the front of the room. "I want you to consider the authors who have affected your lives. Which ones challenged you to take on a new adventure? To look at something as if you've never seen it before? Who inspired you to be a better person? What makes a writer stand out to you as a 'great?' And finally, what written words are your favorites?"

"Sounds like an assignment," Shelley piped in.

"Indeed. I want you to make your own list of influential authors and quotes. You may work with a partner or in a small group. Explain why the author's writing touches your heart." She pointed toward the bulletin board. "On the wall, you'll see the writers I've chosen. Each of you will tack your list there."

"Is that it?" Todd asked with a bubbly laugh. "No home-work?"

"This is a class assignment." Autumn folded her arms around the book she held, her heart still warmed by the poem. "I'll hand out a reading list in a few minutes. I expect you to get started on that tonight."

A few groans resounded, but then, the students turned their chairs and talked about authors and literature with others around them. She listened in on several conversations and was pleased to hear some lively debates.

Her first class was going well. Hopefully, the rest of the day would be as successful. She didn't want to talk about Gar to any of the students. She didn't have answers about doing a production. But the realization that Mr. Whiffleman—or Jewel—might stop by her classroom at any time and pressure her into directing a play weighed heavily on her mind.

Ten

Gar

As Gar removed the flat tire from the customer's rig, he was aware it was the first day of school back home. Did his old students miss him? Or did Autumn fill the void his firing caused? The twist in his gut tightened, a vice squeezing the life out of him.

Even though Kyle was grumpy for a while after Gar avoided meeting up with Ty, he promoted Gar from floor sweeper to phone answering tech and tire repairman. Now he could change tires faster than ever. Was that something worth bragging about? He imagined himself talking to a future employer. *That's right, sir. I have a master's degree in English and a minor in theater but let me impress you with how fast I can change a tire.*

Like anyone would care.

He chuckled, despite the ridiculous scenario. After he put on the new tire and replaced the lug nuts and hubcap, he grabbed the old one, hauled it outside, and heaved it onto a stack of tires behind the building. Then he strode toward the office to fill out the paperwork.

When he heard a commotion, he paused. Glancing into the office, he saw Lacey gesticulating toward Kyle. The whites of her eyes were enlarged. Thanks to the loud sound of the air-powered wrench starting and stopping, her words came in spurts. Ryan, a part-time assistant, used the tool, making Lacey's sentences unclear—but not her meaning. Boy was she irate.

"Gar grabbed a—"

The air wrench revved.

"He needs time," Kyle said in an edgy voice.

More noises erupted.

"—give him a deadline." Lacey tossed up her hands. "Gar can leave now for all I—"

Yep, he'd overstayed his welcome. Five weeks and three days.

He'd filled out a dozen online applications, but no teaching job opened up. What else could he do, other than return home? Of course, he could stick with this job. He drew in a long breath. No, he couldn't. He needed something with a higher pay scale—and work he liked.

The argument between Lacey and Kyle finished. She stomped out the double doors and paused to glare at her husband. Kyle strode into the garage and threw down a tool. The clatter echoed in the tall room. Then he returned to the Mustang engine he was working on all morning as if he didn't just have a fight with his wife. Lacey jumped into her car and sped away.

Gritting his teeth, Gar felt awful that his stay was causing the rift. He entered the information in the spreadsheet they used to document the day's work, then he approached Kyle. "What's next?"

"When I'm finished with this bay, haul in the blue Accent and rotate the tires." Without looking up, he continued tightening something deep in the engine compartment. "Before we leave today, you and I are going to talk." His grease-blackened hand reached for a rag in the back pocket of his coveralls.

"Yeah, sure." Did that mean he was out of a place to stay? Or a job? Guess he'd have to find a cheap motel. Maybe a temp office for work.

The business phone rang, and Gar returned to the office. A guy needed pricing for all-season tires for an SUV. He typed the numbers into the computer and relayed the costs.

As soon as he finished the call, his cell vibrated. One glance at the screen and his heart thudded in his ears. *Sasha Delaney.* He hadn't heard from her since he left Everett.

"Hey, Kyle, I'm heading outside to take a call."

"Uh-huh," Kyle mumbled from under the hood.

With long strides, Gar marched out the large bay doors and into the parking lot where five cars awaited their turn in the garage, including the Accent. That car reminded him of Autumn's.

He took a breath and tapped the screen. "Hey, Sasha."

"Gar"—she dragged out his name—"it's so good to hear your voice."

He gulped. "You too, Sash." Ben's suspicions about their relationship made him feel awkward talking to her. Which was silly since they'd been friends for a long time. "How are things?" Why didn't she call before? Especially considering his removal from the school. Of course, she lost her staging gig too.

She cleared her throat. "Sorry if this is a bad time to call."

"I'm working, but I have a minute." He wished they could chat over coffee like old times. Then they could laugh at the weird things Ben said and mock his old-fashioned sense of impropriety.

The screech of the air wrench escalated in the background. Gar held the cell phone closer to his ear.

"I've missed you," she said with a breathy tone.

"Yeah?" Oh. Did he just flirt with her? He didn't mean to.

"Yeah," she whispered.

"Things didn't turn out the way I imagined for this school year." That was a safer topic.

"For me, neither." A silence. "Gar, I've heard rumors. I wanted your take on them."

"Rumors?" About him and her, no doubt. "Look, Sasha, we didn't do anything wrong. It was all a bunch of old wives' gossip. Don't let it bother you."

Sasha was quiet for a long moment. Uncomfortably so.

"Sash?"

"That's the thing, G-Gar." The tremble in her voice made him think he might not like whatever she had to say. "I, well, this is embarrassing. I shouldn't have called."

"Wait. Say what you need to say."

"I think," she said quietly, "I did—do—feel something more for you than I should have, more than . . . friendship."

In the ensuing silence, he didn't breathe. He'd told Ben, and anyone else who asked, Sasha was his friend. Now, she was confessing she had feelings for him? "Don't you have a boy-friend?"

"Yes." She made an indignant snort. "And you were married. Are you still?" Her voice went soft.

"Last I knew." He pressed his fingers against his forehead. "I don't know what to say. I didn't realize you felt that way." He gulped. Maybe there'd always been something hovering in the air between them. Mild flirting, at least.

"Didn't you?"

Her words, her sultry tone, made his heart beat faster. Thoughts of their late-night set-painting sessions flitted through his brain. Them laughing over coffee. Her hugging him. Had the sparkle in her eyes attracted him in more ways than he realized? He told Ben he wasn't "carrying on" with Sasha.

But she was beautiful. Young. And, it turns out, attracted to him.

A cluster of cobwebs stuck in his throat. "W-why didn't you tell me before?"

"I've kept myself from calling, didn't want to make things worse." She sighed. "But Tawny Richards and I stayed in contact. Remember her?"

"Yeah, sure." Tawny had been the librarian as long as he worked at the school.

"She told me something I thought you'd want to know." Her voice turned serious. "I care about you, Gar. I don't think what the school did to you was right."

It was nice to hear someone say so, but he didn't want to listen to any ECHS gossip. "I'm working, so I've got to cut this short."

"Okay." She spoke faster. "Rumor is ECHS is doing a fall production, after all."

Acid rolled up his throat. "What?"

"That's right." Her voice turned brittle. "Tawny says the parents got in a huff and demanded theater be reinstated—or they'd take their money and find another school. How do you like that?"

A kick in the gut would have been less painful. "You've got to be kidding." He ran his fingers through his hair. They fired him, then resurrected his program? He didn't want to ask but couldn't stop himself. "Who'd they get for a director?"

"You're not going to believe this."

"It better not be Sue Hampton." The band teacher had always been offering him musical suggestions and seemed way too interested in his stuff. "Who is it?" He gritted his teeth.

"Autumn."

A knife slashed through his heart, and he almost doubled over. "I don't believe it." His wife stole his job—and now, theater?

71

"I'm sorry to be the bearer of bad news." She sniffed, almost like she was crying. "About the other stuff . . . if you change your mind or want to talk . . ."

What could he say? *Let's meet?* Guilt spun around in his head, his heart, and he didn't say the words. Even though he walked out on his wife, being unfaithful to her while he wore her wedding ring felt wrong. Isn't that why he ran from Elaine in Vegas?

"I should go. Call me." Again, with the breathy sounds. "I miss you, Gar."

Before he could respond, she ended the call.

He blew out a long breath.

Sasha cared for him. And his wife had betrayed him. Again.

Eleven

Ty

Ty Williams stuck his finger in the neck of his turquoise tie and tugged down, loosening the fabric noose. The late September afternoon was sunny and warm, lacking any chill in the woods along the eastern border of Washington. A perfect day for Josh and Summer Hart's outdoor vow renewal ceremony. Ty, dressed in his best-man tux, linked his fingers with Winter's as they waited for the procession to begin under the shade of two giant cedar trees. She was dressed in a floral turquoise bridesmaid's dress that reached just below her knees. "You look beautiful."

"Thanks." She smiled at him. "You're quite debonair yourself."

Seeing her so relaxed pleased him. They'd been under a mountain of stress ever since a member of their ministry team, Randi Simmons, stole Winter's journal. So far, they hadn't found her. Knowing Randi's dislike for him, Ty figured the woman had something sinister planned. To what extent she'd go to cause difficulties for their ministry—or for him and Winter—he could only guess. For the team, it felt like an attack from the devil, and they were fighting back spiritually. They'd made it a matter of daily, if not hourly, prayer.

But today, they promised not to think about the problem so they could enjoy their friends' celebration. And here he was contemplating trouble. *Lord, forgive me.*

He drew Winter's hand to his lips. "Love you, Sas."

"Love you too." Her green eyes sparkled at him.

Less than a year ago, they had their own second marriage ceremony. Each time they attended a wedding, Ty's thoughts raced to how he felt as a groom. How he waited for his bride to walk down the aisle in her mom's church in Ketchikan, Alaska, him nervous and anxious and eager. Seeing his lovely wife, now, he was reminded of the miracle God performed to bring them together. He felt so thankful for the way the Lord healed their hearts and restored them. The same as Josh and Summer.

As Ty took in the small group gathered in the meadow surrounded by giant pines, cedars, and golden aspens at Hart's Camp, he felt thrilled to be a part of this special day. Chad Gray, a pastor friend who'd performed the wedding ceremony for him and Winter, stood next to Josh, the anxious-looking groom. Chad leaned over and whispered something to him. Josh yanked a hanky out of his pocket, then dabbed his forehead. Apparently, he was sweating, no doubt from the heat. Maybe from nerves.

Josh's aunt and uncle, Em and Mac, and Neil, Winter's co-leader for Passion's Prayer, sat in folding chairs in the audience. An empty chair awaited Ezzie, a kindly older man who'd worked at the camp for fifty years. He'd be the one escorting Summer down the trail and giving her away.

Someone whistled from beyond the tree line, a signal to let them know the bride was ready. Josh pulled on the hem of his western-style jacket and straightened his bolo tie. Deborah, standing at the keyboard they hauled up the hill, played a melodic love song.

Winter slipped her hand in the crook of Ty's arm, and they strolled together along the dirt path they were instructed to follow. He felt such relief that they were already married. That he didn't have to fret about whether Sas might change her mind about marrying him at the last second. Not that she would have. But he'd worried, nonetheless. He bet Josh was concerned about that too. Ty said a prayer for him as he passed Em and Mac. When they reached the point about four feet from Josh and Chad, Ty and Winter separated. Ty strode toward Josh's left. Winter stopped a couple of feet to Chad's right.

A gasp went up from the crowd, and Ty looked up to see what happened. Shua, Josh and Summer's precocious four-year-old daughter, skipped up the trail, tossing daisies in the air and blowing kisses toward Josh. With a wide grin on her face, she waved at him. "Hi, Daddy! *You're pwetty.*"

Everyone laughed.

"So are you," Josh said in a way that sounded like he was choking up. He waved at his daughter, then wiped the back of his knuckles beneath his eyes. Hopefully, the young woman taking pictures captured his tender expression.

Shua skipped and danced all the way to Josh. When she was inches from him, he leaned over and they hugged. Shua kissed his cheek, and then they Eskimo-kissed. Giggling, she twirled her skirt and pranced over to Winter. It seemed the little girl couldn't stop moving. Winter took her hand, stilling her momentarily, probably not for long.

Ty felt a tug on his heart. Seeing Shua next to his wife made him yearn for a daughter of his own. Their own. He'd asked Sas, again, when she'd like to start a family, hoping her answer had changed from the last time he inquired. Her typical answer of "in a few years" didn't seem soon enough. But maybe he was too impatient.

April Gray, Chad's wife and the matron of honor, strolled down the trail, a radiant smile on her face. Her joy, no doubt, not only had to do with this glorious occasion but also because she was a few months along in her pregnancy. A miracle, really, considering her and Chad had almost split up. She walked toward her pastor-husband, and instead of moving to her position, she leaned up and kissed his cheek. An "*awww*" went up around the small group. Chad's face hued red, but he kissed her cheek too. Ty, knowing their story of lost and found love, rejoiced in their renewed relationship. God was so good to bring them all together like this. Three couples who fell out of love with their spouses then were drawn back together by God's grace.

The music changed. Anticipation filled the air. Deborah played the triumphant notes to the "Wedding March." Em and Neil helped Mac struggle to his feet.

Summer—or Summer Day, as Josh called her—strolled up the trail in a flowing white gown that barely skimmed the earth as she walked. No veil covered her face. She'd told Winter she wanted to see Josh clearly and not trip on the trail. A white daisy was clipped in her short hair, just above her right ear. A wide grin crossed her lips, and her gaze was fastened on Josh's.

Smiling, wiping tears, Josh watched his bride drawing closer. He looked so eager as if he might run to her and pull her forward to get the ceremony moving faster.

Summer, her hand linked in Ezzie's arm, paused about five feet from Josh. The two of them just stood there, grinning at each other.

Ty wanted to laugh with joy. But he refrained.

This was their time.

"Who gives this woman to be married to this man?" Chad's voice rang strong in the clearing.

"I do," Ezzie replied. "With all my heart, I do." He kissed Summer's cheek. Then he shook Josh's hand. The two men hugged. Ezzie took Josh's left hand and linked it with Summer's right. "For keeps, this time," he whispered.

Josh nodded.

"Amen," Chad agreed.

Then the older man doffed his cowboy hat and took his seat next to Mac.

Josh and Summer stared into each other's eyes, the love they shared so obvious.

"Mommy, when are we going to get *mawwied*?" Shua asked in an impatient voice.

Chuckles and snickers broke the silence.

"Any second now." Summer took a deep breath.

Josh drew her forward until they were standing side by side in front of Chad and the other attendants.

Through the exchanging of vows, Ty's gaze was focused on the young couple, but every now and then he glanced at his wife. Once, he found her watching him and he winked.

"Marriage is such a beautiful thing," Chad spoke. "Josh and Summer are promising to be true to each other. To love one another above everyone else, other than their devotion to God, as long as they both shall live. Josh, I know your heart's desire is for Summer. You've told me so."

Josh nodded and teared up again.

Ty's reaction was the same. He remembered how this couple planned to divorce each other two months ago. But they attended a marriage seminar he and Winter led here at Hart's Camp, and their hearts were changed by the love of God. Today's renewing of their vows was a miraculous sign of the restoration that took place in their lives.

"Summer, you have opened your heart to love again." Chad glanced from Summer to Josh, then back again. "You want this marriage to last a lifetime, don't you? You told me how you long for your lives together to be a testimony of God's love and second chances."

"Yes." She clutched Josh's hand between both of hers.

Chad led them in traditional wedding vows, and they repeated the phrases. Several times, Shua made comments or twirled her dress, bringing everyone's attention to her. Other than that, Ty's—and he assumed the audience's—gazes were focused on the two who couldn't keep their eyes off each other.

After the rings were exchanged and Chad prayed for their future, Ty, as pre-directed by Chad, grabbed Josh's guitar. Lifting it in his hands, he strode back to the wedding party and handed the instrument to the groom.

Josh nodded his thanks. He removed his black cowboy hat and pulled the guitar strap over his shoulders. After he returned his hat to his head, he stepped back a little and faced Summer. *I love you,* he mouthed. She did the same to him.

"I fell in love with a princess," Josh sang as he picked the strings of his guitar. "With the slightest glance, she can make my heart sing."

Shua left her spot near Winter and danced her way to Josh. As he continued singing, she looked up at her daddy with such love and adoration it took Ty's breath away. She swayed back and forth, and her dress swished in time with the music. Tears ran down Summer's cheeks, and she didn't wipe them away.

"And she's mine, all mine. In finding her, I found myself. In loving her, my life's made new." Josh ran his fingers over the neck of the guitar, all the while his gaze never left Summer's. "Summer Day is the girl in my dreams at night. Summer Day is the name on my breath in the morn. She's the golden beauty who thrills my heart. I'll sing over her until the end of time. And she's mine . . ."

After a couple more verses, Josh finished singing. Even before he took the guitar strap off, Summer lunged forward and kissed him fully on the lips.

Everyone clapped and cheered.

"Hey, you two, I didn't say 'you may kiss the groom!'" Chad spoke in mock disgruntlement.

The attendants and small crowd laughed at the turn of phrase.

Josh removed his guitar and handed it to Ty.

"Hurry up and say it, Pastor Chad," Josh said with a cheeky grin. He took Summer in his arms as if he wasn't about to wait for permission.

Summer laughed. Shua danced around the wedding couple.

Chad cleared his throat. "I now pronounce you husband and wife. Josh, you may kiss your bride."

Josh whooped. "Finally." He tipped Summer back until one of her feet came off the ground and he kissed her thoroughly.

Friends and family made a rowdy noise of laughter and clapping.

When Josh set Summer back on her feet, she blushed. They laughed and hugged each other.

Ty wished he were standing next to his wife. He'd like to be doing the same thing.

"Let me introduce to you, Joshua and Summer Day and Shua Hart!" Chad called out over the noise.

"That's me!" Shua clapped.

Josh scooped up his daughter and held her as he escorted Summer down the trail. Over his shoulders, Shua tossed the remaining daisies into the crowd and nearby bushes.

Chad offered his arm to April. She hurried to him and linked her hand into the crook of his arm, then they followed Josh and Summer.

When Ty met Winter, he held out his hand to her. He grinned, feeling so good for the small part they played in Josh and Summer's reconciliation.

As she linked her fingers with his, she leaned close. "Makes it all worth it, doesn't it?"

His thoughts exactly. "Absolutely." The long days of driving across the country, the hours they spent preparing for events and marriage seminars, the times they sacrificed their own time to give to others, a celebration like this made it all worthwhile. Seeing marriages restored was a blessing beyond anything he could imagine.

He pulled her a tad closer, glad for the beautiful woman at his side. If only they didn't have the issue about Randi stealing Winter's journal to contend with, their lives would be perfect.

Twelve

Summer

After their picnic-style dinner reception, and as nightfall descended on the newly refurbished backyard garden, with guests lingering nearby, Summer watched Shua dancing with her daddy. Tender emotions tugged on her heart. Shua's dream for a daddy and a family had come true. As had her own. She felt blessed and thanked God, again, for healing her heart.

Josh had spent a lot of time over the last two months making Em's garden special. He planted rose bushes, built tiered flower displays, and laid a brick floor centerpiece for tonight's dancing. Shua needed this time with Josh. She'd hardly left his side for weeks. She was so thrilled he was going to remarry them and live with them "fowevew."

Josh did exactly what Summer requested of him that day he asked her to marry him. He dated her, spent lots of time with her and Shua. They went to movies, picnics at Lake Coeur d'Alene, shopping in Spokane, and hiking Schweitzer Mountain. They got to know each other again, and she appreciated the fine man he'd become since coming to know Jesus as his

Savior. She learned to trust him and believe in him. And she'd fallen wildly in love with her husband.

With his help, she successfully finished out the camping season. She thought back to the cougar that charged at her and Ty that summer day. How Josh and Chad chased it with sticks and rocks. She shuddered at what could have happened. How one or both of them could have been killed. Hopefully, she'd never face such a crisis again. But living in the woods as they did had a host of potential threats.

In the aftermath, local game warden, Hunter Thomas, and his men tracked the creature into the mountains. When they found it and tranquilized it, they discovered the animal had been wounded by a previous gunshot. Probably a farmer protecting his animals. No doubt, that's why the mountain lion acted aggressively toward them. Sadly, they had to put it down. But future campers, and Shua, would be safe at Hart's Camp, at least from that animal.

Josh spun Shua off the dance floor. She clapped and jumped up and down. Her tulle yellow dress had a red punch stain down the front. But the joy radiating on her darling face made up for any concern Summer had of trying to salvage the fabric. Surely, no little girl had ever been so happy.

The next song on their playlist was a slow tune.

Josh stepped in front of Summer and bowed. "My beautiful princess bride, may I have this dance?" He offered her his hand, his palm facing up.

She met his gaze, couldn't look away from the stunning warmth in his irises. "I'd love to dance with you, my prince." She laid her palm over his and stood, truly feeling like his princess.

For just a moment, he held her against him. He smelled good, his spicy aftershave mingling with his masculine scent. She gulped, so attracted to him.

He led her to the brick dance floor, her wedding dress

swishing around their feet. The sun had almost gone behind Hart Mountain. Twinkling Christmas lights they'd hung around the fence line circled them in glowing color.

She'd remember this night forever. This sweet moment dancing in her husband's arms. He held her close, her cheek against his chest. The music lulled her, and he whispered the lyrics in her ear.

When the song came to an end, he cupped her cheeks. "I love you, Summer Day."

"Love you, Josh."

His lips lowered, and she melted into his kiss. They broke apart and he held her to him, his heart beating fast beneath her ear. "I can't wait to spend our lives together," he whispered.

"Looking forward to anything in particular?" She couldn't stop her flirtatious grin.

He laughed, the sound washing over her. She'd always loved his laugh, his smile. And he was doing a lot of both today.

"I could think of a few things." He kissed her again. Another song began, and he swayed with her to the music. "Maybe we should tell our guests goodnight, hmm?"

She leaned back and stared into his sparkling eyes. "Ready to take our first walk up the trail as a newly remarried couple?"

His gaze seemed to consume her. "Can't wait."

They'd kept themselves busy for the last two months. Josh lived with Em and Mac. Summer and Shua continued living at the cabin. But she and Josh were eager for tonight. She was ready to sleep in her husband's arms. To spend the rest of her life loving him and being loved by him. The past was gone. A blessed future lay before them.

"Let's say goodnight, then."

They held hands—she wouldn't let go—and talked to each of their guests. Em hugged them and said goodbye. Even Mac, the grumpy codger that he was, accepted her and Josh's hugs.

Shua complained about the evening being over. She didn't want to stop dancing. But when Mac promised to read her as many stories as she wanted, she trotted beside him toward their cabin, waving at Summer and Josh. Shua knew they'd see each other tomorrow—before Summer and Josh left for their honeymoon at the Oregon Coast.

Josh shook hands with Chad. "Thanks for coming from Alaska to perform our ceremony. That meant a lot to us."

"I wouldn't have missed it." Chad patted his back. "You guys have to come up and see us in Ketchikan."

"I'd love that!" April said from beside him. She hugged Summer. "You are a beautiful bride."

"Thank you for all you did to make this happen. For encouraging me to forgive and love my husband. And thanks for being my matron of honor." She smiled at her friend. "I can't wait to hold your baby."

"Me too!" April kissed her cheek. "I'm so proud of you."

"Thank you."

"I don't know what would have happened if you two hadn't been here a couple of months ago." Josh nodded at Chad, then linked his fingers with Summer's again.

"God knew." Chad took April's hand, pulling her closer to him. April's eyes shimmered at her husband like she was silently communicating her love.

"Indeed, He did." Josh nodded at Chad, then he led Summer toward Ty and Winter. "Thanks for being in our wedding." Josh shook Ty's hand.

"It was our pleasure." Winter smiled.

"Our house isn't far." Ty nodded in the direction of Mount Spokane. "Only about an hour. You guys will have to come over for dinner."

"Stop in anytime." Winter chuckled. "Well, anytime we're there."

Josh grinned. "That would be great."

Summer could tell by the way he kept looking at her that he was eager for them to finish their goodbyes. But this was an important part of their evening too.

"Thank you for sharing your wisdom and love in the marriage seminar." Summer blinked back a rush of emotion. "If you hadn't, I don't know where we'd be today."

"She's right." Josh's tone turned sober. "God used you guys to minister to our broken hearts. You were there when we were desperate and needed healing. 'Thank you' doesn't seem adequate."

Ty hugged Josh. "God bless you guys."

Summer hugged both of them, then she and Josh went in search of Ezzie. He was picking up punch cups and paper plates and tossing them in a black plastic bag. When she hugged him, he sniffled and dabbed at his tears.

"You take care of each other." Ezzie gulped.

"We will," Josh promised.

Ezzie squinted at Josh. "You treat her good like she deserves."

"I will, Ezzie. No worries, there."

Summer waved at everyone, storing to memory the garden ambiance surrounding her wedding party.

"Goodnight," Josh called.

She slipped her hand into the crook of his arm, and they strolled toward Haven Trail and their little cabin in the woods—the most fabulous honeymoon suite in the world. While they were gone on their week-long vacation, hired carpenters would be adding on a small master bedroom for their privacy. Hopefully, it would be finished before their return.

The darkness was only interrupted by the full moon as Josh stopped beneath the shadow of a pine tree and pulled her into his arms. His lips fell against hers and he kissed her deeply. "I couldn't wait to do that alone as your husband."

She brushed her cheek against his. "I've looked forward to being with you too."

She heard him gulp. "Summer Day?"

"Yes?" She leaned back and stared into her husband's shimmering eyes.

"Thank you."

"For—?"

"Loving me. For letting me come home."

Home. That sounded so wonderful.

"I'm thankful God brought us together again."

"Me too."

They strolled the rest of the way up the hill, arm in arm, to the same cabin they came back to after their first wedding. But this time, everything was different. He'd changed. She'd changed. They both knew the Lord now. She knew beyond any doubt Josh loved her. And she loved him.

He scooped her up and carried her over the threshold. "I've waited a long time to do that."

She smoothed her hand over his beloved face, so glad they'd come home to each other.

Thirteen

Autumn

Autumn's cell kept buzzing, but none of the calls were from Gar. Instead, parents had questions about her doing a play. Were the rumors true that she was doing a production this year? Did she need volunteers? Could this student or that student be the lead? But she didn't have any answers yet.

The city, the traffic, her job, tension, the calls, her silent house, her sadness. Getting in her car and driving away from all of it sounded like a perfect idea. So when Marny popped into her classroom after school, her cheerful spirit seemed like a godsend.

"I have a brilliant idea."

"What's that?"

Autumn loved Marny's all-natural look. No makeup. A simple hairdo. In her late twenties, she always wore dresses to work in the office. Today, the last day of the school week, she'd pulled her long red mane into a ponytail and wore a blue jumper. Her freckles stood out especially dark after their hot summer. The trait Autumn most appreciated—and sometimes dreaded— was the woman's blunt honesty.

Marny plopped down on an empty student's chair, her arms folded across the desktop. "I think you should stop moping around like it's the end of the world and have some fun."

Did everyone think she was moping? She thought she'd been hiding it rather well.

"What did you have in mind?" Hopefully, not a Mariner's game. Marny asked her to go to one of those last week. She declined.

"Let's go to Edmonds tomorrow." Marny made a playful face. "We could check out the shops. Hang out. Eat great food. Relax."

"Relax" was a magical word. But Edmonds? That was the city she and Gar used to consider *their* town. They'd run down to Edmonds for breakfast on Saturday mornings. Sometimes they put their canoe in the water. Did she want to hang out there with memories looming over her head? "I don't know. I have a lot to do."

"Oh, come on," Marny coaxed. "You said you were going crazy at your house . . . without Gar." She grimaced like she shouldn't have mentioned his name.

Even though she didn't care to talk about him, Autumn didn't want her friends tiptoeing around his name. And while she loved her house, the place she called her *dream* house, it had become more like solitary confinement there.

"We could take the ferry to Kingston," Marny tempted. "Or just hit the coffee shops and stores."

"Okay, I'll go." She said it before she could convince herself to do something else. Like get in her car and chase after Gar. It wasn't like she didn't know where he was, thanks to Lacey. But she was still waiting for some sort of sign from him that he was interested in trying to reconcile. His silence made her doubt he'd be pleased with a surprise visit from her. "Probably not the ferry, though." Or anywhere near the water.

That was Gar's and her special thing to do. "Shopping and de-stressing sound perfect."

Marny pulsed the air with her fist. "Now you're talking."

* * * *

Saturday morning, Autumn rode in Marny's car for the eleven miles to Edmonds. She and Gar had enjoyed the contrast between the bustling metropolis of Seattle where they grew up and the quiet homey neighborhoods of Edmonds, less than a half hour away. Maybe it would be a good place to unwind today.

Marny parked her Corolla on a side street, and they strolled through downtown. Cute shops selling goods ranging from international teas to elegant designer clothes lined the main street, and they took their time window-shopping. In the center where two roads going north/south and east/west met, a fountain sprayed water in the middle of the brick-lined round-about—a photogenic spot.

Autumn didn't like selfies. But Marny, who brought a selfie stick, coaxed her out to the city's centerpiece. Extending her cell phone with the thin metal rod, she snapped several poses of the two of them laughing. When a truck drove the full circle, and the driver honked and wolf whistled at them from his open window, they scurried back across the street. Marny cackled and waved at the guy, single girl that she was. But the male attention made Autumn uncomfortable. The man she still wanted to flirt with was her husband, even though he hadn't acted that way toward her in a long time. Well, maybe she hadn't been that flirtatious with him, either.

"Feels kind of nice to be noticed, huh?" Marny elbowed her and guffawed.

Not exactly nice. But not all bad.

After they strolled down several streets and shopped in a couple of their favorite stores, Autumn was ready for something hot to drink. "Want to hit a coffee shop? I'm on a chocolate binge."

"You read my mind."

Autumn laughed and realized how good it felt. The sea air was doing something positive for her emotions too. Or maybe, just breaking away from the ordinary gave her this lighter feeling. Whatever it was, she was going to embrace it. On the corner of the next block, they entered a cafe with small circular tables arranged around a narrow room. She ordered a mocha. Marny picked a chai latte. Both oohed and aahed over blueberry scones.

"Thanks for suggesting this," Autumn said when they found a vacant table. "I needed it more than you know." Tight muscles in her shoulders eased. The headache she woke up with was gone.

"Nothing like a getaway to turn you into a new woman." Marny raised her mug in a toast. "To new adventures."

Autumn raised her mug. "To a happier life."

"So"—the skin around her friend's eyes crinkled—"have you heard from Gar?" She bit into her scone and shrugged.

Leave it to Marny to cut right to her sore spot.

"Come on, you know I say what's on my mind. You can tell me to shut up."

"Okay. Shut up." Autumn didn't want to discuss Gar. This was her day away from thinking about problems. She sipped her coffee and glanced out the window, noticing a wooden furniture store she'd like to visit. Not that she wanted to buy anything to commemorate *this* time in her life.

Marny cleared her throat. "Well, have you prayed?"

Of all the things Autumn thought the woman might ask— *Did he have an affair? Had they been fighting? Sleeping in separate rooms?*—prayer wasn't on the list.

"Sure, I pray. I'm a Christian." She worked in a Christian school, for goodness' sake.

Marny chuckled.

Autumn, not liking her smug look, felt her ire rising. "What's so funny?"

"Your reaction is humorous."

"Hardly."

"Don't get all huffy. *I'm* not married." Marny pointed at herself. "I can't give you marital advice."

"Good." Autumn thought she'd stop talking about it, then, and they could get back to enjoying their break.

"But here's the thing—"

Oh, great.

"Since we're both serving the Lord, I feel comfortable asking you about prayer." Her mischievous grin smacked of prying. "So, have you prayed about you and Gar?" She leaned forward, her chin resting against the back of her fists, her elbows on the table. Her grin vanished. "Any chance you're mad at God?"

Autumn groaned. "Why in the world would I be mad at God? It's not His fault Gar's acting childish. Shoving Ben. Running away." *Not loving me.* "Can we stop talking about this now?"

"I'm not trying to be snoopy. Sorry about that."

She felt her defenses relax a little. "It's just . . . hard to talk about him."

Marny nodded and picked up her mug. "Thing is, if I had a husband like Gar—handsome, smart, married to *me*—I wouldn't let him go so easily. No matter what he did."

Pain shot through Autumn's heart. Who was Marny to judge her and say she let Gar go easily? What about the tears she shed since he left? Or the fact she couldn't control what he did? "What was I to do? Hang onto his arm? Cry and beg him to stay?"

Her friend took a couple of bites of her scone as if mulling over her answer. "I didn't mean you should have kept him from walking out the door. It was his choice to leave. Like it's your choice to stay."

Even that hurt. Someone had to keep the house running, hold down a regular job. She couldn't take off like he did. But she realized Marny wasn't trying to be mean. "Then, what?"

"God could stop him in his tracks." Marny nodded, like that settled everything. So easy for her to say, from outside all the pain and anger.

"But He didn't." Tears flooded Autumn's eyes, and she fought them. She wouldn't cry. She wouldn't. Ugh. She was. She dug around in her purse for a tissue, then she blotted beneath her eyes. *I'm strong. I don't need a husband. Sure you don't. That's why you've been hiding at home. Not going anywhere. Eating tons of fudge.*

She swallowed down the negative thoughts. She wasn't eating as much fudge since she signed up for a gym membership.

"Back to my question. Have you prayed?" Marny stared at her intently. "I mean *really* prayed?"

"You mean, with fasting and begging God to bring Gar home to me? No." She took a small bite of the white-flour laden treat, not enjoying it as much, then washed it down with a sip of coffee. "I've been eating a lot of . . . comfort food. And praying for peace."

"Peace is good." A blueberry fell onto Marny's plate. She picked it up and popped it into her mouth. "My pastor's been teaching on spiritual warfare. Standing against evil. Speaking the Word over situations, that sort of thing." She leaned back in her chair. "I think it might be worth a try."

Autumn had heard phrases like "fight the good fight" and "put on the whole armor of God." But how did that fit into marriage? Gar walked out. She'd asked the Lord to help her cope. Wasn't that enough? "Gar won't take my calls. I'm trying to figure out where to go from here."

Marny folded her hands. "That must be tough." Finally a hint of understanding. "Don't just *let* it happen, okay? Fight in the spiritual realm." Marny's eyes glowed like she said something weighty.

Maybe she did.

Autumn shrugged, not really getting it. "Have you ever prayed like that? Like it was a fight?"

"Not for marriage, of course. For a sick friend, once." Marny nodded. "Another time, when I was going through a strong temptation about a guy, I faced it with warrior-like prayer."

"A guy?" That sounded interesting.

"Yeah, I liked him a lot. But he wanted more than I wanted to give before marriage." A peaceful expression crossed her face. She didn't seem embarrassed by the personal turn in the conversation. "I prayed fervently and believed God to work everything out for good. I came against sin with the Word of God."

"And—?" Autumn leaned forward, waiting.

"The guy moved to Texas." Marny laughed.

"Strange twist."

"God moved temptation far from me."

"And the sick friend?" Autumn was curious about that too.

"She got well."

"That's awesome." As she finished her snack, she contemplated their conversation, especially the deeper-prayer stuff.

When they left the coffee shop, they strolled through town again. This time, Autumn had a destination in mind—the candy shop.

"I have to see if they have any new flavors of fudge. I've made several batches, but this is the best place on the planet to buy chocolates."

"Sounds fabulous."

Autumn stepped into the cheery shop and, avoiding every other candy, hurried straight for the fudge in the glass display. "Peanut Butter. Mmm."

Marny pointed at a variety called Triple-Decker Delight. "Wow."

One choice wouldn't do. Autumn requested a quarter pound of four different flavors, including the peanut butter and triple-decker. She couldn't wait to try a small piece of each.

"A day in Edmonds wouldn't be complete without a stroll by the water." Marny patted her stomach. "I could use the exercise, and we've got to get pictures by the orca sculpture."

"Okay." Autumn didn't have the heart to say no, and she was more relaxed now. They walked downhill, past the massive group of cars lined up for the Kingston ferry, and approached the water. The wind had kicked up, blowing steadily from the sound. She shivered at the chill and pulled her jacket hood over her head. Even though it felt too cold, she posed by the black and white orca, positioned near the water's edge. Marny snapped her picture, then Autumn did the same for her.

They sat on a rusty turquoise bench with a dedication plaque for a man "who loved the sea." That sentiment made her think of Gar. He loved taking the canoe out on the water. He was always more relaxed after a morning paddling in the sound. Why hadn't she been willing to do that more often, knowing how much it pleased him?

She watched the ferry dock, load up, and disembark. Six people in wetsuits shuffled past them. She was fascinated as they moved into the water and one by one dove under the waves. She observed the ferry and the divers and the seagulls flittering about, and all the while, the conversation she had with Marny played through her mind.

Why didn't she pray more for her marriage? For Gar? Why did she give up and accept his leaving without a fight?

Was it because she felt to blame? As if she deserved what happened after taking his position? Or perhaps it went back further. Like six months ago, when Gar first started acting strange. Or when they found out she couldn't have kids, and she felt as if nothing would ever matter again. Why wasn't she more spiritually aware?

Lord, I think I need to confess some things and have a heartfelt conversation with You when I get home.

Fourteen

Autumn

After school on Monday, following her excursion with Marny, Autumn received an email memo to come straight to the office. She closed her laptop and left the papers she was grading. Ever since the school year started, she avoided the glass case in the hallway displaying pictures of past productions. Today was no different. Staring straight ahead, she hurried to the principal's office. She'd put off talking with Ben about doing a show, hoping the whole mess would disappear. Considering this summons, it hadn't. She loved teaching the seniors, but had she known Gar's theater responsibilities would be thrust on her, she wouldn't have taken the promotion—not to mention all the ways her decision hurt her husband.

Ever since her discussion with Marny, her prayer time was changing. Not quite going to battle—whatever that meant—she'd been talking with God about concerns she stopped conversing with Him about a long time ago. Like her infertility, inner hurts and broken dreams, Gar's coldness, and now, her longing for him to come home. It seemed the more time she spent talking to God, the more she had to say. In fact, she found herself looking forward to morning and evening prayer times, something she never knew was possible before. And even though not many days had passed, something already felt different in her spirit.

Outside the principal's office, white-haired Sandra Nelson typed on a keyboard, her eyes squinting at the computer screen. Autumn cleared her throat.

"Mrs. Bevere." Sandra always called everyone "Mr." or "Mrs." or "Miss." She moved her computer mouse like she was finishing a task. "I'll let Mr. Whiffleman know you're here."

"Thank you, Mrs. Nelson."

While the secretary used the telephone, Autumn read the decorative signs on the wall. *Education Opens New Doors. A Happy Attitude Changes the Atmosphere. Hard Work Never Hurt Anyone.* Ben would probably quote that last one to her.

"Mr. Whiffleman will see you now." Sandra tipped her head toward the closed brown door.

"Thank you." Autumn straightened her dark green skirt and prayed a silent prayer. *Lord, have Your way in this meeting. Guide my footsteps. Be with Gar, wherever he is. Whatever he's doing, remind him of Your love. And my love too.*

A chill rushed up her spine. Before talking with Marny about prayer, she wouldn't have taken time to ask for God's will in a meeting or say a blessing for her husband like that. God *was* doing something. Changing her, perhaps. She hoped He was working on Gar as well. She took a deep breath and turned the doorknob.

Ben stood behind his almost bare mahogany desk. "Welcome. Have a seat."

She crossed the small room and sat down on one of the two black leather chairs parked in front of his desk. "Your note said to come as soon as I could." A shiver skittered over her skin. Even though she'd been a teacher for a decade, sitting across from the principal made her nervous.

"How do you like your new job?" Ben dropped into his leather swivel chair. He rotated the seat back and forth. Was he nervous too?

"It's going well. I enjoy teaching."

"Good. I needed to speak to you about the play. I'm still getting calls." His chuckle sounded forced.

"Mr. Whiffleman, I appreciate the promotion. But wouldn't someone else be more qualified to teach drama? I've never directed a play. Gar rarely needed my help. He had Sasha—"

"You won't have *Sasha* to help you." Ben's face contorted, and he glanced away as if the woman's name sickened him.

What was with that? "She won't design the stage?"

"No." His face reddened. "She's no longer working with ECHS, same as Gar." He picked up a piece of paper. Avoiding her gaze, or distracting himself?

Was he suspicious of Gar and Sasha? Did he know something? Memories crashed into her thoughts. Times she'd come upon Gar and Sasha in a heavy discussion. Moments when a freaky "caught" look crossed the woman's face. But whenever Autumn questioned Gar, he said it was nothing. They were just friends. Had she overlooked the obvious?

"The parents are counting on you." Ben returned to the subject. "Remember our talk about smoothing out their concerns?"

"I do." How could she forget the weight of guilt he placed on her shoulders?

"I need you to do a play—this time. We can't afford to bring on a new hire." He took a long breath. "Mrs. Bevere, our school needs you."

More pressure.

"Parents, such as Jewel Pollard, are driving me insane with

their threats." His voice lowered. "I met with the board. They agreed we should move forward with something theatrical."

"The shows Gar did were expensive." The other day she thumbed through his ordering books and old receipts and was shocked by the prices.

"Nothing costly." Ben pushed himself away from his chair and paced to the window.

"How much money is the board willing to provide?"

A long pause. "Nothing."

"What?"

"Mrs. Bevere, please understand, you'll have to be creative." His voice turned persuasive. "I've observed your classes. I've heard how well you interact with students. I know you can do this."

"Creative, as in *no* money? I'm not *that* creative." She stood up, wanting to run from the oppressive room. "I'm not . . . like Gar."

"I'm afraid you'll have to do your best."

Or what? She bit the inside of her cheek to hold back the words. Would he fire her like he fired Gar? If that happened, how would she pay their mortgage? Other schools in the area had filled their openings. What could she do as a backup plan? Return to serving tables like she did to get through college?

"I'm sure Jewel and the other parents will assist you. They may even donate funds."

She needed Jewel to offer advice like she needed a wrecking ball to demolish her house.

Ben sauntered to the door. "Stop by tomorrow and let me know what production you've chosen, alright?"

He hadn't said "if" she did a show. He expected it.

"How about Shakespeare? It's in the public domain." He raised an eyebrow.

Was he kidding? "That's way out of my experience level."

"It's free." He shrugged as if "free" solved everything.

The phone chirped. Ben hurried back to his desk and pushed a button. "Yes, Mrs. Nelson?"

"Mrs. Pollard is on line one."

"Fine." He held the phone out to Autumn. "We're done here, aren't we?"

Definitely. She trudged out of the office and down the hall. Wait until Gar heard about Ben's plan for her to direct a show. He'd go nuts. She shuddered at the idea of having to tell him what she was going to do. Would he despise her even more?

Frustrated, she paused by the glass display case she'd avoided and closed her eyes. *Lord, I'm trying to be the person You want me to be. Please give me wisdom. You are the strength of my life.* She opened her eyes. In front of her, behind thick glass, a newspaper clipping with a picture of Gar and Sasha onstage caught her eye. She leaned forward to see it better. The realistic carousel painting in the background had to be from *Mary Poppins*. The headline read "Director Loves Youth Theater."

She knew that to be true. And Gar loved the kids even more than she did, it seemed. What had happened to make him so emotionally unstable?

She wiped a tear. Whether she directed a play or not wasn't the most important thing in her life. What she needed to do was find out what went wrong between her and Gar. Where could she start?

Prayer.

Yes, she needed to pray for her marriage as if someone were sick and needed a miracle. Because she was convinced it would take a miraculous intervention to bring the two of them back together.

Autumn returned to her class and continued posting grades for a pop-quiz she gave that afternoon. Her classroom door opened, and Tawny Richards shuffled toward the teacher's desk. What did the senior librarian want?

"Got a minute?" The woman's glasses slipped down her nose, and with her index finger, she pushed them up. Tawny's grayish hair was pressed into a messy knot at the back of her head. Her dark clothes resembled funeral attire.

"Sure. What's up?"

The older woman drew a chair close to the corner of Autumn's desk. "I've heard rumors. Are you doing a play?" She leaned forward. "Hmm?"

Autumn saved her work then shrugged. "Probably. Ben asked me to fill in for that position this fall."

Tawny huffed. "Why would he ask *you*? Have you ever done anything dramatic in your life?"

Autumn didn't know what to say to the woman's critical attitude.

"I'd say you're the opposite of expressive. Passive, even." Tawny scratched at her shoulder.

Was she calling Autumn boring? *I can scream and get my point across as well as the next person.* But she was right. Gar was the outgoing one, while Autumn was reserved. That didn't mean she was weak. She still had opinions.

"Was there anything else?" She nodded toward her laptop. "I'm trying to finish up so I can go."

Tawny stood and pushed the chair in place. "I should have been chosen to fill in for Gar. I acted in community theater when I was younger." Her chin lifted.

"Really?"

"Maria in *Sound of Music.* Katherine in *Taming of the Shrew.*"

"Hmm."

Tawny left the room.

As rude as the woman was, Autumn wondered if she should recommend to Ben that Tawny direct the production. Was he aware of her theatrical experience? Then again, the woman's attitude was questionable. Autumn shook her head and sighed.

It wasn't her place to judge anyone. Maybe Tawny was having a bad day.

She finished entering the grades. Before she went home, she'd hit the gym. It was nice to have that to look forward to. Later, she'd eat a TV dinner and some fudge, then spend time praying. That was the only thing that gave her real comfort.

Throughout her evening, she wrestled with thoughts of her conversation with Ben. Did God want her to do a production? In Gar's absence should she be willing to go the extra mile and become the substitute director this one time?

Fifteen

Gar

In the upstairs guest room, Gar had just changed into jeans and a button-up shirt when his cell phone buzzed. He glanced at the screen. *Wifey* leaped out at him. He'd input that silly nickname for her when he upgraded his phone. Back then, he teased Autumn with names like "Lifey Wifey" or "Gripey Wifey." Sometimes "Foxy Wifey" when the mood hit. He hadn't called her that in months. Now, "Aloof Wifey" sounded more accurate.

The cell phone buzzed a couple more times. Why should he answer and ruin his evening? He was on his way out for dinner and a movie. By himself, but still. The noise stopped. No voicemail followed.

The house phone jingled downstairs.

Lacey tromped up the stairs. "Yeah, he's here. The jerk."

Great. She must have the cordless phone in hand. He hurried to the door and shut it.

"Gar!" Lacey shouted and knocked on his door. "Autumn's on the line. She wants to talk to you."

"Tell her I'll call her back."

"Sure you will." Lacey groaned. "Gar, come talk to your wife."

Gripey Wifey.

"As I said, tell her I'll call."

"Yeah, yeah," Lacey grumbled. But he heard her trudging back down the stairs.

He grabbed his jean jacket but didn't put it on. He might as well face the music. What did Autumn want to talk with him about? Did something break down?

He found *Wifey* in his contacts and tapped her number.

"Gar?" She sniffed.

Hearing her crying, something twisted in his stomach. "What's up?"

"Something I-I"—her voice broke—"need to talk with you about."

"What happened?" He felt concerned, even though he tried to subdue it. This was the first real conversation they had in six weeks, and hearing her sounding upset tugged on his heart.

"Can you talk?"

"I was just leaving."

"Sorry."

He didn't mean to guilt her. He dropped to the edge of the bed. "How are things going?"

She sniffled. "Look, Gar, I just . . . need some advice."

So, something *did* break. "Shoot. What stopped working?"

"Us."

Oh. That's what she wanted to discuss? He knew they needed to face their past—including his mistakes—if they were ever to get back together. But he didn't look forward to that conversation. "Autumn, let's not do this right now."

"Hasn't it been long enough?" More sniffing. "I can't keep going on alone like this."

He didn't want to continue living out of a suitcase and

freeloading off his cousin like he was, either. But he wasn't ready to go back. "I heard you've been busy."

"What do you mean?"

"Sasha called." He gritted his teeth. How could Autumn have agreed to do a show in his place? She knew nothing about—

"Oh, Sasha." Silence. "What did she say I've been doing?" Her voice didn't hold blame, just defeat, which dug at Gar's cold emotions.

She'd never played the theatrics of a jealous wife. Had never accused him of being unfaithful—and maybe she should have. "She heard you're doing a play in my stead." Speaking the words increased his feelings of betrayal.

"I don't want to."

"Then why are you? It seems to me—"

"I need to see you."

"What? No." The news of her directing had sent him into a downward spiral.

"Please, Gar? I need someone to talk to."

"You have your school friends. Marny." He heard the hard edge in his voice.

"Gar, could I see you?"

She lived six hours away, so it was possible. Still, he wasn't ready to meet her and have a knock-down, drag-out argument.

"We could meet somewhere in the middle. Moses Lake?"

The name conjured up a bad restaurant where he lost his clothes and tires. "Maybe some other time." Like at the end of the school year.

"Haven't you been gone long enough?" There, she sounded like *Gripey Wifey*.

"Was that why you called? To harp on me?" He held the phone away from his mouth and glowered at it. She still stirred up the worst in him.

She hiccupped, and he could tell she was close to sobbing. He remembered the last time she cried in his arms and soaked his shirt. That was the night she finally realized she could never have a baby.

The remembrance twisted something tight and awful inside of him. When had he become so heartless that he could ignore the pain in her voice? What was wrong with him? He let out a long sigh. She was his wife. He'd promised to be there for her, and he failed. No matter what she did—or what he did—they were still married. "Why are you upset?"

"Ben's pressuring me to do a play. I'd rather not."

"Well, don't." That would serve him right for firing Gar.

"I tried to get out of it. He says if I don't, some parents will pull their finances—and kids—from the school." She blew her nose. "What should I do?"

"You're asking me?" Didn't she realize how terrible he felt about the whole situation?

"Yes." Again, the quiet, distant voice.

She didn't sound like the complaining, conniving woman he'd pictured since he left.

"You're my husband." Her voice sounded almost melodic.

Heat infused the cold place where his heart had been ticking, but not really feeling.

"Gar, I need your wisdom. I respect you. And I . . . I love you."

How could he say anything unfeeling after that admission? Hot air escaped his mouth as if dredged from the lowest region of his lungs. How long had it been since she whispered those words to him? He swallowed what felt like a lump of clay. He should tell her to figure things out herself. If she refused to do the production and parents left the school, fine. She wasn't cut out for show business. But considering her gentle, almost wooing tones, he'd give her what she wanted—a little advice.

"If you decide to do it—and I'm not saying you should—choose something easy. Non-musical. My theater books are still on the shelf in the home office. Picking a show isn't a big deal. But you might need help with interpreting a play before you could direct one."

"I can't do a show."

"Why not?"

"There's no m-money. You and I don't have any. The school is broke. Ben expects me to be creative. And I'm not." She whimpered. "Then there's Tawny. She's jealous that Ben asked me."

He knew the feeling.

"Maybe she should do it instead of me." Her voice trailed off.

"That would be a disaster." Gar knew Tawny didn't have much patience with kids. "She wouldn't make it fun for the students. What's your deadline?"

"Tomorrow."

"What? How long have you known about this?"

"Since before school started." She groaned. "I've been too upset to consider it. My energy is zapped from doing everything on my own. Living without you is hard, Gar. It wasn't supposed to be this way."

"I know." He gulped down a swallow of saliva.

"I want you to come home." She took a shaky breath, and the sound rattled through the phone. "We could go in for counseling."

Her words gnawed at the thawing edges of his emotions. "I can't. I'm not ready yet."

"Oh."

He was surprised she didn't beg. But he was glad. He didn't need any more guilt.

After a moment of silence, she whispered, "What do you think I should do about the play?"

He let out a long sigh as he contemplated her question. Her asking for his advice and help felt kind of nice. Like she needed him. Even though he couldn't see her pulling it off, an idea he once considered came to mind. "The school isn't offering any funding, right?"

"None."

He could see her getting eaten alive by Ben's demands and parental pressure. Still, his suggestion might be worth a try. "If I were in your shoes, I'd have some of the seniors write a play."

"Together, you mean?"

"Yep. I thought of doing that for a project in creative writing." Now, he wished he'd followed through with his idea. "Get a few seniors together after school and have them each become a character and talk out a story. I bet they'll come up with something interesting in a short time."

"Sounds like a cool idea." He could hear the relief in her voice. "Thanks, Gar."

He gulped at her gentle tone. "Ben might not like it." He had to warn her. The principal didn't approve of a lot of Gar's ideas.

"If he wants a free show"—he heard gumption in her voice—"he'll have to take whatever we drum up. It might work."

"Chase Parker is a natural writer. He's going to major in journalism. Apple Connelly is creative. Those two could write a play in a matter of days." He wished he could be there to encourage them and edit their work. If only things were different.

"You certainly know the students better than I do."

Yeah, he did. "We worked together on a lot of stuff." He loved those kids almost as if they were his own. Pain jolted through him at the realization he might never get the chance to teach or direct students again. His life's work would be gone because he acted stupidly when he charged into Ben's office. No use going down that road. "My digital recorder is in the top drawer in the office. Use that to record meetings and dialogue. Then type it all out later."

"Okay, thanks." She cleared her throat. "Gar, Ben said Sasha can't help me."

"Probably not." He hoped she wouldn't ask him why.

"I feel so alone, but I know God is surrounding me with peace. Nothing is too difficult for Him, right?"

How could he answer that? No doubt, she'd be calling him again, panicked over the next problem.

"I better let you go." She coughed. "Thanks."

The words *I love you* were on the tip of his tongue, something to assure her she'd be okay. He bit them back. "Bye." He stuffed his arms in his coat. He needed a brisk hike down to Lake Coeur d'Alene to rid himself of the feelings racing through his heart. If he allowed such warm thoughts toward his wife to consume him, he'd be hightailing it home tomorrow. No, he had to think realistically. *Remember what she did to you. How she took over your classes. Your stage.* That was the only way he could survive their break long enough to figure out what went wrong between them—and within himself.

He was pretty sure no matter where he went tonight, thoughts of Autumn wouldn't be far away, especially now that she called, crying and asking for his assistance. How could he forget the way she whispered that she loved him?

Sixteen

Autumn

The next day, Autumn invited five students from senior English to come to her house after school. Earlier in the day, she explained her idea to Ben—without mentioning Gar's assistance. The principal didn't act thrilled, but he didn't reject her offer, either. He said he doubted the show's success unless it was a well-known production. Which they couldn't do, anyway, because of the licensing and royalty costs.

A little after four p.m., the students arrived at her house. She barely had time to get home and throw dirty dishes in the dishwasher and toss a couple of frozen pizzas in the oven. She set out water bottles and a plate of fudge on the coffee table. She'd been eating less, so she had more of the chocolates to share.

She powered up Gar's digital recorder and placed it in the center of the room. Thinking of the way he suggested she bring the students together for this activity warmed her heart. He could have refused to talk with her about theater. Instead, he offered her advice. That had to be a positive sign. She wondered if asking his opinion on various aspects of a production might even open the door for them to start talking again. She prayed that would be so.

When it was time to address the group, she stood. Her knees were quaking, not because she feared speaking in front of kids, but she dreaded their reactions. If they hated the idea, she'd be forced to write something herself, tackle Shakespeare, or quit. She'd never been much of a quitter, but this could be her first.

"Thank you for coming on short notice." She swallowed hard. "I have a dilemma and I need your help."

Apple Connelly leaned forward as if eager to find out why this group had been summoned to a teacher's house. "What can we do?"

"I'm told you are very creative." Autumn nodded toward the girl with a unique name.

Apple grinned. "I like to think so."

"What's up?" Chase Parker asked, then guzzled from his water bottle. The plastic container crackled in his hand.

Autumn took a breath. "I asked you to come to my house because I'd like you to join forces and write a play."

"Whoa." Zack, a guy with shoulder-length dark hair, whistled. "What for?"

She'd debated whether to explain the details. But surely these students were mature enough to understand a mess when they saw one.

"Is this because Mr. B. got fired?" Chase tapped a pencil like a drum against his notebook.

She wished that subject could be ignored, especially with the recorder going. Honesty prevailed. "You could say that."

"Where is he?" Apple glanced around the room like Gar might appear any second. "I was hoping to ask him a question about a certain English assignment." She winked.

Autumn grinned, wishing Gar would randomly show up.

111

Oh, if he would but walk through the door, take her in his arms, and whisper that he was sorry, everything could be different. "He's away." What if he never returned? That was something she might have to face, especially considering his aloof reaction to her declaration of love. But right now, she needed to focus on convincing these five students to donate their time and talents to bailing out ECHS drama.

"He's really not directing a play?" Jude, a senior with dark hair and glasses, clicked the keys on his laptop. Doing homework? Or messaging?

"No. That's why I'm asking you to consider developing characters and creating a play." Autumn sat down on a wide stool near the coffee table. "I know it's a lot to ask, but what do you think?" She crossed her hands over her knees and waited for their reactions.

"You mean for this play to actually be performed?" Apple sounded shocked.

"Yes."

"Wow."

"When do practices begin?" Jude glanced at her above his computer.

"Right away."

"What's the theme?" Zack asked.

Autumn shrugged. "What would you like to write about?"

"You mean, we can choose anything?" Zack rocked his eyebrows comically.

"Anything family friendly."

"Medieval would be cool." Chase wrote something down.

"Or futuristic. Robots. Sci-Fi. Time travel." Zack shrugged.

"Medieval could have dragons. Maidens in distress. Kingdoms at war. That sort of thing." Chase's pen raced over the paper, then he paused and chewed on the end of the writing tool. "How about 'Robin Hood' meets 'Lord of the Rings?' Perhaps, 'King Zackery Saves the Day?'"

"Awesome." Zack pulsed the air with his fist.

Laughter erupted, followed by complete silence.

Then, suddenly, they were talking at once like ideas were zinging through their brains faster than they could spit out the words.

"What about a princess who doesn't want to be queen?"

"What about a time machine?"

"I saw this movie where a treasure is found in a castle."

"How about if a king is dying and they have to find his daughter so she can become queen before the bad guy takes over?"

They went on like that for about fifteen minutes, ideas running pell-mell over other ideas. Some topics would be impossible for a stage production, while others were intriguing. Autumn tried absorbing the things the students were coming up with, creative roads she never would have traveled on her own. Gar was right. With all this talent, these five young people, and her transcribing, could put a play together. She'd do a Google search on how to set up a script. Surely, it wouldn't be too difficult.

Having the students over and inventing a make-believe story was exciting. In fact, other than fudge making, their time together was the most enthusiastic she'd felt about anything in months. It seemed God knew just what she needed.

"This fudge is fantastic, Mrs. Bevere." Carly, a studious girl, waved a piece of peanut butter fudge in the air. "Where'd you get it?"

"I made it."

"No way!" Chase bit into an almond crunch variety. "You should sell this stuff!"

She laughed, happy someone liked the dessert—other than her. "Thank you. Now, what do we do next?"

"Let's establish a list of medieval characters." Chase waved his pen in the air.

"How about our names?" Apple asked with a grin. "Chase said 'King Zackery.' How about Princess Apple and Sir Jude? Chase, Captain of the Guard? Queen Carly?"

"I'm in," Jude yelled.

"Cool." Chase nodded.

They all started talking at once again.

By the time the pizza trays were empty, and the fudge was gone, they established ten characters and talked through Scenes One, Two, and Three. It had Autumn looking forward to their next session. She said goodbye to the kids, then cleaned up the mess. She couldn't wait to call Gar and tell him how successful his idea was.

When he didn't pick up, his voicemail started. Autumn had two words for him. "It worked!" Then she laughed, and she hoped he heard the joy in her voice.

Seventeen

Winter

Sitting on the wooden steps leading to the lower level of their home in Spokane, Winter punched redial for Randi's cell. She'd already tried calling a hundred times or more in the last month. This morning alone, she pressed redial five times.

Not expecting a response, at the sound of a connection, she jumped to her feet. "H-hello?"

"Yeah?" a gruff male voice answered.

"Dirk?" Maybe it was the Hart's Camp worker Randi had run off with when she stole Winter's journal.

"Stop calling a million times a day." Whoever he was, he cleared phlegm from his throat. "I'm sick to death of it."

"Who are you?"

"'Who are you?'" the voice mimicked.

"Winter Williams, Randi's previous employer. Who are you?"

"Question of the millennium."

"Put Randi on the phone."

The man chortled. "Lady, if she wanted to talk to you, she would've called by now. Take the hint. Get lost."

Rude, rude man. Definitely not Dirk. He was a hard worker, someone willing to risk his life to help others—even though he'd made a foolish mistake by driving Randi from the camp and leaving his employer in the lurch. The guy on the phone sounded sleazy. Why did he have Randi's cell? "She has something of mine. I need to speak to her."

"Too bad." He guffawed.

Winter's ears burned. "Is she all right?" She still cared about her old friend.

"Stop calling. Stop texting. Leave me alone."

Leave him alone? Well, she wasn't calling for him. "I won't! Tell her to call me back."

Ty unlocked the front door and walked in carrying two brown grocery bags.

"No can do." Click. The connection went dead.

"No!" Ugh.

"What's going on, Sas?" Ty stared at her with concern.

She pushed redial. It went straight to voicemail. She groaned. Disconnected. Then pushed redial again. Nothing.

"I picked up pizza and salad stuff." Ty gave her a toothy grin as if to draw her out of her bad mood.

"Great." She knew she didn't sound appreciative.

"What's wrong, sweetheart?"

She held up the phone. "I finally got an answer."

"And—?" Ty walked up the stairs and set the bags on the card table they were using for a dining area.

"A guy answered, but he wouldn't say who he was."

"Dirk?"

"At first, I thought so." She pulled out a deli-made triple meat pizza, took the plastic wrap off, and carried it to the stove. "The guy was crude. I don't think Dirk would talk to me like that. Made me mad."

Ty followed her and wrapped his arms around her. "Sorry."

She was furious with Randi for stealing her journal then disappearing. "What are we going to do now?"

"Eat pizza?"

Leave it to her husband to have food on the brain. She stepped out of his arms and slid the pizza pan into the preheated oven. "I mean about Randi." It wouldn't be so bad if the book her ex-assistant stole contained only information about Winter. But she'd been privately writing Ty's and her reconciliation story, which included details about his affair and their divorce. Even though she and Ty shared much of their past in marriage conferences, it was their choice what they revealed. She didn't want some blabbermouth publicly humiliating her husband and blasting all the details.

"We can't do anything until she contacts us." Ty stroked loose hairs back from her face. "Seems like she's in hiding."

"Or inventing evil."

"Possibly. But we agreed not to let it consume us, right?" His chocolate-colored eyes gazed at her. "We'll pray together about it again today."

She nodded. He was good to help ground her whenever her emotions got the better of her. Prayer was the best solution to any problem, she knew that. Still, she felt like venting. "The whole situation drives me nuts. What's she going to do? Who's she going to tell?" She grabbed salad makings from the grocery bag.

Ty leaned his elbows on the counter, watching her as she dumped spinach leaves into a bowl. "I like this domestic side of you."

"Don't get used to it." She shoved his arm playfully. "I can cook frozen stuff and heat-ups. Even you can do that."

"Hey, I made omelets this morning." He grinned.

She thought of the cheesy concoction he threw together. "They were fabulous too."

"Thanks." He grabbed a paring knife and sliced a cucumber. "So, why do you think a guy—who wasn't Dirk—answered Randi's phone?"

"She probably gave it away so I couldn't locate her." How would they find her now? "What did I ever do to her to make her hate me so much?"

Ty carried a handful of veggies to the sink. "Married me? Fired her?" He ran a tomato under a stream of water. "Can you forgive her?"

Being a Christian meant forgiving, she knew that. She forgave Ty. She showed Randi mercy and allowed her back on her ministry team. Could she forgive this too? "What if she goes public with our information?" That's the exact thing she feared. Hadn't Randi tried to convince her to write a book once? Her goal wasn't to minister to others, either. Randi wanted prestige and money.

"Let's say she does the worst thing possible—whatever that is." Ty met her gaze. "Can you forgive her? You know, like Jesus forgave you and me?"

"With God's help, I can do anything." But even she knew she spoke the words by rote, not by faith, however, it was a start. "I feel violated. She stole from me." Then she shrugged. "I'm just upset."

"And rightly so." He pulled her against him, holding her close.

Mmm, he smelled wonderful—of musk and manhood—even if she was unsettled.

He leaned back. "Your first women's retreat starts the day after tomorrow."

"I know."

"You want to bring honor to the Lord. To do that, you need forgiveness and love in your heart." He toyed with her wedding ring. "We both know how difficult it can be to speak with bad feelings inside. Those emotions steal your joy. Been there, done that."

A tightness she didn't like squeezed a band around her chest. "Can we just eat?"

"Okay." He gazed at her for a long moment.

She turned away from his knowing expression.

"Sas?"

She gulped.

"Are we okay?" His eyelids blinked slowly.

"Yes," she whispered. "But I don't know what to do with how I feel."

He kissed her cheek. "You do."

"No, I—" What she wanted to do was tell Randi off.

"Come here." He led her to the single piece of furniture in the living room, a tan loveseat they picked up at a yard sale. He sat down and tugged her hand until she dropped onto the cushion next to him. "You've forgiven much worse than this."

She glanced sharply at him.

"That's right. Me." A sweet smile crossed his lips. "You and I wouldn't even be married if you hadn't. I didn't deserve forgiveness, but you offered it to me."

"Because I loved you."

"And I'm glad." He took both of her hands in his and held them. "Randi was wrong to steal your book with your private thoughts in it. She hurt you. Betrayed your friendship."

She bit her lip. "I haven't been able to let it go."

"I know." His thumbs rubbed over the backs of her hand. "Can I pray with you? You said you could forgive her with God's help. Shall we ask for His love and grace?"

This thing with Randi had been digging at her for weeks. Speaking at the three women's conferences Neil scheduled this month would be tough with a cloud hanging over her. "Okay."

Ty closed his eyes. "Lord, we need You. You see how badly Winter is feeling. I ask You to take control of this situation. To help her forgive, even if Randi does us more harm."

More harm? Winter's stomach clenched. She didn't want them to go through some media circus on account of what she wrote in her journal. Oh, how she wished she never penned a word.

"We trust You, Lord."

She focused on her husband's prayer.

"You are greater than our past. More powerful than our future. Bigger than our ability to figure everything out. We come against any evil plans of satan to harm our marriage or our ministry. We commit ourselves to You. In Jesus's name."

"Amen," she whispered. Normally, she would pray too. Maybe she'd go in the bedroom and spend some time alone. "Mind if I pray by myself for a bit? I think I need it."

"Sure."

They both stood.

"Thanks, Ty." She kissed his cheek. "Pizza will be ready in about fifteen minutes."

She trudged down the hall and entered their bedroom. They'd purchased a queen-sized bed, the only piece of furniture in the room. An eighteen-gallon plastic tub lined each side of the bed and served as nightstands. Meager by most standards, this was their refuge, grander to them than any hotel room.

She grabbed her Bible and sat down on the floor in the bare corner. Verses came to mind that she could read to encourage herself. But first, she wrapped her arms around her bent knees and leaned her forehead against her wrists. "Father God, I've got a problem with unforgiveness. I desperately need Your help."

Eighteen

Autumn

Autumn replayed Chase's last line on the recorder—"Men, to arms. We must save Princess Applelyn." She typed the Captain of the Guard's words into the laptop, including the changes they made for the princess's name to be Applelyn instead of Apple, and the queen's name Carlotta instead of Carly, for medieval effect.

One more session with the seniors and the script they dubbed *The Queen's Disaster* should be finished. All she had to do was transcribe and edit the last session. The students had plotted the play and filled it with action and wit and humor. If the rest of the production went as easily, she'd be thrilled. She didn't know how to run auditions or how to organize practices and staging details. Hopefully, Gar would be willing to tutor her. If not? Thinking about the added responsibilities and all the things she needed to learn how to do added to her stress level. The show wouldn't be an elaborate extravaganza like Gar's had been. However, it would be a unique senior project. And best of all, the writers had volunteered to help her.

With a kink in her neck from staring at her laptop so long,

she stretched and headed for the kitchen. Maybe she'd make a batch of white and dark layered fudge. Her experiments were improving. None of the batches had flopped lately. And she needed a distraction from worrying. This time, as she cooked, she'd pay more attention to the timer. None of that talking on the phone with Marny while the candy boiled.

She'd just finished pouring white chocolate over a dark layer and made a decorative swirl on top when her cell phone vibrated. A quick glance at the screen, and she saw it was Marny. "Hello, my friend."

"How's the writing coming along?"

"Better than expected. It's a medieval tale with a good moral." She ran hot water into the large empty pot—and didn't lick the spoon this time.

"I knew you could do it."

Yeah, well, she'd had plenty of doubts.

"I wanted to run something by you," Marny spoke in her no-nonsense manner. "If you don't feel up to this, especially with the play and all, just say so."

"What is it?"

"You've mentioned a desire to help with serving the homeless." Marny cleared her throat. "Still game?"

She'd wanted to do that in the past. Now, between the play and preparing for classes, she didn't have much time. "I have typing and editing to do."

"Let me share what's happening." Marny's voice grew animated. "A crew from my church is taking soup and rolls down to the parking lot of the Broadway Avenue Gospel Fellowship to serve for dinner tonight. One of my helpers is sick. I was thinking you might like to pitch in. What do you say?"

"Sounds wonderful, but . . ." She had so much on her mind. The play. Gar. But he wasn't here. Dirty dishes could wait. So could typing. Helping someone else might be just the thing she needed to lift her spirits. Why not? "Okay, I'll go."

"You will?"

"Yes." Autumn chuckled. "Other than our trip to Edmonds, I've been stuck at the house or at school. I'm ready for an adventure."

"I'm glad to hear you say that."

"Me too."

"I'll meet you there at six, okay?"

"See you then."

As soon as she ended the call, an idea came to mind. If she put the fudge in the freezer for a little while, it would set faster. What if she wrapped individual pieces and brought them with her? Then the people could have a treat with their evening meal—and she wouldn't sit around devouring candy all night.

* * * *

The old brick church on Broadway Avenue boasted a flashing fluorescent sign: "Soup and Rolls—Come and get it!" By the line forming down the sidewalk, people were "coming to get it." Marny and her team had set up two eight-foot-long folding tables with two vats of hot stew and several gigantic silver pans filled with buttery rolls.

Good thing it wasn't raining. The fall, evening temps were getting cooler, so Autumn had worn a hooded sweatshirt over a double-layered shirt.

She'd spent over an hour wrapping one-inch chunks of fudge in plastic wrap. She festively tied a blue ribbon around each piece to secure them. But was handing out candy a good idea? Fudge wasn't the healthiest of foods. Still, it was delicious—she tested it to make sure—and who could resist a little piece?

She hauled the big bowl filled with fudge to where Marny was busy organizing everything. "What do you think of these?"

Her friend, wearing a pink bandana tied around her red hair, smiled and one-arm hugged her. "Your fudge?"

Autumn shrugged. "My experiment."

"What a nice way to share your gift."

"Gift?" Hardly. Her success rate was low.

"You'll see." Marny pointed to a spot at the end of the last table. "Put them there. You and Todd can help distribute rolls and fudge." She nodded toward a guy rubbing his hands together like he was freezing. "Todd. Autumn." She introduced them.

Autumn shook the man's hand and found it was indeed cold. "Nice to meet you."

He eyed the fudge. "Wow. I'd like to try some of that."

"Better grab one, now. They'll be gone fast," Marny warned.

Todd slipped a piece of chocolate into his coat pocket. "For later."

Autumn laughed. It was nice to have someone appreciate her cooking. Even before Gar left, he hadn't been eating at the house much. Alone, she lapsed into devouring prepackaged meals. She felt the familiar tug of emotion. The questioning. The wondering. What had happened between two people who'd been wildly in love with each other to make them grow so far apart? And look at them, now. Separated. Hurting. Not talking.

She'd been trying not to lose hope. But facing facts might be the prudent thing to do. Her husband seemed determined to stay away from her. Her heart ached with loss and grief. But she'd set her mind on not begging him to come home. She drew in a trembling breath. More prayer, that's what she needed.

And faith. *I believe God can work all things for good in my marriage,* she coaxed herself. *All things are possible.*

"Okay, let's get started." Marny waved toward the people in line. "Pick up your bowls and spoons at the end of the first table, then move this way for food."

For the next hour, people of all shapes and sizes, including children, took turns going through the soup line. Autumn smiled and offered rolls and wrapped fudge. She'd never done this type of thing before and didn't know what to say. But a smile was worth a hundred words, right? However, after listening to Todd and Marny chatting and joking with pretty much everyone, she felt herself relaxing. So many people were in dire straits. And while she couldn't relate to not having a house, she was hurting. In a different way, perhaps, but still. The folks in front of her didn't have a place to live and were probably suffering too. Yet she saw smiles on their faces, and many had a kind "thank you" or comment to say to her.

She thought of the cozy house she'd go home to when she was finished. What would happen to her if she missed a couple of payments? She could be homeless too. Alone in Everett. Of course, her mom lived less than an hour away. But things could go downhill rapidly without Gar. Thinking of her own vulner-abilities, something altered inside of her. A warm surge of empathy emerged in her heart. Soon, she was talking to every person in line, feeling like one of them. They were all facing difficulties in life. God loved each of them and cared about their hurts and needs—and so should she.

"Who made this chocolate delight?" a man with a wide gap-toothed smile asked. He stared into the bowl like a kid ogling a Christmas tree. "Mm-mmm. I haven't had homemade candy in years. Mama used to make fudge. Boy, was it some-thing."

Marny scooted over and wrapped her arm around Autumn's shoulder. "My friend made it especially for you."

"Mind if I have two?" The man's eyes twinkled.

"Okay by me." Autumn grabbed a second piece and dropped it into his outstretched hand. "God bless you."

"Thank you, miss." He nodded and grinned.

Autumn sighed. It felt good to do something meaningful outside her job, her house, and herself. Why hadn't she volunteered before?

Eventually, the soup was eaten, the rolls and fudge were gone. The workers cleaned up the area, folded tables, and did a sweep for trash.

A redheaded boy, maybe eight or nine, tugged on her coat sleeve. When he smiled, a plethora of freckles spread over his face. "Sure was good, miss. Thanks for the candy."

"You're welcome."

"I hope you come next time. You make good food." He leaned closer. "And you're pretty." He winked at her.

Autumn chuckled and hugged the boy. "Why, thank you, young knight." Funny that "knight" came to mind. Had to be due to the play she was typing. She breathed in deeply, liking how relaxed she felt. How long had it been since anyone called her pretty? Or since she hugged a stranger?

The boy darted away, leaving behind fragments of joy that danced in her heart.

She found a few more Styrofoam bowls discarded on the church steps and dropped them in her black bag. A sudden chill swept over her. She'd been so busy, she hadn't noticed the cold air. Now, most of the people were shuffling away, searching for shelter. She thought of her house, the one she'd been feeling so alone in, and felt a rush of concern for the homeless. She'd chatted and given fudge, but the little bit she did didn't seem like enough. She carried an empty tray over to where Marny was loading her car.

"You made their day." Marny grabbed the tray and shoved it alongside a table.

"I didn't do much."

"You're kidding, right? Didn't you see the glow on their faces? That fudge was a special treat." She frowned. "Only problem, I didn't get any." She burst out laughing. "Not that I need any."

"I have more at home. Want to come over?"

"I wouldn't turn that and a cup of hot coffee down."

"Good."

Later at her house, Autumn set two cups of coffee on her kitchen table along with a small plate of fudge. Figuring they should have something healthy, she threw together a bowl of salad for each of them.

"What's this?" Marny's lips curled down. "You're going to make me eat green stuff?"

Autumn shrugged. "Vegetables to counteract the sugar. I need healthy stuff in my life too."

"Speak for yourself." Marny held a piece of cashew-topped fudge between her index finger and her thumb. She smelled it, then put the whole thing in her mouth. Her eyes closed. "Mmmm. I can't believe you made this. Better than the fudge we found in Edmonds."

"Oh, get out of here." Autumn took a bite of her salad, even though her mind was on the fudge.

"Where'd you learn to make it?" Marny acted like she was going to grab another piece, but instead, picked up her fork and stabbed baby spinach leaves into her mouth.

"I bought some fudge and tried duplicating it. I've had disasters and successes."

"This one's an A-plus. Why haven't I tasted any before now?" Marny's pouty face made Autumn giggle.

She patted her stomach. "It's right here, my friend." She laughed. Not worrying about Gar or the school or the play felt amazing. "I'm becoming a Mrs. Claus when it comes to fudge." Her cheeks puffed out with a mouthful of air.

Marny bellowed. "Send over fudge for our dinners any time you want."

"Okay, I will." That would keep her from eating so much of it.

"You haven't mentioned him." Marny nodded toward a picture on the fridge of Gar and Autumn canoeing. "Thought any more about our discussion? You know, about praying like your marriage is in a battle?"

Autumn raised then lowered her shoulders. "Sure. I've been reading my Bible more. Writing down verses about prayer. Others concerning marriage. Praying for Gar, *for us*, like I never did before."

"And—?"

She didn't want her friend to get the wrong impression. Like Gar would come trotting back to her tomorrow. "Things have been . . . bad between us for a long time. We weren't talking. He was gone a lot. Preoccupied with theater and—" Funny how Sasha's name came to mind.

Marny nodded, almost as if she knew. Was that possible?

"Thing is, I don't know if anything is changing with Gar. But"—Autumn rested her palm over her heart—"I can feel He's doing something in here. Something beautiful. And I want more of that."

"Hallelujah." Marny clapped her hands. "Desperately seeking God, laying everything down before Him, makes a big difference." She drank from her coffee cup. "When Mom was sick, and the doctors couldn't solve anything, Dad got desperate before God. Fasted. Prayed for an hour or more in the morning, same at night, for days." She shrugged. "Things started changing for good."

That reminded Autumn of when she was undergoing testing to see why she couldn't conceive. She spent a lot of time pleading with God to let her have a child. When she finally accepted that door was closed in her life, she begged Him to make Gar love her.

"Do you even want—" Marny stopped talking, grabbed a piece of fudge, and tossed it in her mouth.

"You might as well say it." Autumn knew she would eventually.

"I don't have any right to ask such a personal question, but you know me." Marny spread out her hands. "I was wondering . . . do you even want Gar to come home?"

The breath Autumn had been taking caught in her throat. Then she sighed. "At first, I didn't. I was mad at him. Embarrassed by what he did to Ben, and that everyone at school knew about it. But I miss him. I still love him. We made vows to each other, promises before God, to stick together through the worst of it. So, yes, I want him home. I want things to be right between us. I'm committed to my marriage."

"Good." Marny patted her hand. "So why let three hundred miles keep you from him?" Her eyes filled with moisture, making Autumn feel like she really cared.

"He doesn't want to see me." If he'd given her the slightest hint his heart was warming toward her, she would have driven east a half-dozen weekends already.

"Then, onward into battle?"

Autumn knew she was referring to a warrior-like prayer. "Absolutely."

"I'll join with you."

"Thanks."

Their conversation melded into discussing school events, including the upcoming auditions. However, Marny's question never left Autumn's thoughts. Why had she allowed three hundred miles to keep her from seeing her husband, even if he wasn't ready to see her?

Nineteen

Gar

Gar assisted white-haired Mrs. Maloney into the shop's waiting area and showed her the magazines and water bottles available for customers. Then he returned to the garage to replace her worn out, sorry-looking tires with all-season tires. Knowing the better tread was bound to keep her safer on the roads made him think he was doing something productive with his life. Even if it paled in comparison to how he'd felt about being a teacher.

"Hello? Anybody here?" a male voice Gar didn't recognize called out.

"Over here." Gar stood and wiped his hands on the rag he kept in his back pocket. He ran his fingers over the beard he was growing. What would Autumn think of his new look? Would she hate it? He'd kept a clean-shaven face for their whole marriage up to this point.

A guy, probably in his mid-thirties, with dark hair and day-old whiskers, walked straight toward him as if he were at home in Kyle's garage. He extended his hand, which Gar shook.

"I'm Ty Williams."

"Oh?" Kyle hadn't told him the other boss was showing up today.

"I guess we just missed each other the last time I was in town." Ty nodded once at him.

"Uh, yeah." What could Gar say? That he ran. Was unwilling to face his failings.

Ty glanced around the shop. "Man, I've missed this place."

"Work here long?"

"Five years. In those days, this was home sweet home." Ty stopped at the tool bench and handled several wrenches. "I've been away too long."

"How long is too long?"

"A year." Ty's hand stroked the surface of the sedan. "I married my sweetheart a little over nine months ago and left all this behind. We've been traveling and speaking around the country."

Speaking on marriage, if Gar remembered correctly. "Congrats on the nuptials." A newlywed? No wonder he seemed so happy.

"Thanks. She's the one I couldn't live without." Ty walked over to the table in the far corner and poured himself a cup of coffee.

"Beware. Kyle makes a mean brew."

"That, I remember." He sipped the drink and grimaced. "Has a real bite to it. Where is he, anyway?"

"He drove to Spokane to pick up an axle." Gar pointed toward the Triumph Kyle had been working on that morning. "So you gave up all this, huh?" He didn't think leaving the mechanic business was such a big sacrifice.

Ty chuckled. "Five shops in all. Kyle and I grew the business together—TK Automotive." He spread his hands out like he was imagining a placard. "But I'd give it up, again, in a heartbeat to be with her."

He doubted Ty was rubbing his good fortune in Gar's face. But something uncomfortable tweaked in his chest. How much did Kyle tell Ty about his situation? "Why are you here now, if you don't mind my asking?" Had he grown tired of married life already?

Ty sipped his coffee and strolled around Mrs. Maloney's car. "I promised Kyle I'd help him a couple of weeks this fall. My wife is speaking at back-to-back women's conferences. It seemed a good time for me to help out my brother-in-law."

"Staying at Kyle's?" If so, Gar might need to find a rental sooner, than later. Kyle had explained Lacey's wishes that he find a place of his own—or return to his wife—but he hadn't asked him to leave the house yet.

"Nah. I have a place in Spokane. Not much furniture, but it's a roof over my head." Ty nodded toward the gray vehicle. "You done with this one?"

"Almost." Gar snagged his rag and wiped down the chrome hubs.

Ty faced the open bay doorway. "Sure have missed Coeur d'Alene. I love fall in the Northwest. Amazing colors. Perfect sky. Fabulous lake." He breathed in deeply. "I grew up here. How about you?"

"Seattle."

A car engine, not Kyle's rig, turned off outside the shop. A customer? Gar moved toward the bay doors but stopped when he spotted Lacey running across the parking lot. Preferring to avoid her, he retraced his steps to the sedan.

"Ty!" she squealed and lunged for him. "When did you get here?"

Ty hugged his sister while Gar busied himself with double-checking Mrs. Maloney's bill. "A little while ago. Thanks for the loaner vehicle you guys left at the house for me."

"No problem. Everything's been so crazy around here. I

couldn't wait until dinner to see you." She tossed a glare toward Gar, but then kept going in her typical rapid-fire talking. "I wish Winter was with you. The four of us could double date. Wouldn't that be great? It's been so long."

"Yeah, it would."

Lacey linked arms with Ty and led him into the office. When the door shut, Gar imagined the topic of conversation— his and Autumn's troubled marriage. And probably, how she was sick and tired of his freeloading. With a heavy heart, he went to speak with Mrs. Maloney.

* * * *

Ty enjoyed catching up with Lacey and Kyle through the salmon dinner his sister made. He loved the way Lacey topped the filets with provolone and turkey bacon and cooked it over sliced onions and coconut oil—she explained the whole process in detail. But the thing that stood out about the meal was how silent Gar was. A strain existed between Lacey and Kyle too. When she pulled Ty into the office earlier, she unloaded her frustrations about Gar staying at their small place so long. Kyle wouldn't make his cousin leave, and Ty understood that. Lacey was convinced they were aiding and abetting a marriage fugitive by continuing to provide him shelter.

Inwardly, Ty chuckled at Lacey's prying. She was sure Gar secretly loved his wife and all it would take was a kick in the rear and he'd be on his way to the big city and his happily ever after.

"Reconciliation is never easy."

She rolled her eyes. "Don't I know it?" Then she complained about Kyle and how they never did stuff together anymore. "At this rate, we'll never have kids."

Ty led her out of the office and back to her car. "I'll be here for almost three weeks. You and Kyle could do a mini-cation while I run the shops."

"I suggested that." Lacey slid into her SUV. "Kyle wants

to work with you on some projects—like the good ole days. And it's not like I don't want to see you. You're my brother." She swatted at his wrist where it rested against the door.

He wanted to hang out with her too. This seemed like the perfect opportunity while Winter was leading the women's conferences. Maybe what Lacey and Kyle needed was to get their house to themselves. Ty knew how tough it could be to have people around all the time—like with Passion's Prayer, although he dearly loved their ministry team. But whether Lacey could see it or not, she was piling on stress to the situation, which was not helping. Gar's silence was proof.

Ty ate another chocolate chip cookie. "These are great, Lace."

"Thanks."

"She's a fabulous cook," Kyle said around a mouthful of cookie.

Lacey blushed, obviously pleased by his praise.

Ty washed the treat down with water. "So, Gar, what did you do back in Seattle?"

Kyle kicked him under the table.

Huh? What did he say?

A grimace crossed Gar's face. "I was a teacher."

Ty met Kyle's gaze, saw him shake his head. A taboo topic? "And Autumn?"

Gar's face tightened. "A high school teacher."

Oh, yeah. Kyle mentioned that a couple of months ago. "Where'd you meet?"

Again, the kick under the table. What was with Kyle? Didn't he ask Ty to help Gar sort through stuff?

"College."

Cryptic answers. He obviously didn't enjoy this line of questioning.

Ty could guess why. Lacey was at the table, and she'd

probably tell Autumn everything she heard. Kyle acted disinterested, but his kicks let Ty know he was aware.

Ty thought of his own living arrangements. All that space and just him. "You know, I have a big house in Spokane. I'll be driving back and forth to Coeur d'Alene during the next few weeks. If you'd care to stay in one of the rooms, you could. There's a studio apartment over the garage which is private. One of our ministry leaders uses it, but he's away at the conference."

Gar glanced at Kyle, then Ty. "Yeah?"

"Sure." Ty wondered what he thought of the suggestion.

Lacey grinned like she'd been offered a trip to Hawaii. "Ty, that's so nice of you."

He swallowed a mouthful of water. "Interested?"

Gar shrugged. "Yeah. Thanks. I appreciate the offer."

Ty would have to broach the subject of marriage and reconciliation carefully. Gar's walls were prison-wire high. According to Lacey, he was defensive and stubborn. But those were qualities Ty recognized about himself from eleven years ago. Back then, he never would have listened to someone trying to convince him to be a better husband or person. He'd thought he had everything figured out. Little did he know he was ripe for a fall.

He could provide Gar a temporary place to stay, an escape, and in doing so, make a way for Kyle and Lacey to have time alone. If, perchance, God opened a door for Ty to share his journey with Gar, so be it.

Twenty

Autumn

Early Saturday, Autumn was wide awake, pacing across the living room floor. She tapped Gar's name in her cell phone contact list knowing he'd hate a call at five a.m. But she had to talk with him. She counted the rings. Three. Four. *Please answer.* Already, this afternoon's auditions had her in panic mode. Twenty students had signed up to try out for ten parts, and she had no idea how she'd choose the leads.

A click signaled a connection, but Gar didn't speak.

"Gar?"

"Why are you calling at such an ungodly hour?" His moan turned into a yawn. "Torture?" Grumpy before nine, as usual. Gar was always the late owl, then miserable to be around the next day before he had a couple of cups of coffee.

She was an early bird. "I have to ask you something. I couldn't wait for a second longer. I'm so—"

"Autumn."

She stopped talking, assuming he was too sleepy to follow. When he didn't say anything else or end the call, she let a breath escape. "How do you know? I mean, how can you really ever know you've chosen the right person?"

She waited in the thick silence.

He growled. "We have to talk about *that* now?"

Talk about what? Did he hate the idea of discussing the play? "I have to know! Please, Gar." She tried to keep hysterics out of her tone, but it couldn't be helped.

"Okay." He groaned. "Answer is, you don't."

"You don't? That's it?" She needed his wisdom. Instructions. And he gave her nothing? "So what do you do?"

"All anyone can do. You try your best."

His raspy voice sent shivers over her skin. She clutched the cell phone tighter to her ear, wishing for a kind word, a whisper of longing, something.

"You hope it works out. Sometimes it doesn't." His voice turned harsh. "Now can I go back to sleep?"

"That's all the advice you have?" She almost howled in frustration.

"Do we have to talk about this before I've had coffee?" Gar moaned. "I can't believe you called to ask me such a ridiculous question at five in the morning. I thought you were *the one* when I married you, okay? I can't help how things turned out."

What in the world? "What are you talking about, Gar?"

"What am I talking about? Us. Who else?" His voice rose. "What are you talking about?"

That's where his thoughts had leaped? She almost laughed. And he'd thought she was the one? A grin spread across her lips, her heart—until she remembered his next words. He didn't think that now? She cleared the clogged feeling in her throat. "I was talking about auditions. Not us."

He muttered something indistinguishable.

"How do I figure out which kid to choose for which part? I need you here, Gar. I need you, and you're off . . . being a bachelor."

"Autumn—"

She wondered if he'd hang up.

He let out a long sigh. "I didn't know you were talking about auditions. I thought you meant . . . something else."

Well, she'd like to talk about that. She knew he was *the one* the day she watched him save a kid from drowning in Lake Sammamish. They'd been at a church college-group picnic, enjoying a meal, when someone at the next site screamed that a boy was drowning. Without hesitating, Gar plunged into the water. His selflessness astonished her. The caring in his eyes when he swam back to shore with the boy in his arms and performed CPR until the ambulance arrived touched her so deeply. She'd talked with him the next day for a long time, telling him how she considered him her hero, how she was so proud of him—especially considering the fact the boy had lived. Gar asked her out for coffee, then dinner. She knew then. She'd never met a man like him—never would again.

She hadn't thought of that day in years. If Gar didn't dive into the water, that child wouldn't have lived. She never would have seen the hero in her future husband. He was still a bit reckless, but he had a good heart and was willing to take risks for others. Why had she forgotten to tell him more often how much she admired him? How she wished she were outgoing and creative like him?

She sighed. "I'm sorry for calling so early. I didn't know who else to try."

"Did you find my audition forms in the file?" His tone sounded gravelly . . . and sexy.

"Ye-es." She swallowed, forcing herself not to imagine his messy morning hair. How his chin would be rough and dark.

"Good." He yawned. "Listen to each student. Give everyone your undivided attention. Trust your instincts." He drew in a long breath. Talking about theater was probably hard on him. "I always loved auditions. Some directors hate them, just something to get through." He sighed. "Picture tryouts as a time to let kids show off their platform skills. Help them relax with drama games. Then, let each one perform. You asked, 'How do you know?' You just do. Anyone else on your auditioning panel?"

"Marny and Tawny."

"Tawny? You've got to be kidding." It sounded like he kicked something. "Ouch."

"She has theater experience. Did you know she played Maria?"

"In the *Sound of Music*?" His voice sounded incredulous.

"Yes. When she was younger."

"I didn't." He groaned. "I wish you weren't in this predicament."

Me too. "I wish you were here with me." She waited, wondering what he might think of that admission, even though she knew he couldn't work onsite at the school anymore. "I could face anything with you by my side." Where had those bold words come from? Would he consider returning home if she begged? But she wouldn't. He had to return because he wanted to and because he loved her. Not because she turned into a whiny wife—or as he used to tease her, a whiny *wifey*. She'd been praying for him and would continue to do so. She'd never prayed for anyone so much in her life. Surely, God was about to do something powerful and healing in their lives.

"I hope it goes well for you." He didn't sound disinterested, but he wasn't warm, either.

"Thanks." Disappointment flooded her. "Gar, I miss you."

"I know."

He knew, but—? Tears swam in her eyes. "Okay, well, have a nice day. Bye." She ended the call and sank to the floor by the sofa. Overwhelming emotions crashed down upon her. She let out the tears and the pain by crying out to the Lord. When she finally collected herself, she knew it was time to pray deeply for a miracle . . . because nothing less would do.

* * * *

As Autumn gazed at the students, grades nine through twelve, who had shown up in the auditorium to try out for parts, she wondered again how she would choose. She led them in drama games, as Gar suggested. Afterward, each of the actors recited a thirty-second monologue. Most knew their parts word perfect. Some recitations elicited deep emotion within her. She felt compelled to cry or cheer, but she didn't do either considering Tawny's stoic expression at the judging table. Only three of the students stumbled over memorization, and she made note of those.

During the cold reads, she enjoyed the actors' unique voices. She watched for those students who exhibited the most confidence. She hid her chuckles over some of their antics. At the end of two-and-a-half hours, she thanked them for coming and dismissed the group. As soon as the last actor exited the auditorium, she let out a whoop, thankful for how well it had gone. Marny cheered too. Tawny didn't make a sound, her face blank, which settled Autumn right down.

"Now for the hard part." Tawny shoved her glasses high on her nose and peered at the forms on the table.

Didn't they just finish the hard part?

"No one stood out as the male lead." Tawny shook her head dismally. "A failure, as far as I'm concerned."

Way to ruin my pleasure over how well the auditions went.

"I disagree." Marny caught Autumn's gaze and made a funny face. "I think it went well."

Autumn fought the urge to snicker.

Tawny harrumphed.

Determined to move on to the next step in the process, Autumn scooped up the cast lists Gar told her to use and passed one to each of the ladies. "Before we discuss the actors, please fill out who you think would best portray each character."

"Without discussing it?" Tawny looked appalled. "I took scads of notes. I want to talk about every actor first."

"No."

Tawny glared at her as if it were a showdown.

Autumn took a steadying breath. She'd taken notes too, but mostly she listened as Gar told her to do. "Before we talk or argue, let's write down our first impressions of the actors we think are best suited for each character. Then we'll compare notes." Ignoring Tawny's glowering, Autumn returned to her seat. She was eager to start casting.

For five minutes the room was silent.

On the line beside "King Zachary," Autumn penned Chase's name. She was thrilled when he showed up to audition. As the lead writer, he'd understand how to interpret the role he created. He was a thoughtful young man with a strong voice who'd make a confident king. She wrote Shelley's name for sweet Princess Applelyn. Despite Autumn's dread of having to work with the girl's mother, Shelley had been dazzling as a royal.

Marny's groan was the first clue all wasn't well. "Harder than I imagined."

"Did you think it would be a picnic?" Tawny sniped. "Of course, it's hard to dash the hopes and dreams of young actors when you only have ten roles for twenty students to play."

Autumn gulped, realizing she may have made a mistake in asking Tawny to help with casting. The woman seemed aggravated about everything. Before today, ten parts seemed like enough characters for *The Queen's Disaster*. What if they had fifteen parts and thirty kids showed up? They'd still be in a pickle. "The seniors worked hard to write this play. It will be a fun production. Although, it may be shorter than usual."

"They needed more experienced guidance." Tawny dished out more sour glares.

Autumn held her tongue. No use getting into mudslinging.

The room fell silent again, except for the occasional pen scratching over a name.

On her paper, Autumn had filled in seven of the ten characters. The last three gave her the most grief. Tawny's words about crushing the hopes and dreams of students gnawed at her. How would the young people react when they didn't get parts? She hated hurting anyone's feelings.

She crossed out two of the names she wrote, churning with second thoughts. Perhaps, someone else should perform the role of the guard. The cook should be more domineering.

"I can't do this." Marny slapped her hand on the table. "Got any fudge, Autumn?"

"Actually, I do." She slipped her hand into her canvas tote and yanked out a Ziploc bag partially filled with chocolates. She passed it to Marny.

Tawny gawked at the bag.

"You're a lifesaver." Marny pulled out a piece of dark fudge with white chocolate chips swirled at the top—one of Autumn's favorites.

"That really is distracting." Tawny stared at the treats, her glassy eyes almost drooling.

"Have some." Marny tossed the bag to the grumpy woman. "It's excellent."

Tawny fingered a piece. When the candy touched her lips, her eyes sprang open, revealing gold flecks in her brown irises. An almost pleasant look crossed her face. "My goodness." Her lips broke into a full smile, then she gobbled down the fudge and reached for another one. "Oh, my goodness."

Autumn giggled. It seemed chocolate could soften the hardest of hearts.

"Told you it was good." Marny laughed outright.

"Best dessert I've tasted in my life." Tawny sighed like she was dreaming. "Now"—her voice turned gritty—"we'd better finish. I still have to cook dinner."

Autumn glanced at her paper. Gar said she should close her eyes and listen, and she'd know. She tried to mentally hear the actors' voices. Who would best portray greedy Queen Carlotta? She peeked at Tawny. Someone like her? Autumn cringed, remembering how Paris had spoken in her audition— churlish. She'd be perfect.

Marny and Tawny set down their writing utensils. Autumn took a bit longer.

"I'll start," Tawny said as soon as Autumn dropped her pen. "I chose Dillan for King Zachary and Izzie as Princess Applelynn. Who came up with a silly name like 'Applelynn?' Sounds as ridiculous as Princess Buttercup. I suggest you change her moniker immediately."

Autumn suppressed her annoyance, but pride in the seniors' work rose too strong not to comment. "The writers came up with that name, and I like it." She explained how the play- wrights incorporated their own names into the characters' world. Tawny didn't act impressed. "Dillan and Izzie, huh?"

"They were obviously the best." Tawny didn't leave room for argument.

Neither were Autumn's top picks.

Too bad Gar didn't warn her how to work out differences of opinions amongst the judges. "Who did you choose, Marny?" *Please, please, let our choices be the same.*

"I had a hard time." Marny rubbed her hands over her eyes.

"You said that already." Tawny tap-tapped the table with her pencil.

Marny smiled tolerantly at the other woman. "I chose Chase to be the king. I loved his voice."

"Yes!" Autumn squealed, so glad her friend shared her opinion. Then, seeing Tawny's scowl, she swallowed her enthusiasm. "Me too."

"I don't believe it." Tawny hit her forehead with her palm. "He doesn't have a shred of theater experience." She shuffled through the audition papers. Finding the one she sought, she pointed. "No experience."

"But he wrote the part. He understands the king's heart. His need to rule well." And since Autumn was directing, she felt she should have the final say.

"So? Dillan has had three years of drama. Not to mention, he has seniority."

"Chase is a senior too." Autumn hated confrontation, but she couldn't sit there and let Tawny run over all her ideas.

They shared their varying views, scraping close to an all-out argument. But Autumn clung to what Tawny had to know—two votes beat one. Despite her objections, Chase would be king.

Two hours later, after they ate the pizza Autumn ordered, they finally finished casting the last castle maid. Exhausted, she thanked the two women for volunteering. Then she scooped up papers and headed for her car. Monday, she'd post the cast list on her classroom door and on the cafeteria bulletin board. Tuesday, practices would begin. Half of the auditioning students would be thrilled. The rest would be disappointed. She didn't know what to do about that.

On the drive home, she thought about Gar. She'd love to call him and talk over the day's events. How would he have handled the disagreements? How would he cheer up the students who didn't get parts? Could she bring out the best in the actors the way he did all those years? In the past, she recognized his creativity but never fully appreciated the work that went into a production, until now. And she'd hardly begun.

When she reached the house, worn out, she slipped into one of Gar's flannel shirts. She flopped down on the bed, grabbed his pillow and laid her cheek against it. The last thought on her mind before falling asleep was praying for her husband and for them to find a way to reconcile. *Oh, God, heal us. Help us to forgive. Please send a miracle.*

Twenty-one

Ty

"Hey, Sas, I couldn't wait to call you," Ty spoke into his Bluetooth as he drove I-90 toward the Washington/Idaho border. Gar sat in the passenger seat, but Ty wasn't about to *not* call his wife just because his housemate might overhear their conversation. If they were going to be apart for a few weeks, he had to talk to her a couple of times a day.

"I miss your waking up beside me in the morning," she whispered in a sultry voice.

"My thoughts, exactly." Ty chuckled at their flirtations and felt his cheeks heat up. "What's your plan for the day?"

"Deborah's speaking on worship this morning. I'm still in bed, sipping my coffee."

"You are the pampered thing." He grinned, wishing he were with her. He enjoyed making her coffee in the morning.

"You know me. I sleep in as long as I can."

"I do know that about you." He smiled. "Gar and I are on our way to work. Kind of nice to head to the job first thing in the morning like most of the rest of the world."

"I'm glad you're enjoying yourself." She sighed. "I can't imagine not seeing you for two more weeks."

"I know. I miss you. Wish I could kiss your dimple."

She giggled, and he missed her even more. They chatted for a few minutes, then ended the call with "I love yous."

Gar stared out the side window. "Sounds like the perfect romance."

"I like to think so." Ty felt so thankful for his marriage.

"Must be that honeymoon, first-year stuff."

Ty heard the smirk in Gar's voice, but he didn't let it get to him.

"If so, I hope it lasts for the rest of my life." Ty steered the car into the left lane to avoid merging traffic. "If you couldn't tell, I'm wildly in love with that woman."

Gar laughed, but his tone sounded more like a man aching with loss than one filled with humor.

Ty reminded himself to tread carefully. Gar hadn't asked for advice. He needed to wait for that open door. Still, he wanted to say something. "Takes commitment and determination to not lose that special connection."

"And if you do?"

"Then it's rough." He passed another car on the freeway. "But not hopeless."

"Sometimes the world caves in on you all at once." Gar sighed like he was in such a spot.

Ty wondered if he should nod and be understanding or be blunt and share. *Lord?*

Gar had been staying in the studio apartment over the garage for the last four days. They'd been chatting and eating dinner together, either at a restaurant or with pizza cooked at the house. Yet Ty had forced himself not to talk about marriage or Gar's situation, instead praying and trusting God to soften the man's heart. Was this the moment he'd been waiting for?

"Do you still love your wife?" Ty asked, feeling trepidation for prying.

The other man shrugged. "Love has various levels. I still love her. Maybe not in the romantic way you're talking about." Gar let out a long sigh. "I'm sure you don't relate to my situation."

Ty ignored the rebuff. He thought of this summer when he asked Josh to attend the marriage conference at Hart's Camp, and Josh grumped that Ty didn't know anything about him. That sort of comment always challenged his inclination to remain silent. "I might understand more than you think."

"You have some deep dark past?"

"Or something." Ty wondered what he could say, considering Gar's combative tone. "If you ever want to talk, say so. You're not alone in feeling the world is caving in on you. Was a time, I felt the same."

He drove another mile without either of them speaking.

"What, no lectures on Christian marriage?" Gar cleared his throat. "Isn't that why you invited me to stay at your place?"

Ty was surprised by his words, but not offended.

"Sorry." Gar huffed. "You're my boss, and you've given me a place to stay. I meant no disrespect."

Sure he did, but Ty would keep praying. "As I said, when you're ready to talk, I'll listen. I'll share my experiences, too. I can't seem to *not* talk about what happened between Winter and me a decade ago."

He spent the rest of the drive praying God would move in Gar's heart, and that He'd open a door of opportunity for Ty to share.

* * * *

"Ever been canoeing?" Gar was rotating tires on a white Silverado. All morning his mind wasn't far from the discussion he had with Ty on the drive to Coeur d'Alene.

Ty's head was tipped inside the engine compartment of a Mazda. "Can't say I have."

"Autumn and I . . . we have a canoe we take out on Puget Sound." He tightened the bolts on the front wheel. "Kyle said I could borrow his. I wondered if you'd be interested in heading down to Lake Coeur d'Alene after work. It's unseasonably warm, wind's calm. Thought I'd give it a try."

Ty stood and wiped thick black grease from his hands onto an old towel. "Sounds fun. Sure. Anything I should bring?"

"Kyle will have everything we need."

"It's a plan."

Gar thought it was strange that Ty didn't guilt him about his marriage like Kyle would have. Lacey would have gone ballistic, shouting at him about the sorry excuse of a man he was for leaving his wife. Words he deserved but didn't appreciate. Didn't seem like any good would come from him talking to Ty, either. Other than the fact he'd experienced a failed marriage. Could he relate to how lost Gar felt? Like he was swimming in quicksand? Drowning in a pond so thick with moss and under-growth he couldn't reach the top for air? It might be worth a shot. Of course, so would taking a flight to Paris and disap-pearing for the next eight months until the school year ended.

Later, they drove to Kyle's. He said they could borrow his truck, so they loaded the sixteen-foot fiberglass canoe, paddles, and flotation pillows from the garage into the truck bed.

"Let's swing by Maude's and get burgers to go." Ty had already taken Gar to the restaurant he called his favorite twice in the last few days.

"Okay by me." His mouth watered at the remembrance of the tasty home-style burgers.

They made a quick stop at Maude's. After Ty paid for the food, the grinning eccentric owner patted his cheeks like she might a grandson and called him one of her best customers.

She gushed about how much she missed him in the last year since he'd been gone.

Gar was laughing about it as they got back in the truck. "That woman scares me."

Ty snickered. "She'd make a great character for one of your plays."

Gar nodded. "You're right." It was nice to have someone mention theater to him as if that part of his life weren't dead and buried.

"Ever thought of writing your own?" Ty asked while driving down Government Way. "A play, I mean."

"Thought of it, sure." Back in college, he wanted to write a script about an inspirational teacher and the long-term difference he could make in the lives of students. Gar hadn't thought much about it since. Still, someone like Maude would make a humorous protagonist.

At the lake, Ty backed the truck into the boat slip. Gar untied the canoe, and they slid the long, narrow craft into the water. Ty parked the truck, while Gar maneuvered the boat toward the dock. He chose the stern bench, the one he usually sat in when he and Autumn canoed. While he waited for Ty, his thoughts flew to other times he went out on the water, the wind against his face, the scent of fresh air and gasoline mingling in his senses, the glances of a beautiful woman's gaze cast toward him—namely Autumn's. And something gripped his chest. He loved those moments with her. Just the two of them paddling on a calm sea. All those years, he looked forward to spending weekends with her. It was their time away from school, the city, the bustle of their lives. What happened to them? To him? When did he wander so far from just enjoying being with his wife?

"All set?" Ty stepped into the bow of the boat.

"Sure." The canoe leaned starboard. Gar held firmly to the rough edge of the dock, balancing them. Even though every canoeist should be prepared for such a calamity, he hated to think of tipping over. When Ty picked up his paddle, Gar released the treated wood he was clutching and did the same. Paddling came back as naturally as riding a bike or maneuvering a sled downhill. Smoothly, they cut through the swells, the water lapping musically against the hull of the boat.

The sun, setting lower in the horizon, glimmered across the lake in streaks of amber. Window panes of houses on the opposite side of the lake, maybe a mile away, reflected the same light. A seagull squawked and flew overhead, searching for its dinner, no doubt. Gar missed the salty air, but this freshwater lake was a good second best.

"This is great," Ty said over his shoulder.

"I love the water." Gar breathed in deeply, the cool air awakening senses dulled too long. "It's like I come alive. Energized, somehow."

"I see what you mean." Ty pointed left, toward a tree-lined hill. "That's Tubbs Hill. Can we veer that way?"

"Why not?" Gar sliced his paddle through a mix of bluish-gray water on the port side, keeping opposite of Ty's stroke through the next wave. He dragged his paddle like a rudder to get them to turn. Then they kept up a steady rhythm, moving forward, then left.

After a while, Ty stopped paddling, his gaze intent on the shoreline. "Right there on the beach, I asked Winter to marry me the first time."

"First time?" Gar lifted his paddle out of the water and let it rest against the gunwale. He stared at the sandy beach with its backdrop of large boulders. "How many times did you ask her?"

"Three times." Ty grinned. "Here about eleven years ago."

"The next?"

"A year ago, in Ketchikan, Alaska, after her dad died. It

was too soon after such a loss." Ty sighed. "Third time, God blessed me with a second chance at love. I'm so thankful."

A second chance. Gar felt a tug on his heart, a longing for things to be right between him and Autumn. A year ago, he'd never have imagined life this far from her. He had been happy back then. Content, even. How could one kiss, one near-miss of succumbing to passion, change everything? Or had that only been the beginning of his struggles?

"Ready to eat?"

"Sure."

Ty opened the food bag and tossed Gar a still-warm burger and a water bottle. With the lake water lapping against the sides of the canoe and the sunshine waning, they ate. The wind seemed to be picking up, but nothing serious. It was a large body of water—some twenty-five miles long. Kyle had mentioned Lake Coeur d'Alene had over a hundred miles of shoreline. Gar wouldn't mind spending a whole day in the canoe, exploring the coves. As he chewed his food, his mind wandered to Ty's story. How did he ever convince Winter to take him back?

"I've missed Maude's cooking. Used to eat there about every day when I was single." Ty scrunched up the wrapper.

"Makes me think of burgers Mom used to make when I was a kid." Gar swallowed the last bite of his double cheeseburger, then dropped the wrapper into the trash bag. "Want to keep going east while we still have a little light?"

"Absolutely."

Gar nosed the boat into the wind. They both paddled, following a steady path along the shoreline. Eventually, Gar maneuvered the canoe 180 degrees so they could face the sunset and make their way back to the dock. He hated to end the outing, but it was nearly dark.

On the return trip to Kyle's, and then the drive to Ty's, several questions churned in his brain. How did Ty and Winter reconcile after ten years? What would it take for him to write and produce his own play? And what was Autumn doing tonight? Somewhere between paddling the canoe and falling into bed that night, it felt like his heart started beating again.

Twenty-two

Autumn

As soon as Autumn walked into the house, she dropped her armload of books and scrolled through her phone's contact list. Just wait until Gar heard how amazing the actors sounded in their third practice. "Come on, pick up."

"Hey." Gar didn't sound enthused about her call.

For a second, she was tempted to be discouraged. "Hi." Did she sound as nervous as when they'd been dating? Because that's how she felt. "I couldn't wait to talk with you."

"What's up?" Again with the dry tones.

Couldn't he sound happy to hear from her for once?

God, are You working in his life at all? I've been praying and praying. Please, change his heart. Help him to love me again. Change me too. Make me into a wife whom Gar will want to love.

"Autumn?"

"Oh, sorry. I wanted to tell you how great practices were going."

"Okay."

Okay? Was that all? She was nearly jumping up and down for joy. Was it painful for him to talk about the play? The thing he loved so much. She wanted to share her experiences with him, knowing he was the one person in the world who'd understand her newfound pleasure. Once again, she wished he'd come back and help her. But if she asked him to do that, would Ben fire her too? It might be worth losing her job to get her husband back.

"You going to tell me about it?"

Oh, yeah. "You should have heard their voices." She didn't attempt to cover her enthusiasm. "You would have been proud. They were like pros."

"That's my team." That sounded more like him.

His team. Of course. How could she think to be on the same level as him? "You're right, Gar. You trained them—except for Chase. I didn't anticipate such enthusiasm, how into their parts they'd be already."

"They'll get better." He sighed. "Some almost direct themselves."

"I noticed that. And the seniors are full of ideas. I couldn't have asked for a better group."

He was silent for a long time.

"Gar?"

"Hmm?"

She wished he'd act like he missed her. Say something about them getting back together. Give her a sign that God was doing a work in his heart.

"I miss you." There, she wouldn't wait for him to say something first. "I'd love it if you could help me with this production."

"Autumn—"

"I know. But you'd figure out what to do. I'm overwhelmed by everything."

"You know I can't." His sigh trembled like he was catching his breath.

She wanted to encourage him, to lift his spirits. If he'd only remember what they had together . . . before things fell apart.

"I'm praying for you. For us."

"That's good."

"You still at Ty's?" Lacey had kept her informed.

"Yep." His short answer and lack of dialogue made her think he wanted the conversation to end.

"Sorry for bothering you." She gritted her teeth. She hadn't meant to sound defensive. "I'll, uh, let you go."

"Thanks for calling." He clicked off.

She exhaled, and her joy evaporated like early morning fog. She stared at the cell phone. Tears flooded her eyes, but she blinked rapidly to ebb their flow. It would probably take a lot more praying before Gar showed any remorse or plans to return to married life. What if he never did?

She plopped down on the sofa and covered her face with her hands. Would she always come home to a silent house? To this emptiness? She didn't have any desire to fix dinner. Not even a prepackaged meal. Exhausted from work and practice, she tromped into the bedroom and changed into her pajamas. Tonight, she'd opt for a quick prayer, then sleep. Maybe hit the gym in the morning.

* * * *

After receiving a memo in her inbox, Autumn hurried to the school office. Marny stood behind the counter talking to a woman who was gesticulating ferociously. Jewel? What had her upset?

"Here she is." Marny waved Autumn over, looking relieved. "Morning, Mrs. Bevere. Mrs. Pollard has some concerns about the drama. Mr. Whiffleman thought you could help?" Marny made an apologetic grimace.

"Hello, Jewel."

A scowl contorted the woman's black-lined eyes. "I expected Ben to hear my complaints."

Complaints? A knot clamped in Autumn's chest. She met Marny's gaze.

Her friend cleared her throat. "You can use the conference room." She rocked her thumb toward the beveled glass door to her left.

One look at Jewel's pursed lips, her haughty lifted eyebrow, and Autumn knew the suggestion was a good idea. No sense in the parent imploding where students might overhear.

Alone, she faced Jewel. "What seems to be the problem?"

The woman's hand fell to her hip. "I'm surprised Shelley wasn't chosen for the lead in your poorly constructed production. She has the most experience. Did she mess up her monologue?"

"Not at all. She did great."

"What, then?"

Shelley had been Autumn's first choice. But Tawny and Marny chose Isabelle. After the practices they had so far, Autumn was convinced they made the right choice. With Shelley's experience, she could portray the more difficult evil queen, while another girl played the sweet-tempered princess.

"Shelley's doing fabulous. Her voice is perfect." Autumn kept her tone calm, thinking of the verse about a soft answer turning away wrath.

"Perfect to represent evil?" Jewel's mocking laugh mirrored the wicked queen's tones Autumn hoped Shelley could imitate. Jewel rested the tips of her hot-pink nails against her silk shirt. "When I spoke to you about theater, I expected a worthwhile production. Not some slipshod play thrown together by a group of high school students."

Ugh. First, she was forced into directing a show. Now Jewel had the audacity to chastise her decisions? "I'm doing the best

I can." She tried keeping her voice modulated but feared that might be impossible. "The seniors have done a remarkable job of writing the play. I'm proud of them. If you'll give their ideas a chance—"

"To fail?" She crossed her arms. "I'll be observing your practices and reporting to the board whether or not your thrown-together show adds value to our school. There's a high standard of excellence expected from productions at ECHS. Your husband, bless his heart, never let us down. He'd be dismayed by such a flimsy production."

How dare Jewel insult the writers of Autumn's production! "For your information, Gar was the one who suggested the seniors write this play. As far as you watching, practice sessions are closed." She gulped, surprised by her own vehemence.

Jewel gasped, her eyes as wide as golf balls. "What are you talking about?"

Obviously, this parent wasn't used to anyone opposing her.

"No one is allowed to watch any of my practices until the final week."

"Don't be silly." Jewel shoved her black purse strap higher on her shoulder. "I've never heard of such a rule."

"Think of the performance as a surprise, then."

"We'll see about that." Jewel stomped to the door. "I got you the position of director, I can get you out of it."

"I'm sorry you feel that way."

"Tawny Richards wants to direct *Romeo and Juliet*. She says my Shelley would make a perfect Juliet."

"I'm sure she would." Autumn clenched her fists until her fingernails dug into her palms. Was Tawny going behind Autumn's back to cause trouble?

With a harrumph, Jewel left the room and marched toward Ben's office door.

Autumn took in deep breaths, trying to calm herself. If the

play were canceled, she'd feel terrible for the kids who wrote the story and for those who got parts. Now that she'd experienced certain aspects of theater—playwriting, casting, and some practices—she'd like to see this drama through to the final curtain. But if Ben gave in to the parent's demands, what then?

She trudged past Marny on her way out of the office, giving her a tight nod she hoped expressed "I can't talk now." The hallway to her classroom felt a mile long.

Since the day she agreed to teach Gar's classes, so much had gone wrong. For weeks she'd been praying and believing. But nothing had changed, it seemed—other than her working out and losing some weight.

Lord, what else can I do? Show me Your will. And can You take care of this thing with Jewel?

Twenty-three

Autumn

Early Saturday morning, after suffering through nightmares about Gar, Autumn sat on the couch sipping a white chocolate mocha, praying and contemplating life. She took a long drink of the chocolaty brew, then set the mug next to the plate of toast and fudge she prepared but didn't eat. Six o'clock in the morning seemed a little premature to binge on chocolate. Now that she was working out, she should limit her sugar intake, but she wouldn't avoid it completely. She enjoyed making fudge, and she couldn't wait for Gar to try some. Wouldn't he be surprised by her new skill?

With her thoughts turning to her husband, she felt burdened to pray some more. She slipped to her knees and leaned against the couch cushions. *Lord, please touch Gar. Strengthen him and give him Your wisdom. I feel so heavy about our marriage. Won't You change him? And me too? I want to be more like You. Help me not to overreact when I talk with Gar the next time. Prepare his heart to love me again. I don't want to lose him.*

After a while, she groaned, pushed herself off her knees and curled up on the couch, hoping to fall asleep. Instead, her thoughts wouldn't rest. When did Gar first start acting detached from her? Last school year? Around Christmas, they had been doing fine. Then he traveled to that teacher's conference in Las Vegas. It was the strangest thing, but it seemed like he came back different. Irritable. Riled by the tiniest things. Changes in school policy drove him nuts. And he spent more time with Sasha. Hours he and Autumn used to spend together—like on their Saturday morning canoe trips.

She remembered one time when she arrived at the school, unnoticed, and stood in the shadows of the auditorium. Gar and Sasha were cleaning the stage in the aftermath of *Cinderella*, and she thought she might help.

"Gar"—Sasha's voice sounded soft and feminine—"can you come here and look at this ding in the floor?"

Gar had rushed to her. Autumn wished he'd hurry that fast when *she* called his name and asked him to take out the trash or help her carry a heavy load.

The two knelt over something on the stage. Gar touched the spot at the same time Sasha did. They looked at each other with an indefinable emotion Autumn interpreted as admiration. In the next moment, it seemed Sasha leaned closer to him than was necessary.

Autumn's foot bumped into a chair leg, making a scraping sound. Gar and Sasha turned and stared at her as if she was an intruder. Had they been two inches closer, their cheeks would have touched. Sasha stared at her with that deer-in-the-headlights look. Gar frowned.

Autumn felt like she was caught spying on them, which wasn't what she intended. She trusted Gar. He hadn't done anything to make her suspicious of him. Although, he had been acting weird lately. Lacking in affection. His ardor tepid.

"I stopped in to see if I could help clean up." She nodded toward the mess on the stage.

Gar stood and stuffed his hands in his jeans' pockets. "That's . . . great." He glanced at Sasha.

"We can use all the help we can get." The stage designer pointed at the gash in the floor. "Want me to deal with that?"

"Yes, we need to leave the place looking as good as we found it."

"Who's to say the band didn't do that with a music stand? We could always blame them." Sasha laughed as if the two of them were sharing in a joke.

When Gar met Autumn's gaze, he smiled. Reassuring her? Surely, he wasn't involved with Sasha. They were only friends. Hadn't he told her so?

Now, laying on the couch, she recalled Ben's reaction to Sasha's name. What did he suspect?

What if . . . Gar did have an affair? Ice water rushed through her veins, bringing a deep chill. Had she been naïve to believe it could never happen when Sasha and Gar spent so many hours alone together? Her heart thudded against her ribs. For a moment, she felt lightheaded.

Then she groaned. All this speculation was ridiculous. She needed to see Gar. What was to stop her from jumping in her car and driving to Spokane? He was there. She was here. Since he was staying with Ty, a little over a five-hour drive lay between them. There were things she needed to ask him. Things she needed to get off her chest. The only question was why she'd waited so long.

Thirty minutes later, she was in her Accent heading down I-405 toward the I-90 intersection. She'd packed an overnight bag which she might not need. That depended on Gar, and how their talk went. Not that she'd want to make the five-hour trip twice in one day.

As she drove, her thoughts whirled in circles about their past and their future. Maybe Gar was experiencing a midlife crisis. Or else he'd become involved with Sasha. Yet, she hated to assume that. Either way, she needed to know the truth. Fifteen years ago, she vowed to stand by him through good times and bad. Today, she'd look him in the eye and ask him what was going on. After she heard what he had to say, would she still want him to come home? She'd been so determined not to beg. To patiently wait for God to work things out. And here she was chasing after him.

Fifty miles west of Spokane, she pulled over and shot Gar a text. *Heading your way. Meet me at Riverfront Park in an hour.* She remembered the city park with the giant red wagon from a previous trip she and Gar made to visit Kyle and Lacey farther east.

A return text came surprisingly fast. *You're coming here? Why? Just meet me.*

She pulled onto the freeway again. Sixty minutes to implore God to prepare Gar's heart to talk with her. Thirty-six-hundred seconds to pray he'd be honest and that they could find a way to work out their differences before she headed home.

Or if things went well, he'd invite her to stay.

Twenty-four

Gar

Ever since Gar received his wife's text that she was on her way to Spokane, his heart had been pounding like he was having a heart attack. Didn't she know he worked on Saturdays, the busiest day at TK Automotive? But he could hardly let her show up and not meet her.

He slammed down a wrench, and it clattered in the garage.

"What's wrong?" Kyle stepped from beneath an SUV raised on lifts. He bent at the waist and stretched from side to side. "You look sick."

Ty rolled out from under a Mini Cooper sitting on hydraulic jacks. He wiped his hands on a rag and stared at Gar. "What's up?"

"Autumn just texted me to meet her in Spokane in an hour."

"That's great." Kyle grinned. Apparently, Gar wouldn't have trouble getting the time off.

Leave it to his cousin to think Autumn showing up unannounced was a perfect solution to their marital woes. Did Lacey put her up to this?

At least Ty didn't say anything wise and full of baloney like he knew just what Gar was going through, because he didn't.

Gar wanted to kick something. Sure, two months had passed, and Autumn had been patient with him. It was time they talked, but he wasn't ready to hurt her with an explanation about Sasha and Elaine, even though he hadn't seen either of them in months. And he sure couldn't go back home—even if he wanted to—with the guilt he still wore around his neck.

A few minutes later, Ty set his hand on Gar's shoulder. "How're you holding up?"

Gar gulped. "Not so great."

"What's the harm in talking things over?" Kyle wiped his finger across his nose and left a black grease smudge. "I mean, it's cool she's driving over to see you."

Easy for him to say.

Ty walked to the coffeepot in the corner and poured himself a cup.

Kyle stepped back under the vehicle, mumbling.

Autumn should have waited for Gar to say he was ready to meet. He'd been contemplating talking with Ty, but he hadn't brought up the subject of marriage yet. Ty continued his daily driving conversations with his wife, and even Gar could tell he was crazy about her. She sounded like some exotic princess by the way he carried on. Of course, their romantic conversations made Gar jealous, and made him long for a stronger connection with his own wife.

"You need time off?" Ty was back beside him, sipping his coffee.

"Yeah. Sorry about the short notice." Hey, if he had to work . . . "Since today's so busy here, I can tell her I can't go."

"Don't mention it. Kyle and I both remember how to change tires." Ty shuffled back to the Cooper and sat down on the dolly.

What did Autumn want to talk about? The play? He doubted she'd drive that far to discuss her production.

He finished changing the tires he'd been working on, then answered a call-in quote request. He removed his overalls and cleaned up in the bathroom.

On the forty-minute drive to Riverfront Park, his thoughts churned. What would she say? Would she give him an ultimatum? *Come home or else?* Or else what—? Divorce? He shuddered at the word, although he'd pondered it enough times. It seemed the walls in his heart rose higher with each mile.

He parked on the fourth level of the downtown parking garage, then headed out the exit toward the park. She told him to meet her at the landmark red wagon. Under normal circumstances, he'd be interested in a closer look at the nearly thirty-foot-long steel and concrete artwork with a kiddy slide for a handle. Not today. If he were in better spirits, he might have stopped to pick up flowers for her. Maybe her favorite, yellow roses. But wouldn't that give her the wrong signal? Like he was ready to make up and come home? He knew that wasn't the case.

His palms felt sweaty. His jaw tightened as he took less-than-eager steps along the cement walkway leading toward the twelve-foot-high wagon. Ducks beside the Spokane River quacked and waddled to him as if eager for crumbs of bread he didn't have. Seagulls squawked and fussed over something on the ground.

As soon as he spotted her sitting on a concrete bench facing the giant artwork, his heart crashed against his ribcage. He paused and drew in a sharp breath as he took a moment to observe her. She looked lovely as she watched two kids playing on the wagon. She hadn't noticed him yet. Her arms were crossed like she was cold, or nervous. Had the sun been shining, it would have brought out red highlights in her dark, shoulder-length hair. He'd always loved her soft tresses smelling of vanilla shampoo.

Suddenly, he felt nervous. He remembered their quarrel before he left. Angry words. An explosion of emotions. The weeks of confusion ever since.

She stood, her gaze meeting his. Then a timid smile.

He stepped toward her. "Hey."

"Hi, Gar."

He wondered what she thought of his beard. Did she hate it? When she offered him another sweet smile, something warm ignited in the pit of his stomach.

He promised her so much, then failed. Her sparkling tear-filled eyes appealed to him to draw closer. He did, and she walked straight into his arms and hugged him tight. She rested her cheek against his chest, and he embraced her too. Not an I'm-madly-in-love-with-you hug. More of an I've-missed-you bear hug. Still, it felt great to hold her. They'd never been apart so long since they married.

For the briefest of seconds, he wanted to impulsively kiss her. To taste her long enough to find out if they still shared romantic feelings. Considering how hard his heart pounded in his chest, he knew the answer.

Her fingers linked with his, and he let her lead him to the bench she vacated. He pulled his hand away as they sat down. Her expression remained friendly, open, not wounded or weepy. Something seemed different about her. Was she more relaxed? Happier? He expected her to be demanding or short-tempered. Relief spread through the tight places in his chest, and some of his trepidation eased away.

Curious why she came, he started with small talk. "Have a nice drive?"

"I did." Again, the smile. "Oh, here." She dug for something in her handbag. "I brought these for you." She handed him a Ziploc bag filled with fudge squares, and their fingers touched.

He stared at the fabulous-looking varieties of chocolate. "Wow. Thanks, I love fudge."

"I know." Her hand lingered near his for a moment. "I made them."

"What?" He perused the bag's contents more closely. "You're kidding me. You made these?" Layered fudge? Cashew-topped? Dark chocolate. White. He'd never known her to be a confectioner. "They look professionally made."

She shrugged. "I've had a lot of quiet hours to fill. I've been experimenting. You know me and chocolate."

"I do." He knew her weakness as well as his own. "Aren't you busy with your show?" Now, why did he bring that up? Way to initiate a sore subject, at least for himself.

"Oh, sure." She twisted her hands in her lap. "Gar, I know I'm pushing things by showing up like this. You may not be ready—"

"I'm not." He swallowed a gulp of air, the old weight growing heavy in his chest.

She closed her eyes, and it seemed she might be . . . praying? *Strange.* When she met his gaze again, her eyes looked moist, but she still smiled at him—without pointed barbs or angry glares.

"You're probably wondering why I had to see you today." She rubbed her hands together like she was trying to keep them warm.

"Yeah." He was concerned about that topic.

Her gaze remained steady on him. "I wanted to see you because I need to ask you something."

"Shoot." He steeled himself.

"Do you see us getting back together?" She ran her fingers along his thumb and wrist.

Mesmerized, he didn't pull his hand away. His heart thumped rapidly in his ears. His breathing rate increased.

"Would you consider coming back home with me?"

In the silence, his lips went dry. He could barely swallow. Given time he hoped to return to her. Right now? More days than not, he felt plagued with memories and that sword of betrayal—mainly his for the bad choices he made. How could he go back before they honestly faced their past?

When a tear dripped down her cheek, he longed to hold her and tell her everything would be okay. They were going through a rough patch. All married couples did, right? But if he followed her home, just because she asked, what then? In Everett, he didn't have a job or any self-respect. Everywhere he looked he'd see the things he still wanted to pursue and couldn't. How could they resume their lives as if he didn't walk away?

Oh, but that smile of hers was doing something astounding to his heart. His stomach felt twisted in knots. How could he have doubted his attraction for her? As soon as he saw her, he wanted to kiss her like he hadn't in months. To love her . . . like his wife. He swallowed a gulp that seemed to land at his feet. What if he invited her back to the studio apartment? What if they could enjoy the rest of the day as if the last eight months never happened?

One perfect day. But then what?

One of them would wind up saying something stupid. Him, most likely. And they'd be back in the same boat, as miserable as ever. He couldn't raise her hopes just to dash them.

Months ago, something bitter poisoned his heart. Maybe grief. Middle age. Temptation. Resentment. Whatever. But it had been a slow takeover, a coup. Until he faced that demon, he couldn't give this woman false expectations.

"You driving back tonight?"

By the surprised look on her face, his words sounded callous. He regretted that more than he could say, but as much as he'd like to make up with her, he wasn't ready.

Twenty-five

Autumn

Autumn stiffened at Gar's abrupt words. Obviously, he didn't want her to stay. Her arrival had been a shock, an unwelcome one, by the look on his bearded face. Seeing him with whiskers had been a surprise. Not a bad one, though. She kind of liked his new rugged look—as long as his eyes still gazed tenderly into hers.

They had, moments ago. Or did she only imagine his pleased greeting? The way his eyes sparkled as if happy to see her? She'd embraced him, and she could swear he hugged her back. Why the cold shoulder now? Because she asked if he'd come home? Because he wasn't attracted to her anymore? She tugged on the bulky sweater she wore over her black slacks.

She watched as two little boys, maybe five and six, raced up the wagon's ladder and came down the slide squealing.

Everything would be different if she and Gar had been blessed with children. When they received the bad news about her infertility, he told her it didn't matter. But she knew it did.

She wasn't enough for him. Their love hadn't been enough to make him stay.

Tears filled her eyes and splashed down her cheeks. She turned and brushed them away before Gar could see.

Lord, I'm a fool for driving over here like this. Look at him. His set jaw. His aloof stance. He doesn't want me. All this time, I've missed him so much, and he's been . . .

She remembered a recent conversation she had with Marny about battles. Sometimes during one, things don't turn out so well. Minor skirmishes are lost. Sustained injuries. Festering wounds. But that didn't mean the war was lost. She'd have to remind herself of that in the days ahead. She needed to continue fighting this spiritual battle she and Gar were in and somehow hang onto hope. *Don't give up.* Yet this very moment, defeat gnawed at her.

Still, her thoughts turned to prayer. *Lord, I commit Gar and me to You. You know our weaknesses and the wrongs we've both done. Please help him. Help me. Change us into who You want us to be. You are the One I trust.*

The two boys flew down the slide again, laughing the whole way.

She stared at the tall wagon, then gazed into Gar's eyes as an idea came to mind. "Want to slide with me?" Even though it was a kid's slide, she could imagine the air blowing through her hair. The butterflies in her tummy as she went down the slide. Just like when she was a little girl.

He frowned. "What?"

She nodded toward the slide. "Let's play." She tugged on his hand that was resting across his knee. She'd been driving for hours. A little exercise sounded great, especially if she had to drive back home tonight. Laughter could be healing too, right?

He shook his head. "No, thanks."

The old Gar would get a kick out of doing something corny and fun.

She stood, determined not to pout or be mad at him. Driving home she could cry all she wanted. "Race you to the top?" She grinned.

He didn't agree but she still jogged over to the ladder and climbed up. Her shoes clunked against the wagon's giant bed at the top. She leaned over the three-and-a-half-foot edge and waved down at him. He raised his hand but didn't put much effort into the motion. She sat down at the top of the slide and flew down.

When she stood on solid ground, she noticed a slight grin on Gar's face before he turned away. So, he wasn't as unaffected by her as he acted.

"That was fun." She nodded toward the river. "Want to walk?"

"Okay." He stood and stuffed both hands in his jacket.

He was probably worried she'd take his hand again. She wouldn't. But how in the world could she reach his heart?

They strolled beside the gray waters, watching ducks searching for food. A bicycler rode past them on the path. A couple of joggers followed.

Silently, they crossed the Monroe Bridge. Autumn stopped and peered into the rushing waters below. She hated the way Gar wouldn't interact with her. When had they become such strangers? Didn't he realize there were things she needed to ask him? Topics even she hated to bring up. Or maybe that was the very reason he was being so quiet.

"Gar?"

He groaned like he hated whatever she was going to ask.

"Did you have an affair with Sasha?" There. She asked the detestable question. The whole drive over she pondered how to approach the subject. But even speaking the woman's name felt suffocating. Like she needed more air than she could draw in to survive his answer. "I need the truth." She fought off sneaky tears. She didn't want him looking at her tears and thinking she was being too emotional for him to be honest with her.

Gar shuffled on his feet, his gaze following the river's edge. "Did Ben say I did?"

"No, why would he?" The way her employer had acted about Sasha came to mind. "Does he know something about you two?"

"No." Gar's face reddened. "Did you actually think I could do that to you?"

She stared deeply into his brown eyes. "No. But I wouldn't have thought you capable of leaving me alone for two months, either." She touched a button on his jacket. "Why did you ask about Ben?"

Gar let out a breathy sigh. "He accused me of spending time with her, inappropriately."

"Oh?" She couldn't imagine Ben saying something like that without cause. "Why?"

"He thought he saw something suspicious. It wasn't." His Adam's apple bobbed up and down as he swallowed. A lie reflex?

"So did I." She watched him, wondering what he'd say to that.

"Autumn, I—" He shook his head like he couldn't finish the sentence.

"Did you . . . cross the line with Sasha?" She held her breath.

"Not in the way you're implying." He turned and strode toward the park.

She couldn't let him end their conversation like that. She ran to catch up with him. "Then what?"

"I don't want to talk about it here. Not like this."

She grabbed hold of his arm. "Please, Gar? I drove a long way to talk with you. I need to know what happened. How did we get like this?" *When did you stop loving me?* But she couldn't ask him that. Not with a mom and her kids strolling past. Not with the way he was avoiding looking at her.

"I'm still trying to figure that out." When he faced her, tears filled his eyes.

Seeing Gar even a little emotional tugged on her heart. "Can't we find out together?" She leaned forward until her forehead rested against his coat. She was close enough to smell his deodorant, his masculine scent. She breathed in deeply, putting it to memory. But when he didn't wrap his arms around her, or say anything reassuring, she backed away. "Are you going to divorce me?" Even though she hated mentioning it, during their two months of separation, she'd imagined the next probable step—unless God intervened. She hated the thought of splitting up for good. She still wanted to keep her promises to him.

"No. I don't know." The skin around his eyes looked pasty and drawn. He stared at her with dread or misery.

He didn't love her, did he? Is that what he needed to say, but couldn't? He denied crossing the line with Sasha. Yet he wouldn't explain—which made her more suspicious. Surely, he'd contemplated making their arrangement permanent, as she had. Only she didn't want their marriage to end. But she made a terrible mistake in coming here. She thought by now there had to have been a positive change in her husband's feelings. That she would see love or at least affection. She was wrong.

Tears burned her eyes again. Not the kind she could simply brush away, either. "I should go." She cleared her throat and wiped her fist beneath her nose to stop it from running. "It's a long drive. Call me when you're ready to talk, okay? Goodbye, Gar." She kissed his whiskered cheek, then walked away as fast as she could. This trip was a waste of time. What was she thinking?

She'd almost made it to her parked car when she heard footsteps approaching from behind.

Gar ran in front of her and stopped, breathing heavily. His face had a pained expression, and his eyes blinked rapidly as if absorbing extra moisture. "Autumn, I-I just wanted to say I'm sorry for putting you through this. I know it's not what you signed up for fifteen years ago. I don't know what's wrong with me."

She longed to fall into his arms and beg him to come home. If he would, they could try to start over. They could go to counseling. She'd love for him to pray with her, to talk to her like they used to when they were younger, to sit in their little backyard oasis and hold hands and dream about their future. For him to love her like he once did. She longed to tell him how sorry she was for taking his job, for ruining the beautiful thing they had. But something held her back. Pride. Or that wary look in his eyes. Instead, she let a smile she wasn't feeling cross her lips.

He pulled her to him for a moment. "Don't give up on me, okay?" He pressed a kiss against her cheek, then he let her go and jogged back the way he came.

Sobs that had been building inside since the moment she laid eyes on his bearded face broke through the dam. *Lord, help. It hurts so badly.* She ran to her car and sat there a full fifteen minutes until her tear ducts were dry enough for her to see the road. Then she drove back home, drinking coffee and praying for Gar and their marriage most of the way. She wouldn't give up on him. But she needed to face her life as a single woman, at least for now, with all the grace and determination she could muster. God was with her. He was the strength of her life. She had classes to teach and a play to direct. *That* would take all her focus in the coming days.

Twenty-six

Autumn

"Mrs. Bevere," Jude, one of Autumn's student directors, called to her from the stage. "We have a problem."

Just one? She sighed. Her crew of assistants made life as a director easier, but there were some theatrical issues none of them knew how to solve. The fact they were cramming in practices and set building sessions every day after school didn't help. And she couldn't call Gar over every dilemma. "What's the problem?" She jogged up the side steps to the stage.

"According to the script, Chase is supposed to enter the last scene riding a horse from stage left." He pointed right, then switched to left, and groaned.

She chuckled at his frustrated expression. She'd had her share of difficulties with communicating stage directions. Left was left if you were onstage, facing the audience. But if she was standing in the orchestra section giving blocking cues, her right was the actors' left. Definitely confusing. "And?"

"A real horse?"

"Oh." That would be a problem. "What else can we do?"

"Know anyone with a horse we can borrow?" Jude grinned impishly. "I looked up a couple of stables online. It's expensive."

Oh, the zeal and imagination of youth.

"With our limited, nonexistent budget, we can't use a real horse." As it was, they were digging through every stored box for costumes, and most outfits had to be altered. Props from previous shows were being tweaked and reused.

Apple walked up behind Jude. "Think of the smell—and the poo you'd have to clean up."

Jude frowned. "So what's he going to ride?"

Autumn wanted to laugh at his crestfallen face. "Put your heads together and come up with a solution."

"A horse galloping across the stage would have been awesome." He thumbed through the script.

"Indeed."

"I have an idea." Apple pulled him toward stage right, er, left.

Autumn's cell vibrated. *Marny* flashed across the screen. "Hey, what's up?" She'd been so busy since her return from Spokane, she hadn't taken time to call her friend. Between grading papers, daily practices, and working out, she'd been falling into bed exhausted every night, then getting up an hour early to pray before she did it all over again. It was good for her to stay active since it kept her from over-thinking about Gar. Not that it was a full-proof solution.

"How are things going with the play?" Marny sounded bubbly.

"We're in practice right now."

"Sorry for my bad timing."

"There's a lull before the final scene. What's going on?" Autumn watched Jude and Apple engaging Chase in their discussion over his horseless entrance.

"I have a big favor to ask. Feel free to say no."

"Okay. Need some fudge?" She had avoided making any since she was exercising on a rowing machine and taking spinning classes. However, she wouldn't mind trying out the new recipe she found for peanut butter and dark chocolate fudge.

"Funny you should mention that." Marny's chuckle sounded like she was nervous—a rare reaction from her typically brash friend. "Remember the kid who was wild about your fudge the night you helped serve food at the church on Broadway Avenue?"

"He was so sweet." She remembered the boy's smile and his freckles, and how they hugged, and she called him "young knight."

"His name's Jimmy. He and his mom need a place to stay."

"They do?" Autumn's heart beat faster. "What do you mean? Is something wrong?"

One of the parent volunteers held out two different cloths for her to consider as a royal cloak.

"This one," she whispered and pointed to the deep purple one. Then she focused on Marny's explanation.

"The short version is our church is trying to find temporary housing for homeless people during the coldest months. My parents are taking in four adults. I wondered what you might think of letting Jimmy and Sarah stay at your place. I know it's a lot to ask. But?"

What could she say? She'd never imagined doing such a thing. Share her home with strangers? She thought of the homeless families and individuals she served rolls and fudge to on that cold night. Didn't she think, even then, how she wished she could do something more for them? Was this it? Deciding such a thing on her own was difficult. If Gar were home— She was already busy, deep in the trenches of directing a play—something she never did before. But wasn't she enjoying it? Didn't she feel much happier and content lately? What if God was leading her to share her home with someone in need? She wouldn't have to return to an empty house anymore. She'd have someone to talk with in the evenings.

"Sorry to put you on the spot." Marny cleared her throat. "I thought since Gar is still away, it might be nice to have company."

Just what she was thinking.

Lord, is this what You would have me do?

Prayer had become so much more spontaneous and less formal to her than in the past. A lifeline. And at home, her deeper prayer time, her battle zone, had transformed into a powerful spiritual experience. Now, she wanted to actively seek God's will, no matter what, whether Gar was part of her life or not.

Her house was a simple three bedroom with more space than one person needed. "Two of them, huh?"

"Yep."

Jimmy could sleep on the futon in the bedroom they converted into Gar's office. A child wandering around her home? Something light and delightful zinged through her heart, compelling her to say yes. Sarah could have the guest room. A friend to share chores and conversation? As soon as she pictured the two of them living in her house, she knew what her answer would be.

"Think about it and let me know, okay?" She could almost hear Marny's sheepish smile.

"Wait. Yes. My answer is yes!" Peace, mixed with a dollop of giddy excitement, infused her.

"You will?" Marny's voice turned high-pitched.

"You asked, didn't you?"

Her friend laughed. "You'll have to attend training at our church. Group orientation."

Something else to do. "Okay."

"Can you expect company for dinner?"

"Tonight?" She glanced at her watch. "My house is a mess and—"

"I'll bring soup—and Sarah and Jimmy."

She could do this. God was leading her. "Okay. Practice is almost over. I've got a bazillion things to do, but I'll see you later."

Autumn ended the call, thinking how her friendship with Marny kept pushing her to do things outside her comfort zone. A mom and a boy were going to come live with her. A smile spread like a wildfire from her heart to her lips. "Thank You, Lord."

Sarah and Jimmy.

Wow. She couldn't wait to see Jimmy again and to meet Sarah.

Twenty-seven

Autumn

The doorbell rang at 7:00 p.m. Autumn rushed through the living room, scooping a pillow off the floor and tossing it onto the couch, tidying Gar's theater books on the coffee table, and then she gave one last look at the room she hastily cleaned. It would have to do. She'd been living alone over two months and had gotten a smidge lazy about vacuuming and dusting—or even caring about how things looked. That was about to change.

She took a deep breath, smiled, and opened the door.

Marny stood on the porch with a wide grin and a to-go coffee cup extended in her hand. Behind her was a small-framed woman, who had to be Sarah, and Jimmy. Both seemed to be hiding behind her.

"Thanks." Autumn accepted the drink, knowing it would be something chocolaty. "Welcome." She swayed her hand toward the living room. "Make yourselves at home."

Marny made introductions. Sarah wore a baggy sweatshirt with a hoodie pulled snug around her face. A backpack slung over her shoulders gave her the appearance of an old hunch-backed woman. She followed closely behind Marny as they walked into the house, gazing everywhere but into Autumn's eyes.

Jimmy stuck out his hand and gaped at her. "It's you. The candy lady." He whistled. "Got fudge?"

She shook his hand. "I sure do."

"Wooeee. This is a mansion."

A matter of perspective, she guessed. She often thought of it as her *little* house.

Marny sat down in the recliner. Sarah lowered herself to the edge of the couch, her lithe body spring-loaded like she might bolt any second. Jimmy dropped onto the couch with a thud, stretched out his legs, and locked his hands behind his head as if he were completely at ease.

"I can show you where you'll be sleeping. I hope you come to feel at home here." She waved for them to follow her down the short hall, and then showed them the guest room and the office with the futon. "Sorry I don't have a regular bed for this room."

"That's okay. I'm used to sleeping on cots at the mission." Jimmy's brown eyes sparkled like it was all an adventure. He set his bulging backpack on the floor and drew out a tattered Denver Broncos blanket. For the slightest second, he rubbed the fabric against his cheek. Then seeming to realize what he did, he dropped it on the futon. "My mom gave it to me."

"Course, I did." Sarah nudged him.

Jimmy's eyes darkened, and he moved away from her.

Autumn was puzzled by the exchange. Sarah looked too youthful to be this eight-year-old's mom. She couldn't be more than twenty-two or twenty-three. That would have made her what—? Fourteen or fifteen when he was born? Her heart went out to the young mother and child. What else could she do to help them, besides offering them a place to sleep?

"I'll let you get settled." Autumn rocked her thumb. "Come

into the kitchen when you're finished. I have grilled cheese sandwiches warming."

"Mmm. And fudge?" Jimmy blinked, his eyes big.

"Jimmy—" Sarah warned him.

Autumn remembered how much he enjoyed the homemade treat a couple of weeks ago. "I'll round up some."

"Yes!"

Marny jumped up from her chair as Autumn entered the room. "I'll run out to the car and grab the soup." A few minutes later, she walked into the kitchen and set a Crockpot on the counter. "I'd like some of that fudge myself."

Autumn chuckled. "All I have are some leftovers. I haven't tried any new recipes lately."

"Ahhh. You get me hooked and then stop creating new combinations?"

Autumn poured tea into the glasses she set on the table earlier. "I've been working out and watching what I put in my mouth. Eating fudge four times a day doesn't complement that lifestyle."

Marny made a rude snort. "Way to ruin a good habit. You turning into a health nut?" A seldom seen frown emerged on her face.

"Hardly. But this"—Autumn patted her stomach, sure she'd lost weight since last week—"has got to stop. I'm taking back my life. Gar is gone for now. I'm focusing on things that make me happy and healthier."

"That sounds good, but I hate giving up your fudge."

"Me too." She dragged a chair to the counter and stepped up to retrieve a covered dish of chocolates she hid from herself on the top shelf.

Sarah entered the room, her hoodie covering most of her dark blond hair and part of her face. Jimmy followed, his head turning left and right as he took in everything. "Your house is a palace, miss."

"Thanks. Come sit down. I hope you like grilled cheese." Autumn set the dessert plate on the table.

"Love it." Jimmy plopped down at the end of the table where Gar used to sit. A perfect place for the young visitor. "Whenever they serve grilled cheese at the mission, I ask for two sandwiches."

"Jimmy." Again, Sarah glared at him.

"We have plenty," Autumn assured them.

Once they were all seated, she cleared her throat. "I like to say thank you to God for the food before I eat."

"That's what we do at the mission too." Jimmy bowed his head.

Sarah shrugged.

Autumn wondered if that was her default response.

"Thank You, Lord, for new friends, and thanks for this food."

"Amen," Jimmy chirruped, then picked up his sandwich with both hands.

Marny dished up vegetable soup into each person's bowl.

"Mmm . . . smells heavenly." Autumn picked up her spoon and tasted the savory broth.

"One place we stayed served grilled cheese with tomato soup every Friday." Jimmy chewed a bite of his sandwich. "'Member that, Sarah?"

Autumn paused with her sandwich mid-air. Wasn't it strange for an eight-year-old to call his mother by her first name?

The younger woman gave Jimmy a reproving glance.

Perhaps Autumn could help the boy have more respect for the woman who birthed him, even if she was young and seemed more like his sister. And maybe she could help Sarah to have more confidence in herself and act more like a mom. Not that Autumn knew much about that. But in her profession, some-times being a teacher felt a little like being a parent.

Marny told Autumn about the meetings she was required to attend. Then she talked about upcoming activities at her church, including a youth event she thought Jimmy might be interested in.

"Sounds like fun." Autumn sipped her coffee, thankful Marny knew her favorite was white chocolate mocha.

"I'll go if Miss Autumn does." Jimmy's face lit up. "We could bring a bunch of fudge!"

Autumn laughed at his enthusiasm. "Looks like I'll have to buy more supplies."

"All right," Jimmy cheered. "I can help with the cooking."

Autumn didn't know when she'd have time to make fudge again, thanks to the play and all her school responsibilities. But she'd be willing to do almost anything to see that kind of joy on Jimmy's face.

Throughout the meal, Sarah didn't speak unless Autumn asked her a direct question. Was she distrustful or naturally shy? Hopefully, she could relax once she settled in. As Autumn glanced around the table, a warm feeling seeped through her. Even though it was temporary, she was sharing dinner with her new family and absolutely enjoying it.

After Marny left and Jimmy went to bed, Autumn hoped to chat with Sarah. But the other woman used the bathroom and slipped into the guest room. She probably felt weird staying in a stranger's house. Autumn was sure she'd feel the same way, kind of like the first week of college when she landed in her dorm and didn't know anyone.

As she got ready for bed, she wondered again why Jimmy called Sarah by her given name and not "Mom." Did the woman call herself that when he was a baby? There didn't seem to be much affection between the two, either. No goodnight kiss or loving words. In the weeks ahead, she hoped she could help them feel secure in her home. She'd do everything in her power to support them and provide for them while they were under her care. She wondered what Gar would say about their guests if he happened to come back unexpectedly. But she wouldn't waste a minute worrying about it. He wasn't here, and she was making some decisions on her own.

Tomorrow, on her way to school, she'd drop Jimmy and Sarah off at the mission. Sarah would receive help with writing a resume and job hunting. Jimmy would attend a nearby elementary school. Autumn smiled, remembering the way he oohed and aahed over the dessert and the way his grin seemed to light up the room.

For the first time in months, Gar wasn't the last thought on her mind before she fell asleep.

Twenty-eight

Winter

Winter had just finished the third evening session of her third consecutive week of women's conferences in Oregon. She was tired, missing Ty, and couldn't wait to call him after she returned to the motel. However, she continued chatting with the ladies who stayed to fellowship and ask for marital advice. Suddenly, voices rose in the foyer in what sounded like an argument. Was that Neil? That was strange to hear him so riled. And Deb? What in the world was going on?

She took off running toward the back door of the auditorium and came to a stop when she stepped into the foyer. Randi Simmons? What was her previous assistant doing in Bend, Oregon? Did she come back to return Winter's journal? To apologize? Seeing Randi's beet-red face, crossed arms, and her gaze shooting fire darts at Neil, Winter guessed none of the above.

Neil—her ministry co-leader and a nonviolent sort of guy—had his hands extended like he was stopping a vicious dog from biting. His back was rigid. His shoulders were bunched up. She'd never seen such a fierce expression on his face.

Deborah stood beside him and spoke to Randi in soothing tones. Winter drew closer to listen.

"We love you, but we're not going to let you cause Winter any trouble." Deborah took a step forward, but Neil laid a hand on her shoulder. "Why don't you call Winter's cell phone? She needs to talk with you."

"That's right, I do." Winter rushed over to stand on the other side of Neil.

"There you are, *Captain*." Boy, she sounded snarly.

"Winter, maybe you should wait in the auditorium." Neil stepped in front of her, becoming a barricade between her and Randi.

Winter shuffled slightly to her right to see her old friend. "What are you doing here? Where's my journal? I want it back."

"Sure you do."

She stared at the other woman, wondering about her glassy-eyed scowl, her scraggly hair, her all-black workout pants and jacket.

Neil resumed his watchdog position. "Stay back," he warned Winter with gritted teeth.

She frowned at him but did what he said. What did he think was going to happen?

Chatter rose behind her, and she realized the ladies she'd been talking to after her seminar had followed her into the foyer. What would they think of this conflict, especially considering her ministry theme about reconciliation? She wished her team didn't have an audience for this confrontation with Randi.

"I need to talk to you alone." Randi squinted in her direction.

"No." Neil planted his fists on his hips, glaring at her.

Winter had never seen him act like this. Apparently, in Ty's absence, he felt a need to be her bodyguard. But this was Randi, her previous assistant and friend. The two of them needed to have a serious chat and work out their differences.

"Let me talk to Winter." Randi's bloodshot eyes focused and unfocused.

Something seemed weird about her. Was she on drugs? Drunk? Maybe Neil was right about not letting Randi speak with her alone.

"Not happening." If there was trouble, Neil could probably haul Randi outside. Although, Winter remembered she knew self-defense and fought like a wildcat. Would she hurt Neil if he tried forcing her out of the building?

"Whatever you have to say can be said in front of Neil and Deborah." Winter crossed her arms, feeling apprehensive.

"I'm talking to you without Superman and Bat Woman, here, present." Randi flattened her hands out as if she were contemplating a martial art move. Had she been practicing? Was that why she wore those clothes?

"No, you're not." Neil maintained his stance.

They were at a stalemate. Dread filled the pit of Winter's stomach. Ty was going to be upset about this volatile meeting. Did Randi know he was back in Coeur d'Alene and couldn't protect her?

"You think you can keep me from talking to her?" Randi yelled at Neil. "Just wait. I'll find my own way." She stomped toward the glass doors.

"Stop." Winter tried following her, but Neil put out his arm, blocking her. "Why did you come here? What's your game?"

"Game?" Randi whirled around and sneered. "No game. It's life or death."

A chill raced up Winter's spine.

"Are you threatening us?" Neil's voice turned gravely.

"Please," Deborah implored her. "Don't cause Ty and Winter harm. They're trying to do good."

"Good?" Randi's laugh bordered on hysteria. "You call kicking me off the team after I sacrificed everything, good?" She lunged forward as if to grab Deborah.

Neil pulled their musician back.

So Randi was still bitter and disgruntled about getting fired. Maybe she had a harmful agenda too.

"You're a sucker if you believe Ty Williams has a speck of decency in him." Randi thrust her hand through her greasy hair. Her voice grew louder. "Read Winter's journal—even she thinks he's a selfish cheat."

Winter gasped. "That's not true."

Randi smacked her lips like she was searching for a taste of something. "Deb's naïve. The rest of you are just hypocrites." She spat the harsh words right at them.

Winter couldn't believe how awful Randi was treating them, since she'd once thought of her as her best friend.

"You should go now"—Neil glowered—"before I call the police."

Randi's gaze homed in on Winter's. "Just you and me for a talk. You owe me that."

"No, she doesn't." Not pausing a beat, Neil turned Winter and Deborah around and led them into the chapel. "Stay here." He closed the doors.

Winter wanted to object. Shouldn't they find out what Randi wanted to say? She didn't like not knowing what was going on in the foyer, either. But it seemed she should let Neil deal with getting Randi off the premises—for everyone's safety.

"How could she hate us like that?" She couldn't comprehend the abhorrence she saw in Randi's eyes. "What did I do?"

Deborah wrapped her arms around her. "Nothing."

Winter blinked back tears. "She's in trouble, I could see that."

"I know." Deborah patted her hand. "We need to pray for her."

190

Neil opened the chapel doors, and he looked frazzled. "Ladies," he addressed the conference attendees still in the foyer, "grab your belongings and go straight to your cars. I think she's gone."

Several of the women hurried into the chapel, scooped up personal items, then dashed for the exit as if running for their lives.

"Goodbye. I'm sorry about all of that." Winter fretted. Would they even return for the other sessions? What caused Randi to show up at an event and act like that?

Neil followed the attendees outside, most likely standing guard while they got into their cars.

Deborah clasped Winter's hands and prayed for Randi and for the team's safety.

A couple of minutes later, Neil strode into the sanctuary. "This changes everything."

"What do you mean?" They still had two more days left of the conference.

"As soon as we get in the car, call Ty. He'll want to be here." His stern expression told her not to argue.

"But Neil, he's working with—"

"I'm serious. Call him, or I will." He shut off the lights at the back of the church. "I parked the Old Clunker next to the entrance. Walk fast and get in the car without delay."

"Okay."

Deborah linked arms with her as they walked outside, then opened the car door. Neil and Deborah took the outside seats, sandwiching her safely in the middle. She felt loved and cared for by these two who'd served with her in the ministry for six years. *Lord, bless them for their sacrifices and love. Keep them safe. Touch Randi. She needs You.*

As soon as Neil started the car, he revved the gas and peeled out of the parking lot.

"Why do you think Randi's doing this?" Winter had to know.

"She's desperate." Neil shook his head. "Willing to do anything to get what she wants—which appears to be some kind of revenge against you and Ty."

"Revenge?"

As they drove away from the church, she peered into the darkness, wondering if Randi might be lurking out there somewhere, watching.

Twenty-nine

Ty

Ty couldn't believe what Winter had just told him. He held the phone closer to his mouth as he paced across the mostly empty living room. "I can't believe this. She just showed up?"

"Yes."

"And threatened you?"

"Sort of." Winter's voice went quiet.

She sounded vulnerable and much too far away from him. He hated that he hadn't been there to protect her. If he saw Randi trying to force Winter into a room by herself, he would have gone nuts. He couldn't predict what he might have done, but he was pretty sure he would have grabbed her and thrown her out the door.

"I don't know what she wanted, other than to speak with me privately." Winter sighed. "How did she even know where I was?"

Oh, man. "The blog." He posted the information himself.

"Maybe it's n-nothing." Her words broke. Was she about to cry?

If so, he'd feel even worse for not being there with her. "It's not nothing, Sas. I'll meet you tomorrow."

"Ty, no."

"If anything happens to you while I'm up here tinkering with cars, when I could have been there protecting you, I'd never forgive myself." He shouldn't have stayed away this long. He'd enjoyed his stint working on engines, but being by his wife's side was his first responsibility.

"Neil protected me. You would have been proud of him." She gulped. "Deborah and I prayed for Randi. Throughout the whole episode, I was worried, but I mostly felt sorry for her. God is with us, Ty. We're trying to follow His will and walking through the doors He opens. We'll be fine. You don't have to drive all the way down here."

"I won't drive. I'll fly."

"Ty—"

He decided to change his tactic. "I want to be with you, Sas. I miss you. We've been away from each other for too long."

"I miss you too, but what about working with Kyle?"

"It'll be fine." Making money didn't compare to being with the woman he loved and assuring himself of her safety. "I need to see you. Hold you."

"Okay," she whispered, then sighed. She was probably exhausted.

"Is Neil there?"

"Yeah, we're just pulling into the motel parking lot."

"Let me talk with him." Ty gritted his teeth, then he forced himself to speak calmly so she wouldn't recognize his agitation. "Don't leave the vehicle until Neil gets off the phone and walks in with you, okay? And stay in your room all night."

"I will. Deborah is with me."

He was glad she wasn't alone, but Deb opposing Randi? She probably wouldn't even defend herself.

"Ty?" Winter whispered his name in the way he loved. "Don't worry, okay?"

That he couldn't promise. "Tomorrow can't come fast enough. Love you, Sas."

"Love you too."

He heard the shuffling of hands passing the cell.

"It wasn't pretty," Neil spoke without small talk. "She demanded to see Winter. I stopped her in the foyer. Otherwise, she would have charged into the auditorium and done who knows what. Her eyes were bloodshot and weird like she's using something. She was bent on causing a scene."

"I can't believe that happened when I wasn't there." Ty kicked the toe of his slipper against the couch. He heard Gar enter the living room behind him. "Thanks for protecting Winter. She means everything to me."

"I know." Neil paused. "I wonder if we should cancel the remaining meetings and head home."

"No." He heard Winter's muffled exclamation. "I'm not leaving because she's causing a stink. Then satan wins."

He was tempted to laugh at her passion, but the situation was too dire.

"I suppose you heard that?" Neil asked.

"I did. I'll fly in tomorrow."

"Let me know your arrival time. I'll pick you up at the Redmond Airport. It's about twenty minutes from Bend."

"Good to know." There was something else. "Did Randi seem . . . violent? Do you think it's possible she'd try to harm Winter?" He had to get down there and protect his wife.

Neil let out a long sigh. "She's had behavioral issues—with you and others. But hurting Winter on purpose seems too extreme even for her."

"Okay, thanks." Ty blew out a hot breath. "I'll let you go. Call if anything—and I mean anything—happens."

"Will do." Neil ended the call.

Ty wanted to buzz Winter again and tell her to stay on the

line until she reached her room. But he didn't want to incite more fear. Deb and Neil were supporting her. He would never have imagined a peaceable group like Passion's Prayer needing security. He wished he'd seen Neil getting all charged up, defending the women, ready to take on an angry ex-employee.

He held his cell to his forehead, then shut his eyes to pray. *Father, I ask You to protect my wife and our team. I come against any evil plan of the devil's to foul up our lives. We trust You to guide us through adversities. Touch Randi. I don't know what's going on in her mixed-up brain. I hardly know how to pray. Please change her heart. Surround the team with Your love and protection. In Your name.*

"Everything okay?" Gar asked from the kitchen.

Ty stuffed his cell phone in his back pocket—where it would be close—and strode to the sink. "Not really." He grabbed a glass and turned on the faucet. As soon as the tumbler was filled with cold water, he guzzled it dry.

"What's wrong?" Gar stood on the other side of the center island.

"A past worker is causing trouble for my wife." Ty leaned his elbows on the island and rested his chin against his fists. "Wish I was there, instead of here."

"What would you do?"

"You kidding me?" Heat spread across his chest, irritation and concern battling within him. Ty stared at the guy who'd become his friend since they were traveling and working together. They still hadn't broached the marriage topics Ty had hoped for, and now he was leaving. "I'd do anything—including risking my life—to save hers. I'd fight or sacrifice or give up every penny I own to ensure her safety and happiness."

Gar nodded. "Because you love her?"

"Because I love her." Ty walked to the fridge and opened the door. Nothing looked appetizing. He shut the door. "I've got to make a plane reservation." He pulled up a travel site on his phone. The earliest available flight was at nine in the morning. He quickly reserved a seat. While jumping in the car and driving for eight hours appealed to him, even if he drove all night, he wouldn't get there much sooner than flying. Especially if he had to pull over and sleep. Although keyed up as he was, he doubted he'd doze all night.

Gar removed some day-old pizza out of the fridge. "Want some?"

"Nah." Ever since Winter called, stress-induced acid had been rolling up into his throat. Pizza would probably make it worse.

Had he made the wrong decision in staying at the house and working with Kyle? Wouldn't his time have been better spent at the conference? But Neil was guarding the ladies. What more could Ty have done? Probably something stupid, like yelling at Randi. More than anything, he wanted to be with his wife. That he was four hundred miles away drove him crazy.

The microwave dinged, and Gar took out a plate with a couple of pizza slices on it. He grabbed two smaller saucers and slid a piece onto each one. He nudged a saucer toward Ty. "In case you change your mind." He grabbed two glasses from the shelf and poured iced tea into both.

The pepperoni and cheese smelled delicious, despite how Ty felt about eating a few minutes ago. Maybe he should try something. "Thanks, man." He grabbed the plate and glass and headed for the couch.

Gar snagged the back of a chair near the card table and hauled it into the living room and set it down across from Ty.

The room was quiet, except for the sounds of them munching their food.

"Can I ask a question?" Gar sipped his tea.

"Shoot."

"What caused your divorce?" Gar took a deep breath. "Maybe you don't feel like talking, and that's okay. I figure you're leaving in the morning. I may not have the chance to ask again."

"You thinking of getting divorced?" Ty cut to the heart of the matter.

Gar winced. "Thought about it."

"I can tell you it's not worth it." Ty exhaled. "If there's anything else you can do, do that."

"I've been away from my wife for over two months. What else is there?" Gar set his glass down.

"Considered going back? Asking her forgiveness?"

Gar cleared his throat. "I'd have a lot of forgiveness to ask for."

"That's a good place to start." Ty didn't know where to go with this conversation. Gar seemed to be reaching out. Yet Ty was distracted with what happened in Bend. What might Randi do? Was she after revenge? He'd like to call Winter again, just to check on her. But if he put off Gar's question, the moment to share might slip away. "Do you still love her? I think I asked you that before."

Gar nodded. "When she and I met at the park, I realized I do . . . love her. Things in the past happened that shouldn't have. I've been living on empty, you know?"

"Yeah, I know."

Gar let out a sigh that sounded like the sputtering of a slow leak in a balloon. "I don't want to drag her through a divorce. Can't stand the thought, actually."

"Good. What do you want? Inside, I mean." Ty avoided the temptation to check his cell. He'd feel the vibration if Winter or Neil called. He needed to focus on Gar's words.

"I suppose I want to feel needed, have a purpose in my life, like most guys."

"Sure." Ty nodded. "Do you believe in God?"

Gar's eyes widened. "Well, yeah, I asked Jesus to be my Savior when I was a kid." He gesticulated as he spoke. "I got my master's in English, then worked in a Christian school for ten years."

Lord, lead me. How do I get him to go deeper with You?

"Would you say you've been faithful in that relationship?"

Gar fidgeted. "With God? Or Autumn?"

Hmm. "With God. How would you describe your relationship with Him?"

Gar talked about going to church, his work with the kids in school, how he volunteered at a homeless shelter when he was younger.

"All great things. Admirable, even." Ty didn't have time to beat around the bush. "But those are things you've done. Maybe for God. Maybe for yourself. My question was about your relationship *with* the Lord."

Ty watched the puzzled look grow on Gar's face.

* * * *

Gar wished he never started this conversation. When had the discussion altered from marriage to religion? He shrugged, pondering his response. "Same difference, right? I put my faith in action by the good stuff I do. I try hard. Or I did once upon a time."

"How about this . . . have you prayed today?"

He met Ty's intense gaze. What was the guy driving at? "Not really, I guess."

"How about yesterday?"

"I don't remember."

Ty leaned forward on the couch, his elbows on his knees, his wrists crossed. "Did you bring your Bible with you when you left Autumn?"

Gar shuffled in his chair, trying to get comfortable,

wishing for a different topic of conversation. Maybe they could talk about the Seahawks or Mariners.

Ty was obviously waiting for an answer.

"No, I was pretty mad when I left."

"At God?"

Gar swallowed. How had he guessed?

Ty leaned back into the couch cushions again, crossed his right ankle over his left knee. "I came to know Jesus in prison."

Whoa. He'd been in prison? That got Gar's attention.

The silence stretched across the room. He didn't ask anything else as he waited for Ty to continue.

"Why I was there doesn't matter. However, I found myself desperately in need of a Savior. I'd ruined my life and landed in a pit. I longed for a way out." Ty pointed at him. "Until you find yourself in that spot—not in prison—at the bottom of yourself, ready to give up your right to be right, your pride, your demands to have your own way, none of what I have to say will make sense."

"I'm a smart man. Educated."

"So was I. MBA."

"Really?" Ty had a business degree? That made Gar respect him even more. It made him more open to listening to what he had to say.

"Still, I was foolish and prideful and a downright idiot." A smile crossed Ty's face, even though tension snapped in the room. "Can you relate to any of that?"

Gar wanted to disagree, but in all honesty, he couldn't. "I've made my share of stupid decisions."

Ty cleared his throat, then he explained his journey from college graduation to prison. His voice softened when he spoke of his love for Winter and how his passion had chilled in the face of temptation and career madness.

Gar made similar mistakes. Wrong choices. Temptations.

His hardened heart toward Autumn, God, and their inability to have kids. The latter brought up a painful sigh of regret.

When Ty shared about reconciling with Winter, about him wanting to do anything to restore their love, about him following her all over the country and giving up his job to have the chance to be her husband, Gar watched as tears rolled down the other man's face. He touched his own cheeks and found moisture there too. He thought of times he bragged to Autumn that he was a guy who didn't cry. Apparently, that was changing.

"Did she forgive you just like that?" Considering what Ty had told him about the other woman, Gar could hardly believe it.

"Not just like that." Ty stared into the distance as if remembering. A sober look crossed his face. "It was a struggle for her to believe I was different. But God changed me. It wasn't me throwing all my strength and willpower into becoming a better man. *He* worked on me, filled me with His love—and I thank Him for it every day."

Had Gar ever been desperate like that for God? Or for his wife, for that matter? Would becoming that way make him willing to fight for his marriage? To be willing to do anything for her?

They talked for several hours. Gar asked questions, and Ty seemed open to answering even the embarrassing inquiries. Two in the morning came before their discussion wound down.

"You should get some sleep." Gar picked up their empty dishes.

Ty ran his hand over his face. "I suppose I should if I can." He lowered his hands and stared intently at Gar. "You can stay here as long as you want. I mean that."

Gar was grateful for the offer. "Thanks."

"But I hope . . . I pray . . . you'll seek God, and soon, experience reconciliation with your wife."

"I'll think about all you said. One more thing." Gar didn't know if he should bring it up. Ty was obviously tired.

"What's that?"

"You didn't ask what caused our split. Why not?"

Ty stood and carried his glass to the kitchen sink. "It doesn't really matter. I told you before that if you wanted to talk about it, I'd listen. What matters is what's in here." He laid his palm against his chest. "Change takes place here first. God can fix everything between you and Autumn if you'll humble yourself and let Him. If you decide you want to get back together, I'll give you some pointers. Main thing? Return to your first love."

"First love?"

"With God. And her." At the card table, Ty stared down at his cell, then grabbed a pen and jotted something down on a scrap of paper. A moment later, he handed Gar a note with a phone number on it. "Call this guy. He's a pastor. He'll help you get through the mess. His name's Chad. Tell him I sent you."

"Thanks." They shook hands. Gar didn't know if he'd be willing to call a stranger and spill his guts. But Ty had given him challenges he couldn't ignore. Gar didn't even know where to start other than the "get desperate" part. And he felt like he was already there. It seemed he had some soul-searching to do. Some praying. Then, perhaps, he'd be ready to honestly talk to Autumn.

Thirty

Gar

For the last fifteen minutes, Gar had been standing in the studio apartment, staring out the window overlooking Ty's backyard. Most of the branches lacked greenery. Brown leaves dangled from rose bushes. All of nature was getting ready for the next season of change. Death. Dormancy. New life. Kind of like his life.

Ever since he woke up, Ty's comments about him returning to his first love hadn't been far from his thoughts. Maybe he should head downstairs and search for a Bible. On the coffee table in the living room, he found one and brought it back to the apartment over the garage. Did Ty leave the book there on purpose?

Using the concordance at the back of the Bible and searching for "first love," he located the verse in Revelation chapter two: *You have forsaken your first love. Remember the height from which you have fallen! Repent and do the things you did at first.*

The indictment hit him like a sword piercing his heart. *Forsaken. Fallen. Repent.* The words replayed in his mind, gnawing at him. He remembered how fervently he served the Lord twenty years ago. How he promised to love Him for the rest of his life. Then how indifferent he became in recent years. Cold, even. He had forsaken God. Deserted his wife. Lust had consumed him. Selfishly, he fell from a life of living for the Lord to demanding his own way. A raw ache he'd never experienced before burned in his chest. A weight seemed to be pressing down on his shoulders, almost crushing him. Ty said Gar needed to return to his first love. But how was he supposed to do that? He knew what it meant to repent, but what then?

He thumbed to the beginning of John and read a few pages. Tears blurred his eyes as he pondered the familiar words from chapter three he memorized many years ago. *For God so loved the world that he gave his one and only Son . . .* He recited that verse many times during his early walk with God. He kept reading, his emotions becoming more and more tender. When he came to chapter twelve, he paused. *Walk while you have the light, before darkness overtakes you.* He sucked in a frayed breath. He'd wandered far from the light. Straight into darkness. Suddenly, he yearned to be out from under the clutches of evil. He longed for peace and the freedom to walk in the light again. *God, help. I need You. I don't know how to find my way back.*

He kept reading, pausing at various verses, considering truths about God's love and how to live more like Jesus, things he knew when he was younger. He imagined himself in the college group a lifetime ago, and the way he believed whole-heartedly back then came flooding into his heart. A knowing that God still cared about him, desired his fellowship, cherished him even, washed over him in waves of understanding. Why did he forsake his faith? Why did he so easily forget what true love was? Tears rolled down his cheeks, and he wept over how far he'd fallen. How cold and indifferent he'd become. Conviction gnawed at him, and by mid-morning, he fell on his knees and cried out to the Lord.

"Father, I'm so s-sorry. I've sinned against You." Sobs tore from him. "I walked away from You—from everything beautiful that You gave me. Please, forgive me." He confessed his sins and continued praying until he talked with God about every failure, hurt, and doubt.

Now, something warm and energizing pulsated in his chest. The rotting guilt he'd lived with for months lifted. Disappointments that wracked his brain with bitterness seemed to have dissolved. It felt like he was breathing deeper, freer, for the first time in a year. The part of him that had lain dormant was emerging back to life again—much like those dead-looking plants outside would do in the spring—and he praised God for this miracle.

He sank into the recliner and thumbed open the pages of the Bible to First John. Several sentences leaped out at him.

God is love.

Gar thanked God for bringing him back into His love.

How great is the love the Father has lavished on us.

He closed his eyes and pictured a bucket of God's love and presence pouring over him.

This is love: not that we loved God, but that he loved us and sent his Son.

He repeated the phrases, allowing the words to soak into his senses. *He loves me. Praise God!*

He remembered how much he used to enjoy reading scriptures. Back when he and Autumn first married, he read a chapter in Proverbs or Psalms out loud with her every morning. Then they prayed together before they left for school, believing God was working in their lives. Somewhere in the doldrums of life, they stopped doing those things. He attended church— it was expected of him as a teacher in a Christian school—but he left his Bible on a shelf at the house. It became a fixture in the room, not something he cherished.

He fingered Ty's Bible in his hands now. The leather cover was cool to the touch, but the words he read earlier burned in him like a fire. *Godly sorrow brings repentance that leads to salvation and leaves no regret.*

No regret. He was forgiven. But he recognized how he'd wronged others, especially his wife. That awareness tore at his conscience, filling him with shame. He turned to the Lord again, knowing wallowing in guilt wasn't God's plan for his life, either.

Lord, thank You for changing me. I'm Yours. Tears filled his eyes, dripping down his cheeks. No longer was he the tough guy who didn't cry. He felt broken and empty, yet full.

Father, I've treated Autumn badly. I'm sorry for my wrongs. Guide me in how You want me to live now. Show me how to make amends.

He thought of Ben, his old employer. *I'm sorry for mistreating Ben. I owe him an apology too. Show me how to do that with humility. I want to live as Your Word says.*

He noticed a strip of paper on the floor by his shoes. *That's right.* Ty gave him a pastor's phone number and recommended that Gar call him. He grabbed the note and found a 907 number written beside the words "Pastor Chad." Should he call? He picked up his cell and pressed the digits before he could talk himself out of it.

"Hello. This is Chad Gray. How can I help?"

"This is Gar Bevere. Ty Williams gave me your number."

"Oh, he did, did he?" The pastor laughed. "How do you know Ty?"

"His sister's married to my cousin."

"I see. So, what's happening?"

How did a guy tell a stranger the deepest secrets in his life? Or maybe because the pastor was an unfamiliar person, it would be easier. "I just repented."

"Wonderful!" He sounded so pleased. "Where are you?"

"Spokane. Ty talked with me last night, but then he caught an emergency flight—"

"Whoa. What's wrong? Is it Winter?"

"Yeah. Do you know the situation about a woman who's causing problems for them?" Gar didn't know how much he should share.

"I was at the camp when Winter's personal assistant stole her journal." Chad groaned. "Is she back?"

"She showed up at a conference in Bend, threatening Ty's wife."

"Is Winter all right?"

"As far as I know. Ty's super worried." That might be putting it mildly.

Chad exhaled. "Hey, you know what, I'll call Ty later. Why don't you tell me what's going on with you? How can I help?"

Gar gulped. He'd fought such a battle by himself over the past months. "I left my wife a couple of months ago."

"And now that you're talking with God?"

"I feel differently. But I'm unsure what I should do next."

Chad chuckled. "I know just what you mean. Let me tell you my story. I'm sure that's why Ty had you call me."

"Okay."

Gar listened for the next twenty minutes as Pastor Chad shared his previous struggles in his marriage, and about his and April's reconciliation. He told of how much he loved their lives together now, and how he can't wait to spend time with her each day. How they were going to have a baby, a celebration of their love.

Gar knew that even if by some miracle he and Autumn got back together, they wouldn't experience that blessing. Still, the interaction with the pastor made a lot of sense. Gar told him about the guilt he'd been carrying. How he grew distant and more susceptible to temptation. He confessed about meeting Elaine. Finally speaking the truth removed a lot of the sting.

Chad didn't act shocked over anything Gar said. He explained how the enemy of our soul picks at our weaknesses in moments when we're distracted or overly busy. And now that Gar had a new understanding of God's love working in his life, Chad said he needed to stay in fellowship with the Lord and other believers.

"And"—the pastor cleared his throat loudly—"you need to be gut-honest about your mistakes. With God. And your wife."

Gar expelled a long breath, contemplating the minister's words.

When the call ended, he dropped to his knees to have another deep conversation with his heavenly Father. But he couldn't imagine how he'd ever be as honest with the woman he hurt.

Thirty-one

Autumn

Autumn's cell phone buzzed early Wednesday morning. The chiming woke her out of a sound sleep. For five seconds, she felt disoriented before she reached out her hand to silence the noisemaker on the nightstand. "Hello?" she answered without checking the screen.

"Hey."

She blinked, swallowed, cleared her throat. "Gar? Oh, hi." Was there an emergency for him to call so early? Usually, he wasn't even awake at this time of the morning.

"I was thinking of you, so I thought I'd check in."

Hearing the warmth in his voice, she swallowed hard.

"That's . . . nice." Could he detect her surprise? This was the first time he called her other than to talk about the house payment or to remind her about a chore since he left. And he certainly hadn't sounded, well, like *that* in a long time. "How are things?"

"Going good. You still in bed?" He cleared his throat as if embarrassed that he asked such a personal question. "I mean, you sound tired. Oversleep?"

She stared at the alarm clock, wondering if she even remembered to set it. "Yeah, I did. I was up later than usual last night." She wouldn't mention the fact she was sleeping on his pillow, still wearing his old flannel shirt to bed.

"Why were you up late?"

How long had it been since he acted interested in her life? His concern made her feel like they almost had a normal, but distant, husband-wife relationship. Something heartwarming and hopeful ran through her. "There's stuff going on." A production opening in a week. A kid and his mom sleeping in their guest rooms. A larger-than-usual food bill. Extra clothes and supplies she'd purchased for Jimmy and Sarah. But she wouldn't mention any of that. He probably called to tell her something.

"Sorry I haven't been there for you."

At his softly spoken words, tears sprang into her eyes. A soothing warmth like honey crept into the hurting places in her chest. *Lord, You are doing something in Gar's life, aren't You?*

He sighed. "I guess you have to get ready for school, huh?"

"Yeah." Did he call for any specific reason? Just hearing his voice made her heart pound faster.

"It's nice to hear your voice. I should let you go." His tone was husky. "And, I, uh—"

She waited, wondering what he wasn't saying.

"Well, have a great day."

"Thanks for calling." She almost clicked off. "Gar? Did you . . . did you call to say anything else?" Dare she allow that little butterfly of anticipation to live?

Another sigh came across the line. "I'd rather explain in person."

What did he need to tell her? That he decided to get a divorce? Wait. Did he say "in person?"

"When's Opening Night?"

Oh, was that what he was concerned about? Did he want to see the show? "Next Wednesday. Speaking of which, I could use your help on a couple of problems." She waited in the silence, wondering if he'd mind her asking for his advice again.

"Things going okay?"

"If I can keep ten yards ahead of Jewel's desire to control everything."

Gar chuckled, and his deep timbre stirred up thoughts of times he laughed with her in the past. "I seem to remember that habit of hers." He took a breath. "I was thinking of heading over this weekend. Would that be okay with you?"

"Really? I'd love to see you, Gar."

"Okay, I'll see you then. Have a great day."

Now, I will. "Bye."

He disconnected, and Autumn held the phone to her cheek. "Thank You, thank You, God, for whatever You are doing. I praise You for it!" She wanted to dance and sing at this glimmer of joy that made her think something good might be about to happen.

She jumped out of bed and grabbed her clothes, and then realized she neglected to tell Gar about her houseguests. The weekend ahead was going to be busy with play practices, the staging committee working on sets, and a training session at Marny's church. When would she have time to hang out with Gar?

She'd find time. That's all there was to it. Gar was coming back! He had something to tell her, and she hoped it was good news.

After showering, she made a latte and whipped up some scrambled eggs. "Come on, you two!" she called to Jimmy and Sarah. "Let's get this show on the road."

Sarah wasn't a morning person, and she exited her bedroom with her hair disheveled, her baggy clothes clutched around her middle, and her gaze focused on the pile of eggs.

Jimmy ran from his room, already in jeans and his brand new Mariners t-shirt, with a big grin on his freckled face. Much more affectionate than Sarah, he charged straight for Autumn and wrapped his arms around her. "You're the best baker."

She laughed at his exuberance and hugged him back. Then she glanced at Sarah, concerned the other woman might resent Jimmy's affection toward her. But Sarah seemed oblivious as she scooped eggs on her plate. She had a hefty appetite for one so thin. Maybe she'd been starving before she came to Autumn's. Poor girl. She pushed a jar of applesauce closer to her, encouraging her to eat more.

After they cleaned up breakfast dishes, Autumn rushed Jimmy out the door. She'd drop him off at the elementary school on her way to work. Sarah would take the bus to the mission later.

As soon as Autumn pulled into the ECHS parking lot, she sent Gar a text.

Loved our chat this morning. Can't wait to see you.

Hopefully, that didn't make her seem desperate. She did want to see him. She longed to hear for herself whether God was doing something in Gar's life like He had been doing in hers.

One more thing needed to be said.

Some things have changed at the house. I will fill you in when you get here.

She couldn't explain the situation in texts. She wasn't a bit sorry she opened their home to Jimmy and Sarah. Being involved with them was giving her a different view of life and a familial feeling she hadn't experienced since leaving home to go to college. And she hoped she was making a bit of a difference in their lives. Besides, didn't God supply her and Gar with the house and rooms to share?

Between her work with the theater kids and spending time with Jimmy and Sarah, she felt herself coming alive again.

Although she hadn't forgotten her disappointment over her inability to have children, she'd experienced so many avenues of joy, she no longer felt that heavy sadness. Through deeper prayer, she'd found peace, and her relationship with God was growing.

Would Gar understand? Or would he demand that everything revert to how it was before he left?

As far as Autumn was concerned, it was too late for that. She couldn't go back. Aside from her relationship with Gar, everything had changed for the better.

Thirty-two

Ty

Ty shifted in the hard, folding chair outside the auditorium doors, trying to find a comfortable position. He'd been sitting in the same place for over an hour, guarding the foyer while Winter was speaking to about a hundred women. Ever since he arrived in Bend, yesterday, he and Neil had been watching opposite exits for any sign of Randi. They took every precaution, making sure Winter was never alone. Even in the bathroom, Deb stood outside her stall. Maybe Randi already left the area, but they had to be cautious, just in case she showed up again.

He picked up the coffee cup he set on the floor, sipped, then grimaced. Cold. He was tired and bored, but he didn't want to leave his watch to find something hot to drink. From inside the sanctuary, he heard Winter encouraging the women to pray for their husbands daily and to believe all things were possible in their marriages. He smiled, then did what she recommended, and prayed for his wife.

A few minutes later, he stood and strode to the glass double doors and peered into the darkness. He thought he saw a flash of light. The more he stared into nothingness, the more he figured it must have been his imagination. Probably a beam of light ricocheting off a passing car's headlights.

He paced back to the chair, wondering about Neil on the opposite side of the building. He strolled toward the hallway and checked down the corridor. At the far end, Neil's feet protruded in front of him like he was completely relaxed. Snoozing? Ty could hardly blame him. He'd been sitting around for days, but they couldn't afford to become lax. He yanked his cell out of his pocket and buzzed the team leader. Neil's feet jerked. Yep, he'd been sleeping.

"Uh-huh," Neil answered the call and yawned.

"Just checking." Ty muffled a laugh.

"Everything's quiet my way." Neil leaned his head around the corner and gave a mock salute. "Yeah, you caught me slacking."

"Guess I did." Ty ended the call and stuffed his cell into his jacket pocket. A hot cup of coffee was sounding better by the second. Another yawn and he knew he better not sit down, or he'd be dozing like Neil. He paced back and forth across the foyer, counting floor tiles, passing the minutes.

Tonight was the last session of the conference. They'd drive back to Spokane tomorrow. They still didn't know what Randi was up to, or why she made that scene a couple of nights ago. She didn't seem like the type who'd travel to Central Oregon to see Winter, and then leave because Neil commanded her to depart. Imagining what she was capable of bothered him the most.

When they returned to their house, Gar wouldn't be there. He'd texted Ty that he was heading home in hope of reconciling with Autumn. He thanked Ty for talking with him and for putting him in touch with Pastor Chad. Apparently, that conversation had gone well. Ty planned to call Gar the first chance he got and remind him that healing could take time. He couldn't show up in Everett and expect everything to fall into place as if he hadn't been away. Ty decided to pray for the couple while they were on his mind.

Lord, be with Gar and Autumn. Help them to be forgiving of each other's mistakes. It seems like Gar's sincere in his desire to face his past.

Wait. What was that sound?

The light in the hallway suddenly went off.

Another sound. All the lights in the foyer went black.

What was happening? Did the power in town go off? Or—? Randi? *Oh, no!*

"Winter!" Scrambling blindly toward the auditorium doors, Ty tripped over his chair and toppled forward. He burst through the double doors into the sanctuary before he caught his footing. The room was pitch dark except for the exit signs.

"Winter?" He rushed down the center aisle. A cell light came on at his left. Several more cell phones made a guided path of light for him.

"What's going on?" someone asked.

"Why's he shouting?"

"Winter?" He didn't even try to disguise the panic in his tone when he realized she wasn't responding.

Thud. He ran into someone in the aisle.

"Ty"—Deb's voice—"she's gone." She gasped and moaned.

"Gone? How?"

She clutched onto his arm tightly like she was in pain. He took out his cell phone and tapped the screen. In the garish glow, he saw she was bent over, gripping her stomach.

"What happened?"

"S-suddenly, she was there."

"Who?"

"Randi."

Cold fury plunged through his veins.

"It happened fast. The lights. Her. I tried to reach Winter, but Randi kicked me." She swallowed. "I fell. I don't know where they went."

"You okay?"

She seemed shaken up, taking in shallow breaths, but she nodded. If Randi had kicked Deb, who was a peaceable and tenderhearted person, what might she do to Winter? Rage spiked adrenaline through every blood vessel in his body.

Deb shoved on Ty's arm. "Go. They couldn't have gone far."

A rumble of female voices rose behind him.

"What's going on?"

"Who's gone?"

"Who did this?"

Ty stared Deborah in the eye. "Calm them down and don't let anyone leave. Randi could disguise herself in a crowd."

"Okay."

He sprinted toward the hallway where he last saw Neil. "Winter?" He kept bellowing her name. If she and Randi were still in the building, he wanted his wife—and her abductor— to know he was coming for her.

"Neil!" Ty shouted and shone the light on his friend who seemed to be . . . just waking up? "Neil, were you dozing again?"

"What? What is it?"

Ty couldn't believe he fell asleep when they needed him the most. "She took Winter." A whooshing sound came from a classroom down the hall. He tapped his cell light off.

On his feet now, Neil groaned. "Randi? Oh, no. I'm sorry, I—"

"Shhhh."

Had a door squeaked opened?

Ty motioned for Neil to follow him and crept along the wall, staying within the darkest shadows. *Lord, please protect my wife.*

So Randi had dragged Winter right past Neil? That infraction would have to be addressed later. He had to find her. Nothing else mattered. If Randi was harming her in any way, the menace would deal with him. He clenched his fists and tightened his shoulders.

* * * *

The auditorium going black had surprised Winter. That had never happened while she was speaking before. Probably a power outage. Ty and Neil were guarding the entrances, right? She just announced for everyone to remain in their seats when hands grabbed her roughly and muffled her mouth. Winter tried yelling and biting the hand that smelled of . . . vanilla lotion? She gasped. *Randi!*

Deborah shouted, then Randi jerked around in the dark and lunged forward. A groan. Had she kicked Deb? *Jesus, help her.* Winter felt herself being hauled out of the auditorium. In the distance, Ty was yelling her name. She tried to answer him, but Randi held her mouth tighter, making it almost impossible to breathe. Winter yanked and tugged at Randi's grip, fighting her forward movement. But despite her resistance, the stronger woman forced her up a staircase. They entered a narrow room, and Randi shoved her to the floor. At the sudden impact, Winter cried out.

"Stay put. And be quiet." Randi pulled her across the rough floor, farther back in the space. She tied a cloth gag around her mouth, then tied her wrists behind her. She moved away, and it sounded like she dragged something in front of the door, but Winter couldn't see anything in the dark.

She tried yelling around the gag. "Why are you doing this?" But it came out garbled.

"Don't talk, or what I do will be on your head. This is your fault. Yours and *his*."

His who? Ty?

"What about Deb?" Winter mumbled.

"I didn't kick her hard enough to do damage. Ty?" She snorted. "If I get the chance—"

"No." Tears flooded Winter's eyes. She didn't want her husband hurt. "Leave him alone." Every time she spoke, the gag gnawed at the corners of her lips. Her jaw ached from her mouth being held open. If she screamed, would Randi kick her as she did to Deb? Like she planned to do to Ty? Winter tried yelling "Help." A slap sent her head reeling backward. Tiny lights pinged around her. She moaned.

"I said be quiet. I'm the one in charge now." Randi's voice sounded high and weird.

Winter couldn't see the other woman's eyes, but she guessed they'd be bloodshot and glassy like they were the other day. Did Randi even realize the harm she was doing? What happened to the woman she trusted as a PA for all those years?

"They'll think we've gone out the window—just like I planned." Randi cackled and plopped down next to Winter. "Won't even check this furnace room. Then we'll make our getaway down the fire escape."

Randi didn't know a thing about Ty if she thought he'd give up so easily. He flew to Bend and sat in the foyer guarding Winter for the last two nights. Unless he was knocked unconscious—or worse, which she didn't want to think about—he'd be searching for her.

She hated the gag touching her tongue. She despised the confined space and the darkness with Randi breathing heavily beside her. Her face hurt. *Lord, I don't know why this is happening. Open Randi's eyes to see Your love. She seems delusional. Show Ty where I am.*

With her hands still tied, she nudged her fingers along the rough floor and the wall behind her, searching for something, anything, that could make noise.

* * * *

"When I say *now*, we'll barge in," Ty whispered outside the classroom where the door had opened and shut.

"Maybe we should call 911," Neil suggested.

"I'm sure Deb did." Ty froze. Had he heard something again? He pulsed his index finger—one, two, three. "Now."

They burst into the Sunday school room, their cell phones shining a light in front of them. Ty felt a cool breeze. An open window? "Oh, no." He rushed to the source of air. "They went out the window!" He charged out of the room and sprinted down the hallway toward the back exit.

Neil plodded after him. "They could be anywhere by now."

Ty couldn't believe the way things had gone down. How did Randi coerce Winter into cooperating? Did she threaten to harm her? Did Randi have a getaway vehicle?

In the parking lot, he raced from car to car searching for anything suspicious. "Winter!" He repeated her name. He saw a pickup truck with a bundle on the back. He climbed onto the bumper, only to find a bookshelf under a tarp.

"Anything?" Neil ran to the truck, huffing.

"No. They're gone." Saying the words made him sick. He promised to protect his wife. "How did Randi sneak in and abduct her? We were right there."

"I was sleeping. I'm so sorry." Neil put both hands on his head and stared up at the dark sky as if questioning the heavens for answers.

Ty wanted to take him to task for his negligence. But he had to use his energy to find his wife. Where could she be?

"We'd better check on Deborah." Neil turned and jogged toward the building.

Ty heard sirens. Two vehicles with flashing red and blue lights pulled into the parking lot, barely stopping before four officers jumped out of the cars. One shined a bright flashlight at Ty. Two pointed guns.

"Whoa." His hands automatically went up. "My wife's been abducted."

One of the officers patted him down and searched him.

"Name?" the gray-haired officer barked.

"Ty Williams."

"ID?"

Ty reached for his wallet and pulled out his Idaho card. "I don't know where Randi took her. She's crazy. Or on something." He knew he was chattering. "Aren't you supposed to be doing something? Calling in an APB? Anything?"

The officer shined his flashlight on Ty's driver's license, then blasted the light at his eyes. He repeated the process like he was checking points on the card. *Brown eyes. Six foot one.*

"I'm Detective Wyatt. This is my partner, Murphy." He nodded toward the redheaded freckle-faced man beside him.

Neil exited the building, and a flashlight beam hit him full in the face. With the firearms pointed at him now, his hands shot up.

"Who are you?" Wyatt barked.

"Neil Quinn. I'm with Passion's Prayer. The missing woman is Winter Williams." He nodded toward Ty. "She's this man's wife."

The man in charge nodded at the officers. They holstered their weapons. Neil lowered his hands.

"Is the suspect still on the property?" Wyatt handed back Ty's license.

"They're gone." Ty covered his face with his hands.

"Describe her." Wyatt pointed his flashlight at Neil.

"Female. About this height." The team leader held his hand out horizontally at his chest. "Shoulder-length dirty-blond hair. Name's Randi Simmons."

"Eye color?" Another asked.

"Blue, I think." Neil shook his head. "Not sure."

"What led to the altercation?"

Neil gave an abbreviated version of what happened at Hart's Camp, the conflict from a few days ago, and what transpired tonight. Ty was relieved Neil was supplying the information. All he wanted to do was get in the Old Clunker and drive up Hwy 97. But what good would that accomplish when he didn't know what type of car Randi was driving or which direction she went? If only the church had installed surveillance equipment as the pastor told him they were planning to do. Frustration gnawed at Ty's gut.

Every second they weren't searching, Randi was taking Winter farther from him. Was this her revenge for him joining the team? For getting her kicked off? For marrying Winter when Randi had been opposed to them being together? Didn't she tell him she'd get even?

While Wyatt took notes, the officers rushed inside to search the building. What a waste of time. Ty was sure Randi took Winter out the classroom window. Why wouldn't anyone believe him?

What-ifs haunted him. What if Randi took Winter from the country? What if she sold her into human trafficking? What if— *Stop!* He had to shake himself free of thinking the worst. *Please, God. Be with her. Help us find them tonight. Keep her safe.*

Murphy exited the building. "Lights are back on. Carson and James are checking the rooms."

Slow. Useless. They needed to uncover what kind of car Randi was driving and go after her, not dawdle in the building.

"Gentlemen, you may wait inside." Wyatt closed his pocket-sized notebook. "Don't leave the premises in case we have more questions."

Questions. "What about closing down the highway? Setting up a roadblock?" Ty's voice rose.

Both uniformed men quirked their eyebrows like they were questioning his sanity. Probably thought he'd been watching too many crime scene episodes on TV.

"She's my wife." He needed to hold her in his arms and know she was safe. "I've got to find her. I'll do anything—"

"We'll find her." Wyatt nodded toward the church. "You a praying man?"

Ty gulped, feeling slightly out of control. "Yes."

"Best you do that and leave police work to us." He took long strides toward the door.

As if Ty was going to sit around when his wife had been abducted. He wanted to get out there, find Randi, and haul her sorry backside to the slammer. He'd been inside prison walls, and normally he wouldn't wish that on his worst enemy, but this was different. The wretched woman took the most precious person in his life. He wouldn't rest until she was behind bars. He stormed into one of the classrooms and kicked over a chair.

Neil followed him. "Feel better?"

Ty wanted to yell at him. He was the one who fell asleep. Ty and Winter had been counting on him to stay alert. "No, I don't feel better."

"Let's do what the officer suggested and pray." Neil nodded toward the miniature table. "If it was someone else, that's what Winter would be doing right now."

"True." Still, anger and worry zinged through his taut muscles.

Neil dropped into a small chair that looked more appropriate for a five-year-old. "We have to come against this attack with prayer. Let's trust God to be working where we can't see."

He was right, but Ty still made a lap around the perimeter of the room to expend some angst. He stopped by the window, thinking of the one he found open in that other classroom.

"Ty?"

He blew out hot air. "I'm sorry. I'm just worried sick."

"I know." Neil's voice softened. "It'll be okay. God will turn this into good. Isn't that the promise?"

"Yes."

"Winter knows you're here, that you came all this way to protect her."

"Lot of good it did her." Ty dropped into a chair, and his knees hit the short table.

A cryptic look crossed Neil's features like he wanted to tell Ty what he thought of his childish behavior. Instead, he bowed his head. "Father, we come before You again. We need You. Please help the policemen and guide them to wherever Randi and Winter are. Keep Winter safe. We're worried, but we ask for the grace to trust You. Redeem this situation. Guard our hearts against fear and bitterness."

At first, Ty felt agony, wishing he could sense something other than frustration, and yes, fear. Hadn't he already gone through enough torment because of Randi's terrible attitude and actions? But Neil kept praying, petitioning heaven for wisdom and strength and grace to endure whatever the night might hold. What exactly did he mean by that? Did Neil think the hours ahead could bring something worse than Winter being gone? Worse than the thoughts swimming around in Ty's mind? Fresh concern clawed at his gut. What if Randi did her serious harm? He blew out a breath. He couldn't ponder that, or he'd go crazy.

As Neil kept praying, beseeching the Lord for Winter's safety and for peace amid turmoil, Ty felt something comforting pour over him. It had to be the love of God because he was feeling anything but loving, moments ago. He swallowed back tears and joined in praying. "God, help us," he whispered. *I'm sorry for doubting and for giving in to panic. Be with Winter. Help me to believe You are working everything out for our good. Rescue her, Lord. I love her. Show us what we should be doing. Help the police.*

They continued praying and quoting encouraging scriptures until Detective Wyatt stuck his head in the classroom.

"We questioned the women who were sitting in the front row. We've sent them home. There's a gal out here who'd like to see you." He opened the door wider, and Deborah rushed in.

Neil stood and embraced her. She was sniffing, her eyes red-rimmed.

"Are you okay?" Ty asked, wondering if she should go to an ER.

"For now." Deb shrugged and clutched her side.

"I suggest you head back to your motel, and we'll keep in contact." The detective wiped the back of his hand over his nose.

Ty stood. "I'm staying here, all night, if necessary."

"You won't be any good to your wife exhausted." Wyatt raised his shoulders, then lowered them. "I promise to call as soon as we hear something."

"Not good enough." Ty moved to the center of the room. "What's next?"

"Next?"

"Tonight? Now? What're you going to do next?" Ty had to do something. He could pray. He could walk the streets of Bend. He could drive back and forth on the highway. But he wasn't going to head back to the motel and *sleep*.

"I'll leave Officer Carson here. It's possible Ms. Simmons wants information and may return Mrs. Williams after she gets whatever she's after."

"Would she go to all this effort for a little information?" Ty looked to Neil to shed some understanding.

"Anything's possible." Neil nodded toward Wyatt.

Wyatt pulled out his notebook and thumbed through it.

"Someone heard her say 'Come on, Winter. You and I have things we need to discuss.'"

"Before or after she kicked Deborah?" Ty heard his voice accelerating. "Do her actions sound like a rational woman who might just bring Winter back?"

"Ty"—Neil clapped him on the shoulder—"let them do their job."

"If only they would." Ty trudged a path back to the window, glaring into the dark parking lot.

"Can I get everyone coffee?" Deborah shuffled to the door.

"I'll go with you." Neil followed her but glanced back as if to warn Ty to be polite.

Yeah, he knew he needed to squash his pride and spitefulness. He glanced at the detective. "Sorry, sir, I'm not usually this tense and rude." He paced along the bank of windows, the leg of his pants brushing the radiator.

"Understood." Wyatt nodded. "I still think it would be better for you to get some sleep."

"We'll stay here and pray—and wait for good news." He spoke words of faith, but inwardly he fought too many doubts.

Thirty-three

Gar

Gar had lots of time to pray and sing worship songs on the late afternoon drive from Spokane to Everett. In fact, the closer he got to home, the more he found himself calling out to the Lord. He also spent time mulling over his conversations with his Alaskan pastor friend.

He and Chad had talked some more on the phone, and Gar appreciated the encouragement. Pastor Chad told him that through his own experience with reconciliation, he was trying to love his wife in a way that wasn't popular, the way Christ had loved the church. It was a new concept for Gar. He'd never thought much about loving Autumn in any way that would be considered sacrificial, and certainly not very humble. In the past, he wanted Autumn's plans to coincide with his. Now, he could see how much he took her for granted. How he almost nurtured an emotional distance between them. Why should he have been surprised when their love fizzled and died?

Chad had asked him something curious, too. He wondered if Autumn might feel like Gar blamed her for the infertility. Gar disagreed. But in retrospect, as he zoomed past the small town of George, Washington, and crossed the bridge over the Columbia River, he had to consider it. Did Autumn think he was upset with her for not giving them a baby? If the roles were reversed and he was infertile, would he worry about his wife's disappointment in him? Of course.

That made him want to pull over and pray or cry. In the last forty-eight hours since he welcomed Jesus back into his life as Lord, he relinquished a lot of his pride and arrogance, and found himself praying more. He'd also been remembering how neglectful he'd been toward his wife for too long. How he flirted with other women—Ty had taken him to task over that one. Gar cringed at the remembrance.

"You can't do that, man," Ty said over the phone. "Think of Autumn as the one and only woman in the world who you're going to flirt with from this day forward. Focus on her. Search for ways to romance her and spend time together. It'll be fun, an adventure."

How could Gar live out that philosophy? He didn't know if she'd accept him back—especially after he told her what happened in Vegas. He still wasn't convinced telling the whole truth was the best way. But Ty had been adamant that if Gar wanted a beautiful healing to occur between him and his wife, he needed to be gut-honest and willing to let her ask him anything. The thought made him want to turn the car around.

About seven p.m., he pulled into his driveway in Everett as he did hundreds of other times coming home late from school on a Thursday night. Everything looked the same as when he left, other than the gorgeous fall colors. Autumn's car wasn't in her spot. She was probably still at practice. With her show opening next week, this weekend would be especially busy for her. But maybe he could be of assistance. Do supply runs, or something. He didn't know if he should go inside the house or not. He could wait until she came home, but he needed a bathroom break after the slow commute on I-405. A cup of coffee would be nice too. Autumn wouldn't mind if he used the facilities and got something to drink, would she?

He'd been planning to stay in the guest room. If she was opposed to that idea, he'd get a room at a motel for a few days. His first desire was to try to make things right between them. Then he'd decide what to do about finding a job.

He left his travel bag in the car and walked up the steps to the front door. Still carrying the house key in his pocket, he fingered it, then unlocked the door. The floor creaked in the exact spot he remembered. Mmm . . . something smelled delicious. Chocolate? More fudge? In that second, he realized he should have bought a dozen roses. What did a man do when he came home after deserting his wife? He gulped. He probably shouldn't have entered the house, even to use the facilities. He should get back in the car and head for a gas station. He took a step backwards.

What was that? A sound in the kitchen?

His footfall froze. After a couple of seconds of silence, he sighed. Must be his imagination. Why was he so nervous? He might as well go ahead and use the bathroom. When he reentered the living room, he noticed how neat everything looked. Maybe he could relax on the guest bed. He'd love to close his eyes for a few minutes after the long drive.

As soon as he walked into the guest room and turned on the light, he stopped. Feminine clothes that didn't look like Autumn's were draped over a chair. Pink tennies with polka dot laces peeked out from under the bed. Not her style. The curtains were floral instead of dark blue as they'd once been. Something smelled different. A flowery-scented soap or perfume? Whose stuff was this?

He backed up and a sharp point—a knife?—jabbed him in the back. *Whoa.* He put his hands up.

"What are you doing in here?" a woman's pseudo-low voice growled.

"I live here."

"Don't play funny." The point pressed into his skin. "Get your carcass out of here before I do some damage to your kidneys."

"Easy." Who was she? And why was she in his house with a knife?

"Move nice and slow. Head out the door or window, whichever way you came in." With her free hand, she jabbed his shoulder. "Don't make any wise-guy moves. Or you'll be sorry."

If he twisted fast, could he take her by surprise and knock the knife out of her hand? She sounded forceful, like she knew what to do with a weapon. "You're making a mistake."

"Wasn't me slinking around." Again with the shove. "Get out, before I call the cops."

Gar decided to go along with her demands but look for a way to disarm her. He shuffled toward the front door and glanced over his shoulder. A twenty-ish woman with dark blond hair glared back at him.

"Go on." She pressed the knife a little harder against him, enough to hurt.

"I'm going, already." He yanked open the door. "I'm Autumn's husband."

"And I'm the Princess of Wales."

Weird. He felt like he'd arrived at the wrong residence despite the fact his key worked. "Who are you? What are you doing here?"

She slammed the door in his face. The deadbolt clunked. *Great.* Kicked out of his own house. That woman acted as if *she* owned the place. Was Autumn letting her stay? A knife-wielding female? He had half a mind to call the police. He huffed as he slid into his car and pulled out his cell phone. He'd text Autumn first.

Just got in town. Stopped by the house. Wild woman inside.

He had to wait a while before a response came.

Oops. I've been meaning to tell you about them.

Them? There was more than one like her?

He tapped his cell against his thigh as he waited.

Still at play practice. Will explain when I get there. Give me an hour.

An hour? Gar sighed. What a reversal. She used to be the one waiting at home for him every night. Time for him to accept some changes—and look for ways to romance her, starting with not being angry or overreacting. He glanced at his cell. The idea of buying roses sauntered through his mind again. A dozen red I'm-sorry flowers might break the ice. On the other hand, he didn't know if he should leave the yard with *that* woman in his house. How long had this been going on? Was Autumn safe with her?

A kid, about eight or nine years old, bounced a basketball up the driveway, then paused beside the car and gawked at Gar. He squinted like he was staring at a caged lion at the zoo.

Gar turned the key in the ignition just enough to lower the window.

The boy's eyes widened. "It's you."

"Yeah, it's me. Who are you?"

The kid shot up the porch steps and pounded on the door. "Sarah, let me in!"

Gar shut off the engine, thinking he'd get out and ask the boy some questions. But the front door opened enough for the youngster to slip inside, then slammed shut. The curtain in the front window shuffled against the glass. Were they peering at him? He sighed. If they were overnight guests, both spare rooms would be occupied. A motel was sounding better all the time. But first, a strong cup of coffee. He started the engine and backed up.

It seemed both he *and* Autumn had some explaining to do.

Thirty-four

Winter

Winter didn't know how many hours had passed since Randi shoved her into the dark musty room and plopped down beside her. With her mouth gagged and her hands tied behind her, it felt like forever. Her jaws ached. She stretched her lips and groaned against the tight gag holding her mouth open. She tasted blood and knew the creases of her lips were bleeding. She tried not to think about disgusting places the cloth might have come from. She had to survive this, whatever *this* was. Her arms were getting numb behind her back. Her shoulders ached. Soon she'd need to use the bathroom. She tried working the fabric around her wrists loose, but she couldn't shift much, or Randi would notice.

Panic and lack of moisture caused an awful taste in her mouth. Swallowing was difficult. Would she get out of this alive? She had to act smart and watch for an opportunity to escape. Randi was stronger and knew how to take down an enemy, but Winter could think things through and was trusting in God. *Lord, protect me from evil. Help Ty find me.* Her husband had to be somewhere in the building, worried sick.

Sitting this close to the woman who took her journal, she wished she could ask her about it. She listened for a moment. Was Randi snoring? Had they waited so long her captor fell asleep? If Winter could inch away . . . but no, Randi would fall over and wake up.

Determined to do something, she shuffled her bottom in tiny increments across the unfinished floor. Randi made a swallowing sound like she was waking up. Winter froze. After a while, she repeated the action, her fingers feeling the outer wall. A warm pipe jutted out. She tapped it with her fingernail, and it clinked. Hmm. Randi shuffled. Faking sleep, Winter breathed deeply and waited for her to be still again.

She tapped the pipe, wishing she knew Morse code. Could Ty hear that? The beat they used to knock on their apartment door came to mind. She tapped, "Shave and a haircut, two bits." It was now or never. She rapped harder this time—with her knuckles.

Randi slammed into her. *Ugh.* Winter landed on her side with a thud. She moaned and tried to lift her cheek off the gritty floor.

"Think Ty will hear that measly sound?" Randi sneered. "I left a window open, and they'll assume we escaped in a car—which we will since my rig's parked down the street. Now you're going to do exactly as I tell you." Randi grabbed her by the arm and squeezed. "You should never have fired me like you did."

Winter cried out, but the gag muffled the sound. So her previous assistant *was* doing all of this because of revenge. Well, she wouldn't go along with Randi without a fight. She'd drag her feet, fall over, kick at stuff, whatever she had to do. If Randi forced her into a car, she'd run the first chance she got.

Randi yanked her into a sitting position. Even that movement hurt. "Be quiet. I'm going to check the parking lot. I repeat—be quiet."

I won't.

She opened the door, and Winter heard her shove something out of the way. Had she put a table or structure in front of the door to make it look like the room wasn't in use?

With Randi gone for a few moments, what was to stop Winter from making noise? She located the pipe again and hit her knuckles against it. Forget the beat. She banged the pipe as hard as she could.

"Stop that." Randi rustled into the space and shoved her so hard she fell over. "Don't try that again." She mumbled something to herself. "Old Clunker's still out there. Why haven't they left?"

Winter lay motionless on the floor and hope rushed through her. Ty *was* still here.

* * * *

The building was old, and the pipes made the weirdest sounds. Ty strode into the classroom where the window had been left open earlier, listening. He paced, praying as he'd been doing for hours. Nothing new had come in from the police department. At the last update from Officer Carson—who had taken his position near the front doors—none of the local rental businesses reported loaning a car to a woman of Randi's description. Even he knew that didn't matter. She could have worn a wig or used false ID. Two vehicles reported as stolen had turned up as dead-ends. No one matching Randi's or Winter's descriptions had purchased tickets at the bus station or the airport. Did Randi want a ransom? If so, where was the demand?

The beat in the pipes started again. Not your typical convection noises, even for an old structure. Wait. That almost sounded like—

He held his breath. Then hummed the beat—*Shave and a haircut.* His heart hammered fast. Was that his wife trying to communicate with him? Could the open window have been a ruse and even now Randi was holding Winter hostage in this building? Surely not. The police searched the place. He swallowed down opposing thoughts. What if . . . Randi had found the perfect hiding place? *Sas!* He wanted to yell her name. To shout to the rafters that he would find her, that he was willing to die for her, if necessary.

Another clunking sounded, more sporadic this time.

That does it. He dashed into the other classroom and shook Neil, who was nodding off with his head tipped back, his mouth opened wide. "Neil, wake up."

He sputtered and coughed. "N-news?"

"Walk around with me, will you? I've been hearing weird sounds in the pipes."

"Ty—" Neil raked his fingers through his graying hair. "Pipes in old churches make strange sounds."

"I know."

A knocking echoed through the convection.

"Hear that? A few minutes ago, I heard a rhythm. Maybe I'm losing my mind—"

"You're under a lot of stress." Neil stood and checked his cell phone. "Two a.m.?" He sighed. "What was the beat?"

"Duh, duh-duh, duh duh, duh, duh."

"Shave and a haircut?"

Ty met Neil's gaze. "We used that knock when we were young. It means something to us." She would know he'd recognize that beat and come to her.

Neil moved to the bank of windows and peered out.

Ty placed his hand on the radiator. "Think these pipes run all through the building? Even upstairs?"

"Yeah."

"Let's go." Ty sprinted from the room and down the hallway. Maybe he'd look foolish, chasing after the cause of noisy pipes.

But his heart drumming in his ears and the adrenaline surging through his body made him feel certain he'd find her.

"What's your plan?" Neil called from behind.

"Look anywhere the police might have missed."

When he arrived in Bend, he and Neil checked over the whole building. They knew the layout. Of course, he hadn't been searching for a hiding place. He'd been hunting for escape routes. An upstairs fire escape seemed the most likely. Was that Randi's plan? What kind of hiding places might they have overlooked?

* * * *

"You were my *friend*," Winter mumbled around the gag.

Randi made a choking sound. "Were we friends when you kicked me off the team? When you made fun of my idea to write a book about you? No, you married *him*. That changed everything."

Winter shook her head. She couldn't defend herself with a gag in her mouth. She needed to reach the pipe again and hit it loud enough to get Ty's attention. Tap, tap, tap.

Randi shoved against her, forcing her away from the pipe.

"I want—"

"Shhh." Randi clamped her hand over Winter's mouth, making it even more difficult for her to breathe. "Someone's coming."

Winter drew in a ragged breath through her nose, praying Ty would find her. Then she feared what might happen if he did. Footsteps in the outer room made her heart race. Ty? A scraping noise came next, like something heavy had been dragged from the door. Randi's thumb pressed into Winter's throat, silencing her, and blocking her oxygen intake. Panic seized her. She sucked in a ration of air. Her heart pounded ferociously in her ears. She didn't want to pass out. She needed to stay alert and warn her husband.

"Stay quiet," Randi whispered, "or I'll kick Ty's head in so bad he'll—"

"No." At the mental image Randi's words conjured up, Winter's desire to create a scene wilted. She concentrated on breathing in and out of the tiny hole left to her for air. Surely Ty would hear her gasping and gulping.

The door creaked open. A ray of light skimmed the narrow space she shared with Randi. The outline of a stack of storage buckets was illuminated in front of them.

"Furnace room? Storage?" Neil questioned.

"Perfect place to . . ."

"Doesn't look like they're here."

Wait! You found me.

"Hey, Neil, wait a second." Ty sounded like he noticed something.

A box scraped across the floor. More light broke through the darkness. Winter felt Randi's tension as she gripped her mouth tighter.

"Sas?"

Ty. Winter wanted to yelp when Randi's fingernail scraped her cheek and tore into the sore place along her lips. The salty taste of blood reached her tongue. Her foot bumped into something solid. Now or never. She bunched up her legs and then kicked out with all her might, sending whatever it was crashing to the floor.

Randi swore.

Someone hit the light switch, but nothing happened. Had Randi removed the light bulb so no one could see into this room?

Two cell phone lights flashed over the storage buckets at them.

"Ty!" she yelled in a muffled tone against the gag and Randi's hand. When Ty's face contorted, she knew he saw her.

"Silence," Randi barked.

"Easy." Ty stretched out his hands as if calming her. "Let her go. There's no escaping now."

"No?"

Her freaky tone made Winter's stomach churn.

"Neil, contact the officer." Ty squatted down on his haunches. "Let her go, Randi."

"No. Get out." She locked her arm around Winter's throat, forcing her body to bend over.

Winter coughed, fighting against the chokehold. *Air. Ty . . . I need you.*

He backed up fast, his hands still extended. "Don't hurt her. Be reasonable. Winter cares for you, e-even after what you've done."

She heard the tremor in his tone and knew he was masking his rage.

"She's coming with me." Randi yanked her to a standing position, her arms still clutched around Winter's neck as they moved into the outer room.

Air became more precious. Suffocating seemed a possibility. She concentrated on breathing, even though she tried to appeal to Ty with her eyes.

"Release her. That's all I want." He swayed his hands toward the door. "You can go."

"I'm not giving you anything you want." Randi tightened her grasp. "Winter and I were friends. I took care of her. Then *you* came along and ruined my life!"

"Steady."

Winter gasped, her lungs desperate. If she knew martial arts, she'd kick or fling an elbow, but lack of air and her current exhaustion kept her from doing anything to free herself. Even the imploring look on Ty's face couldn't make her fight the woman she knew could kill her. "Ty," she whimpered.

"Shut up," Randi snapped. "You're leaving with me."

* * * *

Ty didn't see how he could rescue Winter and fight off Randi at the same time. Where was Neil? How long before the police got here? He read fear in his wife's eyes at a level he never saw before. Finding blood on her face enraged him. "Let her go," he said through gritted teeth.

"No." Randi's eyes were red and wild-looking as she came toward him. "Move back. Let us leave. And nobody gets hurt. Otherwise—" Her gaze darted from him to Winter.

He held up his hands in surrender, knowing his wife needed air. "Take the gag off and let her breathe." He backed away, showing his compliance. He didn't want to let Randi step out of the room, but he had to protect Winter. "She needs air. Remove the gag."

Randi spit. "Don't tell me what to do. This is your fault."

He saw Winter's eyes pulse open, and he gave her the slightest nod. *We'll get through this. You're going to be okay.* He tried to communicate to her.

"Back up," Randi yelled, and she seemed more agitated. "We're going out the fire escape."

So that was her plan. Ty did what she said, but gritty determination raced through him as he waited for his chance to take her down. She might kick his teeth in, but he would not allow her to take Winter from this building.

Neil stepped into the doorway. "Carson is on his way up."

"Get out of my way!" Randi held Winter in front of her like a shield, blocking Ty's ability to grab her.

Neil started praying out loud.

"Randi, please d-don't do this." Deb must have followed Neil upstairs. Hearing the break in her voice, Ty wondered about her injury.

"Go away." Randi glared at Deb. "You're a weak nothing."

"I may be a nothing," Deb said softly, "but all of my

nothingness loves you. Don't hurt Winter. She hasn't done anything against you."

"They deceived us." Randi's glazed eyes took in each of them. "They'll fire you too if it suits their purposes. Come with me. It'll be like it used to be. You, me, Winter."

Ty recognized how delusional her words sounded.

Suddenly Winter went limp. Her body buckled to the ground, taking Randi to the floor with her.

"Sas!" Ty rushed forward.

Randi scrambled to her feet and lifted her hands toward him in a fighting stance, stopping his forward motion.

Ty gulped, breathing hard. At least his wife's chest was rising and falling. Deb rushed to her and knelt without Randi harming her.

Randi's gaze pierced his as she took defined steps in a semi-circle around Winter's form.

Seeing the woman he loved collapsed on the floor ignited a fire of rage in him. When Randi glanced toward Deb, as if making sure she wasn't attacking from behind, Ty let out a yell that came from somewhere in the depths of his gut. He rammed his shoulder full force into Randi, knocking her down, away from Winter. As she regained her footing, he planted himself as a barricade between her and his wife. "No more!" he yelled.

Like a wildcat, she hissed at him, clenching her teeth. Then, as if realizing she'd lost the upper hand, she bolted toward the door.

"There's nowhere to run." Neil blocked the doorway. "It's over."

Randi whirled around and stared at Ty with crazed eyes. She made a high-pitched scream, then she lunged straight for him and threw a side-thrust kick toward his ribs that he couldn't avoid.

"Randi, no!" Deb yelped.

On impact, Ty flew backward, crashing into a whiteboard. He groaned in pain and clutched his chest.

She came at him again, kicking powerfully, the knife of her foot ramming into him as if she were determined to destroy him.

"Stop! The police are here," Neil shouted.

Randi froze, the intensity in her eyes turning from Ty to Deb, who was still kneeling on the floor beside Winter. Was she thinking of taking Deb hostage next? He couldn't let that happen. Despite the agony in his ribs, he lunged to his feet and charged at her like a linebacker. He tackled his wife's assailant to the floor. She clawed and bit and fought him, peppering the room with expletives. He held her down, his knee on her back, feeling a power from inside giving him strength to stop her.

He glanced over and saw Winter—without her gag—leaning up on her elbow, watching him through fatigued eyes. *Thank You, God, she's alive.* She shook her head as if pleading with him not to hurt Randi, but he wouldn't loosen his hold.

Footsteps thundered up the stairs. Carson burst into the room, followed by another officer.

"Let her go!"

Ty slid his knee off Randi's back and released the wrists he held behind her. When Carson took over, Ty stood and gasped. A horrible burning sensation radiated through his ribs. Still, he fell to his knees beside Winter. She blinked at him, sorrow etched in her eyes.

"Oh, Sas." He pressed his lips against her forehead.

"Ty . . ." She sobbed. "I was so afraid for you." She leaned up and wrapped her arms around his middle. He winced before he had time to remind himself not to react to the pain.

"What's wrong?" Her eyes widened.

He shook his head, not wanting her to worry. "It's okay. We're together. That's all that matters." He stroked her hair, so thankful to be near her. She laid her head on his lap and breathed in deeply. He rocked her as the police read Randi her Miranda Rights.

The last he saw of their previous employee was her being escorted from the room, her gaze glinting fireballs of hate at him. "You ruined everything! You swine. Passion's Prayer is destroyed because of you!"

An ache built inside of him at the realization that someone hated him so much. But he couldn't dwell on it. His wife was safe and alive. Their team was a bit battered and bruised, but they'd be okay.

"Ty," Winter whispered, "we can't let them take her."

"What do you mean?" His ribs hurt when he spoke or breathed. "They're going to throw her in jail for a long time, I hope."

"Oh, Ty."

"I have to go with her. Tell her we still love her." Deb stood slowly and moaned as she left the room.

Neil followed her, and Ty figured the team leader would stop Deb from trying to go with Randi to the police station. Most likely, she needed medical attention too.

His chest throbbed, but all he could do was gaze into the green eyes of the woman he loved and thank God for bringing them safely through such a harrowing experience. Blood had smeared up her cheeks. Her eyes were red from crying or strain. From the crease of her lips to her ears, scratches and torn skin showed where the gag chafed. Her bruised jaw looked like she'd been in a fistfight. What had Randi done to her? He wanted to lean in and kiss her but moving even an inch felt impossible now.

"I'm so sorry for what you went through."

She leaned her cheek against his shirt and sobbed. "Why would she do this?"

"I don't know." He smoothed his palm over her arm and shoulder. "What hurts?"

"Everything."

Ty knew what she meant. He sucked in a short breath and swallowed his gasp, certain he had broken ribs.

"I want to go home." Winter curled into him.

"Me too." He gritted his teeth and helped her stand to her feet, knowing they'd need healing and rest in the days ahead.

Thirty-five

Autumn

When Autumn got home from practice, she expected to find Gar waiting in the driveway or eating fudge at the table. Instead, Sarah paced across the kitchen floor tiles, talking faster than Autumn had ever heard her speak, chattering about a guy she thought had broken into the house. The same one Jimmy recognized as the man from pictures in the office where he'd been sleeping—Gar.

"But he had a beard." Sarah wiped her hand under her nose. "How should I know who he was?"

Autumn hugged her and tried to calm her down, but Sarah's shoulders remained stiff and unyielding. "Where is he now?"

"Long gone." Jimmy nodded.

"I scared him off." Sarah twisted the drawstrings from her sweatshirt and squinted at the photo on the fridge. "He looks different. Older."

Autumn dropped into the kitchen chair and pressed her fingers against her closed eyelids. End-of-day exhaustion was settling in.

"He's your husband?"

Autumn held up her wedding ring. "Yes. He's been away."

Sarah harrumphed like she was suspicious of such a man.

Autumn didn't want to get into a discussion about Gar and their marriage. "I should have mentioned he'd be showing up. I got overly busy and forgot to say anything."

"I thought you were divorced." Sarah crossed her arms and hugged herself.

"We're separated, but he's still my husband."

"Is he mean?" Sarah's eyes glinted.

"No, he's not abusive. You don't have any reason to fear him."

Sarah picked up a knife from the kitchen counter. "I protected myself with this."

"What?" Autumn leaped to her feet. A terrifying picture of Gar stabbed, lying on the floor wounded, flashed through her mind.

"I thought he was a burglar."

"Did you hurt him?"

"Could have, but I didn't." Sarah swallowed hard. "He ran out of here fast."

Jimmy bit into a piece of white chocolate fudge. "Sarah knows how to take good care of us."

Autumn groaned. Sarah had defended herself in the only way she knew how, but what must Gar think? She pulled out her cell phone from her pocket and tapped out a message on the screen.

I heard what my houseguest did. I'm so sorry.

"I thought he was lying when he said he was your husband." Sarah's voice rose.

"Could have been a bad guy. Like *Burt Conner* from the mission. He's mean." Jimmy seemed to be trying to smooth out Sarah's frayed nerves. But at the mention of that man's name, she became even more agitated.

245

"I never meant to cause trouble with your man." Sarah tightened the drawstrings until only a small circle of her face showed.

"I'll explain to Gar. It will be fine." Autumn blew out a breath. This wasn't the homecoming she imagined for him, or the meeting she anticipated between him and these two she already cared about so much.

Her cell vibrated.

I never thought I'd be chased out of my house by a knife-wielding woman. Houseguest?

She thought you were a thief. She'd explain the rest later. She couldn't imagine what Gar must have thought when Sarah pulled the knife on him.

Can you meet me at the Red and White?

Glad for the change of subject, she smiled. It was late, but she wanted to see him, even if she was beat. A shower and some coffee would help.

Half hour?

Perfect. Meet you there.

A nervous tingle raced up her spine. Was this a date? Or had he driven over to break the news that he wanted to separate for good? She shuffled to the Keurig. She was going to need a double mocha to get through tonight.

"Do we have to leave?" Jimmy's eyes squinted with concern.

"Of course not. Why would you think that?"

Jimmy glanced at his mother. "Sarah said if your 'Mister' came back, we'd get the boot."

Autumn still hadn't broached the topic of Jimmy calling Sarah by her first name.

The young woman had been more relaxed lately than when she first moved in. But as Autumn met her gaze, her eyes twitched, her shoulders were hunched, and she gnawed on her lower lip. Autumn put her hands on the woman's shoulders.

"Listen, I don't want you to worry. You're welcome in this house whether Gar's here or not. What happened earlier was an honest mistake." She didn't want to come home and find the two of them had vanished. She side hugged Jimmy. "I mean it. This is your home, at least through winter. After that, we'll see. Understand?"

Jimmy nodded solemnly.

Sarah didn't acknowledge her words. It seemed the episode with Gar had set things back between them.

Autumn grabbed the knife off the counter and returned it to the drawer. "Next time you see someone in my house, give them the benefit of the doubt, okay? They may be a friend. Not a foe."

"What's a foe?" Jimmy scratched his ear.

"The enemy." Sarah's voice deepened. "Burt Conner."

"Oh." The whites of Jimmy's eyes enlarged.

When her coffee was ready, Autumn rushed into her bedroom. What should she wear to meet the man she was married to, yet so unsure of? And who in the world was Burt Conner?

* * * *

Gar shuffled from foot to foot as he stood in front of the Red and White, clutching a dozen yellow roses, waiting for Autumn beneath the restaurant's overhead lighting. He'd thought over this first meeting plenty of times since that morning after talking with Ty. He was about to see the woman he loved, the woman he hurt, and the one he prayed he could make amends with.

His heart beat faster. He licked his dry lips. Would she notice the difference in him? Would she care that he'd been through the wringer of expunging sin and shame, or that he finally discovered what he'd been missing the last few years— a deep relationship with God? He had so much to say to her, so much to apologize for and to share, but tonight, he just wanted to be *with* her. To gaze into her eyes and hold her hand, if she'd let him, and promise her things would be different now. He was determined to keep his vows this time—if she'd give him a second chance.

He glanced toward the parking lot, and there she was, walking in the moonlight toward him. She wore a dressy trench coat over black slacks and heels. He loved it when she wore high heels—she knew that about him. He smiled, tempted to whistle at her. She glanced at him, almost shyly. What would she do if he ran to her and kissed her fully on the lips? He could imagine himself doing something dramatic like that, but thinking of her need to hear what had kept him away from her rooted him to his spot on the sidewalk.

When she reached him, he held out the roses to her. The floral scent reminded him of other times he placed flowers in her hands. "You look beautiful."

"Thank you."

She clasped the bouquet, and their fingers touched. Sparklers could have ignited by the jolt of electricity that surged through his senses—just like when they were young and madly in love. She met his gaze and, by her surprised look, felt a similar spark. He touched her ring hand, thinking about how he'd like to pull it to his lips like chivalrous men of old. Instead, she took the initiative and linked her fingers with his. Warmth spread through his chest as he stared into her inviting brown eyes. She still held the flowers in her other hand, but it seemed she was clinging to him. He liked that. And even though they didn't say anything other than those introductory words, kissing her was on his mind. If he could only heal the hurts of the past between them in the way he knew how—romance and gently spoken words of poetry. But thanks to Chad and Ty, he knew true healing and restoration would take time and confession and God working in both of their hearts.

She released his hand and drew the roses to her nose, just like he imagined her doing. She inhaled their fragrance. "Mmm . . . delightful."

He knew this woman well, but he couldn't guess what she was thinking as her eyes shined up at him. Did she still love him? Want him back? Or had she settled into being single so much that she already filled the house with other people? They really did need to talk. "Ready to go in?" He held out his arm to her. "I've reserved a table."

She didn't hesitate to slip her hand into the crook of his arm—which must be a good sign. The adoring way her gaze lingered in his direction made him feel humble and undeserving of her affection, but he was thankful for small miracles. Not waiting to second guess his feelings, he leaned toward her and brushed his lips over her cheek. He wished for so much more, but for now, winning back her love and trust was more important.

* * * *

As Gar led her into the Red and White, a restaurant they'd never been to together, Autumn felt school-girl nerves dancing in her stomach. He was treating her with such gentleness and care, she could hardly believe it was him. And with the way she felt outside under the bower of soft lighting, when he kissed her cheek, goodness, for a second, she wanted to forget the chasm that had been between them for months and meet his lips. She didn't. Of course, she didn't. But the impulse was there, nonetheless.

The way he kept smiling at her made her think something was different about him. He seemed happy to see her. Had he missed her as she missed him? He'd been away so long, and too many problems lay between them, to just resume their lives together. Why did he return like this, with little warning?

After they ordered—he chose lasagna and she asked for a chef salad—she wondered what she should say. Probably an explanation. "My houseguest thought you were a prowler. I'm sorry for what she did with the knife." Her cheeks heated up. "That must have been a shock."

He shrugged. "I should have knocked, but when I saw your car wasn't there, I used my key. My arrival was obviously unexpected." His eyebrow quirked. "Who are they?"

"Sarah and Jimmy." She explained about their homeless situation, how she met Jimmy while serving at an outdoor soup kitchen, about Marny's church's mission to provide warmth and kindness throughout the winter, about how close she'd gotten to Jimmy and Sarah.

"And you didn't tell me because—?"

Irritation bristled despite the warmth she'd been feeling toward him. Was it because she was so tired? "Could we talk about other things before we have a discussion about how I've lived my life without my husband for eleven weeks?" That came out sharper than she intended. She'd have to be careful or this dinner could turn into a disaster. *Lord, help me.*

Gar flinched. "I'm sorry. You're right. I don't have any reason to question the decisions you've made in my absence. I was the one who walked out. I haven't been here for you."

She was glad, and surprised, to hear him acknowledge that. "And now?" Was he returning to Idaho after the weekend?

He stared at her without answering. Was he thinking about his response or avoiding what they needed to discuss? Did he think roses and a little romance—

The waitress set two iced teas on the table then scurried away.

Autumn unwrapped her straw, feeling less eager to chat than when she first arrived.

"How's the play going?" He guzzled his tea without a straw.

"Okay." Did he want to know? Or was he making conversation to avoid her question? She smoothed her hand over the teal shirt that hung down over black slacks, wishing she'd lost a few more pounds. She was working on it. Even this morning, she hit the gym before going to school. "You know how crazy everything can get during the final weeks."

"I do."

"I have lighting issues I don't know how to solve." She sipped her tea. "Squawking monitors. Stuff like that."

"I could help, if you need a hand."

Her eyes had to have jerked open twice as wide. "Really?" *Like actually help?* Or was he just being polite?

"If Ben okays it." He shrugged. "He may still be upset with me. I plan to stop by the school and talk to him tomorrow." His face flushed. "I have some amends to make."

She couldn't believe he'd admit to such a thing.

He slid his hand across the tablecloth and snagged her fingers with his. She was torn. Part of her wanted to pull her hand away. The other part wanted to clutch his hand to her cheek, to kiss it, to weep over the beauty of him making such a move. His thumb stroked her palm like he did a thousand times before.

"Autumn, I have so much to say to you too." Tears filled his eyes. Tears? "I don't even know where to start. But God has been opening my eyes to things I've been blind to in recent years." He released her hand, took a tissue out of his pocket, and wiped his nose. He smiled back at her.

Something warm and powerful rushed through her. Was it too soon to hope he still loved her? Wanted to work things out with her? *Oh, Lord, is this the miracle I've been praying for?*

The waitress set their food down. Staring at her salad, Autumn didn't know if she could even take a bite. All she wanted to do was gaze into Gar's moist eyes and hear what had been going on in his life. How did this change in him come about?

Gar said a simple prayer of thanks and then dug into his food. Apparently, his nerves weren't keeping him from enjoying his meal. That he said a blessing in a public place wasn't lost on her, either.

She toyed with her food and stole glances at him. She loved how he smiled back at her when he caught her looking at him.

"I didn't know if you'd want me staying at the house. When I saw you had company, I got a room at a motel." He took a long drink of his tea.

"You could sleep on the couch." She was glad he knew he couldn't sleep in their room until they got things sorted out.

He shrugged. "Might be kind of awkward."

"Still, you could. How long are you planning to stay?" When he didn't answer quickly enough, she continued speaking. "I hope you can see the play. I know the seniors would love to have you there. I would . . . love for you to be there too."

"Of course, I wouldn't miss it."

His whispered words transformed in her heart to *I wouldn't miss seeing you.* Warmth filled the hollow ache that loneliness and abandonment had left in her chest.

"Back to your first question, I want you to know I'm here to stay."

What? He was staying?

He blew out a breath. "I'm hoping that I can be with you, as your husband, for the rest of my life ... if you'll have me."

If?

His tender smile sent fireworks zinging through her heart. She couldn't tear her gaze away from the sincerity in his eyes.

He twisted his napkin. "I know we've got a lot of things to talk about first, but I'm here for you if you need me."

"I don't know what to say." What had happened to the grumpy, self-centered man who left her nearly three months ago?

"I've been thinking how much we used to love canoeing on Saturday mornings. Would you be willing to go out on the water with me?" His shining eyes told her he was a little insecure about asking.

She had so much to do on Saturday. "I have a long afternoon practice." She cringed and waited for him to say something negative about her directing his show.

"I figured. And that's okay." He leaned back in his chair. "Getting out in the breeze for a little while would be good for you." He rocked his eyebrows and the old eagerness for an adventure was back in his eyes. "Especially on a busy Saturday morning. I'd get everything ready. You wouldn't have to do a thing but show up."

"It would be fun, but I don't know how I can squeeze it in." She thought over her tight schedule.

He took her hand and twirled her wedding ring with his fingers. "I need to talk with you about some things. Preferably not in a public place like this."

The way he touched her hand was distracting. Maybe she could get away from her schedule for an hour. "And we'll talk then?"

"Yes. Out on the canoe with a beautiful lady. What better place to share our hearts?"

He was flirting with her, and that made her heart pound faster.

"Will you join me?" He tipped his head and grinned.

"Um, okay." She swallowed down her concern over what he might have to tell her. Canoeing on the sound with him again would be nice. "Anything I should bring?"

"Have any fudge left?"

She chuckled. "I see where this is going. You like my chocolates."

"I do." He nodded slowly.

I do. Was he still talking about chocolate . . . or their love?

Thirty-six

Gar

On Friday morning, Gar prayed all the way from where he parked his car, through the empty school hallway, to the principal's office. This was where his running started. It was appropriate that he come full circle. He knew the Lord wanted him to make things right with Ben, even though he dreaded facing him. Of course, he'd never work for ECHS again. He didn't know if the principal would see him, but if he would, Gar was determined to be humble and apologize.

"Gar!" Marny grinned at him from behind the receptionist's desk. "It's so good to see you. Welcome back."

Her greeting eased some of his trepidation. "Thanks."

Mrs. Smith glared at him so sternly he didn't know what to do other than nod at her.

"You here to meet with Ben?" Marny hurried around the counter. "I'll check and see if he's available."

Mrs. Smith cleared her throat loudly. She stood and planted her veined fists against her pink skirt. "Is Mr. Whiffleman expecting you, Mr. Bevere? Because if he isn't, you'll have to make an appointment."

Gar knew the woman to be a strict rules enforcer. "I'm sorry for barging in here like this, Mrs. Smith. Would you mind checking to see if he has a moment to speak with me?"

"I'll do it." Marny took several steps toward Ben's closed door.

He felt a sudden thankfulness for Autumn's friend.

"Wait, Miss Blakely." Mrs. Smith strode for the door, effectively blocking Marny—or Gar—from entering. She rapped twice on the wood, then slipped into the office, pulling the door closed behind her.

Marny held out her hand toward Gar. "I'm so glad you're back. I've been praying for you and Autumn."

He shook her hand. "Thanks. I appreciate your checking on her while I've been gone."

"You here to stay?"

Her bold question took him by surprise. But he remembered her tendency to speak whatever was on her mind.

"I know it's none of my business." She grinned. "But are you?" She squeezed her hands together as if eager to hear his answer.

"I do plan to stay." The words felt good to say.

"Yes!" Marny threw her arms around his shoulders and hugged him. Just as quickly, she stepped back. "God sure answers prayer."

"He does." Gar chuckled.

The door swung open and he gulped. Mrs. Smith trudged toward him and pointed her finger at his chest. "He's surprised you're here on school property."

"Will he see me?"

"If you've come with peaceful intent, he has a few minutes." She pierced him with a threatening glare. "Mind you keep a civil tongue."

"Oh, I will. Thank you, Mrs. Smith." He approached the

door where he stood three months ago after foolishly shoving Ben. Had a lifetime passed? His heart was in a different place now. He wanted to follow God and love his wife more than ever. But right that minute, the thing most on his mind was running for the exit and never stepping foot in this school again. His heart hammered in his throat. He'd never apologized to someone like he was about to do. With clammy palms, he twisted the doorknob and walked into the principal's office.

Ben sat behind his wooden desk, his arms folded against the surface, his expression wary. He swayed his hand toward the black chair in front of his desk. "I'm surprised to see you, Gar."

Gar dropped into the chair. "I'm surprised myself." He folded and unfolded his hands.

Ben eyed him curiously.

"I'm here to say, I'm sorry for what I did. Grabbing you the way I did, becoming so angry, was a terrible mistake." He sucked in a breath. "You were right to fire me."

"I appreciate that." Ben visibly relaxed. "What's going on now?"

"I'm back." Gar spread out his hands. "I have a long road of amends to make. Seeing you and apologizing was at the top of my list."

Ben nodded, his poker face not revealing a thing.

In the silence, Gar gazed around the room, taking in framed pictures on the wall, some of them of his theatrical productions. "The Lord has been working on me and changing me. Waking me up, you might say. I strayed, but I've repented. Please forgive me for my grave error in judgment and behavior, and for acting so badly?"

Ben sighed and nodded. "I do forgive you."

Relief washed through his heart. "Thank you."

"But I can't rehire you."

"Oh, no, I realize that." Gar leaned forward. "Honestly, that isn't why I'm here. I've had a lot of time to think things through. I'm praying about what the Lord would have me do next."

"Are you and Autumn—?"

"Not yet. But I hope to make amends with her too."

"She's a real trooper. Taking on your classes. The play." Ben glanced at him sharply. "That's not why you're here, is it?"

"No." Although Gar needed to ask Ben's permission to help Autumn with the staging problems, he felt reluctant.

"Can you accept a word of advice?" Ben's eyebrows drew together.

"Certainly."

"Stay away from Ms. Delaney."

Sasha. "Of course." Gar agreed with that admonishment, although accepting the warning from his previous employer didn't come easily. He knew he'd still have to make a phone call to Sasha—with Autumn's knowledge—to apologize to her also.

"Thank you for stopping by. I appreciate your honesty." Ben stood.

Honesty.

When Ben reached out his hand, Gar shook it, even though he fretted over what remained to be said.

"There is one other thing."

"Oh?"

"Autumn asked for my help with a few staging technicalities." Gar stuffed his hands in his jacket pocket. "I didn't know whether you'd approve of me being on location. I won't go against you and do it without your blessing. But she . . . needs me, and I'd like to be there for her now."

The room fell silent.

Ben seemed to be pondering his request. He sighed. "If Autumn is seeking your help with the show, and since you spoke with me first, I don't see any reason to object." He patted Gar's shoulder. "I'm glad you've turned your life around. I wish you the best."

"Thank you." Relieved the exchange had gone okay, Gar entered the reception area. He waved goodbye toward Mrs. Smith. She hardly glanced up from her typing.

Marny rushed over to him. "Everything all right?"

"Yes."

"Getting your old job back?" Her shoulders bunched up, and she grinned. "Sorry, I'm nosy."

"No, I'm not." He shook his head, trying not to find any sting in her words. He was eager to get out of the school before anyone else saw him and asked the same question.

"Tell Autumn I said hi!"

Gar waved at her as he exited the office, then made his way toward the main doors. The path was bittersweet as he passed the long glass case displaying clippings of his theatrical successes. He paused to notice Dorothy's red slippers. Annie's wig. Captain Hook's hook. Tink's wings. An unexpected rush of emotion gripped him. He'd lost so much. But with God working in his life, he gained a lot too. Then averting an attack of nostalgia too difficult to swallow, he ran the rest of the way to his car.

Thirty-seven

Gar

Standing on an extended ladder, Gar adjusted the lights so they hit the stage without casting eerie shadows on Chase's and Shelley's faces. He couldn't help but detect the flatly delivered dialogue between the two. Something was missing. Where was their heart? Their passion for their characters? Did they always practice with such low energy?

By what he could tell, Shelley was portraying an evil queen conniving to become ruler of two countries. Yet her voice was mild mannered, meek even. Chase lacked a kingly dominance. Wouldn't he be combative toward a wicked ruler endeavoring to take control of his throne? Should Gar mention something to Autumn? Criticizing her first attempts at directing wouldn't be conducive to stirring up romance or healing the past between them. Silence would probably be the better part of valor.

After he fixed the lights, he joined the techs in the booth and helped sort out some of the sound issues. He told one of them to go onstage and tweak the monitors' positions so the actors could hear the entrance music better. He'd noticed the delay in the last two scenes.

"How's it going?" he asked the main tech, Gus Thompson, who'd worked quite a few of Gar's shows.

"Ah, you know, last week flubs." The senior shrugged.

"Worse this year?" Maybe he shouldn't make waves.

"Definitely worse." Gus chuckled. "But we won't mention it."

"Right." What about when Autumn asked him what he thought of the play? Could he avoid telling her the truth? Difficult to do when he was trying to face each situation with honesty. Gar gulped at the thought of critiquing his estranged wife's efforts when they still hadn't had their talk.

Tomorrow morning couldn't come fast enough. This afternoon, after his conversation with Ben, he cleaned out the canoe, double-checked the patch he put on the hull last year, and got all the gear ready. He was excited to take another adventure on the sound. But more than anything, he longed to clear the air with Autumn, even though that conversation might be the thing that ripped them apart for good. Unless God did a miracle—which was exactly what Gar was counting on.

His attention was drawn back to the lines being said onstage.

Chase stood with his hands stiffly at his sides. "You commandeering my throne, my kingdom?"

Gar knew Chase was a new actor, but by now Autumn should have coached him on how to deliver the words as if they were his own, from his heart—like a king—and not simply lines he memorized.

Shelley, whom Gar had directed for three years, laughed, and he was sure her tone was supposed to sound wicked, not girly. "If you are weak, then my country which borders yours is weak, also. Let us join hands so more can be accomplished." She extended her hand to him.

Chase pivoted away on the ball of his foot as if he were a basketball player instead of a royal.

Every impulse in Gar made him want to run down the center aisle and yell, "Cut!" But he didn't have the right. Autumn was the director. Still, his senses were on high alert to challenge the actors to give it their all. The play was in five days. Why were they holding back? Maybe he should leave the theater and not get involved. Autumn asked him for technical assistance, nothing more. Talking to her about her students' lack of stage presence would undermine the real discussion they needed to have.

"Hard to believe the play's a week away." Gus shook his head.

Gar didn't answer. All he could do was sigh. And pray.

At the end of practice, Autumn clapped and cheered and told the kids how well they did.

Really? He'd better keep his mouth shut and walk away. Maybe he could slip out the back door before she questioned him about anything.

"What did you think of that disaster?" Jewel Pollard stood in the doorway of the sound booth, her arms crossed, her french manicured nails tapping a rhythm against the playbook she clutched to her chest.

Man, if only he'd left the building sooner.

"Well?"

"Needs a little work, is all." That was safe. What play didn't need a bit of help the last week?

She laughed like the evil queen should have laughed. "Why Gar, now that you're back, maybe we can have a real show." Her teeth glistened his way, then she twirled around and stomped toward Autumn who appeared to be gathering up her stuff.

Oh, no. What had he done? He didn't want the outspoken parent to corner Autumn and say something obnoxious.

"Jewel, wait up." He rushed after her.

Actors passed him going the other way.

"Hi, Mr. Bevere."

"What did you think, Mr. B.?"

He smiled and said hello, but his main objective was to reach Shelley's mom. "Jewel."

She whirled around and glared at him. "What?"

"What are you doing?"

"I'm having a word with our director." She turned on her four-inch heels.

"Let me." He could kick himself for suggesting such a thing.

She glanced over her shoulder. "You'll tell her the show stinks?"

"Of course not. And neither should you."

"I certainly will tell her that."

"Please, don't."

She arched an eyebrow. "Are you offering to fix it?"

Hardly. He might be back, but he wasn't going to insult his wife. And he wasn't going to allow Jewel to, either. Maybe he could offer Autumn some mild suggestions without sounding critical. "I'll see what I can do. Don't say a word to her, okay?" He held his hands together in a begging gesture.

A smile creased her reddened lips. "You promise to speak with her tonight?"

Gar nodded, hating himself for agreeing.

"Fine." She turned away, and her heels clicked across the auditorium floor.

He let out a long sigh.

"What did she want?" Autumn stepped beside him.

"Not much." He could see how exhausted she looked. He remembered the days of stress and long to-do lists that never seemed to end before Opening Night. He wished for a way to make things easier on her. This production was thrust on her because of his absence. He shouldn't have promised Jewel he'd speak with Autumn tonight. She needed rest—and probably some chocolate.

"Sorry I didn't have time to be with you today." She smiled apologetically.

A little part of his heart tore. "You don't have anything to be sorry about. I crashed in on you during the busiest week of your year."

She seemed to be thinking. "I never realized how involved you were through all those productions, how much you might have needed my support during a show. I'm sorry I wasn't there for you like I should have been. I feel like I've come to understand you better through this experience of directing."

Her words poured over him, sweet and soothing. How could he say what he needed to say now?

His cell phoned buzzed, and he glanced at the screen.

I'm counting on you.

Jewel. If he didn't follow through with his promise, was she warning him she'd take care of it tomorrow?

"How about some coffee?" He grabbed his coat. "I know it's late."

"We're still going out on the water in the morning, right?"

"Yeah sure." His heart beat faster. "You too tired?"

"I'm beat. As much as I'd like to chat with you, I'm so . . . sleepy." She yawned.

"Could I talk with you for just a minute?" Dare he bring up the actors' weaknesses?

She shuffled the load she carried in her arms. "What is it?"

"Let me pack those for you." He grabbed her pile of books before she could object.

"Thanks." She smiled at him. "Hey, thanks for fixing the lights and monitors. That helped a lot."

"You're welcome."

As they walked side by side to the exit, the lights shut off behind them, probably thanks to the stage manager.

"What did you think of—"

Oh, no. The question he dreaded.

"The stage?" she finished.

"Oh, the stage?" A safe topic. "It looks really nice." Simple, but authentic.

"Not as great as you and Sasha would have done, I know." She squinted at him in a way that made him think she suspected something had happened between him and his previous stage designer.

He still dreaded talking with her about that, even though he knew he had to be honest. However, now wasn't the time. "A simple stage is best sometimes."

She nodded, and he wondered if his words had sounded demeaning. *Lord, what do I say to make things better and yet speak the truth? Everything I say seems wrong.*

They reached her car at the far end of the lot where teachers parked.

"What did you want to talk with me about?" She dug into her purse and pulled out her key.

"You've done a nice job with the kids. I can see they really like you." That was the truth.

"Thanks." Her tired gaze met his, and she seemed to relax. "Must have been hard for you to watch and not want to take over directing."

She nailed that.

She laughed. "I wouldn't blame you if you did want to. I'm not as creative as you." She shrugged. "I'm giving it my best shot though."

"Of course, you are." He was more reluctant by the second to mention anything negative.

"What did you think?" She leaned her back against the car.

"I saw Jewel yakking your ear off. She's pretty vocal about her disappointment over my casting, my directing, and my staging." She heaved a sigh. "Name anything having to do with ECHS theater this year, and 'lousy' is written across my forehead." Tears filled her eyes, and she blinked rapidly.

With each indictment, he felt more like a heel. Was he overly critical during tonight's practice? Had the actors, perhaps, just been off? Sometimes that happened. Maybe he shouldn't say anything. Autumn was tired and vulnerable and would take offense easily. But if he didn't relay Jewel's concerns, there was a chance the parent would call her in the morning and unload in a tactless manner.

He met her weary gaze again. "Everything will work out. It always does." He couldn't bring himself to say something that would make her feel worse. What he wanted to do was take her in his arms, to hold her and keep all the bad stuff from affecting her. But he knew he didn't have that right, yet.

"See you tomorrow?" Her eyes glistened in the darkness.

Nights when they were college-aged and they stood on her mother's porch, holding hands, kissing, and saying their goodnights roamed through his thoughts. When did he forget how to romance her?

"Can't wait." He leaned close and kissed her cheek, hoping that wasn't pushing things. "See you at the marina at nine?"

"Okay." She nodded and got into the car.

He waved and watched her drive away.

Hopefully, Jewel wouldn't call before he had a chance to talk with Autumn in the morning. He'd head back to the motel and spend some time praying. He knew tomorrow's discussion could go south in a hurry, but he prayed God would intervene and bring healing between them.

Thirty-eight

Gar

Gar had everything ready in the canoe—two life vests, two paddles, and a thermos filled with coffee—and he had a special present for Autumn hidden in his jacket pocket. He'd placed the boat into the water with the stern partially resting on the cement boat ramp while he waited for her to arrive.

Nine o'clock came and went.

He'd offered to bring her to the marina, but she said she preferred to drive her own car so she could head to the school after their boat ride. He kicked a pebble with his shoe, then paced across the cement, pondering his situation.

On Monday he planned to search for employment. He assumed he wouldn't be able to find an educational job without a reference from Ben. Ty said he'd give him a recommendation for his work at TK Automotive, but changing tires indefinitely didn't sound appealing. Although, after working with Kyle and Ty, he appreciated a laborer's life. Plenty of times, he went home with a sore back and abrasions on his hands to show for his manual efforts. Still, he hoped to find something more in line with his training. Last night, he scrolled through online job listings on his laptop, but nothing stood out to him.

"Gar?"

He turned at her voice. She stood at the top of the boat ramp dressed in dark browns that matched her hair, and her pants were tucked into her wine-colored rubber boots. From here, it looked like she was trimmer than when she drove over to see him that Saturday. Must have been all those days at the gym she told him about. He hated that she might not have been eating well in his absence. He swallowed down the guilt and focused on her. He wished they'd already had their talk and that he had the liberty to hug her to him and kiss her like he wanted to. He'd tell her how beautiful she looked. How much he loved her and wanted to be with her.

"Sorry, I'm late." She stuffed her hands in her pockets, her expression tight. "I had a phone call from Jewel."

A thud landed in his gut.

"She had an earful for me, as you can guess." She met his gaze, hurt etched in her eyes. "You knew she'd call me, didn't you?"

He groaned. "I was afraid she might." Now he wished he explained Jewel's concerns last night.

"Is what she said true?"

"No." Not that he knew exactly what she said, but he could guess. He fingered the little box in his pocket, hoping he'd still get the chance to give her the necklace he bought. "It was an off practice, that's all. It happens." He nodded toward the boat. "Ready to go?"

She didn't move. "Jewel said you agree with her that I'm a terrible director."

"That's a lie. I never said that." Jewel could twist things faster than—

"Says you thought the play was horrible, and the actors don't know what they're doing." She glared at him.

"You've got to believe me, I wouldn't say those things." He swallowed down guilt over the judgmental thoughts he had entertained during yesterday's practice. "When I heard Chase and Shelley, I—"

"You what? Were d-disappointed?"

Anything he said now would be offensive. So much for spending a few hours paddling out on the water with her and finding a quiet place to bare his heart. With a groan, he dragged the canoe across the cement, cringing at the scraping sound it made. He trudged up the slope. "I'm sorry Jewel called you like that." He wanted to take her hand, to reassure her of his love and commitment, but her wary expression kept him from doing so. "Look, she was going to tell you off last night. I stopped her by saying I'd talk to you, but then I didn't want to hurt you."

"More than you already have, you mean?" She turned away sharply, and her sudden sobs took him by surprise.

He blew out a breath of uncertainty. Should he even touch her? Of course, he needed to. He took her in his arms and pulled her against his chest. "I'm so sorry," he whispered against her ear. "I never want to hurt you again." He rocked her and ran his palm down her hair. He held her like that for several minutes, and she didn't resist him. His agenda didn't matter. Maybe now wasn't the best time to talk to her. She had so much on her plate, and this thing with Jewel could fester. "If you'd rather, we could go get coffee and relax for a while before your practice. We can take the canoe out another time."

She stepped back and wiped her face with both hands. She shook her head. "No, I'd still like to go paddling with you. I've been looking forward to it."

That surprised him.

"But let's not discuss the play, okay? It has me feeling too unsettled." Her moist eyes gazed into his.

"Absolutely." He sighed, thankful she still wanted to go out on the water with him. But he didn't know whether he should bring up any serious subjects. Maybe they could just enjoy the experience of canoeing together again.

She walked beside him down the boat ramp. Gar grabbed her life vest and helped her put it on. He shoved the canoe hard to get it moving against the rough slope, and then the bow slipped into the water. He held her hand while she climbed in and sat down on the front seat. Then he pushed the craft fully into the water and leaped into the stern. He dropped onto the back seat and slipped into his own life vest. Both of them picked up paddles and used them to shove against the ramp beneath the shallow water. In moments, as if they were dancers with memorized routines, they were paddling in tandem against the breeze. They didn't need to rehearse instructions or have anyone say in which side to dip the paddle and when. They had their own rhythm.

They cut through minor waves as they passed in front of what looked like a thousand sailboats moored at the marina, their masts pointing vertically to the sky. He imagined how much fun it would be to set sail for parts unknown in such a magnificent craft, just him and Autumn exploring the seven seas. Would she be game for an adventure like that? Maybe when they retired.

They passed a dredging machine, and its rumbling operation seemed like the exact opposite of the natural setting he hoped to find for their talk, if they were still going to have one. "Turning," he called to her. He plunged the paddle into the port side near the stern so the canoe would make a slow turn. Autumn paddled on the opposite side while he steered them away from the noise and Jetty Island—which he'd love to explore with her another time. He paddled hard again, and Autumn did the same. The wind against his face felt invigorating.

He nodded to a guy in a kayak heading back toward the docking area. It was late in the season for boating, but he enjoyed getting to do so without the busy waterways of tourist season. He worked his upper arms and chest muscles as he stroked through deeper water. They kept up their rhythm for a while until they were far into the sound, and then he stopped paddling altogether. He could still see the moored sailboats and the docks in the distance. "Autumn?"

She glanced over her shoulder.

"I brought your coffee."

"Oh, yeah?" She set her paddle down. The canoe rocked gently as she twisted around on her seat and faced him. Gar opened the thermos and poured the steaming brew, then passed the cup to her. Her eyes lit up as she took a drink. "White chocolate mocha. Thanks for bringing my favorite."

"You're welcome." He knew her favorites almost as well as he knew his own.

She nodded toward the trees on the west side of the sound. "This is beautiful. I've missed our Saturday morning outings."

"Me too." He breathed deeply. The water lapped gently against the sides of the canoe, and he hoped no more wind picked up or they'd have to paddle hard for shore. Gazing into his wife's eyes and feeling the slight bobbing of the canoe relaxed him, made him think this moment might be perfect for talking to her.

She passed the cup back to him, just like she did a hundred times before. Their fingers touched in the exchange, and then he drank the hot liquid.

* * * *

For Autumn, paddling was like a hard workout at the gym. Spending that energy helped her tune out Jewel's negative words. How she wished she hadn't taken the woman's call. Then her feelings toward Gar might be more civil than they were. That he thought poorly of her production hurt. Of course, maybe the woman *had* lied. Either way, she and Gar could talk about that later. Right now, she needed to focus on the fact they were together, sharing a cup of coffee like old times. He said he was going to explain everything while they were out here on the sound. How many times over the last two-and-a-half months had she wished for that very thing? She needed to listen to him and hear his heart, despite Jewel's criticism. *Lord, please help me.*

"What did you want to talk with me about?" She wasn't trying to rush him, but she did have to get back to town for this afternoon's practice.

His shuttered eyes seemed reluctant to meet her gaze. He sighed, then pointed toward the shore. "Remember the first time we tried launching the canoe there?"

She remembered. The waves almost tipped them overboard.

"That was fun." He grinned.

She chuckled at his expression. "You recall the story differently than I do."

He leaned forward and took her hand. Instantly, his expression became contrite. "Autumn, I'm sorry for everything. I ruined so much between us."

His unexpected change from laughter to grief tugged on her heart. His dark eyes flooded with tears. She didn't pull her hand from his, couldn't seem to move if she wanted to.

"I know I've hurt you." He swallowed hard but didn't brush the tears off his cheeks. "I left you, lied to you, treated you abominably, but really, the truth is—"

Was he going to tell her they were finished? Would he have gone to all this effort to bring her coffee and take her out on the canoe if he were going to say goodbye?

He looked away, staring at the shoreline as if remembering

that day so long ago when he righted the canoe and kept her from going overboard.

"The thing is"—he repeated—"by the way I was acting, and how I was feeling, I left you before that argument with Ben and the trouble with the school ever started."

She knew that was true.

He rubbed his palm over the outside of her hand. "I failed you as a husband and as a friend. I feel horrible to have sunk so low." A deep sigh rumbled out of him.

She feared what he wasn't saying.

"I-I crossed some lines that I regret."

Her heart beat faster. "With Sasha?"

He stared toward the bottom of the canoe for several moments with a puzzled expression. Was he avoiding looking her in the eye?

"We're taking in water."

That wasn't the deeply honest response she was expecting. She glanced downward. The toes of her boots were covered in seawater. "Uh-oh. What do we do?"

Gar scooped up his paddle. "Head for shore. Fast."

Autumn swiveled around on the bow seat, nearly tipping the canoe in her haste. She scooped up her paddle and plunged it into the sea, but she could see the land was a long way off. "We'll never make it."

"Old patch must've torn," he yelled from behind her. "I checked it yesterday."

They were already shooting through the water, Gar's paddle plowing the waves. Good thing she'd been using the rowing machine at the gym. She might not be able to keep up with his strokes, but she'd make a valiant effort. Plunge, pull, plunge, pull. She glanced at the floor. Four inches? She yanked the paddle to the left, then right, not even caring if she was opposite Gar or not. The canoe was more difficult to maneuver the more water it took in, and way more tippy. Each time she switched sides to paddle, the boat leaned farther in that direction. Six inches of water?

"The crack must be getting wider." Gar sounded panicked. "Autumn"—he shouted—"I'm sorry."

For his wrongs? Or that they might be going down? She remembered the Port of Everett's warning sign: "Cold Water Can Kill!" Could they swim to shore in such chilly seawater? Her teeth were chattering already. "Should I b-bail?" Where was their bailing bucket?

"It's too late. We'll get as close to shore before—"

Panic sizzled up her throat. Before they plunged into the sound? An icy rush of liquid filled her boots. She gasped. *Dear Lord, help. Rescue us.*

Behind her, she could hear Gar's labored breathing. "Take. Off. Your. Boots."

She couldn't believe this was happening. All the times they verbally went through rescue scenarios for canoeing, this had to happen today. There was no way she was jumping in the water. Maybe another boat would rescue them. Still, she tugged off her favorite boots and wet socks.

"Autumn?" That panicked voice haunted her dreams sometimes. "If the boat . . . goes down, stay . . . with it. I'll get you to shore."

Was he trying to be her hero? She remembered the time he saved the boy. "Okay." But she didn't plan to jump into the dark water. Her legs already knew how cold it was. Swimming in such temperatures had to be dangerous—deadly.

"Stick with the canoe and keep your legs moving." His instructions sounded desperate. "You have your lifejacket. You'll be fine."

Fine was an exaggeration. When the water reached her knees and the canoe pitched hard to the left, she screamed. Now she wished she'd agreed with Gar's suggestion to go to a coffee shop instead of doing this.

The splashing sound of Gar plunging into the saltwater startled her. "Gar!" The boat tipped, nearly spilling her into the drink. Did he expect her to follow him? Please, no. *Lord, save us both.*

Gar surfaced and bobbed toward her. "S-sorry. I should have warned you." He grabbed hold of the gunwale. "It's n-not so bad once you g-get in."

"Y-yeah, right." The wind had picked up. She was already freezing, and her teeth chattered. She sucked in cold air, panic racing through her at the thought of joining him in the sea.

This morning when she anticipated him sharing his heart, and perhaps reconciling with her, she never imagined such a catastrophe.

He took her free hand. "It'll be okay. Stay near me and the canoe."

Her body was halfway soaked already, but nothing in her wanted to fall into those waves. There didn't seem to be any other choice. Gar's gaze pleaded with her as if begging her to jump in the water. She shook her head. *I can't.* But then, she lunged forward into the chilly depths, and icy seawater rolled over her head, suffocating her for a few seconds. She kicked her feet and craned her head back until her mouth cleared the surface of the water, then she gasped for air. "S-s-s-o-o cold." Still holding Gar's hand, she kicked toward the canoe and clung tightly to it. Her teeth rattled. Her body felt frozen.

"I need you to float for a couple of minutes while I flip the canoe."

"What? No." She pictured the edge of the boat hitting him in the head and Gar drowning because she didn't know how to save him. "Tell me w-what to do. I'll help you."

He unfastened his life vest and shoved it toward her.

"Clutch this to your chest. It'll keep your upper body out of the cold temperatures longer."

"What about you?

"I have to dive underwater to flip the boat. It'll be h-hard"— he was shivering too—"but I've done this before by myself."

"H-how?" Saltwater sloshed into her mouth and she spit out the nasty taste.

"Trust me. Let go for a few minutes."

Trust him? Let go? In this, or in everything?

She released the canoe and the waves bobbed her backward. She wrapped her arms around Gar's life vest. How could they survive? "G-Gar!" She wanted to touch his face one last time. To kiss the lips she loved and lost. Now she was too far away from him—and shivering uncontrollably. Would hypothermia set in before he righted the boat? Water splashed into her mouth, and she spit again.

Maybe she could swim for shore and get help. But it was too far away. Gar told her to wait. What did he say? Kick her legs? She scissor kicked as hard as she could, hoping not to encounter any fish—or anything else—beneath the surface.

She watched as Gar grabbed the paddles and did something with them, probably secured them beneath the seats. He took hold of the gunwale and rocked the canoe until water sloshed over the edge. Then he lunged upward and with his upper body well above the surface, like a gymnast's rigid form on a pommel horse, he pressed downward against the gunwale. The other side of the boat tipped partway up, releasing more water. She could see his hair was drenched. He spit, then did the same thing again, lunging upward and his muscled arms bearing down on the edge of the canoe. It took several tries, but the whole thing suddenly turned, topside down. Gar lunged out of the way, then lifted his hand and dove under the water.

"Gar!" She kept kicking, but she could tell her numb legs weren't moving as well as before, and she was drifting. She felt sleepy, not as cold anymore, which was nice. She blinked slowly, her teeth chattering. Was today the day she'd die? Before she and Gar had a chance to make up? Before she got to hear his heart? *Even though I walk through the valley of the shadow of death . . .* Wait. No! She would not die that easily. *Stay awake!* She forced her legs and her hands to keep treading water.

* * * *

Underneath the boat, Gar breathed in the air pocket above the floating benches. It had been years since he flipped a canoe, but he remembered succeeding at it back in college. Today he had strong motivation—he had to save his wife. He sucked in a ragged breath, then pressed upward on the portside gunwale while his legs scissor kicked. The canoe broke the water's suction, but not at a steep enough angle to turn it over. Back into the cold water, he dropped. How long could they last in these temperatures that had to be fifty or so degrees? He had to keep moving. He breathed in the air space, then tried shoving the canoe upward again, his muscles shaking with fatigue and cold. When he broke the surface, he gulped in great gasps of air, before plunging into the frigid water again. Determinedly, he shoved upward and flailed his legs. As the boat turned upright, he nearly flew over the top. He held fast to the center thwarts, his body numb with exhaustion.

"Autumn?" Where was she? He called her name again without seeing her. When she bobbed out from under a wave, he heard her sputtering. He slipped back into the water and swam as hard as he could in her direction, hoping the canoe wouldn't float far. "Autumn!"

Her eyes blinked open. "G-Gar?"

As soon as he reached her, he kissed her cold lips. "Come on, love. Let's go home." He kicked and side stroked with one arm while he helped maneuver her toward the canoe. "I'll help you climb in."

"It . . . has . . . a . . . hole." Her words came slowly.

"You need to get out of the water."

"What about you?"

"It will go farther with one person."

"But—"

He helped her reach her arms over the side. "You have to pull yourself into the center. Grab the thwarts." She reached out and gripped the aluminum bars, but he could see she was struggling. He shoved against her backside, and she collapsed onto the canoe floor. Water sloshed in with her, but that couldn't be helped.

"I'll kick at the stern. Can you steer?" *God, give me the strength to see her back to shore.*

"W-want me to paddle?" She grabbed one from under the benches.

"Okay." He doubted she could do much by the way she was shaking, but the effort might warm her a little.

He grabbed the back of the boat and kicked his legs in the seawater for all he was worth. He was so cold and exhausted, but he'd get her back to land, even if he didn't make it. Was this what Ty meant about being willing to do anything for his wife—even giving up his own life? He kicked forcefully, and it seemed a power beyond his own ability fueled his legs.

Autumn dipped the paddle into the water with more grit than he imagined her having. She kept working even though water filled up in the canoe around her. He continued kicking, but his energy was waning.

"Hey!" a voice shouted, not too far away. "Need help?"

Gar glanced up. A kayaker was approaching them fast. "Yes. Help!" Then he thanked God for sending them a miracle.

"Name's Flynn." The single-seat kayak skimmed next to their partially submerged canoe. Flynn pointed at Gar. "Get out of the water, man. You're turning blue."

With difficulty, Gar pulled himself over the gunwale and then dropped to the floor in about eight inches of water.

"Here." Flynn passed him an empty plastic butter container. "Start bailing."

At least Gar was still shivering. That had to be a good thing, even though he felt shaky and clumsy. He grabbed the plastic tub and bailed as fast as he could.

Flynn pulled a rope out of his pack and passed it to Autumn between their bobbing boats. "Tie this to the bow."

Her hands didn't appear to be moving well, but she followed the man's instructions, while Gar kept bailing. It seemed the water was coming in as fast as he was scooping, but he wouldn't give up.

"Let's head for shore. I already called 911." Flynn resumed paddling.

Gar didn't disagree. His body felt wretchedly weak, but he was mostly concerned with Autumn's condition. If he'd only double-checked the patch today. Had it torn when he scraped the hull across the ramp's cement?

"S-sweetheart?"

Autumn gazed at him dully. She'd stopped paddling.

He reached out and touched her shoulder. "You're going to be okay. They'll get you w-warm." He bailed some more, wishing he could paddle the boat at the same time. "Autumn, stay awake!" he yelled at her.

She nodded, then became very still.

"I love you, Autumn Bevere. Stay awake!"

Again, she nodded but gave no other response.

God, have mercy. Please save us. Help my wife.

Flynn paddled with a steady stroke, the tow line taut between the two crafts, but it was slow going. When two ambulances pulled into the docking area with their sirens sounding, Gar felt a rush of adrenaline. He scooped up his paddle and plunged it into the sound over and over, not caring about his bad form, just needing to get them to land so Autumn could receive help.

Flynn led them toward the dock, and Gar used the paddle to steer them closer.

Experienced hands lifted Autumn up on the dock where a gurney waited.

Gar wanted to go with her, but his legs were so numb he could barely move. Two paramedics assisted him out of the canoe and onto another gurney. He wanted to see his wife, to make sure she was okay. As they wheeled him to the ambulance, he prayed and begged God to save her life, and to please give him one more chance to make things right.

Thirty-nine

Autumn

Autumn woke up and stretched beneath a thick and cozy comforter, warmed all the way to her toes—a feeling she'd never take for granted again. It took a few moments to realize she was stretched out on her own couch at home next to—? Mmm . . . a nice warm body. She squinted at wool socks peeking out of the blanket near her face. Gar's? His legs, covered in warm-up pants, were next to her torso. And her legs appeared to be resting against his chest? Where were her feet? She wiggled her navy socks near Gar's ear. An inch closer and she could tickle his temple. When had they become so comfortable with each other?

Must have been somewhere between the hours after arriving at the hospital, the IV units and warming blankets, the doctor saying it was a miracle they both survived, their release to go home and rest, and this moment. Gar wore a peaceful expression at the other end of the couch, his eyes closed, his face relaxed, and she assumed he was sleeping. They made quite the cozy couple, considering they were hardly speaking a week ago.

"Oh good, you're awake." Jimmy popped up over the back of the couch. His wide brown eyes glistened. "Thought you two would never open your eyes."

"How long have I been sleeping?" She rotated her stiff shoulders and groaned.

Gar made a muffled groan of his own.

"Five or six hours."

"What?" Autumn sat up too fast. *Whoa, dizzy.* She dropped back into the nest she vacated. "I have play practice. I can't miss it."

Sarah's humming preceded her. "Here's tea for both of you."

"And fudge." Jimmy grinned and offered her a small plate of chocolates.

"My kind of treat." Autumn scooted to a sitting position and wiggled her fingers to make sure they worked before reaching out for a cup of tea and a piece of fudge. "Thanks."

Gar's eyelids blinked open, and he touched her toes. "How are you feeling?" His voice sounded gravelly. She always loved his just-waking-up tones.

"Tired, but comfy." She sipped the tea. "Tangerine and chamomile. Perfect."

"Here you go, Mr. Bevere." Sarah set his cup on a coaster on the coffee table and smiled at him.

Sarah smiling at Gar? Relaxed around him? That was weird, considering she'd been so suspicious of him before.

"Call me Gar. And thanks." He yawned and plucked a piece of fudge from the plate Autumn had set on her lap. "I hate to tell you, but I think you missed practice."

"I did? What will Jewel say?"

"No worries." Sarah patted Autumn's shoulder. "I called Miss Marny, and she took care of it."

Autumn stared at her houseguest, her reasoning returning slowly. "You asked Marny to cover for me as director?"

"Mmhmm."

"It was my idea." Jimmy thumped his chest with his finger. "Miss Marny teaches Sunday school at the mission sometimes. She's full of good ideas. Always trying to get us to act out one Bible story or another."

"That so?" Gar asked.

"Uh-huh."

"That Jewel-person called and complained about you not being there." Sarah dropped into the chair opposite the couch and shrugged. "I told her where she could take a hike."

Autumn groaned. "She'll hate me forever."

Jimmy grinned. "Sarah and I solved everything."

"I guess I have nothing to worry about with you around." She smiled at the boy.

He grinned as if it were the first compliment of his whole life.

"Hey, now." Gar ruffled Jimmy's hair. "Don't go getting ideas about taking my place as the man of the house."

Jimmy cackled.

"I see you guys have met." Autumn gazed back and forth between the three of them.

Sarah nodded. "We got our little misunderstanding worked out."

"As long as I behave, she won't point a knife at my back." Gar held up his teacup as if to make a toast.

"Hmm." Autumn gripped her cup between both hands, enjoying the heat. "You know, if the play's a flop, Jewel will call for my termination."

Gar chuckled. "Welcome to my world."

Something about that *was* funny. A giggle started in the pit of her stomach and bubbled her tea right up her nose. Soon she was laughing hard, and tears were rolling down her cheeks. She scrubbed them away and sniffed. "I can't believe how awful this day turned out."

Gar shook his head. "Not my most romantic idea."

That started her laughing and crying again.

Sarah handed her a Kleenex.

Autumn blew her nose, trying to regain control of her emotions. "How will I ever pull off this play in four days?"

"It'll work out."

He looked so all-knowing she wanted to kick him. "Easy for you to say."

He tickled her foot a little.

"Don't you dare."

He did it again and grinned mischievously.

She laughed back at him and shoved both feet against him. He toppled to the floor, and whatever was left of his tea splattered all over him.

Jimmy roared with laughter. Even Sarah snickered.

"I cannot believe you did that." Gar stood and glowered down at her mockingly.

"You deserved it."

"Here I was going to offer to help you." He plopped down on the end of the couch and wiped the sleeve of his sweatshirt over his face.

"With the play?"

He stared at her so deeply, his gaze like liquid love washing over her, she could barely swallow.

"Oh, Gar . . ."

Sarah motioned for Jimmy to follow her into the kitchen.

Gar reached for her hand, toying with her wedding band. "I'm not trying to take over. Honest. I just want to help you."

She didn't pull her hand away, since it seemed they were beyond that now. Although, she remembered just before the canoe filled with water, he was sharing something about crossing a line. What did he mean by that? She slipped her fingers free of his. "What did you have in mind?"

He sighed like he didn't want to continue.

She rolled her eyes toward the textured ceiling. "I know Jewel complained about me to you. She said you agreed with her."

"And I denied that."

"Yet you think I need help."

He sank back against the couch and drew her feet onto his lap. "Let's say if you were to ask me to give some last-minute coaching to the lead actors, I might be willing to do that." He shrugged. "It's your show. Your call."

She scooted down into a more comfortable position and heaved a sigh. "More like Jewel's . . ." Her eyelids felt so heavy, she dozed off again.

When she woke up, Gar was still sitting at the end of the couch. Her feet were stretched out across his lap.

"'Love is not love which alters when it alteration finds, or bends with the remover to remove:'" he whispered to her. "'O no; it is an ever-fixed mark, that looks on tempests, and is never shaken.'" He continued reciting the lines of the familiar sonnet. "'Love alters not with his brief hours and weeks, but bears it out even to the edge of doom.'"

They had come to the very edge of doom in the last twenty-four hours and lived. She sighed and stretched. It was good to hear Gar reciting poetry to her again. His wooing tones made her feel safe and cared for.

He clasped her fingers. "I was sitting here, thanking God for answering my prayers. For helping us survive the cold and for sending Flynn to pull us ashore. I'm so thankful you're alive."

"I'm glad you're here with me too." Her gaze became lost in his until, too sleepy to keep them open, her eyes closed again.

But even in her drowsy state, something nagged at her. What was it Gar had been about to tell her before their untimely disaster?

Forty

Winter

Three days had passed since Winter and Ty arrived back in Spokane. Neil and Deb remained in Bend to try to minister to Randi. So far, their efforts to reach the woman in jail had been foiled. She didn't want to see any of them, and they couldn't force her to converse. But Deborah wanted to show their previous teammate God's love, despite the extensive bruises she sustained.

Winter's lips were tender where the rag had been tied. She was thankful no infection had set in. Her jaw still ached, as did her shoulders from where her hands were secured behind her back, but she was feeling better each day. Ty suffered two broken ribs. Fortunately, none of his internal organs had been lacerated. He kept saying he was okay, but she could tell he was miserable every time he twisted or moved.

They spent the last three days resting and praying and wondering if they made the right decisions leading up to the altercation with Randi. Had they grown careless? Did all of that happen because Winter concealed her writings in the first place? The whereabouts of her journal was still a mystery. Randi hinted that Winter would find out where it was soon enough. Whatever that meant.

Winter's mother, Mindy, called from Alaska each day, checking on their condition. Winter assured her they'd be okay. She didn't want her elderly mother flying down to take care of them. She and Ty needed rest and quiet, that's all. After much discussion, Mindy agreed to postpone a trip south, but she planned to visit before too long.

"What if we revised our workbook?" Ty ran his hand through his hair and groaned when he adjusted his seating position on the couch. Their conversation kept returning to ways they could improve their literature for their seminars. "Or how about if we had follow-up material couples could work on together at home?"

"That's a great idea." She patted his knee.

"You know, I've been thinking." He touched her wedding ring. "You should write a book. Randi's idea wasn't all bad."

"What kind of book?"

"What you were writing before—about us." His eyes moistened.

She gulped. "I tried that and look how it turned out."

He shrugged. "Whatever's going to be effective for the Kingdom, that's what satan attacks. We can't let him win so easily."

"Two broken ribs for you and sores all over my mouth are hardly 'easy.'"

"Still. What if we wrote a book together?" Ty shuffled lower on the couch and stared at the ceiling. "When we speak at marriage seminars, I talk to men and you share with the ladies. What if we each wrote from that perspective? Your section could be geared for women. I could write some stuff for guys based on what I already talk about. Then we could combine our thoughts for the ending."

Her heart beat faster. "That is a cool thought."

"We could set up a table with marriage stuff. I could be a salesman. That would give me something to do." He laughed and gripped his side.

"Like you need more to do."

"We should also think about hiring a PR person to replace Randi permanently."

Something in her heart hurt at the mention of replacing her friend, but it was true.

The doorbell rang.

"We expecting pizza?" Ty looked hopeful.

"I wish." She stood up before he could. "Let me. I'm not in pain like you."

"Me, in pain?"

"Yes, you." She nudged his shoulder. "Stay put."

"Yes, ma'am."

She hurried down the split-level stairs. At the door, she ran her hands through her long hair and hoped her mouth didn't look too horrendous. She peeked out the peephole. Flowers? "Hey, Ty, someone sent us flowers." She opened the door to a bouquet of colorful carnations, daisies, and roses being thrust in her hands.

"Surprise!" Two voices rang out.

"Summer! Josh!"

The newlyweds laughed and hugged her.

"I heard from April about what happened to you guys." Summer held Winter's hand an extra moment. "We were heading into Spokane for supplies and thought we'd stop by."

"Come in. What a great surprise." Winter pulled the door open farther. "Thanks for the flowers." She drew them to her nose and sniffed. "Mmm."

"You doing okay?" Summer hugged her again. "I'm sorry about Randi going psycho and hurting you guys."

"Thanks." Winter pointed toward the stairway. "Ty's upstairs."

Josh jogged up to the living room. "Hey man, I heard you were lounging around having a good ole time doing nothing."

Winter laughed at that as she hurried up the stairs.

Ty chuckled, then groaned.

"Don't move a muscle on our account." Josh patted Ty's shoulder gently.

Winter set the flowers on the card table, then grabbed a folding chair and placed it across from Ty. Josh hurried over and picked up the other one.

"Can I get you some coffee?" Winter wiped her lips self-consciously, knowing she still had blisters. "We haven't been to the store, so the cupboards are bare. However, we have an ample supply of coffee and creamer."

"Sounds wonderful. Let me help." Summer scurried into the kitchen.

Winter pointed to the cupboard where the coffee supplies were. "So, how's married life? How was the honeymoon?"

Summer blushed and laughed. "A dream come true. Even the first time we got married, we didn't go on a honeymoon. Getting away by ourselves for a week was fabulous." She seemed to radiate joy. "And the Oregon Coast? I can't tell you how much I loved walking the beaches, holding Josh's hand, just being alone with him." She spooned grounds into the coffee maker.

"I'm happy for you." Winter leaned her hip against the counter. "Being here together in our home is our dream come true." She pointed at her mouth. "But *this*—and Ty's ribs—isn't the way we'd choose to spend a few days by ourselves." She laughed. "How's Miss Shua?" Winter thought fondly of the girl back at Hart's Camp.

"She's in a dream world of her own. Josh had a surprise for us when we got back from the coast."

"What's that?" Winter pulled four mugs out of the cupboard.

"The carpenters built not one, but two small bedrooms onto our cabin." Summer grinned. "Shua has her own room too, and she's thrilled."

"Any plans for more?" Winter couldn't help but ask.

"Rooms or kids?" Summer laughed.

"Both."

"Josh and I have a lot of growing to do as a couple first. Then we'll see."

They finished the coffee preparations and rejoined the men.

"We should order pizza." Ty's eyebrows rocked.

Josh put out his hand. "We wanted to stop by for a minute and wish you well. We don't want you going to any trouble."

"Visiting with you guys is the highlight of our day." Ty's gaze met Winter's.

"Absolutely." She grabbed her phone and tapped "pizza" on the screen. Then she placed an order for half pepperoni/half cheese.

"So tell us what you guys have been up to." Ty set a soft pillow over his chest.

Josh leaned forward, his elbows resting on his knees. "We're closing down the camp for winter, and we've been talking about our future."

"And the future of Hart's Camp." Summer slipped her hand into Josh's.

Winter loved watching these two. Thankfulness welled up in her that she and Ty had been able to have a small part in helping them get back together.

"And?" Ty leaned forward as if to set his coffee cup down.

Winter grabbed it from him and placed it on the table. He said he didn't want her fussing over him, but he'd certainly gone the extra mile for her.

Josh and Summer gazed at each other as if having a whole conversation with their eyes.

"We're thinking of opening the camp for a couple of winter gigs." Josh spread out his hands.

Ty's eyes lit up. "Snow sports? That sort of thing?"

"Could be. Or winter retreats."

"There are a few technical problems." Summer's smile vanished.

"Namely"—Josh shrugged—"it's never been done there. The camp always shuts down after Labor Day. Uncle Mac's a stick-in-the-mud for keeping everything the same."

"How is Mac?" Winter smiled, remembering the older gentleman from the wedding. He didn't look like her father but thinking of Josh's uncle made her miss her dad who was in heaven. He would have been troubled by what she and Ty had gone through with Randi. She could picture him with his arms around her, comforting her, calling her his princess. She blinked back nostalgic tears.

Summer chuckled. "I caught him chopping kindling the other day."

"Me too." Josh nodded. "He used to work up a real temper and then attack the woodpile. Since his heart trouble, his workload has been reduced to chopping kindling when he's upset with Aunt Em."

"You see, we had an ulterior motive for stopping by." Summer made a sheepish expression. "We were wondering if you guys would be interested in speaking at our first winter retreat."

"Oh?"

"What does 'Uncle Mac' say about this?" Ty asked.

Josh grinned. "I have Aunt Em working on him."

"So that's why he was chopping kindling?" Winter smiled, glad for some humor.

"Exactly." Summer laughed. "The marriage retreat this summer meant so much to us. We'd like to offer that experience to others who might be in a similar situation. What better way to fall in love with your spouse than being isolated in the woods with beautiful snow all around?"

Summer and Josh smiled at each other.

"What about your music?" Winter watched Josh's eyes glisten.

The tender look he gave Summer was so endearing like he was writing a song about her in his heart right at that moment. "I'm giving it a break. We'll see."

"And your painting?" She turned to Summer.

The younger woman spread out her hands. "Josh bought me a cabinet full of painting supplies for a wedding gift. I guess that's what I'll be tackling this winter."

"What do you think about doing another conference?" Josh glanced between Winter and Ty.

The doorbell rang.

"Saved by the bell?" She laughed and grabbed her wallet.

Soon they were eating pizza and sharing memories from their last seminar in the woods of Hart's Camp.

When they finished, Summer cleared the cups and plates away.

"Thanks for lunch." Josh shook Ty's hand. "Sorry if we put you on the spot about the conference. We're just excited about branching out and touching lives."

"That's awesome." Ty stood. "Winter and I will pray about it and check with Neil. He's our scheduling guru."

"No worries if you can't." Josh took his wife's hand.

"Wait." Ty clasped Winter's hand. "Let's have prayer before you go."

They prayed together about the possibility of doing future conferences at Hart's Camp with Josh and Summer, and they prayed for Randi. Then their friends left.

Ty pulled Winter close to him. She leaned into him carefully, relishing the feel of his heart beating beneath her ear.

"That's cool, isn't it?" Ty pressed his cheek against the top of her head. "Seeing them together, happy, on fire for the Lord, excited to do something to share their testimonies."

"Yeah." She nodded. "Almost makes all of this worth it."

"Almost?" He chuckled. "We count all things as loss for Christ, right? And"—he lifted her chin so she met his gaze—"I'd go through all of this to be your husband, to be with you in whatever situation we find ourselves, for the rest of our lives." His eyes glowed with some inner fire.

Sore lips or not, she leaned up to meet his mouth in a gentle kiss.

"Love you, Sas."

"I love you."

"What do you think of their winter conference idea?" His eyes sparkled. "I wonder if they might throw in a ski day?"

"I knew that's what you were thinking."

He chuckled. "Doesn't hurt to dream." He swiped his hand over his chest. "Well, maybe, it hurts a little."

She kissed his cheek. "And you're my favorite person to dream with."

Forty-one

Autumn

Autumn read through her to-do list and felt overwhelmed by the things she still needed to accomplish before tomorrow's Opening Night. Good thing she requested a substitute for her classes in the aftermath of Saturday's harrowing experience. This week, she'd been so tired, and her emotions seemed more tattered. Maybe she just needed extra sleep. She held up while Gar had been away. With God's help, she lived on her own and took new steps in her life—like helping Jimmy and Sarah, working out at the gym, and even learning how to make fudge. She'd gone along with her employer's wishes and accepted this crazy challenge of throwing a play together. And through it all, she was painfully aware she wasn't as good as Gar when it came to inspiring students. She didn't need Jewel telling her that to know it was true.

Now, as she checked over her list and gave directions to the parents putting final touches on the castle scene, she listened to Gar, standing on the floor in front of the stage, coaching Chase and Shelley. His tone and encouragement made her feel like the two students could do anything they aspired to. He knew how to instill confidence. That realization made her feel lacking and small . . . and then she felt petty and ridiculous for thinking that way. Gar was helping the whole cast by tweaking the performances of these two actors. But the fact he was here, doing more for the kids than she could, churned an awful angst deep inside her. If only *she* had noticed the play's leads weren't giving their full potential before Jewel brought it to her attention, or before Gar became involved.

And yet, this whole theatrical project, from conception to final curtain, had been his baby for years. It's what he loved, what he should be doing. That he was standing here giving pointers, sharing his heart and wisdom, blessing students with his generous attitude, was a miracle. Even though she and Gar hadn't finished their talk, the transformation in him was obvious. He smiled at her a lot. His eyes twinkled warmly when he gazed into her eyes—and she loved that. One look from him melted her heart. He'd rescued her in the water, putting her needs before his own. He could have died too. That made her feel weak in the knees. He stayed with her all day Saturday and Sunday, resting with her, reciting poetry, and making sure she was okay. Even with all of that, hearing his inspirational talk with those actors didn't make her feel any better.

They'd just finished practicing the bow line. Dress rehearsal had been so-so, according to Jewel. At various times in the last hour and a half, Autumn noticed the demanding parent whispering in Gar's ear, and saw him jotting down notes. What more could they do at this point? The show opened tomorrow night.

"Shelley sounds more confident now that Gar worked with her, don't you think?" Jewel fingered one of her golden dangling earrings.

"Yes, she does." Autumn agreed with Jewel's observation, but she'd say almost anything to appease the woman and keep her from unloading her typically rude comments.

"I'm so glad he came back in time."

"In time?"

Jewel flung her hand toward the stage. "To fix this."

"What do you see that is lacking?" As soon as Autumn said the words, she wished she could take them back. Why bait the woman?

"We need Sasha, that's what."

A knife twisted in Autumn's stomach. She and Gar still needed to broach that topic. Until then, she didn't want that woman anywhere near her set or her husband. "I think the stage is nice how it is." She had to stick up for her volunteers.

"For amateurs." Jewel shook her head like she couldn't believe what she heard.

Autumn groaned in frustration. "That's exactly what we are, Jewel. These are high school seniors and juniors, not professionals."

"But don't you see, it could be so much more. Now that Gar's here, and Sasha—"

"Excuse me." Autumn steadied the stack of papers in her hand and rushed down the aisle away from Jewel. She didn't want to discuss the actors or the stage with the judgmental parent. As she ran up the side stairs leading backstage, it was difficult to concentrate on her tasks. What did she need to do? Double-check that all the items had been returned to the small-props table? Tidy up the Green Room? What she wanted was for tonight's practice to end, and then, maybe she could have that conversation with Gar. As she accounted for theatrical swords and tiaras, she heard his voice.

"Chase, I know this is your first time being a lead."

"Yeah." Chase chuckled.

"With that comes responsibility. It's up to you to step up as an actor, to raise the bar and become the character. In doing so, other actors will step up their game too."

Chase made a nervous sounding laugh.

"It can seem overwhelming, but I believe you can do it. You've got what it takes to walk like a king and think like a man in charge. Puff out your chest a little."

Autumn heard footsteps and imagined Chase strutting across the stage.

"Become a ruler who's in control of great lands and a country." Gar's voice rose dramatically. "Imagine how your character feels toward a manipulative queen."

Chase growled, and Autumn imagined the kingly character pointing his scepter toward Shelley, the one who played the evil queen, and commanding her to leave.

"Shelley, I want a wicked laugh." Gar belted out a maniacal laugh. "Like that."

His commanding tone got Autumn's attention—and probably every other person's in the auditorium. Shelley powerfully mimicked his rendition. Autumn's jaw dropped. Why didn't she think of showing Shelley the kind of laugh she was hoping for? If Gar had been here all along, the play would be so much better. Tears filled her eyes, and she fought them off. She'd tried to be a good director and failed. Just like she botched being a wife who could keep her husband interested in her alone.

The air suddenly felt too stuffy and hot, probably from all the spotlights glaring onstage. She needed to leave the confines of the small backstage area and breathe in some fresh air.

Retracing her path at stage left, she raced down the side stairs she went up moments ago. Then she made the mistake of glancing toward Gar. Her feet stuttered to a halt. Her heart thumped loudly in her ears.

Sasha? Why was she here?

The blond stood like a gorgeous accessory beside Gar, her gaze dripping with admiration—or love.

Gar's gaze zinged toward Autumn's.

She couldn't take any more of the wondering and suspicions. Who called and asked Sasha to come here? Jewel? Or Gar? She dropped her stack of papers on the first seat she came to, then sprinted for the bathroom. Blubbering sounds, too difficult to suppress, wrenched from her chest. Still, she covered her mouth.

"Autumn!" Gar yelled from somewhere behind her.

She didn't want him following her. She ran into the bathroom and rushed into a stall and locked it. Leaning over the toilet, she expected to vomit. Doing so would be a relief. Instead of getting sick, sobs and sorrowful moans burst out from deep inside of her, hardly even sounding like her, almost as if someone else were weeping in the next stall.

Gar pounded on the bathroom door. "Autumn?"

She wouldn't answer. Maybe he'd go away.

Someone else spoke to him. A woman? "Meet me later—

The voices got muffled.

"No, I won't." Gar sounded riled.

Autumn grabbed a handful of toilet paper and blew her nose.

He barged into the bathroom. "Autumn, I know you're in here."

"Leave me alone, okay?"

"I did that for eleven weeks."

So he had.

"What happened? What's wrong?" Now he was standing right outside her stall.

"I-I just need a minute." She sniffled.

"I know this whole thing can be overwhelming." He sounded kind, but she didn't want any of that.

"Especially seeing you with Sasha." She knew her words were sharp.

"Autumn, please. We need to talk."

She shook her head. Of course, he couldn't see that.

"Come out, okay?"

Her tears started up again.

"All right, then, I'm coming in."

Wait. No. He couldn't.

"I mean it."

"Gar—"

Down on the floor, he tucked himself under the door's two-foot-high crawl space. He gazed up at her with puppy-dog eyes. "Please, know this, I want to be with you. Only you. No one else."

She gulped and scooted to the side of the toilet while he crawled in the rest of the way and stood to face her. What an awful place to be standing so close to him. She wiped the back of her hand across her cheeks and under her eyes. Finding black streaks of mascara on her knuckles, she was embarrassed for him to see her in such a mess.

But he looked at her so tenderly, with compassion in his eyes, when he opened his arms, she hiccupped and fell into his embrace. His arms tightened around her, and he held her close to him. When her storm of emotion passed, she leaned against him and allowed herself to rest in his arms for a few minutes.

"Don't worry. I've cried after a few dress rehearsals myself."

"Sure you have."

"I mean it. It's a lot of pressure."

She nodded and sighed. "Why was Sasha here?"

"She offered to help, but I didn't call her."

Autumn leaned back and stared into his dark eyes.

"I didn't text her, either."

"I saw how she looked at you." She watched his every move, checking for any sign of guilt.

His gaze never left hers. "I can't help that. I only have eyes for you."

Was he just saying that to make her feel better? "Is she who you wanted to talk with me about on Saturday?"

"Partially."

"Did you . . . have an affair with her?" Tears threatened, but she blinked them back.

He took her hand and pressed his lips to it. "No."

Relief washed through her chest.

"But there are things we need to talk about. Things I must confess." He released her hand and pushed her hair behind her ear. "Do you want us to get back together?" he asked softly.

She nodded. "With all my heart."

He hugged her to him again. "Then you need to hear my heart, and I need to hear yours." He unlocked the stall door and stepped out. "You're under too much pressure right now. I thought Saturday morning would work. But after our hospital visit, I decided to wait until after the show closes—for your sake."

"No."

"No?"

She shook her head. "I don't want to wait. I . . . can't." She needed to hear what Gar had to say. Carrying the weight of the play and the unknown about why her husband had left her was too much. Seeing Sasha beside him a little while ago had crushed her feelings more than she wanted to say.

"Autumn—"

"I know I'm a mess. I'm not usually like this." She crossed the room to stand in front of the chrome-edged mirror. She scrubbed her hand beneath her eyes, trying to remove mascara streaks. She needed a hot shower and a good night's sleep—and some fudge.

"Let's wait." He stood behind her and met her gaze in the mirror.

She shook her head. "Meet me at Charli's at eight?"

"Tonight? I hardly think you're up to that."

"The wondering is more stressful than knowing." She faced him with what she hoped was a brave face.

He looked doubtful but shrugged. "Okay. Tonight at Charli's."

She'd have to go back in the auditorium and act as if her fleeing the scene hadn't happened. Everyone from stagehands to Jewel would know she had a meltdown.

Four nights of shows, and then it would all be over, but the memories. Where would that leave her and Gar? Maybe she'd know the answer after their discussion tonight.

Forty-two

Gar

At ten till eight, Gar arrived at Charli's, a restaurant in Everett he and Autumn had visited plenty of times. He asked for a table and ordered coffee, figuring he might need several cups. Since it was past the dinner rush, there weren't many customers. A co-ed group of college-aged adults clustered around a table in a corner booth. A younger man and woman toward the center of the restaurant seemed to be having a fervent discussion. The lady gesticulated rapidly, causing her wedding ring to sparkle in the light. "You never do what I ask," she almost shouted.

"Ask?" the man barked. "Command is more like it."

Gar turned in his seat, facing away from them, hoping his discussion with Autumn wouldn't end in an argument and be overheard by others in the room. His hands were already sweaty. His throat was tight. Saturday morning he was more prepared to talk with her, although he was nervous then too.

After working with Chase and Shelley, tonight, he felt elated, especially since back in Idaho he'd assumed his theater days were finished. Trying to motivate two actors to perform at a higher level was fulfilling to him, but something happened with Autumn. Why did she freak out? Preshow jitters? Or was it because Sasha showed up?

He remembered when he ran after Autumn that Sasha trailed his footsteps and grabbed hold of his arm.

"Gar, it's so good to see you," she said breathlessly. "I need to talk with you."

He didn't want to see or talk with her.

"I heard you might need help with the set. I'm here if you want—"

"I don't. And it's not my set. Autumn has it under control."

She laughed like she didn't believe him. "Surely your wife could use—"

"No!"

"Meet me later for coffee?"

He'd answered her sharply, then lunged into the bathroom, leaving Sasha on the other side—for good, he hoped.

Gar poured the creamer into his black coffee and stirred. It had broken his heart to hear his wife crying so hard. At least she let him hold her and comfort her.

Lord, please be with us. I don't know how to overcome our past, but You do.

While he waited, he prayed for Autumn. He thanked God for blessing him with a wife who stood by him all these years. It hit him then, how much she had supported him. All those productions, the gazillion hours he spent with Sasha working on sets, all the teacher's conferences he traveled to, and she never complained, when she probably should have.

He noticed the quarrel at the next table had simmered down, and the couple's hands were linked across the table. Seemed Charli's was the marriage make-up spot tonight.

"Hey." Autumn slipped into the chair across from him.

She wore black slacks and a sweater beneath her jacket. Her hair was shiny and curly, her makeup redone.

"Hey, beautiful."

A blush crossed her cheeks. "Better than when you last saw me, huh?"

He really hadn't complimented her enough over the years. "You look great."

"Thanks."

The waitress hurried over. "Coffee?"

"Yes, please." Autumn slipped out of her jacket and added creamer to her steaming cup. "So—?"

His heart raced. "What did you think of dress rehearsal?" he asked before she could ask him any soul-searching questions.

"Do you mind if we don't talk about the show?" She sipped from her tan mug.

Her request surprised him since as a director he always wanted to discuss some aspect of the production with anyone willing to listen. "Okay."

The waitress returned and took their order. Autumn asked for only a salad. He got a burger, though he doubted he'd do much damage to it. His stomach was churning, but he didn't want to take up a table and not order something.

"On Saturday morning, you didn't get the chance to finish the conversation you started." She seemed to be nibbling the lipstick off her lips. "Something about a line you crossed?"

He still doubted the wisdom of tackling such a heartrending topic tonight. "You sure you're ready to talk about this now?"

"Yes."

He swallowed hard and thought back to when he'd been talking to her before. *Dear God, help us.* He reached across the table and touched her fingers which circled her mug. "I'll tell you anything you want to know. But I think you're under a lot of stress right now. This timing feels all wrong."

* * * *

Autumn *was* under a lot of stress, but Gar was partially to blame for that. "It probably feels wrong because whatever you did *was* wrong." Her answer was edgy, but she was still upset with how Sasha waltzed into the theater and cozied up to him. What really happened between them? "Maybe this isn't the best place for talking. Our house would have been better, but I didn't want Sarah and Jimmy hearing us."

"You really care about them, don't you?"

"I love them." She spread her hand over the smooth table-top. "Sarah feels like my little sister, even though she's a bit prickly and protective. Jimmy's like my favorite nephew."

"Or a son?"

"Or that." She shrugged. "But he has a mother, and we're getting off topic. You said you didn't have an affair with Sasha. Why did Ben think you did? He still acts weird at the mention of her name." She took a breath and blew it out. "Earlier, when I saw her looking at you with such adoration, I knew something was going on."

He shook his head. "Nothing physical ever happened between Sasha and me."

"No kisses?"

"None."

"Holding hands?"

"Never."

That was a relief. But why did he still look guilty? "What, then?"

He interlocked his fingers with hers. "I let her come before you."

Autumn felt those words all the way to the pit of her stomach. "You loved her?" She slipped her hand free of his.

"Not romantically." His shoulders lifted. "As a friend and someone who understood me creatively, yes."

"In ways I didn't relate to you?" That hurt even though it made sense.

"Maybe. What I've come to realize is I can't have that kind of relationship with her or anyone else, other than you. I only want such closeness with my wife, my lover, my best friend . . . you. I mean that."

His words soothed something raw in her spirit.

She knew there were times when she hadn't been attentive to him, like when he talked about his ideas and dreams. For too long she was lost in her own troubles, her own heartache, and it was easier to ignore him than deal with more stuff. "I could have been a better listener, more supportive of you."

Gar shrugged. "It's an area we can work on. I liked feeling as if we were sharing the experiences of the show the last couple of nights. Even though I know it's *your* play."

"Hardly mine."

"Are you kidding me?" He set his cup down hard. "This program wouldn't be happening if it weren't for you being brave and bold enough to see it through to the end."

It was nice to hear him voice that opinion. Especially since she'd worried for so long that he might resent her for taking on his roles.

"Ben and his board should be kissing the floor for all the hard work you've done."

She appreciated the sentiment, but they were veering away from the subject again. "Why does Sasha seem to think there's hope for the two of you? I can see the attraction for you in her eyes, and I don't like it." Heat infused Autumn's cheeks. "I want to know why she thinks you're interested." If Sasha had no hope because Gar had *never* returned her interest, she'd have gone away by now. So, clearly, he'd given her reason to hang around on the sidelines.

He tapped the table with his knuckles, a nervous gesture. "She called me when I was working in Idaho."

"And—?" Anger tightened up her throat muscles. So the other woman pursued him while he and Autumn were separated? Did they talk a lot on the phone? Meet up? Now that he was back, did Sasha think she had a chance with him?

"She made it plain she wanted our friendship to go further." His face hued ruddy, even beyond the whiskers of his beard.

"What did you say?" Picturing him flirting with Sasha twisted a knot in her stomach.

"It was before my turnaround." He swallowed. "But even then, I didn't want to do anything that would hurt you."

"More than leaving me would?" Anger heated up the blood pounding through her chest. She bit her lip to keep from saying something uglier. "Look, I'm sorry." She shouldn't have met him like this. Her emotions were too close to exploding. She shook her head and blew out a hot breath. "I'm way too tense with the play opening tomorrow and now Sasha showing up."

Gar nodded like he knew this discussion was a bad idea.

But she wasn't about to quit now. "Do you have feelings for Sasha?"

"Like a girlfriend?"

Autumn nodded. "What else?"

"No."

"But you let things go too far? Isn't that what you said?" Why was it so hard to pull the truth from him?

"I got close to her at the expense of our marriage, so yes." He wrapped his hands around his coffee cup and looked her in the eye. "Perhaps, it was an emotional affair. Though I never would have admitted that before. Only because of the change in my heart am I open to such a confession now. Even when Ben asked me about her, I told him no."

If that's all the further their friendship had gone . . . and he wasn't attracted to her romantically, the two of them could surely move on from this and start over. She felt herself relaxing. Maybe she could go home and finally get some sleep without lying awake fretting. But something didn't make sense. What wasn't he telling her?

* * * *

Gar knew he'd explained only part of the story. There was still the matter of Las Vegas. The waitress set down their food. The hamburger looked about as good as a chunk of leather. "Thanks," he mumbled as the woman dressed in black walked away.

"Is that it?" Autumn frowned. "You fell out of love with me because you were preoccupied with Sasha?"

If he were living as the man he'd been previously, it would be easy to agree and end the conversation right there. He knew he couldn't. Honesty was more important to him than preserving his pride. Besides, he wanted to come clean with her and be free of the past, even though he knew his confession could hurt their chances of reconciliation.

Autumn ran her fingers through her hair. "For months, even before you left, you've acted indifferent to me. Why? Because I couldn't have kids? Because I gained weight?"

Gar glanced around the room and noticed a few gazes meeting his. "Autumn, no, please. I—" He lowered his voice. How stupid he'd been. So many mistakes. How could he tell her that Sasha hadn't been the only threat? He already saw her fall apart tonight.

"Tell me." Her dark eyes appealed to him. "I need to know what terrible thing I did to cause the man I loved to not want to be with me anymore."

Her words hit him hard. "I do want to be with you. I'm so sorry—" An ache churned in the pit of his stomach. But he met her gaze and forced himself not to look away even for a second. Not when tears rolled down her cheeks. Not when the waitress poured coffee into their cups and asked if everything tasted all right. "I was having problems, and my self-worth was deteriorating. About the only thing I felt good about were the plays. And that was all tangled up with Sasha—which wasn't healthy. I wandered far from God too. But you know that more than anyone."

She nodded slightly. "What brought you back?"

He loved how her eyes brightened to umber when she looked at him. Yet her vulnerability gnawed at him.

"Ty talked some sense into me." He picked up the ketchup bottle, then set it back down. "He and his wife got back together years after divorcing when God changed both of their lives. He was straightforward about me needing to get right with the Lord. And about me being honest with you."

"And have you been?"

He coughed. Could she see right through him?

* * * *

Autumn couldn't eat her salad. Instead, she toyed with water droplets on her glass, waiting for her husband's answer.

"I know what I still have to share will hurt you." He gulped. "It's what drove a wedge between us."

At his warning, she had the strangest urge to run for the door. To not sit here and listen to his confession or blame casting or whatever. But didn't she want him to talk to her and be honest? Didn't she pray for that very thing? She swallowed back her fear and insecurities. She was a stronger woman now. She sat up a little straighter. "What is it?"

"I'm so sorry, but there was someone else." He covered his face with both hands and groaned.

Someone else? She could barely swallow. "You mean, other than Sasha?"

He nodded, lowering his hands. His troubled gaze clashed with hers.

"Who?" A cold chill sped down her spine. "When?"

"Last spring when I went to the teacher's conference in Las Vegas."

Hadn't she thought something about him changed then? Intense pain twisted in her chest. "What happened?" Not that she wanted details, but she had to know the truth.

"I met a woman I was attracted to." His cheeks flamed crimson. "She w-was a teacher. Younger than me." He inhaled sharply. "Attracted to me, it seemed, and fairly pushy about it."

Blood pounded in Autumn's ears. So he had been unfaithful? "How far did it go?"

"I'd rather say it went nowhere."

That's what she wished he'd say.

He blew out a breath. "I didn't sleep with her. I could never do that to you, to our vows."

She sagged with relief against the chair. He hadn't had a physical affair, but she could see by his hesitancy there was something more.

"I was consumed with shame over my feelings—and my inappropriate thoughts." His voice went quiet. "I couldn't seem to . . . forget her."

She gasped. "You loved her?"

Gar shook his head. "Not loved. Bedazzled? Yes. A beautiful young woman attracted to *me*—a thirty-seven-year-old has-been?"

Autumn would never have thought of him in those terms. She was still attracted to him. Still loved him. But his words ripped apart her hope for an easy reconciliation. If he still cared for this woman, where could they go from here?

"Do you remember how I returned home from the conference early?"

She nodded.

"I wasn't sick. I ran."

"But you were tempted to stay?" Even though she knew she'd made her share of mistakes too, hearing his confession, this kind of confession, scorched a path of anger and jealousy over every rational thought. How dare he fall for a younger woman!

His nod was slight, but there.

So that's what had been wrong between them. Not her infertility. Not her being self-conscious about her weight gain. He almost had an affair. Lusted after another woman. She didn't want to break down and bawl, but her emotions felt far too tender to ignore. She picked up a tissue and clutched it in her hand. Had Gar kept in contact with this flirtatious teacher?

"After I came back, I begrudged everything in my life. I wrestled with sin. Guilt. My desire to leave." He leaned his arms against the table, his face drawing closer to hers. "Pastor Chad said the devil was tempting me to yield to something that would have harmed both you and me. At the time, that one thing I couldn't have was driving me crazy." Tears pooled in his brown eyes. "I'm sorry for how far I strayed in my mind and my heart."

At least, he had the nerve to finally tell her the truth. But how could she forget the fact he almost gave in to temptation? "H-how do you feel about her now?"

He kept his gaze on her. "Like a distant memory. I've confessed all of this to God. But I need to ask your forgiveness."

His candidness and humility touched her. Not that it eased her heartache.

"What was her name?" Maybe she didn't need to know, but he said she could ask anything.

"Elaine."

The softly spoken name on her husband's lips was a sting of jealousy.

"There's one other thing."

The muscles in her stomach clenched. What else could there be?

"We, um, kissed," he whispered almost too faintly to be heard.

She pictured him embracing a younger woman, kissing her deeply in the way she thought only the two of them had shared together, and something inside of her died. Her trust in him. The fantasy she'd conjured up of them kissing and making up. Her hope for a happy future with him. She'd been wrong to think she was tough enough to handle whatever he had to say to her. Maybe her frayed nerves were due to the stress of the play. Sasha's flirtations. Jewel's annoyances. Or now, finding out about the woman her husband wanted instead of her. Whatever it was, she needed to find a private place to weep and process what he told her.

She remembered recent battles she fought on her knees. The heartache as she cried and begged God to change them and bring healing to their hearts. Praying that He'd touch Gar and bring him home to her. Didn't the Lord answer her prayers? Her new understanding of prayer and spiritual warfare changed her life. But she'd anticipated a tidy package of healing and closure for their marriage. She didn't envision the muck she had to slosh through to reach a place of reconciliation.

"I'm so sorry for hurting you." He touched her hand. "Please forgive me?"

A volcanic rush of emotion churned in her, stifling a charitable response. What she wanted to do was tell him just what she thought of his flirtations with other women and his neglect toward his wife. Sure, he humbly asked for her forgiveness, yet the anguish of three months of feeling wronged wouldn't be appeased easily. "I'm sorry too." Her words came out sharp, but she didn't soften them. "I'm sorry for not being *attractive* enough for you." She thought of the hours at the gym and her struggle with her weight. "For not being an *adoring* wife who could meet your every need." A picture of him with a young teacher flashed through her mind. She shoved away from the table and stood. "I need to go and think about what you've said." To give way to the tears bunching up in her throat. To release the pain squeezing her heart. Then somehow, she had to find a way to pull herself together so she could face the pressures of her production week.

He stood too, his expression cautious. He grabbed his wallet and threw down two twenties. "I'll walk you to your car."

"That's not necessary." She pushed her hands into her jacket and hurried toward the entrance.

"Is everything all right?" the waitress asked.

"I left money on the table. Thanks." Gar rushed ahead of Autumn and opened the glass door for her, his eyes glistening with unshed moisture. He remained at her side until she reached her car. "Goodnight," he whispered. "Call my cell if you need anything."

She unlocked her door and slid onto the seat. "What could I possibly need?" Other than a faithful husband. As she drove out of the parking lot, hot tears rolled down her cheeks, and she let them fall. It seemed she wasn't as strong as she'd imagined.

Forty-three

Gar

Gar paced across the low-rise carpet in the meager motel room, his hand gripping his cell phone. "Things are a mess. I had to call."

"I'm glad you did," Pastor Chad assured him. "By the panic in your tone, I assume you had 'the talk.'"

"Yep, and it didn't go well." Gar bit the inside of his cheek, regretting that he'd been so vulnerable and open when he talked with Autumn. Maybe he shouldn't have told her about his temptations—even though Chad and Ty had assured him that was the only way. What good had it done?

"'Didn't go so well' as in she was upset?" the minister asked.

"Quite." Gar trudged across the room, venting his frustration the only way he could. "I don't know if she even wants to get back together with me now."

"Hold on." Chad's voice sounded calming, but Gar didn't feel any calmer. "Don't throw in the towel so fast. She probably needs time to consider everything you told her, and to pray about it."

"I don't know." Fear crawled through his senses. What if

Autumn didn't want him back? What if their marriage was over because of him?

"Listen, when I had my talk with April, she didn't accept my explanation right then, either." Chad sighed. "It took time and a lot more sharing and honesty. You love her, right?"

Gar stopped frantically pacing. "Y-yes. More than ever."

"Good. Then you'll get through this. God is with you."

"I just don't know what to do." He felt a panic attack coming on like he hadn't experienced since directing his first full-stage production. He frowned at the remembrance. No wonder Autumn was so emotional last night. Sasha's arrival was rotten timing. And he knew they shouldn't have had that discussion when Autumn was so stressed out, but she wouldn't listen.

"What did she seem the most upset about?" Chad asked.

Gar thought for a second. "That I was attracted to another woman."

"That would be hard." Chad made a humming sound like he was thinking. "Consider the situation from her perspective. How would you feel if she confessed to making out with another guy?"

A sour taste crept up Gar's throat. "I'd want to punch whoever he was. But I didn't make out with her. I only—" Gar stopped talking. He'd already told Chad about his experience with Elaine, and he remembered the other man's response.

"But you thought about it, right?"

The same glug he felt during their last conversation settled in his stomach like a rock. "Yeah," he admitted quietly.

"So, were you able to help Autumn see how much you care about her? Assure her of your love and devotion?" Chad sounded so wise. It was hard to imagine him making the kind of mistakes in his marriage that he'd told Gar about.

"I tried." Gar groaned. "It didn't work out as I'd hoped."

"It never does."

Whoa. "What do you mean? I thought if I were open and honest, she'd see how serious I am about changing. How much I want to be a better husband." Gar dropped on the edge of the bed he'd barely slept in last night due to pacing and worrying.

"It takes time." Chad drew in a long breath. "It took a while to get in this situation, right? So it's going to take time and prayer and wisdom to get out of it."

"I'm not the most patient guy."

"Are any of us?" Chad laughed. "So what's the next thing happening in Autumn's life where you could make a positive difference? Not a pushy one. But showing kindness and endearing yourself to her. Being a blessing."

"Her play opens tonight." Not that he wanted to go now.

"Perfect. You're going, right?"

Gar rubbed the side of one shoe against the other. "I was thinking of staying in my room."

"No way."

Gar stood and paced again.

"If you bail"—Chad paused—"you'll miss an opportunity to show her you really love her. That you're willing to sacrifice your pride to support *her*."

"I don't see what I can do."

"Opening Night? How about buying her flowers?" Chad's thoughts seemed to change direction. "Based on what you've told me, you have a lot of experience with theater. You know the exact places to have her back. Know what I mean?"

Gar pictured Jewel Pollard and her tendency to say rude things. Maybe he could absorb some of that. "Yeah, I suppose. Thanks. I was going crazy."

Chad chuckled like he understood. "God wants you and Autumn to mend your relationship. He's for your marriage, but there are consequences to sin. You left. Checked out on your vows. Now you need to be loving and gentle. Woo your wife, so she can heal from her hurts."

Some of his words felt like darts piercing Gar's heart, but he knew what the pastor said was true.

Chad cleared his throat. "I know this is hard to hear, but don't forget to be humble. Assure her that you know it may take time to win back her trust. That you're going to be there for her the rest of her life—and mean it."

"I do." If only Gar could convince Autumn. "Thanks for talking with me."

After Chad prayed with him, Gar ended the call. Then he dropped to his knees and cried out to the Lord to heal his wife's hurts and for him to become the man God would have him be.

He spent time reading his Bible, then he put on his leather jacket and headed out to his car. First stop, the florist. Then the jewelry store. All the while, he'd keep thinking of ways to show Autumn how much he loved her.

Forty-four

Autumn

Autumn hadn't seen Gar all day. Would he even attend the show? Chase was asking for him for last-minute pointers, but all she could say was she didn't know where Mr. Bevere was. He could have left town, for all she knew. She hoped not, but it was possible.

About thirty minutes before showtime, she checked everything backstage one last time. She breathed in, then reminded herself to exhale, to avoid the overwhelming panic that kept hitting her. It was almost time for the curtain to open on her first, and probably last, production. Despite her lack of abilities, this was it. Strangely, her thoughts were more on Gar than on her actors.

"Mrs. Bevere, there you are." Jewel, dressed in a sparkly silver gown, scurried over to her. "The newspaper reporter from the *Herald* is here. Can he take a picture of you?" She grinned like they were the best of friends.

"Oh, sure."

"How about in front of the castle scene?" Jewel swished away, obviously expecting Autumn to follow her.

"Okay." Now her mug shot would be seen in the school's glass display case with her standing in front of the scenery Jewel had labeled "tacky and lacking."

A younger man stood onstage behind the closed curtain and extended his hand toward her. "I'm David Jensen from the *Herald*."

"I'm Autumn Bevere."

"Nice to meet you. How about sitting on the throne?" He pointed at the king's chair set on a raised dais covered in rich-colored maroon fabric.

As she listened to the crowd gathering in their seats on the other side of the curtains, butterflies flitted around in her stomach, no doubt, as rampantly as the new actors were experiencing. She stepped on the platform, then sat down on the gold-cushioned throne. "Like this?"

"Perfect." The reporter snapped several pictures, then asked her some questions.

Yes, it was her first time directing. Yes, she was an English teacher with a voracious love of books. Yes, she was married to Gar Bevere, the *well-known* director in the area.

"Are you filling in for him?" David tapped his fingers against his smartphone.

"Sort of."

"Will he be back next year?"

"Well, I'm not—"

"Oh, look at the time." Jewel grabbed Autumn's arm and nearly dragged her off the throne. "The director's needed backstage."

What happened? Did Jewel think she was going to say something embarrassing about Gar or the school? Autumn pulled her arm free of the woman's clutches. She'd had quite enough of her controlling ways.

"I think I've got what I need." David held up his digital camera.

"Thanks." Autumn hurried backstage with Jewel almost pushing her along. Behind the wall of flats, she whirled around. "What is wrong?"

The parent wagged her finger. "Directors must be careful of what they say to the press."

"I was only answering his questions."

"Exactly." Jewel gave her a sour look. "Now, I'm going to go find my seat. In a few minutes, we'll see whether your little show works or not." With a swish of her gown, her heels click-clacked offstage.

Autumn groaned, then breathed in deeply. Relieved to be alone, she checked over the small-props table. Chase kept forgetting to return his crown. Good. It was in its marked location.

"Fifteen-minute call," the stage manager whispered.

"Thanks, Justine."

Shelley, dressed in a deep purple medieval gown, rushed up to her and handed her a dozen red roses.

"What's this?"

"Guess who it's from?" Shelley's giggle contrasted with her mean-queen costume and makeup. "There's a card." She pointed at a white envelope. "Mrs. B. has an admirer."

Autumn smiled and stepped away from the actor to open the card privately. Even though she was still reeling from Gar's disclosure, the thought of him sending her flowers and writing something romantic made her heart flutter.

Have a great show. Break a leg. Your biggest fan, Gar

Maybe not romantic, but thoughtful. So he was in the audience? Would he hate the show like Jewel did? Would he critique it like he did all the other productions he attended? Or could he sit there and honestly cheer for her and the kids?

Despite how brokenhearted she felt after last night's talk, today she sensed a nudge of hope that in time they could work things out. She was thankful Gar had been honest with her.

They both made mistakes. The verse about *love covers over a multitude of sins* had been replaying in her mind all day. Could God's love heal their wounds? And since He wiped out every one of her past failings and sins, how could she hold Gar's wrongs against him?

"Mrs. Bevere?" Chase stood beside her.

She'd been standing in front of the props table just staring at the objects.

"Aren't you going to say something to the cast?" His hands clenched and unclenched in a nervous gesture.

"What am I supposed to say?"

Chase shrugged. "A pep talk? Prayer?"

"Oh, of course." Why didn't someone mention that before?

She followed him into the Green Room. A buzz filled the area. As soon as she walked to the center of the hairspray-laden space, everyone stopped talking.

"Gather around." Chase waved his hands. "Mrs. B. is going to talk."

The cast surrounded Autumn.

"Five-minute call!" Justine stage-yelled into the room.

Autumn gulped. What inspiring words or quotes would Gar have shared? She knew he would love this moment and have something profound to say. She glanced at the actors, most of them wearing heavy theatrical makeup. Joy and enthusiasm radiated from their wide-mouthed grins, their high energy, and their laughter—even though they had to be nervous too.

She pulled in a raspy breath and let it ease out. "We've come a long way on this journey together—the writers, actors, and techs. We've worked hard, and I'm so proud of you." Emotion gripped her. "I love all of you, and I can't wait to see you perform." What else could she say? "This is it. The moment we've all been waiting for. Do your best." She made eye contact with each of the students.

"Let's give it all we've got." Shelley lifted her hand. "May I pray?"

Autumn nodded. "Of course."

Shelley thanked God for the participants and for Mrs. Bevere's dedication to the show. She asked Him to help them share their gifts for His glory. As soon as she said "amen," she thrust her hand toward the middle of the circle and whispered, "For God's glory."

The cast members each placed a hand on top of hers. "For God's glory!"

Laughter came again. Then silence.

It was time.

"Have a good show." Autumn nodded toward Chase and Shelley.

"Break a leg," Shelley whispered in her ear.

"Oh, right." Autumn chuckled. "I'm new at this. Break a leg." She hurried from the Green Room to find her seat near the front section in the auditorium.

Jewel, representing the school and the parent association, welcomed the guests and asked everyone to silence their cell phones. Autumn dropped into the seat she reserved for herself earlier in the day and was surprised to find Gar sitting in the chair next to hers. They exchanged glances, then Gar rocked his thumb toward the person next to him. Jimmy leaned forward with a wide grin and waved. Then Sarah and Marny did the same thing. She smiled back at them, then glanced at Gar. He brought them here and bought their tickets, didn't he? *Thank you,* she mouthed. He drew closer to her and brushed his lips against her cheek.

A wonderful awareness rustled through her. This was her family. She'd taken in Sarah and Jimmy, and there was no way she'd send them back into the cold after winter. Marny was her truest friend, almost like a sister. And Gar? The only man she ever loved was still watching her like he was very attracted to her.

She gulped. Then she remembered the flowers he sent. Where did she set them down? On the prop table? In the Green Room? "Thank you for the flowers," she whispered.

"You're welcome."

Just then, two actors—the princess and an orphan—dashed up the center aisle searching for a hiding place in the forest surrounding the castle. Jimmy laughed when medieval knights brandished swords.

Even though Autumn had heard the actors reciting their lines over and over, tonight it was as if she were seeing it all for the first time. An audience made a big difference.

At the end of every scene, her row cheered. When she looked beyond Sarah, she realized Jewel and her husband were there, clapping. Apparently, the parent in Jewel surpassed the critical feelings she harbored toward Autumn. Several times, she heard Gar chuckling too. She glanced at him, and he met her gaze with the sweetest smile. That he was able to relax and enjoy himself at her show pleased her so much.

When intermission was announced, Gar stared pointedly at her.

"What?"

"It's your time."

"I don't know what that means." She shrugged.

He took her hand in his. "Why don't you go backstage, love?"

Love. "Am I supposed to do something?" That panicked feeling was back in her throat. "The stage manager has it under control. The actors did great. Nothing went wrong." So far.

"Go on." He nudged her arm without explaining.

Puzzled, she retraced her steps from earlier. As soon as her shoes hit the tiled floor in the Green Room, she felt like the star of the party. The actors clustered around her with shining smiles, laughing and asking a million questions at once.

"What did you think?"

"Did you hear how they laughed?"

"Which scene was the best?"

"Did you see—?"

"You were all amazing!" she said back to them.

They laughed and cheered and chattered some more.

She helped fix a few makeup smudges. Chase asked her to repair the neck of his costume where he tore it. Dillan misplaced his cane, and Autumn scurried to the props table to hunt for it. Fifteen minutes of intermission passed like a whirlwind backstage.

"Two minutes!" Justine bellowed.

Two minutes? Autumn gazed at the actors staring at her. "Go out there and do it again. The crowd loves you." She turned to race back to her seat, but Chase tapped her shoulder.

"Thank you, Mrs. B." He grinned. "I love being the king. Thanks for letting Mr. B. help me with my part." Then he hugged her.

"Yeah, thanks, Mrs. Bevere," several others called and hugged her too.

Gar had understood she needed this time with the kids when they were wound up and bursting with excitement over how they portrayed their characters in front of a live audience. Tears kept her from seeing clearly as she returned to her seat—and him.

* * * *

Four performances of *The Queen's Disaster* passed too quickly. The last minutes of the final performance were bittersweet. Tomorrow, when it was all over, she could sleep in without a to-do list hanging over her head. On Monday morning she'd go back to her regular routine of being a teacher and a house-mom to Jimmy and Sarah—and very possibly, someday soon, a normal wife again. But she'd miss all of this. She'd never forget the closeness she felt with the actors this week.

Gar sat beside her every night and seemed to enjoy the performances as much as she did. He remained supportive, running to the store for anything she or the cast members needed. He swept the stage before every show, tweaked lighting, and helped in any way he could. They hadn't mentioned their conversation again. Without agreeing to a truce, they'd seemingly put their past on hold while she finished her role as the director.

Tears dripped down her cheeks as Chase gave his final kingly decree onstage and then clasped the princess's hand. The music rose to a crescendo, and the cast rushed downstage to join the royals for their last bow line. The audience rose to their feet, clapping and cheering.

Then Chase did something irregular. Stepping from his lead position in the line, he ran down the side steps and stopped beside her chair. When he offered her his arm, Gar nudged her. She glanced between him and Chase and saw a look pass between the two. What were they up to? She stood and laid her hand in the crook of Chase's arm and allowed him to lead her onstage. A roar of clapping and cheers and whistles resounded in the auditorium—as if they were giving her a standing ovation. Under the spotlight in front of the packed auditorium, she felt overwhelmed with joy and humbled by their exuberant applause.

Chase held up his hand toward the audience, and all went quiet.

"The cast and I want to thank Mrs. Bevere for directing this show. We almost didn't have a production this year, but she saved theater for us!"

Again loud cheering and clapping erupted.

Autumn laughed, feeling a mixture of embarrassment and nostalgia.

Shelley pressed several bouquets of roses of various colors in her hands. "Thank you, Mrs. Bevere."

"They're beautiful." Her house was going to smell delightful.

"We all have a question for you." Chase grinned from ear to ear.

What would the actor ask her in front of this crowd of several hundred people?

"Will you direct the spring show—please?" He held his hands together in a begging gesture.

The spring show? Direct again? She chuckled nervously. Surely, they didn't expect an answer right then. In the ensuing silence, her gaze sought Gar's. There he was standing and smiling at her. Was he nodding?

"We'll see." That's all she'd agree to.

The music started up. The actors bowed one last time. And the curtain closed to a thunder of applause.

Behind the thick red fabric, one by one the actors hugged her and expressed how much performing in the play had meant to them. She didn't know how she could contain all the emotion, but she kept herself from crying.

She still had a cast party to attend, but right then, what she wanted more than anything was to be alone with Gar, to talk over every detail of the show—and to initiate a discussion about plans for their future. After the sweet way he treated her this week, and the things she'd been pondering about God's love and forgiveness, she felt ready to put their past behind them.

Forty-five

Gar

A little after noon, Gar sat on the front steps of the house waiting for Autumn. He'd already checked out of the motel, and he was hoping to move back home. But he didn't know if his wife was ready for that. The night they returned from the hospital, he stayed with her, slept beside her on the couch, and she didn't seem bothered by his closeness. Of course, that was before he'd destroyed her trust in him. He let out a sigh, then said a little prayer asking for God's mercy.

He touched the jeweler's box in his pocket, hoping Autumn would like the gift he bought. The necklace he lost in the sound wasn't engraved. This one was.

Her Accent pulled into the driveway and he stood. As she got out of the car, he watched for a sign that she was ready to work with him toward reconciliation. When she waved and gave him a welcoming smile, a mix of relief and hope washed through him.

"Sorry I'm late." She carried a grocery bag. "I stopped and picked up supplies for spaghetti and fudge."

"Fudge?" He reached out and grabbed hold of the bag to help her.

"Thanks." Her eyes sparkled in the sunshine. "I thought it might be fun if you and I made a batch of double-layered white over dark chocolate together."

"Oh, yeah?"

"I've heard a man who helps in the kitchen is a man who loves his wife." Her voice softened.

Was she flirting with him?

His heart beat faster.

She touched the button on his shirt and gazed warmly into his eyes. "We'll be alone for a little while."

He gulped. "I'd like that . . . a lot." Not that he knew how to make fudge. But being alone with her? Beyond amazing.

She leaned toward him, almost as if to—

A dark blue official-looking sedan pulled into the driveway behind Autumn's vehicle.

Looking as disappointed by the interruption as he felt, she turned toward the unfamiliar car. "I wonder who that could be."

Sarah climbed out of the vehicle, a deep scowl on her face. A man in a dark suit who looked like a government agent exited from the driver's seat.

"Sarah?" Autumn walked quickly to her. "What happened?"

Gar set the bag on the step and hustled over to stand beside his wife. He didn't take her hand, but he wanted her to know he was there if she needed him.

When Jimmy jumped out of the car, he dove at Autumn, crying and hugging her.

What in the world? Poor kid.

She held the boy to her, stroking his back. "What's wrong, honey?"

Jimmy didn't answer, just shook his head.

Sarah broke down crying too. Autumn held out her arm, and she fell into her embrace.

"Autumn Bevere?" the dark-suited man asked in an official tone.

"Yes." She nodded toward Gar. "And my husband, Gar Bevere."

Husband. Liking the sound of that, he moved a bit closer to her.

"Frank Donnelly. Child welfare." He showed them his ID.

"What's going on? Sarah and Jimmy are staying with me."

"That's the thing." Frank gave Sarah a stern look. "Sarah's been posing as Jimmy's mother, but she isn't his legal guardian."

* * * *

"What?" Autumn set Jimmy at arm's length and gazed into his weepy eyes. "Sarah isn't your mom?"

Jimmy shook his head and scrubbed the back of his hand across his nose.

"But I thought—" How could this be? "Sarah?"

The younger woman jerked away and stuffed her hands in her coat pocket, avoiding looking at any of them.

"Where's Jimmy's mom?" Had she been harboring runaways?

"She d-died." Jimmy sniffled.

"Oh, no. I'm so sorry." Autumn pulled him back into her arms. Did that mean he was an orphan?

"I brought Jimmy here to gather his things." Frank's voice deepened. "I'm taking him to Child Protective Services."

"Do you have to?" She wanted Jimmy and Sarah to stay with her—with them—and become a real family. How could that happen if he took Jimmy away?

Jimmy sobbed. "Burt C-Conner said the bad guys were gonna come and throw me in kid's j-jail. He was ri-i-ight."

"Oh, Jimmy." Autumn was close to crying too.

Gar put his hand on the boy's shoulder. "No one's taking you to jail, son."

Son? Did he mean that?

Jimmy maneuvered himself between Autumn and Gar, his skinny arms wrapped around both of their waists. "I don't want to go. Please. This is my home. You said so."

"Get your stuff. I'll come with you." Frank pointed toward the house. "May I?"

Autumn needed more information first. She faced Sarah. "I told you I was here for you, and I mean it. My home is your home. Now, please, tell us what's going on."

Sarah kicked at a pebble on the ground, her gaze averted.

Frank nodded toward Jimmy. "If you want your things, grab them now."

"Wait." Autumn held out her hand toward Frank. "Can't you give us a minute?"

He glanced pointedly at his watch but didn't deny her request.

Jimmy was clinging to Gar as if he'd never let him go. The soft expression in her husband's eyes as he gazed at the boy let her know he didn't like Jimmy being taken away like this, either.

"Sarah, how did you get Jimmy?"

Sarah crossed her arms and pressed her lips together.

Jimmy broke away from Gar and rushed forward. He braced his arms in front of the woman who'd been posing as his mother as if he were her protector. "When Mom got sick, Sarah promised to look after me. And she did. Even if she's not my mom, Sarah and me need a family."

A family. Just like Autumn wanted. A motherly affection for Jimmy, and Sarah too, spread through her, soothing the aching, hurting places she'd carried in her heart ever since the day she heard she couldn't be a mom. With tears flooding her eyes, she gazed into Gar's equally tear-filled eyes. He nodded at her, and she knew he had to be thinking the same thing.

"Frank, can Jimmy stay with us? We'd like to become his parents. Whatever it takes, that's what we'll do."

"Parents? You mean it?" Jimmy lunged for her, almost knocking her over. Gar's hand at her back kept her from falling.

"You have to go through proper channels." Frank ran his hand over his full head of black hair. "There's paperwork. Classes. Getting approval, and so on."

"Okay, but can he stay here while we accomplish those tasks?" Autumn didn't want to raise false hope in Jimmy, but she had to ask.

"No." Frank tapped his phone. "I have my orders. When Jimmy wrote his story for an assignment in school, his teacher was obligated to call us."

So that's how the facts had been discovered. "Sarah has done a good job watching out for him." Autumn clasped Sarah's hand, wanting to stick up for her. "You kept your promise to his mother."

Sarah nodded, and some of her sadness seemed to lift.

Gar cleared his throat. "Isn't there an emergency provision where Jimmy could stay with us while everything is settled legally?"

That he was stepping up, trying to help take care of things for Jimmy, pleased Autumn.

"I thought you weren't even living here." Frank pierced Gar with a dark look.

"I was away for a few months."

Hearing the embarrassment in Gar's tone, she linked her fingers with his, felt him squeeze her hand. She liked standing by him like this, feeling as if they were a couple again. "He's home to stay now." She met his gaze. "And we'd like to become foster parents with the intention of adopting Jimmy."

"Adopting?" Jimmy jumped up and down and clapped.

"That's right." Gar ruffled his red hair.

"Wait till I tell the guys at school."

"I have to take him now." Frank's face was set in a stern glare, but he sighed and seemed to relent. "You can come down to the office tomorrow and fill out the application."

"Then that's what we'll do." She leaned down to Jimmy's eye level, blinking back her tears. "Young knight, you have to be brave and go with Mr. Frank. But Gar and I will do everything we can to bring you home again soon."

"As your son?" Bright, trusting eyes glistened up at her.

"Yes, as our son." Gar put his arm over Autumn's shoulder.

"Okay." Jimmy ran inside to gather his personal items.

Autumn followed him and grabbed the picture of her and Gar from the fridge and a Ziploc bag partially filled with peanut butter fudge and tossed them into his backpack. Jimmy hugged Sarah, then with a mournful glance, he left with Frank. Gar walked them to the car.

Autumn sniffed back tears.

"I guess I should gather my things too." Sarah's hands twisted over her baggy coat.

"Why?"

"I only came here to watch out for Jimmy. It's not right for you and Mr. Gar to give up a room on account of me."

The thought of losing Sarah tore at her heart. She moved around the center island and hugged her. Sarah sagged against her and let out quiet sobs.

"I-I tried to do my best by Jimmy."

"I know you did. He loves you."

Strange how Sarah seemed fatter in her belly than Autumn had noticed. How could she be chubby there when she was so skinny everywhere else? *Ohhh.* Was it possible—? Had Sarah's baggy clothes hidden that she was pregnant?

Autumn held her at arm's length. "Please stay here with us."

Sarah's dark eyes stared at her as if lacking comprehension. "Why? I'm too old to be your daughter. No one's ever wanted me before."

"Now someone does. I do. You may call this place home for as long as you want." She wiped dark smudges from Sarah's cheeks where her tears had fallen through her mascara. "And maybe, I could be your baby's auntie or grandma?"

Sarah gasped. "You knew?"

"I just realized." Joy filled Autumn's heart in waves. "Sarah, will you join my family? Daughter or sister, whichever you're comfortable with?"

"I'm keeping my baby." Sarah placed her hands over her stomach as if protecting her unborn child.

"Good." Autumn felt her smile all the way to her toes. "But if you'll let me, I'd like to help. Hearing a baby in the house will be soothing to my ears—and my heart."

"Even when it cries its lungs out at two in the morning?"

"Especially then."

Sarah stared out the kitchen window as if pondering Autumn's offer. "Okay, I accept. We"—she rubbed her stomach—"accept."

They hugged and laughed.

Gar strolled into the kitchen and set the grocery bag on the counter. "Still game to teach me how to make fudge? I heard someone say something about a man who helps in the kitchen . . ."

Ahhh, yes. Autumn released Sarah and walked into her husband's arms. She leaned her face against his smooth jacket, and she heard Sarah close the door to her room. Autumn breathed in the musky scent of the man she'd loved for over fifteen years. He'd made mistakes—so had she—but she wasn't going to hold his wrongs against him anymore. God had changed them both. She wanted Gar to stay with her and for them to fall in love again. To be a family . . . with Jimmy and Sarah and her baby. She gazed into his chocolaty eyes filled with a bit of surprise, and the idea of planting a whopper of a kiss on his lips was a temptation she couldn't ignore.

* * * *

Gar's heart pounded a double beat in his ears. Had he just witnessed a miracle? Or two? They were going to have a son. And Autumn was in his arms?

When she gazed sweetly into his eyes, all he could do was grin. What would it be like to press his lips against hers and kiss her passionately like he hadn't done in far too long? He wanted to romance her with poetry and words of love, but instead, they stayed as they were, grinning and gazing into each other's eyes.

Maybe he should apologize one more time. "Autumn, I'm so sorry for the ways I hurt you."

"I know." Slowly, as if they were about to dance, she ran her hands up his chest, over his shoulders, her fingers linking behind his neck. "I forgive you, Gar. I'm sorry too."

He stroked her back, liking how close she was standing to him. "I love you so much."

She licked her upper lip as if anticipating his kiss. Welcoming it? Her mouth drew nearer to his, inviting him closer, it seemed. His heart thudded a wild drumbeat against his ribcage. His gaze got lost in her dreamy expression. It had been so long since they kissed like a married couple, he felt a need to ask her permission. "May I . . . kiss you?" He brushed his fingers over her soft cheek, following the familiar contour of her face.

"If you don't, I'm going to beat you to it." Her flirting got to him every time.

He leaned toward her, and that first touch of her lips

against his was like chocolate fudge melting in his mouth. *Mmm.* It made him want more. He kissed her deeply, hungrily. She was water to his thirsty spirit. Air to his oxygen-starved lungs. She was all he needed. His lips trailed from her cheek to her ear. "So"—he whispered—"may I move back in?"

She laughed and the sound was music to his ears.

"Yes, you may." Her eyes sparkled up at him. She took a step back and touched his wedding ring. "I want you to stay here with me ... as my husband."

A rush of emotion went through him. "Thank you. There's nowhere in the world I'd rather be than with you." He pulled her to him for another kiss. And he thanked God for blessing him with this second chance.

Then he remembered he had gifts for her. "I'll be right back." He ran out to his car and grabbed the package he brought, then returned. He placed the thin parcel in her hands and kissed her cheek. "I love you."

* * * *

Autumn adored the way his eyes stared into hers like he truly wanted to be with her. "I love you too, Gar. More than when we first married. More than five years ago. More than yesterday."

When tears filled his eyes, she knew her words touched him.

She tore back the wrapping paper and found a framed picture of the newspaper clipping of her sitting on the throne. The headline read "Teacher Captures Kingdom." In the corner, Gar had signed it "Director of my dreams."

"What a thoughtful gift."

His finger slid across the edge of the black frame. "Think you'll direct again?"

She shrugged. "I don't know. It's your thing. You're the one who helped Chase and Shelley." She set the picture on the table near a vase of roses the actors had given her, then she linked both of her hands with his. "What would you think of us working together on a show? I think we should go in and talk with Ben about it. Or else, we could start over somewhere else—you and me, the directing duo." She chuckled. "I bet you could even write your own play. What do you say?"

It seemed like he froze. Did she say something wrong? "Gar?"

"I would l-love that s-so much—"

She watched as tears rolled down his cheeks and disappeared in his beard. And she loved him for his tenderness. "You've changed. You never used to cry."

He nodded and wiped his sleeve over his face. "The Lord changed me. I feel different inside. Now, what I long for more than anything is to be a good husband for you. From this day forward, I promise to love you, Autumn Bevere, and to be there for you all the days of my life."

His words—just like the ones he promised in their wedding vows—touched her deeply.

He let go of her and dug his hand in his jacket pocket. Then he placed a small jewelry box on her palm.

When she opened it, a necklace with a beautiful silver heart lay on a cushioned bed. She read the inscribed words: "My wife, my love."

"Oh, Gar."

He took her hands in his. "Will you be mine?"

She nodded, so thankful he came back to her. "Forever."

He brushed his lips softly against hers, almost as if it were their first kiss. Then he drew her closer and held her against his chest, his heart beating a familiar rhythm beneath her cheek. She felt loved and cherished, knowing Gar had truly come home to stay.

If you enjoyed *Autumn's Break*, or mostly enjoyed it, please leave a review wherever you purchased this book. They say reviews are the lifeblood for authors, and I would consider it a personal favor if you wrote one. Even one line is great. Thank you! ~Mary

Check out the next book in this series!

Season's Flame

How can Season commit to renewing her efforts in their relationship when her husband won't even try?

If you'd like to be one of the first to hear about Mary's new releases and upcoming projects, sign up for her newsletter!

As a thank you gift, you can receive two pdfs: "To Winter, With Love—Romantic Letters Between Ty and Winter," that takes place between *Winter's Past* and *April's Storm*, and "Rekindle Your Romance! 50+ Date Night Ideas for Married Couples."

Check them out here:

www.maryehanks.com/FREE.html

Special Thanks to . . .

Paula McGrew ~ for being my amazing critique partner and reading through my work in its rough stages. I appreciate your kindness and encouragement so much!

Michelle Storm ~ for being a beta reader for all four books in this series. Thank you for helping bring out the best in these stories.

Kathy Vancil, Melissa Hammerstrom, and Joy Calkins ~ for testing this story and finding all those things I overlooked. You are amazing! I appreciate your heart for second chances.

Jason Hanks ~ for reading this story and encouraging me to live the writer's life. Thanks for telling me I could when I thought I couldn't.

Annette Irby ~ for fine-tuning my words. The story is always better because of your critique.

Suzanne Williams ~ for a sweet and endearing cover. Your gift for artistry shines through your work.

John Andrianu ~ for reading the action scene and offering pointers about martial arts. It was nice to have a previous student as an adviser.

Steve Peterson ~ for checking my canoe scene. That time you demonstrated flipping a canoe at youth camp in Alaska was my inspiration.

Daniel & Traci, Philip, Deborah, & Shem ~ My life is sweeter because of you.

Friends & Family ~ for helping with research questions and for letting me borrow your names.

The Lord ~ for blessing me in so many ways.

Books by Mary Hanks

Second Chance Series

Winter's Past

April's Storm

Summer's Dream

Autumn's Break

Season's Flame

Restored Series

Ocean of Regret

Sea of Rescue

Bay of Refuge

Tide of Resolve (July 2020)

Marriage Encouragement

Thoughts of You (A Marriage Journal)

Youth Theater Adventures

Stage Wars

Stage Woes (2020)

maryehanks.com

About Mary E. Hanks

Mary's favorite stories are inspirational tales about marriage reconciliation. She and Jason have been married for 40+ years. They've been buffeted by their share of storms—kind of like the couples in her stories—but by God's grace they have stayed together. Whenever she can, Mary likes to include her love for romance, chocolate, second chances, and ocean settings in her books.

For many years, Mary worked in Christian education. She still loves Youth Theater and has written and directed over twenty full-stage productions. Her love of theater inspired her to write the Youth Theater Adventures for readers age 10-14, beginning with Stage Wars.

Besides writing, Mary likes to read, do artsy stuff, go on adventures with Jason, and meet her four adult kids for coffee or breakfast.

Connect with Mary by signing up for her newsletter on her website—www.maryehanks.com.

"Like" her Facebook Author page:

www.facebook.com/MaryEHanksAuthor

You can email Mary at maryhanks@maryehanks.com

www.maryehanks.com

Made in the USA
Las Vegas, NV
13 October 2022

57193703R00198